Much later, Burlane heard the unmistakable chatter of automatic rifles in the streets below. Three quick bursts. Then two. A siren began wailing, then stopped. There was another burst of automatic fire, then another. Then firing broke out in several places.

THE SIEGE HAD BEGUN . . .

Nye's people had allowed themselves a three-to-one fire-power advantage at every point of resistance and had attacked simultaneously and without warning.

In Washington, D.C. and London, England plans began to form.

On the Rock, Burlane had some ideas of his own. . . .

Also by Richard Hoyt
Published by Tor Books

Dragon Portfolio
Fish Story
Head of State
Siskiyou
Trotsky's Run

RICHARD HOYT

SIEGE

TOR

A TOM DOHERTY ASSOCIATES BOOK
NEW YORK

SIEGE

Copyright © 1987 by Richard Hoyt

A TOR Book

Published by Tom Doherty Associates, inc.
49 West 24 Street
New York, N.Y. 10010

Cover art by Bohdan Osyczka

Map by Alan McKnight

ISBN: 0-812-50029-6   Can. ISBN: 0-812-50030-X

Library of Congress Catalog Card Number: 86-51488

First printing: July 1987
First mass market printing: August 1989

Printed in the United States of America

0 9 8 7 6 5 4 3 2 1

For Harriet McDougal

The author would like to apologize to the Royal Navy for suggesting that Arabs might somehow grab Gibraltar. The Rock is impregnable. Everybody knows that. Laura Hoyt, twelve, lagged marbles to determine the names of the television networks; the characters are pretend only. Also, special thanks to Janice Johnson and Ted Magnuson.

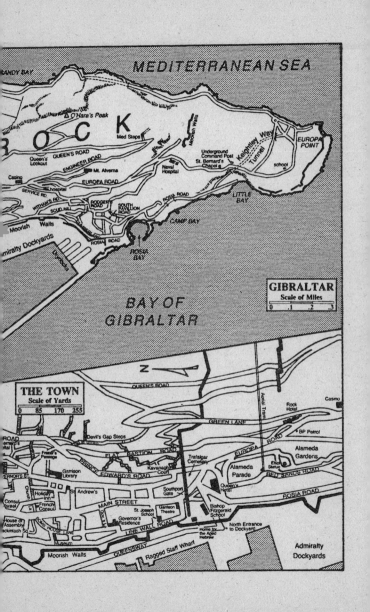

PART ONE

La illah il-Allah

1

THE FORTRESS AT Gibraltar had suffered fourteen sieges over the years—beginning in 1309, when troops under the command of the Archbishop of Seville loosed His Grace's catapults on the barbarous Moors who had occupied the Rock since A.D. 711. Over the centuries some of the sieges were real beauts.

Within weeks after Britain's Admiral George Rooke captured Gibraltar in April 1704, eight hundred soldiers on the Rock withstood a seven-month siege by eight thousand Irish troops in the service of France. After Gibraltar was rescued by the British fleet, the fortress became a symbol of steadfastness and fortitude—safe as the Rock.

In 1726, Spain's King Philip set upon Gibraltar with an Irish brigade of twenty thousand—this one also containing Flemings, Germans, and Scots and Englishmen. The enthusiastic Irishmen fired upon the Rock until the barrels of their cannons melted—fourteen thousand rounds in four days, it was reported. The Rock suffered but twenty-six casualties, and held firm.

But the definitive, no-fooling-around siege was the Great Siege, ending as it did with the Chevalier d'Arcon's bittersweet moment in history's wonderful parade.

The Great Siege began on July 11, 1779, and lasted for three years and seven months. Both France and Spain set upon Gibraltar, commanded by the redoubtable General George Augustus Elliot. In preparation for the siege, Elliot had the tops of churches and tall buildings lowered to give the enemy a poorer target; he had the streets plowed to prevent skipping cannonballs, and once lived for a week on four ounces of rice a day to prove it could be done.

3

In the beginning, the French and Spanish amassed one hundred and twenty thousand men to surround an area of some three square miles, outnumbering the British ten to one. The French and Spanish gave the Brits everything they had, and then some. On July 12, the Spanish bombarded the city with 60,000 thirteen-inch shells and 150,000 cannonballs. During one six-week period in 1781, the attackers fired 20,000 shells and 56,000 shot at the Rock. They killed seventy British defenders.

The shelling of the Rock continued daily, unabated, for the duration of the siege. Alas, the Royal Navy was at the time occupied with an uprising in America, and the Gibraltarians could be resupplied but once a year. Each time they were relieved, however, the disheartened besiegers, having wasted millions of francs and pesetas, had to begin again. The plucky Gibraltarians endured; the British even had the cheek to send two thousand defenders out one night to spike the enemy's guns.

By the third year of the siege, 1782, the attackers were desperate for a solution. Their inability to capture the Rock was an object of laughter and derision by neutral countries. Something had to be done. A competition was held, won by the Chevalier d'Arcon, who envisioned a flank attack with floating batteries.

Using cut-down ships, the attackers built ten such batteries. They were heavily decked and protected with thick timbers. Following d'Arcon's vision, they stretched rope nets and hides across the timbers. Upon each of these rafts were mounted ten to twenty heavy brass cannons. News of this pending gambit spread and became a matter of international curiosity, and observers began arriving to observe the sport.

In April 1782, the French and Spanish anchored their entire fleet—and their floating batteries—a half mile offshore of Gibraltar's fortified western slope. As word spread that the operation was set to begin, spectators gathered with their lunches on the hills surrounding the bay. The gallery included reporters representing newspapers throughout Europe.

As the floating menace formed offshore—forty-seven

sails-of-the-line, frigates, xebecs, battering ships, gun and mortar boats, bomb-ketches, cutters, and d'Arcon's special floating batteries—General Elliot's Irish deputy, Lieutenant General Robert Boyd, began tinkering with an invention of his own. He began heating cannonballs.

At the appointed hour, the French and Spanish, with five hundred cannons at their disposal, unleashed a terrible rain of shot and shell upon the beleaguered Gibraltarians.

The British, whose upper lips were as stiff as their ramrods, replied from behind the safety of their battlements with ninety-six guns and Boyd's red-hot cannonballs. The poor Chevalier d'Arcon had apparently not considered the accuracy of shore-mounted batteries against immobile rafts. True, some of the British rounds went *ker-plunk,* sizzling into the Bay of Gibraltar, but enough found their mark that the floating batteries were soon smoking, then burning.

With journalists from all over Europe scribbling the details so their readers might enjoy the spectacle vicariously—misadventure become spectator sport —fifteen hundred French and Spanish sailors were killed.

2

IT WAS THE wonderful bounty of Bah that caused the apes to wait in anticipation on the high side of the narrow road far, far above the great blue water. The waiting was part of the daily ritual for the apes in which Bah was properly worshiped and his blessings gratefully received.

Bah was no less revered by ordinary apes in the pack than He was by the maximum ape, although his rewards were far greater than theirs. Bah did not preside over a random world. There was a reason for everything, as the apes understood intuitively.

The maximum ape waited for the skinfaces to come

bearing Bah. Several of the skinfaces were preferred by Bah; that much was clear. The maximum ape looked down the wide-hard-path for one of the noisy-moving-things to arrive bearing with it Hairy Lip, Things Around the Eyes, or Big Nose. They were the best of the skinfaces.

The lonely Bah lived in strange black snouts that made a whirring sound or went *click-clack*. But as the apes had discovered in a long-ago and now forgotten time, Bah had a strange power over the bearers of the black snouts:

First, Bah made the skinfaces show the apes the snout in which He lived. This was so He wouldn't be lonely and so that the apes could see that they were made in His image.

Second, Bah made the skinfaces give the cooperating apes nuts and fruits to reward them for their company. All the apes wanted to see Bah, the rewards being what they were.

There was one thing, however, that the apes had observed over the years. It did no good to quarrel and push to see Bah. The skinfaces did not point the black snouts at fat apes, or at apes with scabs on their fur, or at apes who picked at their orifices, or at apes who chattered and jumped around. Whether these prejudices were Bah's or those of the skinfaces who pointed the snouts was unclear.

The bearers of the black snouts preferred to arrive and show Bah to the most perfect apes they could find. Thus it was that the maximum ape, who was calm and had perfect fur and sincere eyes, became leader of the pack. He stared at Bah each day until he became bored and full, making noises out of both holes; then he went off to vomit and have a nice nap. In the absence of the most handsome ape, the second-best-looking ape got a turn before the black snouts. When one leader got too fat to attract Bah's attention, he was replaced by another, more attractive ape.

Owing to the fact that he vomited after every turn, the current maximum ape had stayed trim and sleek and so had the longest run as favored ape than anybody could remember.

The apes had taught the skinfaces how to behave.

6

Skinfaces were to back up to an ape, not approach him straight on. Skinfaces were not to reach out at the apes with their stupid-looking hairless hands. When the skinfaces breached these rules, the ape whose turn it was to see the ape god would bear his teeth and call "Bah! Bah!" and the creature in the black snout would make the skinfaces back off and do it right.

Skinfaces, lackeys of Bah, were big and dumb and easily trained.

Because of the sweltering September heat, the traffic was terrible in Manhattan. There were too many cars, as usual, and on top of that the drivers were hot and irritable. Although it was a four-master of automobiles among dinghies and Hobie Cats, Gerard Thompson's NBC limousine had to wait its turn in the snarl just like everybody else. This gave Thompson and Tony O'Brien more than enough time to study the consultants' report.

Consultant reports were smoking cannons in the ratings battle between NBC and CBS news. Ever since Tom Brokaw and Dan Rather went down in a Nebraska cornfield on their way to the Republican convention in San Francisco, the struggle for Nielsens was reported as if it were a basketball game or hockey match. Brokaw had been killed outright, but Rather lingered in an uncertain coma. The doctors said his case would very likely go one way or another: he would either recover and be back on CBS News as good as ever or . . .

Well, this presented problems for the other networks. NBC first tested match-ups between likely successors to Brokaw and Dan Rather, should Rather survive. Rather beat them all, beat Gerard Thompson, beat anybody NBC could hire from another network. They then matched Thompson against Harry Gilchrist, Rather's likely successor. Thompson had a slight edge.

While publicly professing great sorrow for Rather, the folks at NBC kept their fingers crossed. For a while, Rather's vital signs showed a distinct improvement; there was hope, his doctors said. It was during this worrisome

7

time that the NBC brass met in a top-secret meeting during which, Thompson was later told, there had been a discussion of hiring an Italian to give Rather a little nudge.

Two days later, NBC and CBS were spared. Dan Rather died in his sleep and the nature of the ratings competition was redrawn. It was now Gerard Thompson versus Harry Gilchrist. ABC had come upon awful times and merely lurked in the bay of Nielsens, rather like a plastic shark in Long Island Sound.

Gerard Thompson retrieved a bottle of Stolichnaya from his stock. "You got the full report, I take it."

"Got it, Gerard. Late last night." Tony O'Brien tapped the bound report in his lap. O'Brien had cast his lot with Tom Brokaw's replacement much as a cowbird picks a choice beast upon which to stake its fortune. Everyone at NBC knew he wanted to anchor a weekend news show or be the network's White House correspondent. O'Brien walked like Thompson, talked like Thompson, and was Thompson's favorite correspondent. O'Brien signed his name "T. Anthony O'Brien." The T. stood for Timothy. At NBC the T. was said to stand for Today, although this euphemism was ordinarily replaced by coarser, if more honest, epithets. There were those who maintained that if Gerard Thompson ever turned a corner too sharply, Tony O'Brien would surely lose his nose.

"Ahh, well," Thompson sighed.

"Everything's here. The numbers on the match-up. Summaries. Their recommendations."

"I can't wait," Thompson said. Thompson and his friend, NBC correspondent Tony O'Brien, rode with that day's issue of *Variety* on the seat between them which they avoided touching or looking at. The paper might have been a hand grenade with the pin removed.

Thompson poured two neat vodkas and popped a videotape into the VCR. He punched the start button and on came CBS's Harry Gilchrist, giving his version of the evening news.

"The truth is, he's not that good," O'Brien said.

Thompson and O'Brien watched Gilchrist deliver the news with the sound turned off. They sipped their vodka.

When they finished the first round, Thompson poured them more. Finally Thompson said, "So what did our consultant friends find out, bottom line? They say their system is more accurate than Q-Scores. What do they say?"

"They're not sure, Gerard. It's complicated."

Thompson looked amused. "We paid them half a million dollars and they're not sure? Oof!"

"They matched you up, one-on-one, in all the important variables: warmth, believability, indices of trust, attractiveness of voice, projection of character, sincerity of eyes, masculinity, sexiness, the works. They dragged in experts from Harvard, Yale, West Texas State."

"West Texas State!" Thompson smirked.

"I just made that up, Gerard. Little humor there."

"Sure, laugh." Thompson looked at himself in the reflection of the tinted window, then at Gilchrist delivering the news. Thompson had a more attractive face; there was no doubt of that. His features were more even. Gilchrist, in fact, had too big a nose. "Tell me what they found, Tony. Give it to me straight."

"You edged him on the biggies: warmth and trust. That much is clear, Gerard. Then it starts to get muddled. You're in a virtual draw for warmth; you get the men, but more and more he's getting the women."

"He's getting the women?" Thompson was surprised. That wasn't good. Women controlled the dials, everybody knew that; she who lowers the zippers calls the shots.

O'Brien waved his hand. No problem, the gesture said. "*Nada. Nada.* Nothing to worry about. A point or two spread, no real difference. You have to figure the margin of error." O'Brien opened the report, running his finger down the conclusions and recommendations at the end. "They say you have more wry in your closing grin by a factor of two point seven two. They have a bunch of numbers explaining what that means."

"Get to the gritty, Tony."

O'Brien sighed. "For some inexplicable reason, women think Gilchrist is sexier than you."

"What?" Thompson paled, not because of any blow to

9

his ego or knee to his balls. Sexiness was critical to staying on top; Gerard Thompson had never had any reason to feel personally insecure.

"Woman think he looks commanding. There's this Latin thing, Gerard."

"Harry Gilchrist looks about as Hispanic as Clint Eastwood looks Chinese." Gilchrist was light-complexioned and sunburned easily. And his mother, a professor at UCLA and the daughter of a Costa Rican diplomat—this was included in every Gilchrist fact sheet distributed by CBS—was in fact a green-eyed blonde of Spanish ancestry. Thus the bilingual Gilchrist was a two-fer: his Anglo surname and appearance were acceptable to Norwegians in Seattle and Poles in Buffalo, while every Hispanic in the United States knew about his mother, the subject of frequent features in Spanish-language magazines and newspapers.

O'Brien fell silent, watching the blue-eyed Gilchrist. Gilchrist had first caught the public's eye with his coverage of the Iranian hostage crisis and then, owing to his dramatic account of the hijacked airliner in Beirut, had become a celebrity journalist.

"Give it to me straight, Tony."

O'Brien frowned. "Of course he beat hell out of you in Los Angeles, Miami, and the Puerto Rican sections of New York, but . . ." He hesitated.

"But what?"

"He beat you in Beverly Hills and Palm Beach too." O'Brien cleared his throat. "But that's just one score, Gerard. Nobody wins them all. It's the balance that counts, you have to remember."

"What it comes down to is that women like me and trust me, but they'd rather be fucked by Harry Gilchrist. If their husbands would only take the time to satisfy them, for God's sake, maybe they wouldn't let their twats decide which channel to watch. Did you ever stop to think of that, Tony? Did you? Why the hell aren't they running Dr. Comfort on public television? They've shown raw tit on *Masterpiece Theater*—I saw it." Thompson was distraught.

10

"It's not as simple as that, Gerard."

"Of course it is. If they start thinking of you like you're their father, your Nielsens drift."

O'Brien braced himself as a cab pulled in front of the limousine and the driver braked.

Thompson said, "We gotta get their pussies singing like Jim Henson's puppets." Thompson poured himself another vodka and rolled up the copy of *Variety* on the seat. He began bouncing the paper on his knee. "I can flog and whip and whack this son of a bitch until it's limp, but the facts remain the same: last week Harry Gilchrist beat my Nielsens and now these bastards are speculating on how long I'm going to last."

"That was last week, Gerard. We had some good stuff this week. The baby sliding under the Missouri. The interview with the serial murderer."

"Interviews put people to sleep. Gilchrist had fresh blood oozing from under the door in the Tucson murder. His people are hustling out there. Where were we?"

"We could have been faster off the dime, that's true."

"And just what is it these whiz-kid consultants recommend that I do?"

"They've got some nickel-and-dime stuff mostly. For example, they think you should increase your gym time. A few more curl-ups, a few more laps."

Thompson groaned. "I knew that was coming. They think they have to throw that in there or we'll think they're amateurs."

"There's that, and they think the colors are off on your neckties and the stripes of your shirt. There's a lot of talk about various hues of blue, and a report by a psychologist at the University of Rochester. They want the network to invest in some special organic dyes for your ties and shirts."

"Organic dyes!" Thompson shook his head.

"Whatever."

"Ridiculous, is what it is. What's the biggie recommendation? What do these assholes say that's supposed to save the day? What?"

"They think you should be sent to do a special report

11

on some dangerous hot spot—Nicaragua, say, or Angola, or Afghanistan, someplace like that—and come back with a short beard. It would grow in silver-gray, they believe, and if it doesn't, the makeup people could . . ."

Thompson shook his head. "The old 'he's been around' routine."

"No, no, now, just a second. Let's see what they have to say here: 'Increasing Thompson's ratio of ruggedness and experience, critical parameters in projecting masculinity.' Here's a quote: 'He would be someone who gets out there where the story is, a masculine intellectual who'll wear a beard if he wants.' Here's another: they want you to develop a 'touch of the renegade.' You're really very serious, see; you'll stop at nothing to give the public the truth. Dan Rather had that quality. They say—let's see here—they say 'this suggestion of independence' should swing the Nielsens back your way."

"Note that they say *suggestion* of independence. Heaven forbid I should actually be independent. And it's *should* swing it back my way, not *will*. If I had a dime for every *should* or *could* or *might* that I've seen in a consultants' report, I'd be richer than the Rockefellers."

"This'll give you a good idea, Gerard. Listen to this one: 'The object is to leave Harry Gilchrist looking like the earnest Lieutenant Fuzz in "Beetle Bailey."' They want you to wear very high quality British suits to maintain your credibility. They say it will be a good contrast with your silver beard. They say you should wear shorter sleeves in order to take advantage of your hairy wrists." One corner of O'Brien's mouth raised slightly.

Thompson looked at his wrists. "Do you suppose sexy wrists can get a guy laid? Maybe they'd like me to stuff my shorts with balls of rolled socks."

O'Brien pretended to check the report for that suggestion.

"What they're saying is that I have to go out there and slap mosquitoes and eat food with dirt in it so we can give the ladies Papa Hemingway after supper."

"Not Hemingway, Gerard. If the public got wind that you shot ducks, that'd be the end of it."

"Dumb shits." Thompson left it unclear whether he meant the consultants or people who watched the news.

"Ladies, here's a guy who's been around. Give him sass, and he'll turn you over his knee and warm your buns. That's what they're really after."

"No wonder the feminists won't leave us alone."

"Except for sports, women turn the knobs, Gerard, not the men. By the way, the consultants think you should have the skin tightened up under your eyes."

Thompson turned on the seat. "They what?"

O'Brien cleared his throat. "They say you're developing bags, Gerard. Uh, bags aren't, uh, sexy."

"Oh, for Chrissake!"

"They have this idea, Gerard. Eyebag surgery is minor stuff, see, but if they do a proper job, it'll naturally take some time to heal. The problem is how to get the job done without the public getting hip. You can't be on camera with baggy eyes one night, then go on vacation for two weeks and come back with eyes looking twenty years younger. It just wouldn't work. So the idea is to give you the surgery, then cover it with makeup to give you a pair of the biggest fucking black eyes you've ever seen."

"Worded a little differently in the consultants' report, I take it. Are they going to hire somebody to biff me around a little? Is that it?"

"What they propose is that we say you were assaulted in Central Park by these two big assholes, see, and you duked it out with them, and wound up with these shiners. Dan Rather got roughed up on Park Avenue, remember? The public'll buy Central Park, no problem. Little by little, day by day, the surgical puffiness and any bruising will subside. Your makeup man will remove the black-eye makeup to match the healing. When your eyes clear, *voilà!*—eyes as young as Harry Gilchrist's, a smooth transition from mature but baggy eyes to mature but, uh, vigorous eyes."

"All the better for gazing at the ladies across a candlelit table."

"You're fifty-four and he's forty-two, Gerard. They say you can make that work for you or allow it to work against you. The reason for the mugging business is to show that you can take care of yourself. If you want to walk in Central Park, you by God walk in Central Park. You can handle yourself. You might have wound up with a couple of terrible eyes, but you got in a few blows of your own, and walked away with your wallet intact."

"A man's man."

"The idea is that the shiners are badges of honor. The consultants say it's guaranteed to boost your masculinity numbers, Gerard. They say you shouldn't make any fuss about it. You got jumped and you took your lumps; it happens all the time. No big deal."

"It's hard for me to see what a woman would see in that little twit. Look at him." Thompson gestured at Gilchrist reading the news. "His mama's probably watching the taping."

"They, uh, they want to go back to an old-fashioned kind of set, with books and everything. The idea is to showcase biggie American writers. Let people see their titles back there behind you. Gives the authors a little ride, but why not?"

"We can afford to be generous."

"Sure, Gerard. Shows class on our part. The books'll give you a little Edwin Newman, they say, and just a touch of Bill Moyers."

"A guy who knows a comma or period comes before the quotation marks."

"They want you to be, where is it now?" O'Brien moved his finger through the report. "Ah, here it is: 'a Renaissance man, a man who knows history and history's ills.'"

"A guy who knows that 'hopefully' is an adverb."

"Exactly."

"And these authors on the shelves, who would they be?"

O'Brien checked the report. "They recommend Barry Lopez and Peter Matthieson to show that you're sensitive to nature. They did a survey and found that when people think poetry they think Robert Frost."

"Frost is dead."

14

"John McPhee's books are suggested. He's published in *The New Yorker* and is approved of."

"No Roy Blount, I don't suppose."

O'Brien smiled. "Humor is touchy, Gerard. Too many people suspect they're being laughed at. Publishers even back off. For every reader who likes to smile, two more want to suffer—"

Thompson fished a Tums out of his jacket pocket. "I don't suppose I could slip Donald Westlake in there?"

"They say we have to be careful."

"So who chooses the titles?"

"A network committee."

Thompson slumped in the seat.

"All this is small stuff, Gerard. Nothing we can't fix. What we need is a good story, something dramatic and fast-moving to show your stuff. Put Gilchrist and you on the spot and see who gets the Nielsens then. We'll make their nipples stiffen."

Thompson laughed. "We'll have them singing 'Moon River' with their pussies. Next dynamite story up, you've got it. Guaranteed." The studios were coming up. Gerard Thompson studied his reflection in the window of the night.

3 _____

JUST UP FROM the football pitch maintained by Her Majesty's Navy, the young Englishman and the curly-haired Arab hitched a ride on a vegetable truck. This was on Queensway, which paralleled the harbor; the driver was delivering Spanish vegetables to a greengrocer who served the flats at Europa Point. It was a balmy October day. The temperature was in the low seventies; warming sunlight shimmered on the large, nearly round bay.

Ordinarily the driver would have taken Europa Road

up past the naval hospital, but he was in no hurry, and went via Rosia Road so he could drop the Englishman and the Arab off at Camp Bay.

Terry Holmestead, the Englishman, had three awful pimples on his reddened face—one by his mouth, another on his chin, and a third just above his left eyebrow.

The Arab, who was older and handsome in the manner of Omar Sharif, sat close to Holmestead, arm against arm.

Holmestead fingered the inflamed pimple by the corner of his mouth. "They can't find a bloody soldier smart enough to do it, so they have to hire me. They b-bring me down here from London, Mr. Holmestead this, and Mr. Holmestead that. Then they treat me like a bloody private." Holmestead fingered the pimple on his chin, using his hand to hide the fact that he didn't have much of a jaw.

"They can b-bloody well take their proper accents and shove them." Holmestead laced his fingers together and cracked his knuckles. He gave a peremptory squeeze of the pimple by the corner of his mouth and winced slightly.

The three rode in silence for a moment, then the Arab asked the driver, "How long have you been doing this?"

"Four years. I got a girlfriend across the bay and one here, just like Alec Guinness in that movie. The *señoritas* are lovely, but they all want to get married. I make a couple of trips a day. Back and forth. Back and forth."

"Across the border?" the Arab asked.

"Oh, sure. I deliver fish, vegetables, and beer." They were now on Rosia Road with the Admiralty Dockyard on their right. "My company handles everything but red meat. Another company has that, but probably not for long. It's a matter of time."

"How's that?" Holmestead asked. He stole a secret glance at the handsome Arab.

"We're supposed to be owned by Salvatore Sabatini, a gentleman who lives in Palermo."

"I read about him. Mafia everywhere." Holmestead grabbed for the pimple on his forehead and inadvertently said, "Ooo!"

"I heard a bloke say it was hollowed out in there," the

16

driver said to Holmestead. "High-tech stuff, right out of *Star Wars*."

Holmestead laughed derisively. "Let me tell you a little secret. It takes two blokes to do everything in there: to open the lid of an Exocet tube, to open a perimeter door, to do whatever." Holmestead interrupted his story to finger the pimple by the corner of his mouth.

He continued: "You have to have six blokes to cover three watches, and these are rotated to provide backups. Each of the six has a secret code that lets him work his part of the function, whether it's letting someone through the main entrance or firing a SAM. There's a secret code for just about everything anybody does down there."

"A Sam?" the driver asked.

"I don't understand this." The Arab looked confused.

"It means surface-to-air missile," Holmestead said. "Do you think they have cannons in there?" he asked the driver. The traffic slowed as the highway followed the Moorish wall around Rosia Bay.

The driver said, "What is it you do in there?" He meant in the underground headquarters of the British garrison where Holmestead worked.

"I was supposed to program, but they've got me servicing the terminals . . ." Holmestead cracked his knuckles again. He fingered a pimple. "Maintenance! Well, I said to meself: they're so bloody smart. The impregnable Rock and all that rot. I can beat their system for a few quids' worth of equipment."

The driver and the Arab waited for Holmestead to tell them more.

Holmestead obliged: "The entry codes come in seven digits. Suppose I service the terminal where the security people monitor the perimeter alarms. Do you know what a ROM is?" he asked the driver.

The driver shook his head, slowing for a Fiat.

"ROM stands for 'read only memory.' This comes from the factory with a source code built in. These machines also have what is called EROM, which stands for 'erasable read only memory.' This is a clear glass lid over silicon dye. Every month a man flies out from London and

17

uses EROM to change the entry codes in the ROM. Now, there is available on the market a pin-compatible RAM —'random access memory'—that's powered by a tiny lithium battery that you can buy almost anywhere. What you can do in a few minutes . . . what *I* can do, is use the EROM to tell the ROM to pick up the entry code and write it in the RAM."

The Arab furrowed his brow.

"What do you mean 'pin compatible'?" the driver asked.

"It has the proper twenty-four wire pins to plug into their terminals. Ordinarily the RAM would forget everything the instant the operator turned off the machine."

"The battery!"

"The lithium battery saves it. All I have to do is unplug the RAM and slip it in my pocket. It's a silicon chip with legs, hardly larger than a fifty-p coin. With a little planning, it could be done. I could record the entry codes, the instructions to the machine, whatever. I could open the perimeter barriers if I wanted. Anything."

The driver looked at Holmestead with astonishment. "Don't the security people check for things plugged in where they don't belong?"

"Oh, sure. Random checks. But they're a cheap lot, they are." Holmestead winced as he pinched a pimple.

"Why is that?"

"Security uses me to run the checks." Holmestead laughed.

The driver whistled. "If I were you I'd watch who I told that to."

"I'm afraid I don't understand any of it," the Arab said.

As the truck emerged from the first tunnel at Camp Bay, the driver let them off at Little Bay Beach and continued on his way. They found a place to sit at the base of the limestone cliffs that were the southern boundary of the beach. The cliffs rose from the water all the way around Europa Point.

The Arab scooted next to Holmestead so that their

arms sometimes touched when they moved.

They spent the afternoon at Little Bay Beach; the sun was warm and the Arab had brought along a Berber pipe and a good stash of hashish. The center of town was less than a mile away, so they waited until the sun was well down before they set out for Camp Bay Beach. They walked on the water side of the Moorish wall that flanked Rosia Bay—a neat, round little inlet. At the northern end of the wall around the bay, they looked at the one-hundred-ton cannon on display.

With the beaches behind them, they walked along Cumberland Road. The four huge cranes that served the harbor's three dry docks rose on their left, behind another stretch of Moorish wall. The cranes looked like huge mechanical birds above the Moorish embattlements. The dry docks had names: King Edward, Queen Alexandra, the Prince of Wales. There was a modest repair yard next to the dry docks, then the base of Her Majesty's Navy, then the Gun Wharf and the Ragged Staff Wharf—all facing the longest uninterrupted stretch of Moorish wall on the peninsula.

It was now late in the afternoon, and the sun, turning orange, was sinking toward the ridge on the far side of the bay, as clouds gathered and a cooling wind began blowing off the water. Holmestead and the Arab started up the hill, beginning with one of the many alleys of steep steps that separated the parallel, terracelike streets. They took Cumberland Steps to Scud Hill Road, and Rodgers Steps to Rodgers Road which became Hospital Service Road. Hospital Service flanked the uphill side of the lawn tennis club and the golf course.

As they walked, feeling the wind coming from the west, looking down on the golf course, the Arab's hand bumped Holmestead's and lingered. It was a steep walk; nevertheless, the higher they got, the longer their hands touched.

The Arab finally took Holmestead's hand when they reached the grounds of the casino. They watched the sun set across the bay. Europa Point was to their left; the golf course was directly below them, and to their right, a maze of narrow streets and a tangle of rooftops and television antennas.

At first this holding of hands was tentative on Holmestead's part, then he gripped the Arab tightly.

The Arab said, "Have you ever heard about a town called Chaouen?"

"No, I haven't."

"The Djebala tribesmen live there. I don't suppose you've heard about the Djebala. The men are like us; it is their way of life." The Arab squeezed Holmestead's hand. "They live in Chaouen, many of them. It can be a fabulous place."

"Really?" Holmestead was excited, and allowed the Arab to put his arm around his waist.

"I have friends in Chaouen, and a place to stay anytime I want. Of course, it isn't possible for an Englishman to go there by himself. You have to know someone. Can you get a few days off? We can take the ferry to Ceuta and go by bus from there."

"Well, I don't know . . ." Holmestead was clearly eager to go. "If they ever found out, I'd lose me job. They've got security people wanting to know every b-bloody thing I do."

"I can get us all the kif we can smoke," the Arab said. "We will ride the wind of Allah."

"This is nice, the wind off the water."

"In North Africa this wind is called *imbat*; here it is *datoo*. The wind is important in the Mediterranean. Everybody has a name for the wind."

"If it comes from the east, what's it called?"

The Arab said, "In Arabic it is called *sirocco*, meaning from the east; this is the hot wind. The east wind is called many things, Holmestead: *shamal* in Iraq; *sharav* in Israel; *sharkiye* in Jordan; *khamsin* in Egypt; *chili* in Tunisia; *chergui* in Algeria; *leveche* in Morocco; *levante* in Spain."

"And in Libya? You mentioned all of North Africa except Libya."

"In Libya they call it the *ghibli*," the handsome Arab said. He squeezed the pimpled Englishman's hand.

20

4

THE MEETING WAS held in Tripoli, at the Al Sahra, a colonial hotel that seemed to be a composite of every classical cornice, cupola, and column its frenetic Italian architect could imagine. Alas, the splendid mix had long since succumbed to heat and neglect. Originally white on the outside and an opalescent cream on the inside, the building had apparently never been repainted; the exterior had turned chalky and yellowish, then had peeled, leaving scabrous walls streaked as high as men could piss. The Roman columns in front were brown as high as the hands of leaning Libyans could reach. Curling scabs of paint hung from the ceilings. The hotel reeked of sweat and lethargy.

Boris Suslev arrived first, stepping confidently from the black Mercedes that had brought him from the Soviet embassy. The huge Russian had a square jaw, small gray eyes, and short brown hair. Suslev obviously enjoyed his freedom to travel outside of the Soviet Union. His stylish Italian blazer—a proper blue with gold buttons—and his pin-striped broadcloth shirt appeared to be immaculately tailored, but neither did much to hide his astonishing neck and shoulder muscles. Here was a man who had apparently pumped everything: iron, beetroots, steroids.

Muhammad Aziz, wearing a flowing white thobe and a white kaffiyeh on his head, met Suslev in the portico of the Al Sahra, the carpetless floor having been swept of sand and litter for the occasion. "Comrade Suslev, it is so good to see you."

"Comrade Aziz." Suslev glanced at his wristwatch.

"Qafi will be here momentarily," Aziz said. "He has been delayed, I'm told."

Suslev grinned, showing gold caps on his teeth. "I

suspect Comrade Qafi has been delayed for quite some time."

Suslev and Aziz chatted about the weather until Qafi arrived, chauffeured from his headquarters in a black Mercedes-Benz. Qafi wore an Arab headdress over a smart military uniform that overflowed with decorations awarded for high valor in Libya's many campaigns against the French imperialist lackeys in Chad. He was clearly excited, animated, and rushed to meet them, clutching a video cassette in one hand.

"Salam alekum," said Aziz. Peace be unto you.

"We alekum salam." Unto you be peace.

"How are you, Comrade Qafi?" Suslev said.

The three men shook hands.

"Did you hear? Did you hear? I did it again!" Qafi said. "I faced them down, the American Sixth Fleet. I waved my finger like a sword, pilots at the ready, and they stayed back, cowering like puppies. Cowering! Whimpering! It's on television all over Europe and America. The line of Allah's justice!" The excited Qafi drew a dramatic though imaginary line in the air with his finger.

"I just got in from Moscow," Suslev said mildly.

"The Swedes're saying I humiliated the Americans. Humiliated them! I am the leader of the Arab world."

Suslev said, "As I understand Comrade Aziz's proposal, it has the possibility of a little humiliation as well."

"Well, yes, Aziz," Qafi said. It was with some effort that Qafi directed his attention from his imaginary line to Aziz and the proposal at hand. "I am the leader of the Arab world," he said again, obviously unable to restrain himself, and wanting to remind Aziz of his station.

Aziz led the two others to an aged elevator with folding iron gates and whirring cables; they were taken to the roof, which was given over to white metal tables under red parasols. Here Italian colonial administrators had once sipped red wine and looked out over the Tripoli medina; here Libyans now drank tea and considered their country's crumbling economy and Qafi's next mad sortie against the Americans and Israelis.

Tuxedoed waiters hovered like excited moths as Aziz,

22

Qafi, and Suslev settled around a table overlooking the medina. The rooftop was theirs. They were served hot tea under the shade of the parasol. It was a pleasant North African day, not too hot, and the humidity was low; a cooling wind blew off the Mediterranean.

Muhammad Aziz sipped sweet mint tea and told Qafi and Suslev how one of his agents had curried the favor of a young English homosexual who serviced computer terminals in the bowels of Gibraltar. There was a full minute of silence as the participants in the meeting considered the consequences of Aziz's find.

Suslev said, "This English queer can let your people into Gibraltar, then."

"At their Europa Point command center. Yes, he can," Aziz said. "He can and he will if we ask him to, although I'm not sure we would want to get inside. What would be the point in that?"

The Russian looked puzzled.

"I've been told it's impossible to recruit mercenaries with sufficient training to run the weapons system on Gibraltar. In fact, the British have only recently introduced a new missile system, their own new SAMs and French Exocets, for the Strait."

"We're all curious, Comrade Aziz. Tell us, then, if it's impossible to operate the British defenses, how would you take advantage of this queer's clever idea?"

Muhammad Aziz gave Suslev an envelope. "I've spelled out my plan in detail, which you'll want to consider at your leisure. I'm open to recommendations, of course. But enough for now. You'll want some time to think it over, Comrade Suslev. Right now, I've brought a special lady here from Beirut I thought you might like to meet."

"Oh?" Suslev looked interested.

"A special lady?" Qafi said.

"Her name is Fatima."

"Fatima, the Los Angeles belly dancer?" Qafi was impressed. "She's here? I saw her in Beirut last summer." He smoothed his black hair with the palm of his hand.

Boris Suslev was clearly amused at Qafi's primping. "You know of her then, Comrade Qafi?"

23

Qafi smiled. "A sultan's harem in one woman, they say."

Boris Suslev did not believe in small talk or foreplay. He entered the room growling like a bear. "Lady Fatima! Ggrraagghh!" Suslev started taking his clothes off before he closed the door. He grabbed his crotch. "Ggrraagghh!"

Ella Nidech retreated, tripping over the base of a lamp. He was Russian, so she should have known. What an asshole!

Suslev threw his Italian blazer to one side. He growled and stripped the silk necktie from his shirt. Then came his shirt, revealing a torso strapped with muscles upon muscles. Without taking his eyes off Nidech he unzipped his trousers slowly.

Nidech swallowed. Male spooks didn't have to do this. James Burlane got to roam around killing people, all good clean fun for the delicate man. If he had to seduce a lady, it was with a man's ability to distance himself emotionally. He never had to put up with this kind of bullshit.

Suslev removed his trousers and stood naked save for tiny white shorts covered with a polka-dot pattern of tiny hammers and sickles.

Nidech moved backward, her hands behind her groping for obstacles. She bumped into the bed. She had nowhere to turn.

Suslev removed his shorts.

"My God!" Nidech's eyes were wide with shock and disbelief.

Boris Suslev had the tiniest, most pathetic excuse for genitals that she had ever seen. His cock wasn't more than three inches long in its erect state. His balls, the size of spring peas, were covered with blond hair. They reminded Nidech of cottonwood seeds that floated in the air in springtime.

"Yes, you see it is a fearsome socialist cock. Take off your clothes."

Ella Nidech couldn't believe what she was being called upon to endure. Belly dancing was one thing, but this was too much. She swore that when she got out of this mess, when she was safely out of harm's way, she would tell President Charles Barbur to shove his "delicate woman" business. She would get herself an academic appointment at a university somewhere and grade papers like any sane woman. She couldn't take her eyes off Suslev's eager little worm that was standing rather at parade rest.

The delicate man had encouraged her to take the assignment. You're the best female agent in the world, he had told her. He said there were things he couldn't do because he was a man. The president needed a delicate woman. She had been flattered. When she got ahold of James Burlane, she swore, she would grab that lanky prankster by the throat and shake him until his eyes popped.

Ella Nidech had told herself that she could do what she had to do and at the same time blank the experience out of her mind, that she could remain somehow detached from what was happening to her. Such nonsense! Nidech, thoroughly disgusted, looked frantically about her, hoping against hope that there would be some way to escape the Leninist Don Juan advancing toward her, eager to bestow upon her the blessings of socialist accomplishment. If she surprised the jerk with some of the karate blows she had been taught by Company instructors, she would blow her cover. There wasn't a damned thing she could do.

Boris Suslev growled. "We Russians are great fuckers, the greatest. It is cold in the Soviet Union. In the winter there is nothing to do but crawl under the covers and fuck, fuck, fuck." He lapsed into Russian, then back into excited English: "We love to fuck people in the USSR!"

5

THE MOSSAD CHIEF Saloman Schechter made the original request. He asked the Company if it had a good-looking female agent who could speak Arabic and pass herself off as a Los Angeles belly dancer—a sexy and liberated American woman who was returning to her Lebanese homeland. If the Company did, Schechter said, Mossad could place her close to Arab terrorists plaguing the Mediterranean. Mossad had tumbled onto a fabulous opportunity but lacked the right woman.

Something like this comes along once in fifty years, Schechter said. Please, please, do you have a woman?

The Company did have such a woman, Ella Nidech, but Nidech—after her performance in the battle of Fong Wai Chow—was assigned as the president's delicate woman. The delicate man, James Burlane, was the man who got things done. He could poison people without their suffering ill effects before death; he could loft a .22 slug into the pupil of an eyeball at two hundred yards; he once burned the oil lobby's building in Washington, D.C., to draw attention from a crucial second-story job. The man from Umatilla, Oregon, was a linguist of accomplishment. But there was one thing he could not do.

Burlane could not get men to talk by blinking sexily over a cocktail glass; neither could he turn men's mouths dry by undulating his belly. Ella Nidech could. And so it was necessary, human desires being what they are, for Nidech to become the delicate woman, joining Burlane as the president's free-lance assassin and spook. The delicate couple orbited the planet separately, each doing what had to be done in whatever way he or she found to do it.

President Charles Barbur didn't like the idea of loaning the delicate woman to Mossad. "Is this . . . is this delicate work?" the president asked. "I thought . . . I thought they were to be reserved for delicate work." Delicate work was anything the president didn't want to be published in *The New York Times* or *The Washington Post* or to be discussed before any nosy committee of Congress. The need for a delicate couple was one of the lessons of *Ivan Oopsie II,* and the misadventure of Colonel Oliver North.

Something was bound to go wrong; everybody knew that. However, in their rush to find out what the Arabs were doing, Schechter and the Americans carefully placed logic aside, like an empty salad plate, and consented to Ella Nidech's becoming Lady Fatima, a Los Angeles belly dancer returning to Beirut.

In no time at all, with Mossad's connivance, Lady Fatima was rolling her belly for Abu Nidal, Yasir Arafat, and Muhammad Aziz. Lady Fatima confirmed a rumor long popular in the Middle East—brought back by students returning from UCLA and USC—that the best belly dancing in the world was found in Los Angeles.

The call came in Tuesday, the fourth of February. Ara Schott was already on the safe line to Mossad's headquarters on Oliphant Street in the Talbieh section of Jerusalem when Peter Neely stepped into his office. Sit, sit, he told Neely with his hand. Ordinarily protocol demanded that the Company director talk to the head of a foreign intelligence service. But Neely felt insecure in the presence of men with first-rate minds; hence Ara Schott was delegated to speak to Saloman Schechter, who was the Memuneh, or head of Mossad; by law, his identity was not made public in Israel.

It was clear also that the Memuneh preferred to talk to Schott as well.

The call was coming over a safe phone, meaning that it was encoded and decoded on its satellite trip from Tel Aviv. Schott wouldn't have minded Neely's participation —Neely, after all, was supposed to be in charge of the Company. But Schott knew Neely didn't want to take part.

Ara Schott declined to have a speakerphone on his desk, citing vague security reasons. He scorned a second receiver as well, so that any form of conference call was impossible in his office. When an intelligence officer of a NATO country or an Israeli called, Schott took the call in his office, with Neely listening in, assured that at a minimum the Company wouldn't be embarrassed.

This arrangement was arrived at by the DCI and his deputy without any kind of discussion that hinted at the truth of their relationship. Peter Neely appeared before congressional committees—Schott did this in instances where real questions might be asked—read about himself in *Time* and *Newsweek,* appeared on Sunday afternoon news programs, went to parties at the White House. For these duties he was paid handsomely. Ara Schott saw to it that something approaching rational decisions were made, although he was paid far less than Neely and wasn't invited to parties.

Schott, a career officer, had become the Company's deputy director through merit—as was alleged to sometimes occur elsewhere—whereas Neely, a dilettante who dressed properly, had been elevated to the top strictly according to the American plan: he was a longtime supporter of the president.

There were those in the Company who claimed the relationship between the two men was reversed outside the battlements of the secret war. For example, when the two men ate lunch at a proper restaurant, it was said, Ara Schott watched Peter Neely to see which fork went with the asparagus salad and what to do with the escargots.

"Aziz and Suslev!" Schott, glancing at Neely, bit his lip. He pinned the telephone receiver to his ear with his shoulder; he caught Neely's eye and wrote in the palm of his left hand with an imaginary pen.

Neely, who in fact acted as Schott's assistant when there was a nondecorative decision to be made, gave his deputy a notepad and pen.

Schott scrawled "Qafi" on the pad and handed it back to Neely.

"Omar Qafi!" Neely was scornful. He hated Qafi. This wasn't so much because Qafi sponsored terrorism. The Syrians and Iranians were just as guilty of chickenshit bombings and airline hijackings. The problem was that Qafi loved the camera and loved to brag. The network anchors all feigned objectivity and neutrality, as though they were the very soul of *New York Times* responsibility, but they really loved Qafi's antics, and everybody knew it. Neely wanted to tack Omar Qafi's balls to the wall and fire at them with a rifle.

"Seville?" Schott said. "What are they up to, does she say? Yes, it does bear close watching. I think so too, Saloman." To Neely, he mouthed: "Se-vill-e."

Neely didn't understand, which wasn't unusual, but this time he had reason.

Schott scrawled "meet Spain" on the pad.

A meeting in Seville. Neely understood.

Schott wrote "Thurs morn" and showed it to Neely. "That's coming right up. What? I'm very sorry to hear that, Saloman." To Neely, he mouthed: "Mos-sad has a mole."

"A mole! Mossad?"

"I see. I see," Schott said to Schechter. "Well, yes, what with our woman involved, of course we're willing to help. Anything at all, Saloman. Name it."

Remembering that he was in a position of responsibility, Peter Neely listened, frowning.

Peter Neely lived in an imitation antebellum mansion in Virginia that was forever plagued by moles. No matter what Neely's gardener did, he couldn't get rid of them. He tried to poison them. He smoked their tunnels with calcium bicarbonate. He set traps. Nothing worked. The little bastards were always leaving their calling cards on his rolling lawn, upwellings of dirt that were as cancers on the immaculate green. Neely's neighbor's lawn was wonderfully free of moles. He even had a putting green to one side of his house that helped keep his game several strokes below Neely's. This was the way Mossad had always seemed to Neely: neat, and tidy, well trimmed, miraculously free of moles.

Although Saloman Schechter had never overtly gloated at the Company's occasional misfortune, Neely was convinced that the Israeli felt himself and Mossad superior to the bumblers in the Company. Peter Neely had a political imagination; he was secretly pleased at Mossad's bad news.

Ara Schott was not at all pleased. He was a committed cold warrior; when he was younger and they were popular, he had been an enthusiastic devotee of crew cuts. The Company and Mossad were fighting the same enemies, the Russians, who were pricks with ears, and Muslim fanatics, who were just as bad. A blow to Mossad was a blow to the Company and everything Schott held to be valuable.

Schott was dismayed at the turn of events, and his face showed it. He said, "The worst of it is that it's almost impossible to know everything they did, Saloman. Oh, no!" His eyes were grave. He shook his head. "I see. So how long, do you think?" He listened. He pressed his lips together until they were colorless. Schott's head bobbed up and down in agreement with the Israeli. "It's our agent with her rump on the line, remember. We're not going to leave her dangling. No way, Saloman."

Peter Neely knew he would find it hard not to gloat a little. It was good that Schott was talking to Schechter.

Schott wrote on the pad and showed it to Neely. "Del w. needs hlp del man."

"James Burlane?" Neely mouthed. He wrote. "Is he well enough?" He meant well enough to travel.

Schott read the note, his brow furrowed. He wrote: "Mossad needs Thursday."

Neely shrugged. He hoped Burlane was resting and drinking fruit juice as he had been told.

Schott said, "Saloman, we'll send our best. An ace. Oh, yes, I understand that too. What?" Schott laughed. "No, no, no. You don't have to worry about that; we've told everybody here that he died of dysentery in Mozambique." Schott paused. He listened to Schechter, then laughed. "No, no, Saloman. You will not see this on the front page of the *Post* or the *Times,* I guarantee. It's our lady, remember. You do? I see." He laughed again. "Okay, okay, I'll put it in words for you, Saloman: you will not find our man profiled on *60 Minutes.*" Schott listened and grinned. He scrawled on the pad: "Wants file mugs." He showed this to Neely and said to Schechter, "Our man can shoot pictures from a plane or on a table. You want mugs, you'll get all the mugs you can handle, no problem. Of course he does tech work too. Sure, sure. He has a license and has used it. He's good, believe me."

"Parabolic?" Neely asked.

Schott nodded his head yes, pleased that the DCI, after six years in charge of the Company, knew that tech work very likely had to do with eavesdropping. That Burlane had a license meant that he was an assassin if need be. "Listen, Saloman, consider it done. I'll get back to you so we can work out the details. Certainly. No problem." Ara Schott made a note to himself and hung up.

Schott studied the note and said, "Peter, remember in October when Ella Nidech told us that Muhammad Aziz, Omar Qafi, and Boris Suslev met in Tripoli? They spent the whole afternoon engaged in serious palaver. Mossad then wanted to know if we would be willing to share our satellite photographs of Libyan military activity and we agreed. Well, Ella has now been entertaining Muhammad Aziz's friends, including Boris Suslev. Suslev went south for six weeks, Ella said. Our satellite photos show what we believe to be Arabs being trained by Libyans with Russians at Jebel As Sawda, the nearest thing the Libyans have to mountains. This is about three hundred miles southeast of Tripoli."

"Arabs!"

"Ella thinks they're getting ready to do whatever it is they're going to do. Just what, she doesn't know. She's convinced it's something big, but she has to be extremely careful. She now says that Aziz and Suslev are going to meet someone in Seville on Thursday. That's the sixth."

Neely obviously didn't remember Mossad's October inquiry or its request for photos of the Libyan desert. He said, "Why Seville?"

"Ella says the ostensible reason is that Boris Suslev wants to watch Viktor Barakov run the Seville Marathon. Schechter would have handled this himself and used however many reps were required except that Mossad is trying to rid itself of a mole. He doesn't want to risk Ella

31

until they know the extent of the damage. Mossad wants file mugs of whoever is participating at the Seville meeting. Schechter wants someone who can do photo and sound work, and to join Nidech in some scrub work if necessary. Mossad wants things tidied up at the end." This meant simply that after the Israelis had identified the conspirators in the Palestinian plot, they wanted to shoot a few of them.

"Burlane can do that."

"Schechter is very, very pleased at the quality of Ella's work. He says he frankly doubts that we can come up with a male as good as she is."

Neely laughed. "Burlane does his best."

"It's essential that we help her out, Peter. We put her out there." Schott read from his notes. "Burlane'll have to work it alone with Ella until Schechter and his people find their mole. She says Aziz and Suslev will be registered under assumed names at the Hotel Andalucia near the fine arts museum."

"What if Burlane's too sick to move?"

Ara Schott grimaced. "The bad part of it is when I tell Burlane he has to travel as Larry Schoolcraft. He likes all the whistling and noisemaking but hates to lug those lenses and microphones around. Since he's sick, it'll make it even worse."

Peter Neely said, "Tell him to take a hot bath, then rub his chest with Vicks. Tell him to sweat it out. That's what my grandmother said, and she was right. Tell him to turn his blanket to eight." Neely was pleased to have something to offer at clutch time.

6

JIM QUINT, STILL burping cannonball pie—shepherd's pie in any other Commonwealth country or British colony —was halfway through his second pint of John Courage when his portly old friend Bob Steele appeared at the door. Quint looked forward to much beer drinking and bullshitting in the manner of middle-aged men.

"Hah, Jim Quint, you bloody Yank!" Steele called. "You got my note. Glad you could make it."

"Of course I made it. Park that behind of yours," Quint said.

"Good, good." Steele took a barstool. "Have you got a place?"

"Full up, but I can always get myself a room in La Linea."

"A pint of Courage, please," Steele told the bartender, a young woman wearing jeans that were too small for her. "Thought you might have a time of it. This is supposed to be the low season, but they're almost full up on the Rock. Jorge Muldoon, the chap at the Queen's, says it's an invasion of camel jockeys. There are Arabs everywhere, Jorge says. He's never seen anything like it."

"Except for the most expensive rooms, naturally."

"Naturally. Those are always free. However, Jimbo, let me tell you that Jorge is an obliging chap and booked us into a double but jiggered the receipt to look like a single. This was after I laid a liter of scotch on him."

"All right!"

"*The Daily Telegraph* springs for the room, thereby assuring itself of its Barbary apes story, and in the process contributes to the arts."

"In a manner of speaking."

"How's Humper Staab doing these days?"

33

"I've got him in Berlin. I've got French spies, British spies, East German spies, West German spies, Polish spies, the KGB, of course, not to mention Mossad, and The Hated Company—a traffic jam of spies, Bob. The Humper's square in the middle of it, naturally, pursued by beautiful women who want to impale themselves upon his schlong, and by villains he has to waste. Great sport! I haven't figured out how to get Nazis in there, but that'll come. I want to have a swastika *and* a hammer and sickle on the cover at the same time. You can't miss with a swastika; swastikas sell books. Publishers know that. But it's getting harder and harder to bring the Nazis back; it's been so long, most of them would be old farts now."

"And a hammer and sickle too. That is ambitious. How do you propose to do that?"

"I was thinking maybe of having an anti-Semitic KGB officer find an SS unit that got lost in a snowstorm during the siege of Stalingrad. The Germans froze to death, see, and their corpses were thrown into a deep pit and covered up. Well, it never gets above freezing at that depth, and the Soviets find them when they're excavating for a bomb shelter. Russian physicians are always having to deal with people nearly frozen to death, a country like that, cold all the time. Wouldn't you imagine, Bob?"

"Oh, certainly. Poor blokes have to suffer those incredible winters."

"The Russians have discovered that if you thaw a corpse out gently enough and at the same time goose it with gentle waves of electrical energy, then *presto!*—life! This won't work with other kinds of death, only death by freezing. My publisher could put a foil swastika on the cover, see, only with a Soviet hammer at the end of one line and a curving sickle at the end of another. Best-seller, Bob! We're talking movie money here." Quint giggled at the fun of having the KGB thaw out an SS unit to do its dirty work. "Can you imagine a crazed KGB officer with a unit of pissed-off SS types ready to pick up where they left off? Hey, you're talking hammer and sickle and swastika. This one's breakaway, Bob. Breakaway. I can feel it."

Jim Quint—that is, Nicholas Orr, his nom de plume —did his damnedest to get in step with serious-minded authors who made real money, but it was a tough go because his imagination was slightly bent and wouldn't straighten out. He'd done his best, in fact strained furiously at the keyboard of his computer. In the end he learned he couldn't write any other way. He was trapped by a skewed imagination. "How's your monkey business going?" he asked Steele.

"I got most of it taken care of today so we can get on with the drinking."

"You get everything you wanted in one day?"

Steele looked mock offended, his voice turning very proper—heavy public school. "Well, I should say! I'm a journalist, James, a professional. I'm now an expert on the subject of Barbary apes. Ask me anything. Anything at all."

"Well!"

"Jim, old chap, you're looking at a man who covered EEC cheese negotiations in Brussels. I covered Daley Thompson's decathlon win. I covered Prince Bill's first bout with gas on the stomach. When my bloody sod of an editor decided to bore our readers with yet another Barbary apes story, who do you think he'd turn to?"

"Experience. Bob Steele, a writer's writer."

"He turned to a man with sense enough never to let the truth stand in the way of a good story, that's what he did. The apes are interesting in their way, Jim. They're monkeys, actually—identical to monkeys who live in the Atlas Mountains across the Strait of Gibraltar."

"I see. And did they swim or come by raft like Thor Heyerdahl? That's fourteen miles."

"They were either brought over in the eighth century by the followers of Tarik Ibn Zeyad, a soldier of Allah, or they're the sole survivors of monkeys that once prospered in southern Europe. Take your pick."

"Moorish monkeys!"

"That was in 711 when this place was named Jebel Tarik." He retrieved a small notebook from his jacket

35

pocket and printed J-e-b-e-l T-a-r-i-k, then crossed off the *i* and the *k*. "What do you get?"

"Jebel Tar."

"Say it quickly now."

"Jebel-Tar. Gibraltar."

"That's it: Tarik's Mountain. I've found it spelled several ways, and the definitions vary. It could be Tarik's Hill or Tarik's Rock. I think mountain's got it, though. There are two packs of apes, a friendly one that lives halfway up the Rock, at Queen's Gate, and a wild group near the top. The two packs had quite a history of fighting over the years." Steele pulled his reading glasses from his pocket and put them on. He deciphered the squiggles and scrawls for Quint's ape education. "Let's see, here we are. They've had quite a time of it. There were two hundred apes in 1910, which is just about when they split up into two factions and began fighting and killing one another over territory and females."

"Oh, the Hatfields and the McCoys, they were reckless mountain boys." Jim Quint sang a happy tune.

"By 1913 there were only three females left to carry on the race." Steele seemed perplexed at his own handwriting. "This is when the Royal Regiment of Artillery stepped in to help feed them and keep the packs separate. But the ape packs kept raiding one another, so that by 1924 there were only four left."

"Four?"

"It was close. They laid off killing one another for a while and grew to twenty-seven in number, but were down to ten in 1931, which is when the governor imported seven apes from Africa to help out. They were down to eleven by 1939, and to seven in 1943 when Churchill, on his way to the Teheran Conference, ordered more imported from Africa and said their number must never be allowed to fall below thirty-five. I ought to be able to do something with that, don't you think? Have a little fun. Remember the legend: when the apes leave the Rock, the British will go with them."

"You got some good art, I take it."

36

"I have made certain inquiries. A photographer for the *Chronicle* has Saturday off and can shoot them for me. For a few quid, I get a professional. We could take a car to the apes and hike on up to the top, what do you say?"

"We'll do it," said Quint, who wanted to know what the town and bay looked like from up on top. "I've never seen so many pubs in any one town in all my life. Pubs everywhere."

"And these hours, open until the wee hours." Steele was clearly excited at the prospect of drinking and talking uninterrupted by Her Majesty's odious drinking laws.

"An oasis."

At seven, the Spanish-language program on the television above the bar was switched to the Gib, the English-language station. Before the station was given over to *The Sea Urchins,* a children's adventure produced in New Zealand, an announcer told the viewers to stay tuned for a news special on the terrible storm that was howling across Europe.

Quint went to the men's bog where he took a seat on the toilet, latched the door, and had a couple of leisurely hits of hashish from a pipe made out of a matchbox and aluminum foil, holding the smoke in his mouth before he inhaled. He returned to Steele red-eyed, feeling drifty.

The gray-haired man on the Gib was saying how the "most savage blizzard in forty years" had ravaged central and northern Europe that day, killing scores. "Meteorologists say no end is in sight, but more on that later," the announcer said.

There followed shots of bundled people standing in a wind that moaned like suffering monks, sending snow fleeing. A Scottish fishing vessel was reported in trouble at sea. A German official was shown standing next to a snowdrift that had halted snowplows on the autobahn. Hardy Danes were shown chopping ice off streets. Swedes were shown skiing to the store in a snowstorm. All manner of fires were reported to be breaking out because of overworked, inadequate heating systems; an entire block burned to the ground in Stuttgart, captured at the peak of its fury by a German television crew. Frozen people were shown being taken into a Dutch hospital. The images of suffering were crowded together in a fast-paced montage.

Then a television weatherman explained the whole thing. He said he had access to photographs taken from a European communications satellite. He used plastic overlays with colorful arrows to indicate the direction of the wind.

What the arrows showed was that the terrible winter low, ordinarily centered around Irkutsk in Siberia, had moved twenty-five hundred miles to the west, settling over Sverdlovsk in the Urals. This in turn had pushed the Siberian cold over Eastern and Western Europe. The westerlies coming off the Atlantic were being deflected to the north.

Similar conditions had obtained before and would again, viewers were told. Eventually the low-pressure area in Siberia would drift back where it belonged and normal winter weather would return to Europe.

7

THE CAB SLOWED for a red light. James Burlane blew his nose and looked out into the snow. He tapped his toe with his thin black walking stick. He wet his dry lips with his tongue and whistled a low *weet-wit, weet-wit.* He said, "You ever hear one of those?"

"Hey, that's good! Over on the Jersey shore, I think." The cabdriver was from Brooklyn and pronounced it "shaw."

"Good ear. That's a purple sandpiper and they are indeed found on the Jersey coast."

The driver was pleased at his success. "Yeah, there's a place over there me and the old lady likes. You ever notice how a woman never feels like doing it at home, but if you get 'em in a motel room they just go crazy? They love it."

Burlane made a rasping *cheezp!* sound with his tongue. "That's your red-backed sandpiper, a lot harder to imitate."

The driver laughed. "Those are really good."

Burlane made a shrill, plaintive *kree-e-e-e* whistle, the call of Swainson's hawk, and fell silent. Burlane regarded himself as an artist and liked the whistling part of his Larry Schoolcraft cover. But he didn't like lugging the gear required. Ordinarily he insisted that technicians do tech work, not him. But this assignment was different. There was no arguing with the logic of the Israeli request; he had to do it.

The traffic, which had finally begun creeping again, stalled once more. Burlane could see miles of red taillights up ahead. Snow swirled under streetlights on both sides of the Queens arterial; snow scurried over curbs, and whooshed up walls, and whistled up and over eaves. Parked cars, heaped with snow, looked as if they were large white bugs. Such snow-laden bugs so brave as to venture into the storm crept slowly, *cl-clack* on chains, down the icy streets.

"Hey, we lucked out." The cabdriver had a shot at an off ramp and took it, gaining a traffic-free block before he had to stop at a red light. "Weathah like this, a guy's better off on the side streets," he said. "That crap ain't gonna clear," he said, gesturing with his head at the traffic he had abandoned. "Why don't you do some more calls, help pass the time."

"Sure," Burlane said. "What do you like? Ducks, thrushes, or what?"

"Gimme a medley."

Burlane made a trilling whistle, *tup, tup, tup, checheche, wiwi,* then *tup, tup, tup, cheche whew.* "Those are different kinds of warblers, also hard to do. I like shorebirds the best, grebes, and shearwaters, terns. Gulls too. Gulls are flying rats, did you know that? They'll eat anything."

39

The driver, laughing, turned his head. "Hey, that's a good one. You could never tell that to my wife, though; she'd kill ya. She's got a thing about sea gulls, my wife does. Thinks they're romantic. Every time we go to the shore she drags back a sea gull of some kind, a little wooden one, or a ceramic one, one made out of beach sand mixed with glue, or one made out of sea gull dung encased in plastic."

"Sea gull dung?"

"Sure, white there, with a few streaks of gray. She bought it two years ago in Atlantic City. She's got sea gulls clutterin' up the coffee table and sea gulls on shelves and windowsills. Fuckin' dog's always knockin' 'em over. Her sistah's the same way about unicorns. She's got unicorns all over the place. I tell her old man she's just horny is all, but he says that's a laugh."

"It's freedom and power, don't you think? Gulls and unicorns have got all the freedom and power they can use, but women ordinarily don't have a whole lot."

The driver didn't say anything.

"Want to hear my special bird?" Burlane said.

"Sure, let's hear it."

James Burlane cupped his hands around his mouth and made a crazed yodeling sound which he replaced with quavering, demented laughter.

The driver laughed too when he realized his passenger was just getting warmed up.

Burlane repeated the yodeling and laughing, getting louder and more frenzied each time.

When he stopped at last, the driver, who was still laughing, said, "I give up. What bird is that?"

"The Pacific loon in its breeding grounds. I grew up in Oregon."

"Is that really the way they sound?"

"You should hear them out on the water just going nuts." Burlane glanced at his wristwatch and coughed. He felt the cold window with the back of his hand. He hated the cold, hated the awful wind that had whipped Manhattan for the last four days. He'd stayed holed up in Jeffer-

40

son's loft the whole while, sweating, and swallowing aspirin like popcorn. He'd eaten half a slice of pizza from a place on Seventh Avenue, and that was it. He should have told them no.

The driver said, "I'd be goin' someplace warm if it was me."

"I'm going to record a few calls along the Spanish shoreline, take a few pictures."

"Ahh, warm. None of this crap. One of these days I'm gonna take my wife to Europe. She's always wanted to go to Paris, a romantic city, she thinks."

Burlane was overwhelmed by a fit of coughing.

"You could use a little sun, a cough like that."

"It'll get better. Takes time is all." He should have told Ara Schott to find somebody else. If he had any brains, he'd stay in New York and rest. But what was he going to do, sit around and eat Tylenol, and watch television, and listen to horns honk and people yell at one another, while someone else pursued Arabs?

James Burlane insisted on inventing his own covers. He had once traveled as a troubleshooter for a company that manufactured ovens for commercial bakeries, this following the logic that people bake bread just about all over the world. He had once traveled as a rep for the Coca-Cola company because Coke is consumed almost everywhere. In similar spirit, he had once attended a hamburger college so he could pass himself off as a McDonald's executive. In these covers, he traveled fast and light.

Ordinarily, Company reps had high-tech spook gear smuggled by the State Department in diplomatic baggage, where it was then stashed for pickup. This all required planning and coordination. Occasionally there was an emergency that demanded the ability to move gear quickly across international borders. Contemplating this problem one day in his Virginia home, Burlane was watching hyperactive finches attack the seed in his feeder, when he came upon the idea of Larry Schoolcraft.

There wasn't going to be any hanging around for

41

James Burlane. Mossad had called. The zits were clear: trouble in the Med. He had a job to do. This was go time. Show time. Larry Schoolcraft time.

The delicate man used his walking stick to tap along as he sang, "Be kind to your web-footed friends, for a duck may be somebody's mother." He started coughing again. His tongue tasted awful. He hoped he would still be able to whistle when he got to Spanish customs. Anybody could do ducks or Martin Denny jungle birds. It took real skill to do wrens and finches.

8

IT WAS SERGEANT Miguel Cigueres's first day on the job as a Spanish customs official, and as he had recently undertaken the responsibilities of marriage and family—his bride was already pregnant—his performance was of some consequence. For the occasion of Cigueres's first day, his captain, a self-impressed man, stood over his shoulder and watched his every move. This was to ensure that the standards of the service were upheld and so that the captain might leave the boring confines of his office and intimidate travelers with his impressive uniform.

Cigueres and the captain both heard the bird whistles before they saw the passengers. The passengers, having retrieved their luggage at last, burst into the room and headed toward them. Cigueres thought they resembled anxious cattle. On second thought, because of the oversize luggage they dragged with them, he decided gypsies. They looked like crazed gypsies. He glanced quickly at the captain.

The captain said, "You'll bear up, don't worry. This time next year you'll have to stay awake half the night burping a baby."

42

Above this, Cigueres heard what he thought was the excited chatter of a bird. "Captain?"

"I hear it."

They both saw him at once. He was a tall man in a tweed jacket that could have used elbow patches. He wore an ancient V-necked brown sweater over a pale yellow cotton shirt, blue jeans, and tattered running shoes. Under the floppy brim of a British desert cap, a long face with a large nose. He wore a pair of earphones that ran to his jacket pocket, and was twirling a walking stick like a baton.

Such a man imitating birdsongs would have been one thing: this man also pushed three huge suitcases that had wheels mounted on the bottom. He pushed, and whistled, and gyrated to his Walkman, and twirled his baton/walking stick all at the same time. It was incredible—as though the dancer/pusher/whistler could somehow juggle torches and swords and naked women all at once.

And he was headed their way—an interesting case, since most travelers grow somber and wary when they approach customs, not wanting to draw attention to themselves lest they be considered somehow suspicious, possibly worthy of searching. The whistler was either a harmless eccentric or indeed somebody who should be searched.

Cigueres looked to his superior for support. He had been told there would be an occasional loco in the line.

The man who had stood on that same line for eighteen years blinked uncertainly and adjusted his spectacles.

The dancing, whistling man was to be Cigueres's first traveler. Cigueres could hardly believe it. The other inspectors were looking at him, he knew, amused that he had to suffer so. He felt his mouth turn dry.

Before he knew it, the whistler was upon him. His rangy body never ceased to move, although he did stop twirling his walking stick and instead bounced the tip of it up and down on the floor to the beat of the music. He moved his pelvis suggestively. His shoulders moved. He might well have been an African. He gave a lopsided grin when he ceased pushing his luggage. He slipped an American passport out of his jacket pocket and gave it to

43

Cigueres. He snapped his fingers to the music on the radio. He whistled a *chip chupp-ee, chip chupp-ee, chip chupp-ee* that was startling in its clarity.

At Cigueres's side, the captain said, "No music, please, señor."

The whistler adjusted a diminutive cassette player in his jacket pocket. He whistled *quink, quink, quink, quink, what cheer, what cheer, quink, quink, qu . . ."*

The captain put his finger over his mouth to shush the American.

". . . *ink.*"

The captain said, "I think I'd better handle this one, Señor Cigueres."

Cigueres stepped aside, both relieved and disappointed. He'd wanted to show that he could handle anything.

The long-nosed man waited patiently while the captain read his American passport: Lawrence Schoolcraft, age forty-four. His passport had four pages filled with customs chops. "And the purpose of your visit, Señor Schoolcraft?"

"To record some Spanish shorebirds."

"Mmmmm," the captain said. Schoolcraft had two heavy suitcases and one valise. The captain unzipped the valise and removed a book entitled *Schoolcraft's Bird Calls of Europe,* followed by *Schoolcraft's Bird Calls of Asia, Schoolcraft's Night Birds of the World,* and *Schoolcraft's City Birds of the World.* The books had the traveler's picture on the back of the dust jacket. The captain opened one and read the biography of the author.

The jacket copy said Lawrence Schoolcraft had received a doctoral degree from Harvard University and was an ornithologist employed by the San Diego Zoo. He was regarded as a world authority on bird calls and had imitated birds on *The Tonight Show* for Johnny Carson, and for the benefit of Her Majesty the Queen.

While the captain examined his books, Schoolcraft whistled *weeta-weeta-weeta-wee, weeta-weeta chilp-chilp-chilp.*

44

"What do you have in these suitcases, Doctor?"

Tsit, tsit, tsit, twee, tsaay. "A camera and lenses and tripod and microphones for recording birdsongs. Also tape recorders." *Whoit, whoit, whoit; cheer, cheer, cheer.* "Shall I open them?" *Sweet, sweet, sweet, twiiirrrrr.*

Schoolcraft's whistling had everybody in the room smiling and looking their way. "That won't be necessary."

"Well, thank you." Schoolcraft zipped his valise back up and turned on the music.

Cigueres said, "What's the music?"

Schoolcraft, moving to a lazy, slow beat, said, " 'The Dark Side of the Moon.' "

" 'The Dark Side of the Moon'! Pink Floyd!" Cigueres was surprised.

"They say the back side of Gibraltar is as mysterious as the dark side of the moon," Lawrence Schoolcraft said. He coughed and went on his way, pushing his wheeled suitcases, dancing, twirling his walking stick, whistling.

If he hadn't been so sick, James Burlane would have been euphoric over his Larry Schoolcraft entrance. He had pulled it off, and without dropping his baton. He was out of practice with his bird whistling, so had cheated by whistling along with his Walkman tape while he pretended to be dancing to music.

Burlane took a bus into Madrid. The countryside looked remarkably like that in eastern Oregon where he had grown up; it was high and wide, slow rolling and nearly barren. He was discouraged to see that the Spaniards had managed to plant locust trees along their avenues, no doubt because they didn't need watering. Burlane thought locust trees had the ugliest bark of any tree on the planet. He had come to that conclusion as a boy and refused to part with it. Such Spaniards as were on the streets were bundled in layers of sweaters and coats and walked with their shoulders turned into the biting wind.

He decided that if he was going to spend only one night in Madrid, the least he could do was hang out in Hemingway territory. So he told the taxi driver to take him

45

to the Plaza Santa Ana; there were said to be lots of hostels in the area. Shivering, he settled into the back seat, glancing every so often at the traffic to the rear.

When he got out of the cab, James Burlane could hardly believe the cold. How did these Spaniards do it? There would be no central heating in a hostel, he knew, just big, cold rooms that were centuries old, and wind leavened only by an occasional space heater.

He knew he shouldn't stay out in the cold. He turned his own shoulder into the frigid wind, and set about finding himself refuge.

9

JAMES BURLANE WAS awakened by a full bladder and sheets that were soaked and cold from a long night of sweating. He opened the shutters of the Central Hostel to find Seville shrouded in a cold, wet fog. Walking stick in hand, and his Nikon slung over his shoulder, he set out to have himself some coffee. He saw from some posters that this was the morning of the Seville Marathon.

Burlane ran a routine down the Avenida de la Republica Argentina across the Rio Guadalquivir to wash himself of anybody who might have followed him from Madrid, and doubled back to Calle Zaragoza. He took a seat in a hole-in-the-wall bar not twenty yards from the front door of the Central Hostel. He had a clear view of the narrow street. If there were any poor little lost Libyan or KGB reps out there, they'd come back to wait for him, poor dears. Burlane wanted to know what they looked like.

The delicate man had two cups of coffee and a small plate of *churros,* light, sweet, deep-fried pastries that were turdlike in appearance—a special machine extruded them into hot oil from which they emerged in long, crisp, pale

46

brown curls—but were delicious dipped in hot chocolate or Spanish coffee.

Burlane savored his *churros*. No frustrated spook lingered in the street. He was clean. He checked his watch; it would be another hour before the runners got to the center of the city. Aziz and Suslev would still be having coffee in the Hotel Andalucia. Outside, the fog was beginning to thin.

Luck, if not health, was with him; James Burlane found another bar with a reasonable view of the main door of the Hotel Andalucia. This one was filled with people waiting for the runners. The leaders were now approaching the city from the south on the Calle del Torneo that flanked the west bank of the Guadalquivir. The route turned left up the Calle de Alfonso XII—past Burlane and the rabbits in the Hotel Andalucia—then right onto the Calle de las Sierpes for the run to the center of the city. Unmindful of the pathetic capacity of his bladder, Burlane had another cup of coffee.

He took just one sip before the rabbits emerged from the front door of the Andalucia: Muhammad Aziz, wearing gray slacks and a proper blue blazer; the mammoth Boris Suslev, looking like a bookie at Pimlico; and . . .

Ella Nidech.

James Burlane was stunned. Ella Nidech! It was Ella Nidech who needed help. Ella Nidech in deep cover as a belly dancer. Ara Schott, following Company policy to the letter, had told him nothing except that the Mossad's woman was on loan from a Western intelligence service.

Suslev checked his watch, and he and Aziz and Ella Nidech joined the thin crowd gathering at the curb.

Burlane watched the delicate woman's rump as she walked up the sidewalk and remembered that long-ago night in Hong Kong, after the two of them had taken on the Society of the Red Lotus on Fong Wai Chow. He watched Suslev check his watch again. The crowd got thicker. Soon Burlane heard applause, first faint, in the distance, then louder as the lead runner turned the corner from the Calle del Torneo. Burlane eased closer to the rabbits in case they

47

moved in the crowd. He heard Suslev say, "Barakov will win. He is Russian and has the best training in the world. He will win in Seoul. The best."

The applause drew closer.

A motorcycle appeared, parting the crowd for the leader.

"See! Barakov!" Suslev shouted. "Barakov! Barakov!"

Sure enough, the lead runner, a blond with leather muscles, wore a bright red outfit with a yellow hammer and sickle on the jersey, proof to the world that socialism produced the best marathon runners and was therefore best at everything.

The excited Suslev raised a triumphant fist and shouted, *"Da! Da! Da! Da!* Comrade!" as the motorcycle passed. Barakov, soaking wet from sweat, face racked with pain and fatigue, acknowledged Suslev with a fist of his own.

Suslev brushed past a Spanish policeman and ran beside his comrade for ten yards, shouting, *"Da! Da! Da! Da!"* Suslev returned to Aziz and Ella Nidech. Even from across the street, Burlane could hear the excited Suslev:

"No one is close. Not even close. Do you hear applause for the second-place runner? I don't hear it." He grinned broadly, triumphantly. "Barakov trains on the taiga!"

On the far side of the street, Burlane dropped well back—he wasn't interested in hearing Suslev's enthusiasm for Barakov—and followed the trio to the Calle de las Sierpes which became the Avenida de la Constitución. They passed Seville's grand cathedral, said to be the largest Gothic cathedral in the world, from which—in one of Christendom's more questionable hours—the Catholic Church had conducted the Inquisition.

The rabbits joined a tanned, middle-aged man at an outdoor table where the Avenida de la Constitución became the Avenida de Roma. The man appeared to have stepped out of a Dewar's scotch ad. He sported a handsome mane of silver hair and a neatly trimmed silver beard. Burlane recognized him immediately. He was Bobby Nye, a former British colonel turned mercenary.

Burlane found himself a table by the entrance to the café. This was well back of his rabbits; there he could drink a *tinto* and watch both marathoners and rabbits. Muhammad Aziz and Boris Suslev meeting with Bobby Nye. This was an interesting turn of events. He found it hard not to stare at Ella Nidech.

Burlane surveyed the area, trying to pick the Mossad rep, but couldn't find a candidate. He noted that the Spanish runners were less given to dramatic grabbing of paper cups from outstretched hands than were the Americans he had seen on television.

The café was less than four hundred yards from the finish of the marathon; the cheering could be heard as one runner after another reached the blessed end. Ella Nidech got up and started walking Burlane's way. Burlane concentrated on his *tinto* as she passed him on her way to the women's toilet.

Burlane whistled the brown creeper's *see-ti-wee-tu-wee* as she passed on the way back and a spitball of thin paper tumbled at his feet.

"Very good. Could you please light my cigarette," she said. She murmured, "Bobby Nye is coming with us. They're being watched by the one to your far left in a brown jacket, and one to your right with the trousers that're too short."

Burlane lit her cigarette, catching her green eyes for the briefest of moments. This was the first time since she had become the delicate woman that they had been on the same job together.

Nidech continued on her way.

Burlane watched his rabbits talk and drink tall glasses of Spanish beer. He unfolded Nidech's spitball. She had typed it neatly for her assigned partner in the case, not knowing it was to be Burlane:

Welcome to the fun. Muhammad Aziz and Boris Suslev are traveling together. I have them covered. Bobby Nye will be coming with us. You have responsibility for whomever it is they meet. Maybe it will be a man named Borodin. Suslev is

49

sore and resentful of someone called Borodin. This Borodin is obviously Suslev's superior, and it seems that he has taken over whatever it is these people began. I think he is the Mr. Big to whom they report. We'll need mugs of everybody possible, especially this man Borodin when we find him. I sense that they're about to do something big in the western Mediterranean, though of course I'm never included in their discussions. We're scheduled to take an eight o'clock flight to Tangier for another meeting of some kind. I don't know the flight, but there can't be that many. I am the belly dancer Lady Fatima!

On the bottom of this she had scrawled, *"Yr lft, brn jckt. Yr rt, sht pnts. Pcs plse."*

Burlane lit the note and watched it burn in the ashtray. A belly dancer!

A few minutes later Nidech and her companions rose and moved through the spectators toward the cathedral, away from the Plaza de España and the finish of the race, where cheers could still be heard.

Burlane's Nikon was strapped over his shoulder, tourist fashion. He casually put it to his eye, pretending to follow the runners. He focused the 200mm zoom onto the face of one, then the other bodyguard, and snapped their mugs. If their luck held out, he and Ella Nidech could give European customs officials a whole bunch of photos to help them grab assholes at the border.

After they were gone, Burlane ordered a sandwich of *jamon serrano,* a salty Spanish ham, and a glass of San Miguel. He had a few hours to himself. He called the airport in his best Spanish and found there were plenty of seats remaining on the flight to Tangier. He strolled over to the Plaza de España to watch the excitement at the end of the race. When the fog cleared and the afternoon sun came out, he took a walk along the Paseo de las Delicias and the Paseo de Cristobal Colon, both of which flanked the Guadalquivir, where lean Spanish crewmen leaned into the oars of racing shells.

At five o'clock he returned to his room to take a nap. He had three hours before flight time. This is when the gods of crappy luck intervened.

At first, Burlane thought a cold front must have arrived in Seville because even in bed he was freezing. His fingers were especially cold. He tried to warm them between his legs and under his arms but to absolutely no avail. He wondered if he would ever be warm again. He couldn't stand it. He got up, determined to get warm once and for all. In addition to the runner's sweats and T-shirt he used as pajamas on the road, he put on his two pairs of blue jeans and one pair of chinos, this plus three shirts and one turtleneck sweater. He pulled on all five pairs of socks. Aside from his extra underwear, this was everything Burlane had with him.

He got back into bed, barely able to bend his elbows and knees, and forced himself into a fetal position. Ahh, now, he told himself, I'll be warm.

He was freezing.

Burlane lay there shivering, staring at the shutters and the electric wall heater that was turned on but didn't produce heat. Those bright orange Spanish oranges were in season; Burlane had seen workers harvesting them as he had come down from Madrid on the train. The orange groves looked loaded. How could it possibly be this cold in an area that produced oranges of such health and abundance?

The cold was Siberia-like, outrageous. Burlane's feet were chunks of ice. There was no sufficiently warm refuge for his fingers, none. Suddenly he knew he had to vomit. Had he gotten sick from the *churros* and coffee? Had his ham sandwich been bad? He couldn't get into his shoes because of all the socks and so went pad, pad, pad down one flight of stairs to the john.

When he got back into bed, braced for the cold, he found it wasn't so bad. Then he actually got warm. Nice. Then toasty. Okay! Well, then a bit too warm. Then hot. Then hot as hell. He began stripping layers of clothing. He was roasting. Heat wafted up from his face.

Burlane looked in the mirror. A bead of sweat formed

on the end of his nose. Sweat streamed into the corners of his eyes and began burning. He held out his hand and droplets of sweat formed instantly on each finger. It was as if he were riding a body-temperature roller coaster.

Then he coughed up some gunk from his lungs: once, twice, three times. Frothy and bright pink each time. The pink was caused by blood, he knew. Pneumonia. He looked at his watch, startled to see that it was seven-thirty. Bobby Nye! He hadn't been paying any attention to the time. He had to follow Bobby Nye to Tangier. He had to get a taxi for the airport. He got up, feeling light-headed, and had to grab onto the sink or fall down.

James Burlane knew he couldn't possibly get to the airport on time. He had screwed up once trying to catch a plane, had taken the plane to Portland, Maine, instead of Portland, Oregon, and had left Ella Nidech in the lurch in the South China Sea. Now this. Pneumonia. If he had blood in his lungs, it was only going to get worse, not better; he knew that. He didn't want to leave the Mediterranean, but he didn't want to go to a Spanish hospital either; he didn't know the language well enough to talk to a doctor. Returning to the United States was out of the question. Something big was coming up with the asshole Sovs right square in the middle of it. Ara Schott told him Saloman Schechter's people could not give this agent protection because they had a mole in their yard. He would not leave Ella Nidech by herself.

Ella Nidech aside, Burlane had his pride. He'd accepted an assignment. It was a point of honor to deliver.

He dug out his paperback atlas to see what the possibilities were. He turned to a map of Europe and the Mediterranean. France? London? They had good hospitals there. London, maybe. The Dutch. Possibly. Burlane thought the Dutch were wonderful people, and he couldn't believe their medicine would take second place to anybody's.

He mopped the sweat from his forehead with the tail of his T-shirt, and when the shirt was soggy, he turned to the bed sheet, and finally began squeegeeing sweat with the back of his forefinger. He flip, flip, flipped it on the floor, more sweat, and more and more. It was coming so fast he couldn't see without the squeegeeing. If he hadn't been sick and a little scared, he would have laughed at the deluge.

With sweat dripping on Bavaria and the Swiss Alps, Burlane considered his predicament. He was a professional, a survivor. He was determined to be calm and logical. He had faced down East Germans, and Colombians, had gone one-on-two against KGB agents on the Trans-Siberian Express. He tilted his head so the Warsaw Pact countries got drenched. Burlane knew damn well he wouldn't be going there.

Then Burlane spotted his refuge. Physicians trained in the United Kingdom. Okay! Grinning through the sweat, he looked up the weather stats: an average of sixty-two degrees in February. Yes! He would go to Gibraltar. He would stay in the western Mediterranean. He would get well and catch up with Ella Nidech and the whole pack of them, Bobby Nye, Muhammad Aziz, Boris Suslev, and Borodin, too, whoever the hell he was.

10

BY FRIDAY MORNING the storm over central Europe had broken and the weather had improved over the Mediterranean as well. Jim Quint and Bob Steele hiked to Mackintosh Square to meet the photographer and driver who were to take them to the Barbary apes' den. Quint wanted to have a picture of himself with a Barbary ape for the dust jacket of his next novel. He said he'd leave it to his readers to decide which one was the author and which one was the ape.

The driver was a curly-haired man with thick-lensed eyeglasses set in black plastic frames. He had taken a lot of tourists to see the apes in his time. The driver knew his apes.

As if to prove his point, he tossed the photographer a bag of chocolate-covered peanuts. The photographer gave the bag to Bob Steele.

"They just love 'em," the driver said. "There's a good-looking one you'll see today who just hogs them down, hogs them. Puking Max, we call him. He's the maximum ape. Primo. He packs it away, then brings it up. He never gets fat."

Steele looked shocked. "He vomits?"

"Every day, we think. We've seen him do it enough. You'll meet him today. Loves the camera, that one does!"

"A bulimic ape! Good stuff! Yes! Yes!" Steele beamed. He took out his notebook and scrawled a note.

The custodian of ape lore drove the black Mercedes up the narrow, steep Engineer Road, on the city side of the Rock; they were headed south toward Europa Point. Engineer Road doubled back and became Queen's Road and rose even higher, toward Mons Calpe. The Bay of Gibraltar was soon far below them on their left. Then the road leveled off and they came around a curve to find three cars pulled to the side of the narrow road. A gathering of tourists were looking at something in the heavy brush on the upper side of the road.

"We're here, lads," the driver said.

The tourists, brandishing 35mm cameras, some with huge, impressive lenses, were taking pictures. The apes were sitting at a respectful distance on branches of the underbrush.

The bespectacled driver shook his head.

"They don't look very friendly to me," Steele said.

"These people know *nada* about apes. *Nada,*" the driver said.

"Is Max here?" Quint asked.

The driver pointed to a handsome ape with sleek, clean fur. "He knows who I am. He'll be coming over to have his picture taken."

Indeed, Max, who had been indifferent to the other visitors, stirred at the sight of their driver. The photographer began adjusting his camera. Steele scribbled a note. "You go first, Jim. I want to see Max in action."

The driver put some chocolate-covered peanuts in Jim Quint's hand and slipped some into Quint's jacket pocket. "Back up slowly to him. He'll hop up on your shoulder." Max did exactly that, settling himself comfortably.

"Hold some in your hand," the driver said.

Quint did as he was told. He could feel Max's warm body against the side of his head. Max hardly weighed anything. The photographer moved in close, snapping shots; Puking Max, contentedly chewing his peanuts, obliged by looking at the lens straight on. He seemed fascinated by the lens, in fact.

When they reached the summit of the saddle-shaped ridge between Mons Calpe to the north and O'Hara's Peak to the south, Bob Steele took his jacket off and swabbed his face with a handkerchief. He sat down on an outcropping of limestone and sighed heavily. "Why in the sod are we doing this? We should have gone back with them in the taxi. We're pub adventurers. This is work. No sane person works when he could be sitting on a barstool. We could be having ourselves a pint by now."

"It's the spirit of Sir Edmund Hillary and Tenzing Norkay." Jim Quint, too, was breathing hard. He read the names of flowers from a tourist brochure. He stuffed the brochure back in his hip pocket and looked back down at the Bay of Gibraltar. "Man, that's way, way, down there." He looked back at the city of Gibraltar far below.

"About twelve hundred feet to the summit of Mons Calpe and almost thirteen hundred to O'Hara's Peak. We should have stayed in the pubs, Jim."

It seemed to Jim Quint as if, in some long-forgotten time, in one of the planet's periodic internal wrenchings, the earth had suddenly tilted, leaving part of the crust sticking up at a forty-five-degree angle, and that had turned out to be Gibraltar. The peninsula that was the Rock sheltered a small town on the base of its steep western slope. The city soon gave way to a dark green thicket called maquis, mottled by outcroppings of light gray limestone, rising up to the crest of the peninsula. It was nearly a solid limestone cliff.

On the Mediterranean side of the peninsula, a great vertical fracture of limestone, including Prudential's famous rock, looked down on the water. Mons Calpe—the northeastern base of the peninsula—overlooked the Mediterranean and narrow beaches to the east, and the Gibraltar airport and the Spanish mainland to the north. The limestone cliff was broken by concrete water catchments that collected Gibraltar's drinking water.

Quint said, "Look at that belly on you; it'll do you good to air your shorts out. Maybe we'll find an ocellated lizard. They have ocellated lizards here, whatever they are. A pint of John Courage would hit the spot, I agree."

"I should have told you I didn't like heights," Steele said.

"No one with any sense does."

"We could have bought postcards, Jim. The trick is to stay in the pubs and buy postcards. You'll note that the tourist bureau attributes this trail to the Moors. No sensible Englishman would have gone to all the effort to carve a trail out of limestone way up here. What's the point?" Steele lay on his ample belly before he peered down at the dramatic vista of the Mediterranean—straight down.

Quint joined Steele staring down at the concrete catchments. "You never see those in the Prudential ads."

"I get the shivers climbing over the edge of a bathtub. Mons Calpe was supposed to be one of the two pillars of Hercules, who guarded the gates of the Mediterranean. Did you know that?"

"Well, sure, I like a good story as much as the next guy. And the second pillar?"

"Mons Abyla across the Strait. It's now called Sidi Musa—Ape's Hill."

"Fourteen miles across." Quint looked to his right, south, toward the African shoreline, which he could see clearly.

"Right, as German U-boats found out during the Second World War. Franco let them into Cadiz, where they refueled, but they still had to run the Strait. Even then the British could shell Tangier if they felt like it—that's about thirty-five miles to the southwest."

Quint looked down at the concrete catchment that collected the Rock's drinking water. "And now? A person'd never know you. Brits even had a garrison here."

"They say a garrison of two thousand, but bodies don't mean anything. The word is, NATO was concerned about outdated batteries on the Gib, so the government rearmed the place. *Jane's* says they have French Exocet missiles. Nobody runs a fourteen-mile bottleneck with Exocets pointed at them; our chaps learned that in the Falklands. At Europa Point—down there on the southern point of the peninsula—Her Majesty's Navy has banks of sonar listening to the sweet songs of screws passing in the night."

Quint held his hand over his left ear, squinted his eyes, and said, "*Ping! Ping! Ping!* I love those old submarine movies. *Run Silent, Run Deep. Navy Hellcats.* 'I hear it now, sir. Hard on our port, coming straight at us!' All that sweating and being knocked around as the depth charges go *boom! boom! boom!*"

"They have IBM computers to tell them whose screws these are, whether they're surface or submarine, plus a complete identification of the vessel including age, speed, weapons, range, and capabilities. That's your superb American technology. If the Russians break out of the Black Sea, there's Suez at one end . . ."

". . . and Gibraltar at the other. This must annoy the Soviets, the pricks."

Steele laughed. "I can't imagine they're delighted. They have a huge navy, but your American Sixth Fleet has the run of the Med. I'm bloody pooped. I can't imagine why you haven't passed out, all that gray hair. What color did it used to be?"

"The color of rich manure. I looked like a skunk in reverse until the top turned gray too. Shall we push on for Mons Calpe?"

Bob Steele eased back from the precipice that overlooked the water catchment. "Tell my editors I was game to the end, Jim. Tell my brother Bill I did him proud. Stay away from my sister Nell, though. Women get emotional and weak at funerals, and I wouldn't want her bunking up with an American."

"You'll be a legend on Fleet Street, Bob. Are you up for it?"

"I'm ready." Bob Steele followed his friend north. The narrow trail followed the spine of the summit toward Mons Calpe. Talking as he walked, Steele said, "They say—if one uses one's imagination—that from Algeciras, Gibraltar looks like a woman on her back. The head, Mons Calpe, points toward Spain. Her breasts are there at Middle Hill. Her knees are drawn up, you see, at O'Hara's Peak on the south. I don't suppose I have to ask a chap like you if you can imagine it."

An hour later they had straggled down to Castle Road, not far from St. Bernard's Hospital, when they had to stop for a taxi.

Bob Steele, shaken by something he had seen in the cab, grabbed Jim Quint by the collar and yanked him sharply back.

"What the hell . . . ?"

Steele stared after the cab, which had slowed to a stop in front of the hospital. "Come with me. Quickly now. Quickly. Quickly."

Quint followed quickly. "What's going on?"

"Remember me telling you about meeting that guy on the Trans-Siberian Express who was introducing himself as you? Said he was from Bison, Montana. Wrote Humper Staabs. The works. Loose, just like you. Don't stare. Don't stare."

"What about him?" Jim Quint turned to see a tall man step out of the taxi. The taxi driver had to help him with his gear. He had a walking stick poked under his belt and was struggling with two heavy suitcases in addition to an airline carry-on.

"That man right there went after two Russian agents, John Wayne style, pistol blazing, and killed them both cleanly. I thought they only did stuff like that in the movies. I helped him push the bodies off the train. I could hardly believe it. That's him, Jim. I wonder what he's doing here, dragging suitcases around?"

11

JAMES BURLANE, FEELING a stabbing pain as he breathed, suppressed a wince and leaned slightly to the left to appease his distressed lung. Dr. Michael Maskill, a slender man with a thoughtful face and intelligent eyes, said, "So what can I do for you, Mr. Schoolcraft?"

"I have an infection in my right lung. I ran a fever and didn't eat for four days before I left New York, and when I got to Madrid, it was cold enough to freeze a penguin. And that wind. In Seville last night I got twisted with an awful fever and started spitting up pink gunk. I was weak and hadn't eaten and insisted on traveling, and this is what I get. I rode the bus down from Seville today."

"What was the consistency? Thick? Thin and frothy?"

"Thin and frothy."

"Only in your right lung?"

"The left one's still okay, I think. The stuff was pink. That means blood, doesn't it?"

"That's possible. Would you take your shirt off, please?"

Maskill used his stethoscope to listen to the slurging and gurgling in Burlane's beleaguered lung. It was the usual drill: Maskill moved the stethoscope from spot to spot with Burlane breathing as deeply as he could each time. Burlane could see him eye the terrible scar on his right shoulder. When Burlane turned for Maskill to listen in from the back, he said, "I was lucky."

"I should say you were."

59

"They were small caliber. I was in Thailand looking for a kind of small parrot and wandered into a bad part of Bangkok."

"I see. Breathe, please, Mr. Schoolcraft."

Burlane breathed. "There are four holes there, actually. He piled one slug on top of another."

"Breathe."

Burlane breathed. "I say 'he.' I never did see the son of a bitch."

Maskill gripped Burlane by the abdomen just under his right ribs. "Is this sore?" Burlane knew there was a question Maskill was dying to ask but was too polite.

"Yes, it is," Burlane said. "I got the cut on the left shoulder there in San Fernando de Apure. I took a boat up from Ciudad Bolivar."

"Which is?"

"That's in Venezuela. That happened just eight months after I got shot in Bangkok. I'd just gotten out of the hospital when I took off after parrots' calls again. I did a whole book on parrot calls." To prove his point, Burlane began squawking and cawing.

Maskill looked amused. He looked at the scan, then at Burlane. "He must have taken it to the bone."

Burlane ran a finger along the white ridge. "A little run of bad luck. I suppose we've all got scars of one sort or another. He did take it to the bone, you're right."

"You must lead an exciting life."

"I got bushwhacked in Port Moresby two years ago. That put me in the hospital, too, but didn't leave any scars. Guy whacked me alongside the head with what I think was a cricket bat, although I can't imagine they play cricket there. Too damned hot." Burlane gave his *oo-loo-woo* call of the mating prairie chicken, followed by the *tsee tsee tsee tsee tsee-o, teetsa teetsa teetsa teetsa teet* of the American redstart. He opened his camera case and valise and pulled out his publications for Maskill to examine.

Maskill read the blurbs on the backs of Larry Schoolcraft's books. On the back of the dust jacket of *Schoolcraft's Night Birds of the World,* four distinguished ornithologists pronounced the tome the "definitive book on the little-understood behavior of nocturnal birds, with rare and fascinating photography made possible by recent advances in infrared telescopic lenses and parabolic microphones."

"I was on my way to shoot some Spanish shorebirds, but now I guess I'll have to concentrate on Gibraltar. You've got two kinds of vultures here, the Egyptian and the griffon. You've got Scops owl and the rock bunting, but the best of all is the Barbary partridge, which I'd like to get on tape." Burlane grinned. "Who knows, maybe I'll add him to my repertoire." To sink home his cover, Burlane gave Maskill a diving duck, the *onk-a-lik, ow-owdle-ow* of the old squaw.

Maskill smiled. "Mr. Schoolcraft, I suspect you have a patch of pneumonia in your right lung. I think we should start feeding you antibiotics through your arm and have a look at your blood."

"How long will I be in the hospital?"

Maskill shrugged. "Three days, maybe. Perhaps a week. It depends on the kind of infection and how it responds to drugs. You'll be weak for a while, so I wouldn't be thinking of returning to the field right off. You'll want a good long rest. Since you're not entitled, there'll be some people from accounting coming around."

"I'd like to have a telegram sent, if I might. It can be sent collect. My Uncle Paul has more money than he knows what to do with."

"Certainly. I'll have someone run it downtown." Maskill gave Burlane a pen and a notepad.

Burlane wrote a Fairfax, Virginia, address for one Paul Fuller, and wrote:

Dear Uncle Paul,

Boy, this trip is really turning out to be for the birds. Was it ever cold in Madrid! I almost froze my yo-yos off. I did get to meet Margaret's friend Elizabeth in Seville as we had planned. Such a surprise! You dickens you for not telling me

61

earlier. But then again I guess a surprise once in a while isn't so bad. I saw some interesting birds in Seville. Took their pictures but got sick before I got a chance to mike any of their calls. Elizabeth is going to Tangier. She says I can mike the same birds there, and asked me to come along. Alas, I started coughing blood from my lungs late yesterday. I had quite a time of it, you can be sure.

I took a bus to Gibraltar today and wouldn't you know, Dr. Maskill here at St. Bernard's says I have a patch of pneumonia in my right lung. He says I'll be here four or five days although you know me; I'll be out there taking pictures of birds quicker than the doctor might imagine. When they let me out, I'll catch up with Elizabeth. If you hear from her please tell her what happened to me and tell her I'm sorry to be such a party pooper. Tell her if she lets me know how I can get in touch with her, I'll make everything up to her. No bird escapes Larry Schoolcraft. Do keep in touch.

Your faithful nephew,
Larry

Burlane was taken to Room 5 of the private ward. It overlooked television antennas and clotheslines on the roofs of bars and flats, and beyond that the Bay of Gibraltar, and the Spanish city of Algeciras on the far side.

Burlane was given some cotton pajamas that were too large around the waist. Maskill inserted a needle into a vein on the side of Burlane's wrist. A plastic bottle of saline solution at the top of the I.V. stand filtered, drip, drip, down a clear plastic tube into a solution of penicillin, then drip, drip, down the tube into the needle and into James Burlane's blood to enter combat against the assembled pneumococcus bacteria, vicious little bastards.

Pneumonia! James Burlane looked at the needle taped onto his wrist. Pneumonia! Now he knew what happened to spies who stayed out in the cold.

* * *
62

Muhammad Aziz was commander of the operation, assisted by Colonel Bobby Nye. It was Nye who had been in charge of the three weeks of training on the slopes of Jebel As Sawda, which weren't much in the way of mountains, but were the best Omar Qafi had in Libya.

The high command met for a final briefing in a banquet room in the Central Hotel overlooking the main square in downtown Gibraltar, and across Main Street from the House of Assembly and the city hall. Muhammad Aziz's instructions were preceded by roast beef and Yorkshire pudding served by comely young Gibraltarians.

The Arab commanders were all English-speaking, so they would be able to follow the instructions of Bobby Nye. It would be Aziz's responsibility to smuggle four hundred Arabs onto the Rock from Spain.

As usual the Russian, Boris Suslev, looked on in silence. Suslev, whose assignment apparently was to see to it that Moscow's rubles weren't wasted on a bunch of excitable camel jockeys, had been with the Arabs from the beginning of their training. It was an inexpensive operation as such matters went, but Moscow was protective of what rubles it had.

Bobby Nye's services, on the other hand, had been expensive. Nye's knowledge of the Rock's geography and defenses—he had served a tour there—was essential, and he knew it; he had demanded payment in advance and had already banked it in the Cayman Islands. This arrangement was made with the implicit understanding that if he pulled a skip, he would be run down by the KGB and made to regret his decision.

Colonel Terry Holmestead, whose acne had taken an unaccountable and repugnant turn for the worse, licked his lips when Aziz's briefing came to his part.

Holmestead's uniform had been fashioned by a Lebanese tailor working from Libyan and Iranian patterns. The trousers had parallel red stripes running down the sides. Three rows of colorful ribbons and two golden medallions were pinned on the left breast of the tunic; two medals dangled on the right side. One medallion had Omar Qafi carved in relief; the second contained the Ayatollah Khomeini. One medal featured a golden pyramid; the second offered a scarlet, running camel that reflected the light. Holmestead's hat was adorned with golden scimitars crossed over ropes of silver braid.

Holmestead showed no indication of being embarrassed or self-conscious about his uniform. On the contrary, he slumped about, looking excessively casual. This Steve McQueen slouch was broken only by Holmestead's need to give relief to his inflamed face.

"Colonel Holmestead will disable the alarm system with his computer, then he'll take their communications, and the doors." Aziz gestured to Terry Holmestead.

"Men," Holmestead said. He bowed awkwardly, grabbing for his billed officer's cap to keep it on his head. Then he stood, shifting from foot to foot, apparently uncertain what to do next. Holmestead's left hand sought a lump of reddened pimple on his neck. The fingers were poised to squeeze—seemingly yearned, ached, to squeeze—but stopped. Holmestead, glancing about the room, removed his hand; his eyes narrowed momentarily, and he inhaled quickly, his teeth grinding. He sat down abruptly, and crossed his arms and clenched his fists.

"We'll review the operation in sequence, starting with the border crossing tomorrow afternoon," Aziz said. "The crossing is my responsibility. Then we will review Colonel Nye's mission of getting Colonel Holmestead to the proper computer terminal. Colonel Nye?"

Bobby Nye wore jeans and a dark blue sweater, Nike running shoes, and a jaunty black beret. Nye ran the palm of his hand over his neat beard. "I know you chaps are probably tired of listening to me, but we shall have to go over it one more time. We must know it one hundred percent, all of us. We shall move quickly and quietly. If every one of us knows his job and does it, we'll be fine. We're a unit, chappies; we move as one."

Aziz said, "While we are securing the inside, Colonel Nye will be leading the assault on the surface barracks, the police, and the airport. Colonel Nye?"

64

"We've been over it and over it," Nye said. "The Gibraltar defense is aimed at conventional attack by sea or air. Britain has the responsibility of defending the entrance to the Mediterranean. We move quickly, hitting the police station, the border, the surface units simultaneously—to the second." Nye swept his forefinger from his left to his right, pointing at each of his subordinates, looking them square in the eye. "To the second!"

"You all have Colonel Holmestead's rough drawings of the interiors that he has seen. These will be supplemented with drawings by Colonel Nye. Colonel Nye will answer questions you might have about their exits to the surface."

"It's crucial that all these are covered," Nye said. "One mistake and we'll find ourselves swimming for Africa. If you have any confusion at all about your assignment, don't hesitate to ask me. Remember, if they choose to make a break at your sector, hit them with everything you have. Your Kalashnikovs aren't very accurate"—he glanced at Suslev—"but you can put down a lot of fire. You'll be at point-blank range. Don't hesitate."

One of the Arabs signaled with his finger. "And the flamethrowers?"

Nye smiled. "The best the Warsaw Pact has to offer. Your LPO-50s have a range of twenty meters; if you have to toast a few Brits, then toast them. More questions?" Nye waited. "The assignments up top are crucial. I want you people to move very quickly indeed. Go in sprinting. I want to hear those Kalashnikovs singing. We've been over it all before; I'm sure you're tired of hearing it." Nye was finished.

"Colonel Holmestead?" Aziz said.

"I will answer questions so everything will be c-clear," Holmestead said. He removed the heavy officer's cap. His forehead was sweaty. He mopped it with the sleeve of his jacket. He seemed in pain.

"May I help you, Colonel?" Aziz asked.

"I say, where's the b-bog?"

Bobby Nye gestured with his thumb to a door in the

rear of the room. "On the right there, sir." Nye watched the awkward Colonel Holmestead pick his way through the crowded room. When he had disappeared, everybody in the room grinned and a few stifled laughter, but nobody said anything.

Holmestead didn't want to miss out on what was being said. He urinated as quickly as possible. Unfortunately, he stuffed his member back into his pants before he was finished and soaked the crotch of his fancy uniform. "Bloody damn!"

Holmestead returned quickly, holding one hand in front of his crotch to hide the wetness. Using the other hand to finger a burning pimple, Colonel Holmestead leaned against the wall. He tried to appear nonchalant. He wore his hat at a jaunty, cocky angle.

12

THE MOST AMUSING drill at St. Bernard's was the ritual bashing of James Burlane's rib cage. This low-tech medicine—it had yet to be replaced by an expensive device—was as available to a GP in Keokuk as it was to the Mayo Clinic. James Burlane was assured that the bashing was entirely for medicinal reasons and in fact worked superbly—which is to say it worked as well as the limits of nature allowed.

The first basher, an attractive young lady with a neat little diamond pin in her nose, arrived shortly after breakfast, looking cheery in her crisp blue uniform. A pin on her lapel identified her as a "physiotherapist," which Burlane took to be Britishese for the American "physical therapist."

"Will you turn on your side, please?" The basher pushed the sleeves of her sweater up on her arms. When

she had the unsuspecting James Burlane properly curled
onto his left side, hands above his head, she began pum-
meling his ribs with the edges of her hands. "Breathe," she
said. "Breathe deeply. Do your best." She turned her
hands into fists and really began to pound him. His body
shook from the blows. "Keep breathing. Breathe. Breathe.
Raise your hand when you have to cough something up."

Burlane, jolted by the blows but breathing the best he
could, suddenly began hacking and raised his hand for
time out; he spit some phlegm into the lidded gunk pot.
Grinning, he settled back and braced himself. The attractive basher folded a towel across his ribs.

She said, "Breathe now. Breathe." She began slugging
him in the ribs with her fists, saying, "Yes, yes, that's it," as
Burlane breathed as deeply as he could.

Which is when an Anglican priest popped his head in
the open door, a shocked look on his face. "My word!" he
said.

"We-'re ha-ving a g-o at Ya-nk bash-ing," Burlane said
as the physiotherapist hammered at his body. He raised his
hand for another time out and spit in the container again.
"You can take a turn after the young lady if you'd like."

The physiotherapist, unrelenting, resumed bashing.

Burlane coughed some gunk up.

"Good! Good!" the basher cried, slamming her hands
into his ribs with as much energy as she could muster.

"I was looking for the sailor," the priest said, and
continued down the hall.

"I hope I'm not bruising you," the physiotherapist
said.

Burlane raised his hand for a go at the gunk container.
"Oh, you savage woman," he lisped. "Don't stop! Don't
stop!"

After the first basher had departed, leaving Burlane
grinning but breathing easier, he was given an antibiotic
capsule, after which he was tormented by cramps that
twisted his insides. In the afternoon a nurse stabbed him in
the rear with a hypo of muscle relaxant to stop the stomach
pains. He was blessedly free of the cramps for a half hour,

but then they returned, little by little, stronger each time. With two hours to go before the next shot, a second basher showed up to pound on his ribs and yell at him to breathe, breathe, breathe. He thought she was an attractive little sadist.

Although the mass media made much of President Charles Barbur's famous loyalty to his subordinates and supporters, it was equally true that privately he could be both sensitive and compassionate. As the director of the Central Intelligence Agency, his old friend Peter Neely felt compelled to maintain an attitude of omniscience. While it was obvious that Neely couldn't possibly know as much about the situation in the Mediterranean as Ara Schott —whose job it was to follow reports from the field —Barbur joined in the face-saving conspiracy of pretending Neely knew almost everything.

Barbur, who liked to pace during these briefings, looked at Schott and said, "So what is the latest, Peter?"

Responding as though he were Neely, Schott said, "We had Tripoli on October fourth—a meeting that included Muhammad Aziz, Boris Suslev, and Omar Qafi. Ella Nidech smuggled a beeper into Suslev's personal belongings and found he went somewhere south of Tripoli during December and the first two weeks of January. During that time, our satellite cameras tell us, the Libyans and Russians were training Arabs in some hills south of Tripoli. Suslev and Aziz met again in Seville on February fourth, this time with a British mercenary named Bobby Nye. Nye was a colonel in the British army, was a hero of the Falklands, and served a tour of duty on Gibraltar. They met again in Tangier on February fifth. Unfortunately, Ella couldn't mike them safely. She did pick up the Russian surname 'Borodin' in a conversation, the context of which suggests, she believes, that this Borodin is an important Soviet player in whatever is developing.

Another Russian! President Barbur narrowed his eyes. His lips tightened into a colorless, determined line.

"Mr. President, we ran the name through our computers, which contain identifying data on any Russian of any conceivable interest to us. Well, it turns out Borodin is not an uncommon name in the Soviet Union. There are all kinds of Borodins working in the KGB and the foreign service. The computer gave us Borodins who were rocket experts, Borodins who were scientists, Borodins who are athletes and chess players; we even got a Borodin who is a public relations man."

The president laughed. Barbur knew *that* Borodin all right, the man behind Premier Petr Spishkin's pose as a civilized human being. There was no politician in the world who wouldn't like to have Leonid Borodin giving him advice. "Surely, one of those KGB officers."

"One would think so, and I agree, Mr. President. But we've checked them out one by one and they're all accounted for, with nothing to suggest they could be linked to anything developing in the Med. We'll send the computer through the Borodins as many times as it takes to find the right man. Unless 'Borodin' is a cryptonym, he has to be in there, Mr. President." Elia Nidech had engaged in some dangerous eavesdropping to give Schott a surname and he'd been unable to do anything with it. He took this as a personal failure.

Barbur gripped Ara Schott by the shoulder and gave him a squeeze of confidence. "You'll find him, Ara. You always do. I tell people I have this man who is a regular hound when it comes to tracking Russians. You can almost smell the bastards, can't you, Ara?" The president brightened. "Besides, we've the delicate couple out there, don't we? Ellen Mydick and Jones Voorlaing?" The president couldn't help but grin every time he pronounced Ellen's name.

The president's hearing aid served him well on most occasions, but too much confusion was hard for him. For some reason the sound of James Burlane's name reached him distorted. For a while Barbur had called him Jack Verlain, but eventually Jones Voorlaing became permanently etched somewhere in the presidential cerebrum. No matter how Neely or Schott might pronounce James Burlane's name, he was Jones Voorlaing to Barbur. Ella Nidech was forever Ellen Mydick.

Voorlaing and Mydick were the two people who got things done for the president without anybody being the wiser, although Mydick had requested and was granted the same privilege as Voorlaing—namely, she could refuse to make a hit. In fact, Mydick refused the president's first request to burn a Mexican cocaine dealer who had allegedly ordered the torture of an American drug investigator, saying she wasn't certain of the man's guilt. Burlane, who had looser standards of proof and no patience with cocaine dealers or torturers, burned the Mex *con mucho gusto* the following week.

Ara Schott glanced at Neely. "He . . ."

The expression on Peter Neely's face said he'd prefer that Schott be the bearer of bad news.

"Mr. President, James Burlane came down with pneumonia and is in St. Bernard's Hospital in Gibraltar."

"Jones Voorlaing? Pneumonia?"

"A virulent bacteria in his right lung, Mr. President."

Barbur looked concerned. "Will he be all right? He's a good man, Voorlaing."

"He's taking antibiotics intravenously, but he'll be all right in a few days, his doctor says. Up and around. After that, he'll rejoin Ella Nidech in Tangier."

The president looked uncertain.

"His trigger finger still works, I'll bet, Mr. President."

Barbur was relieved. "Nothing stops the delicate woman. We've got ourselves a winner there, Schott. Mydick and Voorlaing will take care of whatever it is the Arabs are up to."

"He's using his birdman cover, Mr. President," Schott said.

After Burlane had learned a repertoire of calls for his Larry Schoolcraft cover, he had given a little performance for Barbur in the Oval Office. Barbur had loved it.

"Is, ah, Mydick still a belly dancer?"

"Yes, Mr. President." Schott cleared his throat.

Barbur grinned hugely. "Boy, oh, boy! A birdman and

a belly dancer. What a team. By golly, Voorlaing's good with those whistles and honks of his, you have to give him that." Barbur looked outside. He whistled softly to himself, apparently considering Burlane's skills. Then he said, "Boy, can you imagine Ellen Mydick belly dancing?"

Schott said, "She's a professional, Mr. President."

Barbur looked outside again and said, "I loved the snow when I was a kid. We used to slide down a hill on pieces of cardboard. That was fun. Voorlaing's in the hospital on Gibraltar, you say?"

"Yes, Mr. President. He got sick in Seville. Ella Nidech believes Muhammad Aziz is about to make a big move of some kind, but she has no idea what. She's temporarily out of touch."

"Aziz is not that guy. *Achilles Laurel.* You know the one," Barbur said. His face tightened in rage at the memory of that outrage in which ragheads had pushed overboard a man in a wheelchair. His eyes focused on the snow again. "If you get the snow packed down enough, you can really go on a piece of cardboard."

"Aziz has been a member of the Palestinian brain trust for three years, but he has had no real power in the post. He's believed to be soft, Mr. President."

"My mother used to make us ice cream by adding sugar, cream, and a little vanilla to the snow. Was that ever good!" Barbur paused, remembering. "He's no crazy, then, this . . . this . . ."

"Muhammad Aziz. He doesn't seem so, Mr. President, but the truth is, we don't know. Mossad doesn't believe he's had the authority to lead his own operation. Now we have a new report, a little delayed, from the Italians. A week ago, they say, Aziz spent four days with a Mafia chief in Palermo."

"Ahh, the Mafia," Barbur said.

"The Sicilian controls most of the produce shipping in Spain, southern France, and Italy. No Spanish orange or Italian tomato makes it to Germany without this man profiting."

Barbur's mouth began to move, then it stopped. He

71

frowned. "Have you told the British all this? I mean about this fellow Nye and everything. What do you think they're after?"

"Maybe Gibraltar. Gibraltar's right there in the middle. Maybe James Burlane went to the right hospital."

"Gibraltar? The Rock? Surely that can't be." Barbur looked alarmed.

"The British say there is no cause for alarm, Mr. President. Gibraltar's defenses are secure. They hooked everything up to computers three years ago. Nobody gets through the computers without top-secret entry codes. It can't be done, the British say."

"Aren't those computers wonderful nowadays? Just wonderful."

"Gibraltar is hollowed out, Mr. President. Impervious, the British say. It can field hits by nukes."

President Barbur looked relieved, then laughed nervously. "Well, now. It was stupid to worry about Gibraltar, I suppose. We're talking the Rock here." He was suddenly in a jolly mood. "You know, we should get us some sleds and go for a ride. I could share my piece of cardboard with a little kid. The television people would love it."

13

TERRY HOLMESTEAD JUST couldn't believe that his acne had chosen this time to break out; it was as though all the wretched poisons of ill fortune that had plagued him his entire life had chosen to well up at once, both mocking and punishing him. The night before had been bad enough. Holmestead wanted to be a dashing, silver-haired mercenary like Bobby Nye, but what had he done? Rushed himself in the bog and pissed his pants. Now, tonight of all nights, his pimples were even worse. His face seemed like it was on fire. Before he went to work he stared at it in the mirror. Suddenly he wondered if there might not be a God after all, a vicious, vengeful God who caused his face to swell and burn.

He kneeled and laced his fingers together, a pious Terry Holmestead. He bowed his head and closed his eyes and said, "Dear God, if You actually exist, please see to it that Muhammad Aziz's plan works. I'd like to be something in life. Somebody owes me. Thank You." Then he concentrated hard, in fact furiously, on the existence of God—just in case. Did it all begin with You, God? he asked. He pursued the question into the void, his face contorted from the effort. For a fleeting second he thought he believed, thought he had found Him, Faith, whatever. Then he lost it. Pumping metaphysics was a bloody taxing piece of business. He knew if he tried it again, he'd get a headache. He rose, giggling at the absurdity of prayer. As a businessman adjusts his necktie, Terry Holmestead squeezed one last pimple before going to work.

It was a Saturday night, and such British sailors and Royal Marines who weren't on duty were chasing *señoritas* and smoking hashish in Algeciras, or tipping pints of ale down on Irish Town and along Main Street. This was a good tour for the men of the Royal Navy—British pubs with Mediterranean closing hours. A man could get properly pissed on Gibraltar.

Holmestead reported as usual at a restricted building above the Europa Point underground headquarters of the British command at Gibraltar. He took an elevator down the vertical entrance burrow carved out of solid limestone. The car stopped, and he stepped into a small white room watched by two remote-control television cameras—one on either side of the two-way mirror in front of him. The door closed on the elevator. He listened as the car returned to the surface.

Prime Minister Deborah Fielding's White Paper on the readiness of the regiment later claimed that two thousand men were assigned to Gibraltar on the night in question. The regimental commander, following directives of the Royal Navy, regarded the protection of the Gibraltar sealane as his primary mission.

A voice said, "Good evening."

"Evening, Louis." Holmestead put his card in the machine, and after the machine spit his card back, he entered his personal code into the keyboard. He said his name into a receiver recessed into the wall.

"Proceed, Terry," Louis said.

It was typical, said Mrs. Fielding's report, for there to be four hundred communication and weapons systems specialists in the Europa Point underground command at any one time. A second group of four hundred specialists were on standby, either sleeping or doing barracks detail. A third group of four hundred were on routine pass. The command was supported by an administrative and logistics staff of six hundred. Two hundred rotated the routine duties of guard duty at the border, at the Admiralty Dockyard, and at the surface entrance to the Europa Point command. The rigor and quality of guard duty was "of department store quality, given the importance of what was being guarded."

Holmestead stepped through an airport-style metal detector and waited as a steel door slid aside. He entered a tunnel which led to a second barrier, past which lay the bowels of the underground command. It was just behind the second barrier that Holmestead worked. Or rather sat. Her Majesty's Regulations required that a human being be able to take command of the backup computer should anything happen to the main system that controlled the perimeter barriers and alarms.

The White Paper explained the ease with which the Arabs assembled the terrorists necessary to ambush the skimpy British guard detail. With the reopening of the border by Spain in 1984, Gibraltar aggressively pursued tourist dollars. It was a pub town. There were pubs everywhere—all needing tourist dollars to keep running. Tourism had been encouraged by London, hard pressed to find the money necessary to keep its expensive little colony running. The result was that crossing the border became routine; luggage was rarely checked. The White Paper said the volume of traffic at the Spanish border was simply too great for the customs officials.

Ordinarily Terry Holmestead read motorcycle magazines or English spanking magazines. When he got bored with that he sat down at his keyboard and roamed the main computer to see what he could find and how everything worked. But tonight was different. Tonight he was wearing a fancy new watch, and he was—unknown to poor Louis behind the mirror, or the machine that had approved his card, or the machine that recognized his voiceprint—a full colonel in the army of the People's Republic of Jebel Tarik.

For dinner, the nurses' assistants brought James Burlane a baked leg and thigh of chicken, a plop of mashed potatoes, and some leaves of romaine lettuce glistening with vinegar and oil. But James Burlane, who had suffered from stomach cramps the entire day, was still in no mood for food.

On the wall opposite his bed there was a print of a watercolor by someone named Jas. R. Richardson. For all Burlane knew, Richardson was an English master, but the painting, of a cottage and garden, was just awful. Richardson loved blue, and so had flowers of various hues of blue, a bluish path, blue trim on the cottage, and, of course, a cloudless sky.

Burlane had been told when he came in that his room had one of the best views of the city that could be had. The window shutters had been open all day, but the city was so steep that all Burlane could see was the tops of the nearest buildings, the harbor and the bay with Algeciras on the far side, and a ridge on the horizon. He studied his map of Gibraltar.

The town was on the back side of Gibraltar—fortified by Muslim defensive walls—that had borne the brunt of all the storied sieges.

St. Bernard's Hospital sat on choice high ground, and he was on the bay side of the top floor. St. Bernard's was two blocks uphill of the center of a town that was only three steep blocks wide. The city center included Mackintosh Square, around which were clustered the Israeli consulate, the city hall and the city telephone exchange, the central police station, a synagogue, and Barclays Bank.

Willis's Road and Flat Bastion Road were just behind St. Bernard's. Above that, as Burlane had seen on his way to the hospital, there was nothing but dark green scrub brush and outcroppings of gray limestone, rising at nearly a forty-five-degree angle, a thousand and more feet to the top of the ridge, and twelve hundred feet to the summit of Mons Calpe.

Burlane wanted to see what the town looked like at sunset. He took the heavy IV stand in his left hand, careful not to set the plastic jar and feeding apparatus swinging, and closed the door to his room. Then he inched his way to the glass French doors that were shuttered from the inside. He opened the shutters and doors, and leaned against the iron railing, careful not to lose the IV needle in the side of his left wrist.

The city was so steep, it was a maze of rooftops as seen from above. There were clotheslines and television antennas everywhere, even on the tops of government buildings it seemed. The rooftops were largely red, and the walls gray, and beige, and white to reflect the summer heat. Curiously, a greenish-yellow mold grew on the east sides of buildings rather than the north as Boy Scouts were taught in the United States. Burlane assumed this was because of the long shadow of the Rock.

If mornings arrived late for Gibraltarians, their sunsets were splendid. The sun was a lazy yellow, then orange, then reddish-orange as it settled over the ridge beyond Algeciras. The bay, mirror flat, glowed with color.

Much later, as Burlane lay in bed pondering his bad luck, he heard the unmistakable chatter of automatic rifles in the streets below St. Bernard's. Three quick bursts. Then two quick bursts near the border. Then silence.

A siren began wailing, then stopped.

Was this what Muhammad Aziz, Boris Suslev, and Bobby Nye were discussing in Seville? An assault on Gibraltar? He knew intuitively that it was. Was Ella Nidech still in place? he wondered. He was weakened from his illness—pooped from the pneumonia. There was nothing he could do to help her now.

Burlane checked his watch: 2 A.M. He didn't want to

turn on the lights of his room lest a nurse think he needed help. He got his ballpoint pen, his pencil flashlight, and his map from his nightstand. Taking care with the IV stand, he shuffled to the window.

There was another burst of automatic fire, then another. Then firing broke out in several places. He checked his map. The gunfire on his right would be at the Spanish border and the airport police. The commotion straight below would be the central police station. The chatter on the left would be the police detachment at the north entrance to the dockyard.

Gibraltar was a very small town at the foot of a very large rock. It was no more than a hundred yards to the central police station and less than a half mile to the Spanish border.

Burlane made a note. He looked up and for the first time saw three freighters in Gibraltar Harbor and two in the bay waiting their turn to enter.

The shooting ceased, then started up again.

Tugs were guiding the freighters to the unloading jetties on the north mole of Gibraltar Harbor. The freighter captains seemed unworried. Burlane could make out canvas-covered vehicles on deck. The lights went on at the receiving jetties.

The freighters were flying the Libyan flag. The booms of the unloading cranes began moving.

What kind of vehicles were under the deck canvas? What the hell had happened to the Royal Marines? Nevertheless, Burlane now knew what the Arabs were up to in the western Mediterranean. He had work to do.

Burlane moved to the case that held his heaviest piece of equipment, the yard-long, twenty-five-pound Modulux 125. The Modulux 125, manufactured by Davin Optical Ltd of Barnet, England, was capable of multiplying available light times seventy thousand, which meant Burlane could take telephoto shots by starlight using short exposure times. Without his Schoolcraft cover, he'd have had to use a special fast film that accommodated a camera setting up to ASA 64,000.

He unfolded his tripod and screwed on his Nikon.

Struggling to manipulate the telescopic lens without pulling the needle from his wrist, Burlane popped it onto the camera. He was starting to shoot the Libyan freighters when the alarm went off on his digital wristwatch: someone had dumped a high-speed, coded message into his Mazumo. This was called a squirt: an encoded message —babble—sent in a quick burst too fast for its origin to be traced. Burlane returned to his bed and retrieved what looked like an AM/FM radio/cassette player from his nightstand. He set two knobs and punched a button, instructing the machine to decode the scrambled words of his correspondent.

His correspondent's message began appearing on the eight-line light-emitting diode, starting at the bottom of the screen:

CHINESE GORDON. GLAD YOU COULD MAKE THE PARTY. EAT LOTS OF CHICKEN SOUP NOW. TAKE A MORNING WALK ON MAIN WHEN YOU FEEL BETTER. MAMA GIVE YOU A GREAT BIG KISS IF SHE COULD.

Ella Nidech was okay. All right! He laughed out loud at her calling him Chinese Gordon. Chinese Gordon was a nineteenth-century British general who refused to withdraw from Khartoum and was eventually overwhelmed and killed by Muhammad Ahmed, whose followers called him the Mahdi. The Mahdi—"he who is guided"—was the Shiite term for "the expected one," a messiah who would appear to establish a reign of righteousness throughout the world. Burlane acknowledged her message with a squirt with no ID:

A KISS, SCHEHERAZADE? WHERE WOULD THAT BE?

James Burlane dragged the IV stand back to the window and started shooting close-ups of the cargo being unloaded from Omar Qafi's ships. Burlane wondered if Ella could see his telescopic lens. He would like to see her answer to his question about the kiss, but, like him, she had been taught to keep her squirts to a minimum.

On the other hand, if she were as much like him as he suspected . . .

Forty minutes later, Scheherezade sent Chinese Gordon another squirt:

NEVER MIND JUST NOW, BIG BOY.

Colonel Bobby Nye received reports on a walkie-talkie from his Arab commanders on various parts of the peninsula. One by one his subordinates checked in, their accented English solid amid the popping and snapping of static. Nye, grinning, marked each positive report off on a checklist of police stations and substations, plus units of Royal Marines guarding the Admiralty Dockyard, and the border guards, and the unit guarding the entrance to the Europa Point underground command.

Nye's Arabs had allowed themselves a three-to-one firepower advantage at every point of resistance and had attacked simultaneously and without warning. They were experienced in attacking from ambush, and the surface takeover went as expected. This was not an unassisted Arab triumph; it could not have been done without Bobby Nye's almost photographic memory of Gibraltar's defenses.

The problem now was what to do with the four hundred Brits underground on Europa Point. They were down there, and, well . . .

Colonel Terry Holmestead put his trembling hands over his ears and puffed air out between his cheeks. "I . . ." His mouth started to move, but he didn't say anything. Had he blown everything? What would they do to him? A pimple at the corner of his mouth burned.

"You what, Colonel?" Muhammad Aziz said evenly.

Holmestead said, "I shut down the perimeter warnings. Then I tapped out their communications. It was easy. The system responded perfectly. I took the outer perimeter barriers and they went. Then . . ." Holmestead licked his lips. He moved his hand to his face, and hesitated. The

79

pimple by his mouth burned, but he couldn't squeeze it, just couldn't. His fingers were right there close. He could do it quickly. No. He clenched his jaw and damned his accursed face.

Bobby Nye put down his clipboard and lit his briar pipe. "Twelve of our own dead and maybe nineteen wounded," he said to Aziz, an interjection to assist his beleaguered countryman. He puffed twice and said, "Then what, lad? We didn't especially want to get in there anyway, but we have to know what happened. Things go wrong in battle. That's expected. We have to know clearly and concisely what happened. Tell us, please."

Of course; obviously things did go wrong in battle. Holmestead blinked. "I . . ." He swallowed.

"Go ahead, lad."

"I tapped the first two digits of the c-code to the inner perimeter and a program in the backup cut in and t-took over." Holmestead's face was shiny with oily sweat. His pimples blazed.

"We're not blaming you for anything, son."

"I told you that might happen. They could program an automatic response to any given sequence. I'd have no way of knowing."

"No matter. They're trapped in there, is that or is that not correct?" Aziz looked at Nye.

Nye removed a receiver mike from his ear. "All their holes are covered. You're looking at a solid limestone prison. We can go in after them if we want, but the casualties would be high now. There's no harm waiting. I say we begin our deployment. We'll need everything in place quickly or they'll be right on top of us."

"The British down there can't do any harm."

"Not that I can see, but eventually we're going to want them out of there."

Aziz paused. "For now they add to the hostage count. Colonel Holmestead, I assume there's a way I can communicate with the commander inside?"

"That would be Colonel Givings, sir."

"Yes, Colonel Givings."

"He can't communicate to the outside, as I said, but we can call him with this phone, sir."

"But they have their own generators in there?"

"Oh, yes. They've got food and water. They're self-sustaining, sir. The place is built to take a siege."

Nye said, "That's why we didn't fly in or come by boat, son."

"Fabulous strategy, sir." Holmestead liked it when the famous Bobby Nye called him son. Maybe Nye liked him after all.

Aziz said to Nye, "Are the ships in yet?"

"They're in and unloading at the north mole. Morning comes late here, so they should have time to get everything in place by daylight."

Aziz said, "I'll want to communicate with Borodin. After that I want to talk to the British prime minister and the American president."

Nye's face tightened at the mention of Borodin's name. But he said nothing. He made a note.

"We'll proceed according to plan, Colonel. You'll need to find out if there are any foreign journalists in town. I'll be needing them for a short briefing."

"Consider it done."

"I want all guests removed from the hotels and sent across the Spanish border. The same is true of all wounded and dead from the attack, both ours and theirs. Get them all off where they'll receive good medical care. Take care that nobody suffers unnecessarily. Cooperate with the doctors and ambulance people, but get them off. We have enough hostages without crowding our hospitals."

"Yes, sir."

Aziz turned again to Holmestead. "We might as well keep you busy, Colonel. I want you to stand by until we're certain we have our obliging gophers securely trapped in their various tunnels. Tomorrow morning I want you to begin training some replacements who know how to operate the alarms and barriers. We don't want you on duty twenty-four hours a day. We'll need shifts, so everybody can keep fresh and alert, yourself included."

"Yes, sir," Holmestead said. "No problem, sir. Sir, would it be possible for me to see some of the real action?"

Aziz said, "You lived here for a year. You know the legend of the Barbary apes?"

"Yes, sir. As long as the apes stay, the British will be here. I know quite a bit about the apes, sir. There are two packs, sir. One for the tourists at six hundred feet—that's just above the casino—and a wild one higher up." In fact, Holmestead's knowledge of the Barbary apes was limited to summaries in tourist brochures, but he knew Aziz wouldn't know the difference.

"Do you think you could lead a detail to get rid of the apes?"

"Yes, sir!" Holmestead was relieved. He had never been made privy to Aziz's entire plan of battle, and had assumed the Arabs wanted to get all the way inside. Holmestead was eager to see some real action; against Brits or apes, it didn't matter to him.

"We'll need to videotape them being loaded on the ferry to Morocco," Aziz said. "The local television station will have video cameras and cameramen."

"Yes, sir!"

Aziz said, "Is it true that the apes are very friendly?"

"They're tourist attractions, sir."

"Capture them if you can. Get them in a cage if you can. If you can't, then shoot them. We'll need apes or ape corpses on videotape."

Nye raised an eyebrow. "Comrade Borodin's idea, I take it?"

"Comrade Borodin's, yes."

Colonel Terry Holmestead didn't know who Borodin was, but he could tell from the manner of Aziz's response that he was somebody important, Boris Suslev's superior, perhaps. Holmestead felt flattered and proud to be chosen to lead the mission of anybody so important. He was to take care of the apes. Comrade Borodin's right-hand man. He savored the sweet connotations of the phrase. What if Holmestead himself became powerful? No emperor has pimples. Mmmmm. Such delicious dreaming.

14

Ara Schott was at home in his apartment in McLean, Virginia, reading Barbara Tuchman's *The Guns of August* —in which Tuchman detailed the multiple screw-ups and stupidities that led to World War I—when his Buck Rogers wristwatch went into its buzzing act. He punched up a Langley code on his Company safe phone. When Peter Neely answered, he knew he wasn't being invited out for pizza.

"I'm afraid we've got some very big mud in the western Med, Ara, and our delicate couple is right in the middle of it." Big mud was Company lingo for trouble. The western Mediterranean. Ella Nidech and James Burlane.

Schott put a bookmark in Tuchman's history. He'd have to postpone the details of the next pointless slaughter of young men.

Neely said, "Ara, we've got Arabs on the Rock."

"What are you talking about, Peter? Where are the British?"

"I'm talking about Muhammad Aziz, calling himself a Palestinian, and thirty thousand hostages—including what's left of the British garrison."

"Oh, my God!"

"Yes. Yes. My sentiments."

"We should have done something. We had a smell. We told everybody. Why the hell didn't someone do something?" Schott's voice rose.

Neely's sigh was audible. "Does us a whole lot of good now, Ara. We've got the delicate couple in place, even if one of them has come down lame."

"What do the Brits say?" Schott was angry at the

British. It was their damned colony. Why didn't they take care of it?

"Kaplan says Deborah Fielding is thinking Falklands."

"Thinking Falklands?"

"She wants to send in the Royal Navy. Royal Marines. Loose Gurkhas and Sea Harriers, whatever."

Schott said, "I thought the damned thing was supposed to be impregnable."

"That's a matter of definition. Mrs. Fielding is saying it hasn't been captured because the British garrison on shift, four hundred of them, were trapped in its underground compound. The commander hasn't officially surrendered and won't, she said. The president will have to talk to the press, Ara. He needs a briefing on the western Med. I've got a car on the way."

Schott looked at his watch. "It's what, Peter, two in the morning on Gibraltar? We'll have to get somebody down there to whatever Spanish town it is that's across the bay there. Our people are both carrying Mazumos."

"Two A.M. it is, Ara. I'll have the updates when you get here."

"See you in a few minutes, Peter." Schott hung up. He'd have to make sure he had the facts right for President Barbur. The administration didn't like it when the president screwed up a fact in a press conference. He'd have time to study the Med-Sum updates on his way to the White House. Langley was just two miles down the road, so he'd have to hurry. Schott's mouth felt dry.

He stripped off his chinos and comfortable shirt on the way to his bedroom. He slipped into gray slacks and blue blazer, and snatched an atlas off the shelf on his way to the door.

When he got downstairs, the driver said, "Little excitement tonight?"

"I think so." Schott settled into the back seat. The driver sped off with Ara Schott wondering whether Ella Nidech had managed to make it onto Gibraltar as well, or if Aziz and Suslev had left her in Tangier. She would be checking in if she'd made it.

Schott wondered about the man named Borodin. The Company computers had no Borodin listed who was close to commanding such power as this one apparently did. There were plenty of Borodins in the KGB, but they were technicians, or minor, or out of favor. Schott had combed the list again and again, frustrated.

The Company car came to the end of Dolly Madison Boulevard and passed under the Chain Bridge Road. Ara Schott reminded himself that the next time he saw either Burlane or Nidech, he would tell them he loved each of them, which he did. He wouldn't, he knew. He wished he would, though, just once. Although he did his best to hold it in, sentimentality of this sort occasionally dripped out of Schott like oil from the bottom of a decrepit old klunker.

The snow was back, falling into the darkness of the Potomac under the Roosevelt Bridge. The lights were on and shining in the Kennedy Center. Concert time, dress-up time, Ara Schott thought, quiche and white wine time, with a nice salad lightly dressed with vinegar and oil with just a hint of tarragon. He smiled to himself. Up ahead he could see that the lights were on at the State Department as well; it was pizza and maps of Gibraltar in Foggy Bottom.

The Company car, its chains clicking softly, eased down Constitution Avenue in a gathering snowstorm. To the south the Mall looked cold and gloomy under its mantle of snow; Schott could see, on his right, the Lincoln Memorial, which was lit; the long, narrow, reflecting pool where ice skaters were defeated in their effort to keep it clear of snow; the Washington Monument, also lit and standing tall in the falling snow; then, in the far distance, on a hill, bathed white by floodlights, the Capitol.

Ahead and on Schott's left, blue lights flashed at the southern entrances to the Ellipse. The driver turned the Company car left off Constitution onto 17th Street; more blue lights flashed ahead, at E Street.

All the streets surrounding the grassy Ellipse and the rear lawn of the White House were blocked off so that helicopters from the Pentagon might land on the great expanses of white space. Schott watched military officers being disgorged from the choppers. They were trying to appear casual and heroic at the same time. There was an emergency and they were professionals; they had been summoned to the White House and it was snowing and cold. It was to be a night to remember; everybody knew that.

The Company car slowed at a two-way roadblock at E Street and 17th. They stopped for a district policeman with a long flashlight and a notebook. The driver punched the window button. The cop copied the license number on his pad and asked, "Do you have a card?"

Ara Schott drew an ID card out of his wallet, and they waited while it was checked by radio.

The cop returned the card and said, "A couple of TV vans crashed into one another up ahead here at Pennsylvania. It's okay to turn right here at E Street; we've got it blocked off."

"TV vans?" The driver smirked.

"Going full tilt in this snow." The cop shook his head in disgust.

They *cl-clicked* their way east on E Street for a block, and the driver took a left onto SW Executive Avenue. As they passed between the Executive Office Building on their left and the White House on their right, they were able to see, for the first time, the scene on the front lawn.

Peering into the snow, the driver said, "Well, a little action at the White House tonight."

Owing to the crashed vans at one end and a police roadblock at the other, the long block of Pennsylvania Avenue was free of traffic and given over to the television and newspaper people. Television vans were parked at odd angles, and men were unloading cameras and gear in the snow. On the lawn itself several reporters dressed in hats and overcoats peered into video cameras with dramatic faces. They were standing in a driving snowstorm. The White House was in the background. Their mouths moved earnestly, describing the opening moments of the Gibraltar crisis.

The driver looked back at Schott, one professional to another; what the fuck is this all about? his face asked.

"Arabs grabbed Gibraltar." Schott didn't see any way Deborah Fielding and Charles Barbur were going to keep this oopsie from the public.

"No shit? The Rock?" The driver burst out laughing. He stopped so Schott could show his pass to another guard, and they drove slowly down the driveway to the White House.

Schott stepped out of the car with his briefcase of Med-Sums. He showed his pass to a uniformed guard, who escorted him to a security desk where his briefcase was X-rayed and checked for metal. A woman at the desk punched his name and card number into a computer terminal. When the computer okayed him, he was given a mint green security badge for his lapel, and told to proceed down the hall to the next security desk.

Ara Schott thought he heard the bellowing and mawing of cattle through an open door but realized quickly that it was the press room, where imaginatively dressed reporters and photographers, competing to see who could make the most scornful, sardonic speculation about the British fuck-up on Gibraltar, waited for the president to speak.

Schott stepped quickly through the Pentagon contingent, which seemed to have been herded into the hallway. They had ridden helicopters in with much racket and dramatic billowing of snow and now waited in a hallway. Schott knew they could have waited comfortably in the Executive Office Building until the president was ready for them; instead they chose to stand, bored, so they could later say they were there in the White House as the action unfolded, witnesses to history. They didn't want to have to admit they had waited across the street.

The admirals and generals were used to having people wait for them, not the other way around. They wanted to appear casual, yet powerful and central to the coming action; they didn't know what to do with their bodies when they weren't in charge. Ordinarily they moved through groups of people like mammalian icebreakers, crushing ego with bows of privilege. Schott suspected it would always be like this—decisions of consequence made in total confusion, amid much posturing. Later, historians, insisting on the existence of logic and order in public affairs, seeking sequence and evidence of intelligence, demanding an accounting, would find few heroes among them.

The officers were issued yellow badges that allowed them to wait in the hall until the president was ready for them. They weren't really actors in the drama at all; they were there in case they were needed by people with more prestigiously colored badges. Generals were stepped around and ignored as if they were children or privates. They were stiff and awkward; some were obviously sore that their fictitious relationship to Barbur had been exposed. It was an emergency that the British should have handled immediately, in their opinion.

Schott's mint green badge was identical to the one worn by Peter Neely. Schott had to brief the president while he was on the toilet, if necessary, and so his had to be mint green.

He saw the officers watching him surreptitiously. They wondered who this bespectacled man was. There was no arrogance to Schott's stride; he looked a bit like a befuddled professor. His shoes were polished, but were neither new nor expensive. Their eyes challenged him, said, Just what did you do to deserve a mint green badge? They were powerful because they ran the Pentagon, thus claiming the largest budget in the federal government. Virtually the only thing they coveted—besides a mistress who was more enthusiastic about oral sex—was better access to the president.

Schott knew they remembered well how Richard Nixon had chosen Alexander Haig to be his chief of staff. There were those among them—latent Haigs, he suspected —who would have killed for a mint green badge, and were angered when they saw an unfamous, commonplace, apparently unpowerful individual sporting one.

Schott was escorted by a Secret Service agent to a small room where President Charles Barbur, his face soaking under a steaming hot towel, lay back on a barber chair that was upholstered in a soft, tan leather. The Secret Service agent said, "Ara Schott, Mr. President."

"Mmmmm. Mmmmm," Barbur said from under the towel. He raised one finger and gave it a small twirl. A black man in a white smock and a pale blue badge removed the hot towel. The president said, "I think you can get started now, Duane. You don't mind if I talk at the same time, do you?"

"That'd be fine, Mr. President," Duane said. He put a new blade in a safety razor.

"They're afraid to let Duane use a straight razor for fear he'll cut my throat," Barbur said. He and Duane had a good laugh at that. "I can't face cameras without a shave for fifteen hours." Barbur gestured at the Secret Service agent with his hand. "I think we'll be just fine, Stan. If Mr. Schott rushes me, Duane will take him on with his safety razor."

Duane grinned. "You bet, Mr. President."

The Secret Service agent, not liking to leave Barbur alone, did as he was told and left the room.

Barbur closed his eyes as Duane began brushing on hot lather with a shaving brush. "Boy, that feels good," he said. "This Gibraltar situation is something you Company people call . . . what was that?"

"Mud, Mr. President. A swamp. The Big Muddy."

"Fig Duddy?" The president's face bunched under the lather.

"Big Muddy," Schott said, louder, slower, trying not to be obvious.

"Mud. That's it. Bad mud. It looks like we've got a little bad mud, doesn't it, Ara." Barbur tilted his chin up to tighten the skin on his neck. He talked and kept his skin tight at the same time. "On the other hand, we've got Ellen Mydick and Jones Voorlaing on the Rock? Both of them at once, that's not bad."

"We don't know whether Ella made it onto the Rock or not, Mr. President, but she should be checking in shortly. We have to remember that Jimmy Burlane's in the hospital with pneumonia."

"Isn't that Ellen Mydick something. She knows all of those languages and can shoot people and belly dance

89

too!" The president puffed one cheek to tighten the skin for the barber. "You know, I don't think I ever paid any attention to her belly." The president stopped. His eyes glazed, possibly locked in concentration at the problem that confronted his government, possibly in memory of seeing Ellen Mydick in slacks; the president was an upfront admirer of the delicate woman's derriere and everybody knew it. "When Ellen checks in we'll have to get back on the horn with Debbie Fielding, tell her we've got our two best people on the Rock. Whatever Debbie Fielding needs done is as good as done with Mydick and Voorlaing on the spot. Mmmm. Say, wasn't there a Russian involved somewhere? Didn't you mention a Russian mixed up in all this?"

"If it's the same people with whom Ella Nidech has been traveling, there is a Boris Suslev, Mr. President, but I think perhaps you are thinking of the man named Borodin."

"Baurodeen, that's it!"

"We're still running our checks, still coming up negative. We now believe it's a cryptonym, Mr. President. At this point we don't have any proof that these are the same Arabs that Ella Nidech has been following. They could be somebody else entirely."

The barber was finished with the presidential neck. The president, running his fingers over the now smooth skin on his neck, lowered his chin. "Boy, nothing feels better than a good shave. We'll let Jonesie whistle a little tune. We'll turn Mydick loose, give her license." President Charles Barbur grinned his affable hound-dog grin. The incident in which Ellen Mydick had filed sexual harassment charges against Jones Voorlaing had long been forgotten by the president, a thing of the past. "That Mydick, now there's a real woman. Educated. Smart. Does everything. And her . . ."

President Barbur, frustrated, reached for an imaginary Ellen Mydick rump. Every time President Charles Barbur remembered his interview with the delicate woman candidate, his eyes glazed and he looked wistful.

President Barbur, enjoying strawberry ice cream, yelped in triumph when word came in that Ella Nidech was safe and in place on Gibraltar. The Arabs who had grabbed the Rock were in fact the Arabs she had been entertaining with her dancing. "Yessiree! Yessiree! Voorlaing said she was a good one, you know. He said trust her. Turn her loose. She'll be belly dancing one minute and slitting throats the next if she's anything like Voorlaing. Those Arabs better not turn their backs on Ellen Mydick. By golly, there's a woman of substance."

Barbur, grinning broadly, peered at Ara Schott over the rim of his coffee cup, then returned to his strawberry ice cream. "He's got a feel for the action, Voorlaing does. If he says Mydick's a money player, so she is. Voorlaing anticipates. He comes down with pneumonia and where does he go? Gibraltar. For a spy that's like running for daylight, like knowing the end zone, you know what I mean? Remember Don Hudson? There's a man who could catch a football. Raymond Berry was good, too, and Tommy McDonald. I suppose it's true a president gets better ice cream than most people, but isn't this wonderful? These strawberries aren't frozen, either. They're fresh. Fresh strawberries in February. Where do they grow these, do you think?" He looked at Schott.

Schott hesitated just a tad. He was not an encyclopedia. He certainly didn't read thirty-year-old sports magazines to prep for conversations with the president; Schott knew that Peter Neely and several members of the president's cabinet did exactly that. It was said that anybody who had ambitions of a Supreme Court appointment had damn well better know his or her Chicago Cubs. "The strawberries are from Mexico, I think, Mr. President," he said. He hoped that Barbur wouldn't lapse into sports talk.

"From Mexico?" Barbur sounded surprised that Mexicans could grow sweet strawberries. "They're delicious!" He took a spoonful of ice cream and held it in his mouth, savoring the strawberry flavor.

"We have to remember that Burlane has pneumonia, Mr. President. Ella Nidech is in a very, very dangerous position, square in the middle of the Arabs."

"Oh, pshaw!" Barbur waved that objection away with the back of his hand. "We're talking Voorlaing and Mydick here. They're professionals. Pshaw! And that Mydick." The president, remembering Mydick's wonderful keister, perhaps, appeared to be drifting off. Suddenly Barbur tightened his lips until they lost their color. "Well, we'll give him all the help we can."

"There's not much we can do for the moment, Mr. President."

"And . . ." Barbur stopped. Deep in thought, he savored another spoonful of strawberry.

"Mr. President?"

President Barbur smacked his lips. "Boy, this is good. Mmmmm. I wonder what Voorlaing's got up his sleeve. He's a never-say-die kind of guy. He'll come up with something. He comes from that crazy place in Oregon, you know, Umatilla. He'll come up with something, if I know him. Remember Bart Starr standing there in that snowstorm? Seconds left. A field goal will tie, but"—Barbur squinted his eyes, remembering—"no, he goes for it! Follows Kramer in for the score! Voorlaing's Bart Starr, see, and Mydick's Max McGee. Voorlaing drops back, cool as you please. Mydick runs over the middle, juking this way and that with her hips." The president did an imitation of Max McGee/Ellen Mydick running a pass pattern. The action was all in the hips. President Barbur alternated McGee's left-right juking and faking with a belly dancer's forward-backward pelvic undulation. "I'll bet that Mydick has some real moves." Charles Barbur was amazingly limber; he made some moves of his own, his hips going this way and that. This could only have been done by a man with jet-black hair.

Schott, who remained amazed that the nation had elected an elderly youngest son to be president, waited for the animated Barbur to complete his imaginary touchdown run. He said, "Burlane has to get his health back before he can throw very long, Mr. President." Was that what quarterbacks did, throw long? Schott hoped he hadn't screwed up.

92

"Voorlaing? Oh, pshaw! Pshaw! Jones Voorlaing is a professional! A professional knows how to play hurt, Ara. Remember when all of Baltimore's quarterbacks were wiped out? Tom Matte was all beat up himself, but he went in there, a running back with the plays taped to his arm, and hell, you'd have thought he was Norm van Brocklin. That's what being a professional is all about. Let them call their own plays, Ara. You know that. When you've got players like Voorlaing and Mydick, you let them do what they do best. Give them the ball. They're shooters, both of them. They'll be going straight for the hoop. Bob Petit had some sweet moves. Remember Nellie Fox. Nellie always got wood on the ball, always."

"I'll tell them to be sure to get wood on the ball, Mr. President."

"No, no, no! They'll be wanting to drill one, Ara. They'll be swinging from the heels. You're talking big timber here. Mickey Mantle. Duke Snider. Ernie Banks. I . . . I . . ." Barbur looked as though he had remembered something terrible.

Barbur looked ill; Schott was concerned. "Mr. President?"

"They . . . I . . . They made me put my stock in a trust fund when I took office, you know." Barbur looked dismayed. "I had about five thousand shares of Prudential Life, something like that. A lot of money. Buy a piece of the Rock, they said. You can't go wrong. Solid." President Charles Barbur dug into his dish of ice cream again, seeking comfort.

15 _____

PLAGUED BY THE implications of six straight weeks of trailing Harry Gilchrist in the Nielsens, Gerard Thompson resorted to a sleeping tablet and a movie in which Tony Curtis was playing some sort of Mongol warrior. Curtis rode a horse as if he were stapled to the saddle. Thus prompted, Thompson fell asleep.

An hour later Thompson dreamed that the red light was on. The camera was running. He had nothing to say and the prompter was blank. He woke up, startled. His eyes were clear. Vincent Price was applying a stethoscope to the admirable bosom of a young maid. Thompson, wide awake, watched in fascination as the camera closed in on the stethoscope that descended onto white skin. He wondered where the producers had found an actress with breasts like that. Mt. Ekbergs, they were.

The public had added Thompson versus Gilchrist to its list of fun contests; their Nielsen duel had thus joined the Kentucky Derby, the Superbowl, the NCAA basketball championships, the presidential election, and contests featuring television actors and actresses. Gerard Thompson had been a winner all his life, and he was damned if he was going to buckle at this stage of the game.

Thompson took another tablet, but knew he wouldn't be going back to sleep for a while. He poured himself a neat shot of scotch.

Naturally, the poobahs had ordered the usual outside consultants to make a recommendation. The consultants' report was doo-doo, of course, but it was a required drill when the Nielsens were down. The network executives felt they had to do something to face down Harry Gilchrist. They couldn't stand around pulling their chickens. So the network had been forced to buy expensive organic dye for

Thompson's shirts and ties. He'd exercised until he had Stallone's stomach.

A report two years earlier had carried a ten-page addendum on the shape of Thompson's eyebrows. In it, Chet Huntley's eyebrows were said to be both fatherly and expressive, and Thompson was asked to watch old films of Huntley delivering the news with a young David Brinkley. A young man with limp wrists was dispatched to "sculpt" Thompson's eyebrows, making insane eeny-teeny snip-snips with wee little scissors for an outrageous hour.

The poobahs were exercised that their man, inexplicably, had now trailed Harry Gilchrist for a month and a half—this after organic dyes and a month-long trek with the contras in Nicaragua. The contra series had been miserable, as Thompson had known it would be: he had had to sleep on the ground, eat food with bugs in it, interview hyperbolic beaners, and suffer the accursed crotch crud and the Nicaragua quickstep. He still suffered night sweats as a result of the experience, and he still trailed Gilchrist in the Nielsens.

Thompson's apartment was well insulated and on the top floor, but he could still hear the distant, dim buzz of New York.

Of all the days of the month, the Day of Fabulous Hormones was the lousiest for Thompson to take his sixth week of Nielsen hits in a row. Felicia Thompson had developed a series of hints designed to let her husband know she might not object to some playing around. Many of these messages were so subtle they passed him by even after several repetitions. Was the cover just accidentally lying at a tantalizing angle or was she maybe in the mood? Was her hand accidentally draped over her groin or was she suggesting something fun? Her one, unmistakable, clear-cut message, a flag waving an erotic Mayday, was her naked rump up high and in the presenting position as she was ostensibly going to sleep. This indicated the Day of Fabulous Hormones, and boy, did she ever want to fool around then. Her wonderful odor rose and drifted, as sweet as fried onions at a county fair.

This was Thompson's monthly opportunity to explore

95

a little kinky territory if he wanted, and did he ever. He was a fried onion man and resented interruptions of that blessed day. Of course, Felicia had her Day of Lucifer's Hormones, too, but she could feel that day coming on and tried to give him warning.

Two hundred curl-ups each morning. Two hundred! God! Thompson had read once where the body releases chemicals called endorphins to combat physical pain and that research showed people found this to be sexual. And it was true that Thompson liked to pursue Felicia after their workouts. Well, that is, after their workouts and a little nap. Thompson believed endorphins were the real reason for the hard-body craze that had swept yuppiedom a few years ago and lingered, threatening his Nielsens.

The way Thompson saw it, the high cost of the paraphernalia of masochism gave voyeurs an innocent pretext to gather in suburban health clubs. He believed the real reason for all this sweaty activity was for people to scope potential lays. For the men this was any woman with a minimum of cellulite. The women were after men with buttocks that supported large wallets. Thus both sexes put their bodies on display; they sweated and strained, pedaled and pulled. As they showered, their endorphins churned.

He felt there must be something he could do besides more curl-ups, sit-ups, and laps. He had gone to college because he was appalled by the idea of physical labor. Now he had to do curl-ups and laps to read the news, although jaws in working order, and presumably a brain, were all that was really needed.

Thompson slipped in a videotape and watched Harry Gilchrist reading the news; he grew angrier by the second. New Jersey Senator Ben Greene had been sent to the federal prison in Allenwood, Pennsylvania, for income tax invasion. CBS had Greene giving the press a raised knuckle, clearly the finger, and yelling "fuck you"—with the reporter doing a voice-over during the no-no word. Good stuff. Professional work. What did NBC have? Greene's sleazy lawyer saying how the conviction had been a "tragic miscarriage of justice" and he would appeal it to the Supreme Court if necessary. Sleazy lawyers were always saying something was a "tragic miscarriage of justice." For having the ability to repeat such clichéd lies with a straight face, lawyers were able to bill their clients unconscionable sums of money.

Thompson wondered if there were any miscarriages of justice that were not tragic. The blue telephone rang, the NBC hot line. Thompson answered almost before the ring was finished.

"Gerard? Tony O'Brien."

"What's happened, Tony?"

"Gerard, we've got a big, big, big, big one on the line. Arabs hijacked Gibraltar less than forty minutes ago and have proclaimed it the sovereign People's Republic of Jebel Tarik."

"They did what? Which?"

"Gibraltar. They grabbed the Rock and are calling it Jebel Tarik."

"What the hell does that mean?"

"We don't know what it means either, Gerard. Hill or rock or mountain or something. We've got research scrambling on it. The prime minister, as he calls himself, is someone named Muhammad Aziz, claiming he's a Palestinian."

"How the hell did they do that? Gibraltar and everything. How?"

"We don't know, Gerard."

"I thought that place was supposed to be impregnable. You're telling me a bunch of Arabs . . ."

"That seems to be it. Nobody's denying anything."

"Jeee-zus!"

"Aziz has thirty thousand people hostage, Gerard. That's twenty-eight thousand Gibraltarians plus a British garrison of two thousand."

"How the hell did he pull that off? I still don't understand. Gibraltar guards the entrance to the Mediterranean."

"I know, I know, Gerard. The map says the Strait's only fourteen miles across. It would take a pretty stupid missile to miss at that range."

"Do we have any kind of correspondent there?"

97

"All communications were cut by the Arabs. Everything we're getting, they're telling us. We have no independent confirmation on any of this. Aziz is letting the Red Cross in to check everybody's identity and to observe his treatment of his hostages. We don't have any idea if there are any Americans there or not. The Red Cross will let us know, but that will take some time."

"And Washington?"

"The president put the Sixth Fleet on alert. He's on the hot line to Moscow and to Mrs. Fielding. The Sovs are neutral so far. Our people in Washington say the Pentagon is buzzing with activity and the lights are on in Foggy Bottom. Listen, Gerard, this thing's shaping up to be an around-the-clock thing."

"What do we have from the White House, Tony?"

Tony O'Brien cleared his throat. "Well, we've got a little problem there. Our van collided with an ABC van at the corner of Seventeenth and Pennsylvania and . . ."

"And what, Tony?" Thompson's heart sank. What could possibly have gone wrong now?

"Our good camera and our sound equipment got smashed, Gerard."

Thompson said nothing.

O'Brien said, "But we've got another camera now and more sound gear. We'll have a shot of Angie Rollins standing in a snowstorm in front of the White House. Very dramatic."

All the networks would have people standing in the snow. Thompson still said nothing.

"Gerard? Are you still there? Listen, I've just been told Muhammad Aziz will allow two flights of journalists in on Wednesday afternoon."

"Wednesday?"

"No reason given, Gerard. No journalists in until Wednesday and that's it, apparently. No arguments."

"Wonderful."

"The flights'll be leaving from Heathrow. The Palestinians want small news crews only. They say they don't have hotel space for a mob. Gibraltar's too small a place."

98

"I guess you'd better pack your bags, Tony. You can use the time to work out the jet lag."

"This one's better than the Munich Olympics or the hijacked TWA plane, or that ship."

"No comparison, Tony."

"Are we gonna kick ass or what, Gerard? This is your kind of story. Made to order."

The problem of crisis coverage was that nothing happened most of the time. A good anchor had to keep things moving, had to pretend there was tense, unrelenting drama when there demonstrably was not. Thompson was an acknowledged master at keeping his mouth moving and his voice serious, if not ominous, for hours on end while saying absolutely nothing. He could take a few sketchy facts and repeat them different ways to give the appearance that the story was rapidly changing and volatile—something not to be missed by the viewers.

Thompson regarded ideal viewers as having tremendous bladders so that they could sit back in sofas and quietly fill up, human balloons of urine, never missing a commercial. In a variation of George Orwell's observation that the function of political language is to give the appearance of substance to pure wind, there were those who said Gerard Thompson was able to confer solemnity to the passing of gas.

James Burlane finally nodded off at five-thirty, only to wake up at six, startled by the wavering call of a man's voice broadcast by loudspeaker.

"La illah il-Allah!" the muezzin called—there is no God but Allah.

Burlane sat up in his bed, wide awake. From missions in the Middle East he had memorized the English translation of the call:

> Allah is most great,
> There is no God but Allah, and
> Muhammad is His Prophet,

Come to prayer, come to salvation,
Allah is most great, there is no
God but Allah.

The muezzin's voice rattled, spit, soared, part Caruso,
part bookie with a smoker's hack, *"La illah il-Allah!"*

PART TWO

Lights, cameras . . .

1

GIBRALTARIAN POLICE AND members of the Royal Navy who were captured above ground were taken to the football stadium, which was lit and surrounded by Arabs with AK-47s. There they were interrogated as to their duties and job skills. Those deemed necessary for the smooth administration of Gibraltar were kept. The remainder were taken to the Spanish border and released.

At 4 A.M., with the British defenders either evicted to Spain or imprisoned under Europa Point, Colonel Bobby Nye and his Arab subordinates turned their attention to the weapons and gear being unloaded from the Libyan freighters.

Nye, who had proper training in military tactics, took the responsibility for deploying Muhammad Aziz's missile batteries.

The first thing Nye needed to do was prevent the freighters from being sunk from the air before they were completely unloaded. To this end he first unloaded the ten half-tracks bearing Italian Indigo-MEI surface-to-air missiles. These missiles—six were mounted on each half-track—had a 6.2-mile range, which covered the airspace above the Strait of Gibraltar and the bay, and the Spanish communities around it. Each driver of a half-track knew exactly where his missiles were to be deployed and was on his way within seconds of his vehicle being free of its unloading straps.

Nye put one battery of missiles in the middle of Church Lane with the Roman Catholic church on one side of the street and Barclays Bank and the French consulate on the other. He deployed a second half-track just outside the southern entrance to St. Bernard's Hospital. He put a third in Mackintosh Square by the rear entrance to the Gibraltar House of Assembly. He deployed a fourth in the middle of a triangle formed by the Norwegian consulate, a synagogue, and the Gibraltar Museum.

Nye placed a fifth between the Home for the Aged Hebrew and the Bishop Fitzgerald School; a sixth in Governor's Lane alongside Kings Chapel, the convent, and the governor's residence; a seventh in the parking lot between the Garrison Library and the offices of *The Gibraltar Chronicle*; an eighth halfway between the Holiday Inn and St. Andrew's Church of Scotland; and a ninth and tenth in the housing estate on Europa Point.

Facing west, these missiles covered the bay and beyond; facing south, they covered the Strait of Gibraltar; facing north, they covered the narrow, flat isthmus connecting the Rock to the Spanish mainland and the hills beyond.

The Indigo-MEIs were in place before sunrise, after which Nye deployed his eighteen three-missile batteries of British Tigercat surface-to-air missiles. These mobile missiles, towed by Land-Rovers and guided by radar for night firing, had a three-mile range.

He deployed eight Tigercat batteries in the spaces between the high-rise flats of the Varyl Begg Housing Estate. Varyl Begg was the largest, highest density housing project on Gibraltar, the perfect spot for Muhammad Aziz to exploit Western European softness and sentimentality. From the housing estate—located at the base of the north mole jetties where the Libyan vessels were being unloaded —Nye's defenders had an unobstructed view of the connecting isthmus.

He scattered the other ten banks of Tigercats in a variety of locations: two between the Pentecostal church and the Italian consulate on Main Street; a third by the synagogue on Engineer Lane; a fourth between Barclays Bank and the synagogue on Irish Town; a fifth by St. Joseph's School; a sixth by the Mount Alverna Home for the Aged; a seventh by St. Bernard's Chapel on Europa Point; an eighth by a school on Europa Point; and nine and ten on either flank of the Caleta Palace Hotel on the Mediterranean side of the peninsula.

Only when the Tigercat carriers were unloaded and on their way to their assigned positions did Bobby Nye turn his attention to his allotment of seventy-two German Cobra antitank missiles.

He deployed the Cobras behind the Moorish walls facing the connecting peninsula and in the British fortifications dug into the solid limestone of the north face of Mons Calpe. Any attempt to attack the peninsula by crossing the tarmac of the Gibraltar airport would meet with impossible firepower; the same was true if anybody wanted to try mounting an amphibious attack from the bay.

The Mediterranean side of the peninsula—hardly more than a narrow road and skinny beaches at the base of a limestone cliff—required less attention. If the British tried landing on the Mediterranean beaches, they faced the task of circling the rock at Europa Point to the south or around the base of Mons Calpe to the north. If they tried that, they faced Nye's highly mobile firepower—brought to bear on passages from ten to twenty yards wide, or straight down from the top of the Rock.

Bobby Nye covered the fourteen miles of the Strait of Gibraltar, plus the entrance to the Bay of Gibraltar, with twenty-four French Exocet missiles installed on Europa Point. He covered his Exocets with Gibraltarian lives by removing the furniture and knocking the windows out of randomly selected flats. Each bank of missiles had an inhabited flat on either side, above and below.

To see to it that U-boats might not pass the Strait without risk, Nye installed Norwegian Terne Mk 8 antisubmarine rocket depth-charges on Europa Point. Only then were the Soviet howitzers unloaded. The howitzers, in fact old-fashioned field cannons, were added for just a little insurance.

By 7:30 A.M., the last missile was declared ready to fire if necessary. Muhammad Aziz used the Gib radio to declare a public holiday in Jebel Tarik. He told the twenty-

105

eight thousand permanent Gibraltarians that only essential workers were to report to work the next day.

· Gibraltar was thus transformed into a technological porcupine; the Rock bristled with missiles deployed among people, holy places, and the artifacts of history. The British defense of solid limestone that had seen the hardy Gibraltarians through many a siege was replaced by the flesh and blood of civilians.

The employees of the Gibraltar airport had little choice but to continue work as before. The Arabs had no air traffic controllers of their own, but they did know how to pull the triggers of Kalashnikov automatic rifles. The air controllers, not wanting to be air-conditioned by 7.62mm holes, did as they were told.

The Arabs had obviously not moved on Gibraltar without considering British counterploys. Wary of a repeat of Israel's Entebbe gambit, they instructed the controllers to deny landing permission to any plane not approved in advance. An Arab in radio communication with Aziz's surface-to-air missiles monitored the airport radar screens. The message was clear: an unauthorized airplane risked getting scorched by an Arab missile.

That done, a detail of Arabs—terrorists turned defenders—began practicing a drill in which they surrounded a plane as it taxied to a stop.

Accompanied by a squad of uniformed soldiers with their Arab headgear rustling in the slight breeze coming off the Bay of Gibraltar, Boris Suslev arrived at the airport at three o'clock. He ordered the terminal cleared of everybody but essential workers, then retreated to the bar, declaring that bartenders were essential workers. He told the bartender to put all bottles of vodka in a refrigerator; while his men went about their duties, and the refrigerator did its job, Suslev drank his vodka warm and enjoyed the view of the north face of Mons Calpe just across the runway.

The sun had turned orange and was low over the hills behind Algeciras, and the bay was bathed in color when the Gibraltarian air controllers received a request for permission to land from the pilot of an Air Libya plane. His coordinates placed him one hundred miles east of Gibraltar.

The Gibraltarians checked with Suslev, who was by then enjoying chilled vodka. Suslev asked for more identifying data, then told the controller to grant the plane landing permission and to cooperate with the pilot in any way he requested. They did as they were told.

The blond man who stepped off the plane first looked at all the AK-47s pointing at him, and grinned his approval. The blond man wore an elegant three-piece suit and a stylish fedora. When he got to the bottom of the exit ramp he turned to Mons Calpe, which reflected the last red rays of the dying sun, then he turned and grinned at Suslev, who was coming to greet him.

"Hello, Boris," the blond man called.

The blond man was not alone: he had with him a party of thirty to forty Europeans who joined Suslev in the bar overlooking the tarmac. A detail of Arabs arrived to supervise the unloading of the aircraft that—judging from the labels on the sides of the boxes—had brought numerous Sony television sets and Panasonic VCRs.

The newcomer joined Boris Suslev in the upstairs lounge overlooking the airport as the television sets, VCRs, and other gear were loaded on trucks. The two men chatted, and drank cold vodka. Then a convoy of taxis arrived. The blond man and Suslev went downstairs and got into the lead taxi of a caravan of twelve that followed four loaded trucks across the airport.

The trucks slowed on the far side of the sundial: this marked the southern edge of the airport apron and the northern limit of the city. The lead truck turned up Main Street and stopped at the Continental Hotel, whose guests had been evicted and were standing along the street with their luggage, wondering what was going to happen to them.

The Arabs who had unloaded the plane at the airport arrived to move the equipment inside the hotel, as the mysterious man's entourage went inside with their suitcases and luggage.

107

Gibraltarians had been put on a dusk curfew by Muhammad Aziz. The streets were deserted except for soldiers on duty at their missiles and howitzers.

The blond man and Boris Suslev stood in the early evening. They admired the sailboats in the marina and looked across the water at Algeciras. They smoked cigarettes and enjoyed the warm air.

Gerard Thompson was as cool as Joe Montana under a pass rush as he delivered the hook: "Good evening. As those of you who have been watching television or listening to the radio know by now, Palestinian terrorists ambushed the British garrison on the Rock of Gibraltar late last night, and now occupy the famed fortress that guards the entrance to the Mediterranean Sea. We will devote the entire program tonight to what we have been able to learn about this stunning turn of events. Stay tuned for details."

Thompson relaxed as the monitor was given over to a reeling montage: John Kennedy being ripped by bullets; a Vietnamese officer shooting a captured Viet Cong with a pistol; Richard Nixon stepping aboard the plane that was to take him into internal exile; Reggie Jackson leaning into a fastball; a woman astronaut stepping aboard a rocket; Mount St. Helens erupting; a shapely, high-stepping baton twirler with an American flag on the derriere of her costume.

"A special edition of NBC News . . .

". . . with Gerard Thompson."

2

THE MONDAY HEADLINES in the fun-loving tabloid press said it all. "Shamed!" cried *The Express*. *The Daily Mirror* went up-market and chose the fancier, five-syllable "Humiliation!" "All Mourn the Rock!" claimed *The Sun*. "Resign!" said *The Daily Star*. "Take It Back!" added *The Express*.

This latter idea had indeed occurred to Prime Minister Deborah Fielding. The problem was, nobody knew how without an uncivilized loss of lives and property. It was as though the residents of No. 10 Downing had been saying over the years, Oh, well, yes, we did lose the empire, but that was a political thing, out of our hands; it was inevitable, surely, and in the long run for the best. But we will never, ever, lose Gibraltar. Gibraltar is impregnable and will remain so. You have our word on it.

Unfortunately, Arabs now occupied Gibraltar, and on Deborah Fielding's watch. Astonishingly, it appeared the Rock was impregnable only to the Royal Navy.

Although Deborah Fielding was born the daughter of a London cabdriver, conception through upstairs loins was not needed for her to recognize a bunch of confused, befuddled males. In Fielding's experience, women were generally smart enough to allow for some insecurities. But men? No, no, no! Their precious egos wouldn't allow for anything other than utmost confidence.

A sprint by tank and armored personnel carrier from the north across the airport tarmac was militarily the best alternative, which the Spanish generals had figured out immediately, moving their own units onto the isthmus leading to Gibraltar. The message was clear: the British were either forced to bargain with the Spanish for help in the only invasion route that made sense militarily, or they could recapture the Rock by themselves in a bloody air or sea battle.

It didn't take the foreign secretary, Sir Ian Tovey-Rundel, to tell Fielding what the Spanish price would be: eventual Spanish sovereignty over Gibraltar. The Gibraltarrians had several times made themselves clear on the issue: they did not want to be ceded over to Spain. They regarded themselves as Gibraltarians first, British second, not Gibraltarians first, Spanish second.

Mrs. Fielding would have no part of dealing with the Spanish under those conditions.

The idea of turning to NATO for help was out of the question for the same reason. Spain, now a member of NATO, would almost certainly use the occasion as an excuse to press Spanish claims to Gibraltar.

On Sunday afternoon, First Sea Lord Sir Denis Parsons had called for a meeting at the Ministry of Defence, including his senior advisers, the Commander in Chief Fleet, Admiral Sir John Keeble, and Rear Admiral Sir Cecil Whitehead, the logical commander of any invasion flotilla.

It turned out that the Royal Navy was somewhat short on contingency plans about what happens next after Arabs grab Gibraltar. Parsons and his officers turned their attention to the possibility of an amphibious attack. The best beaches were on the Mediterranean side—Eastern Beach, Catalan Bay, Sandy Bay—at the eastern end of the airport runway and along the base of the famous limestone cliffs. As beaches go, these weren't much. The British marines would have to assemble in a concentrated area, giving the Arabs a wonderful target. The Arabs, in their turn, could fire straight down on the hapless British with rockets and artillery, without exposing themselves in the least. "It would be like dropping turds on turtles," Sir Denis commented.

Brigadier Harry Tomlinson, senior fighting commander of the Royal Marines, and his advisers at the marines' Plymouth headquarters at first suggested that paratroopers be used. Tomlinson said hand-to-hand fighting would

110

spare the maximum of civilian lives. There would be no need for any kind of bombardment. There was no bloody raghead in the desert who could survive one-on-one with a British commando.

Later, Tomlinson backed off a bit: a jump onto the Rock was impossible, he said. Gibraltar was too small a target and the cliffs were dangerous. And if the wind shifted and they landed in the water . . . well. And besides which, Aziz's missiles could easily knock out the aircraft before the pilots could get their paratroopers over the jump zone.

Tomlinson repaired to Plymouth to rethink the problem. One of Tomlinson's four commando brigades, 3 Commando, which had borne the brunt of the fighting in the Falklands, was in barracks and hit the track immediately, triple-timing in combat boots and jockey shorts featuring the Union Jack fore and aft. His other brigades, 40 Commando, 42 Commando, and 45 Commando, on training exercises in Scotland, Norway, and the Black Forest, were recalled to Plymouth immediately.

The west slope of Gibraltar, with its town and harbor, offered no satisfactory sites for an amphibious assault. What's more, any attack on the west slope exposed civilians to the greatest of danger. The west slope was impossible.

There was an argument that the best plan would be to send commandos ashore in scuba gear night after night until a strike force could be assembled to liberate the men trapped inside. This would take longer, true, and might have had some merit had not the Arabs anticipated it, sending word through Omar Qafi's ambassador to Switzerland that for every British spy caught, twenty-five British soldiers would be removed from their prison and quietly executed. As it was inevitable that some of the commandos would get caught under this plan—a form of political suicide for its sponsors—enthusiasm for it waned.

The danger of postponing an attack was that the Arab claims of sovereignty might be considered a fait accompli if too much time passed. And if Debbie Fielding lost

Gibraltar, her government would surely fall to the boorish proles and Marxists in the Labour party; everybody knew that.

The leader of the loyal opposition was William Fluute, originally Flwte, of confused origins but held by Fluute as being Welsh. Fluute had a large head of white hair that the papers all called a "leonine mane." He suffered grievously from a limp—he'd been shot in France during the war —and from a severe case of egalitarian sympathies. Fluute was a passionate speaker, and one night—he was then Lord Fluute—he had renounced his hereditary title in a fervor of righteousness, a move his close friends said he later regretted. Fluute was drunk and showing off, they said. Sober, he would have never given away his title; a good-looking bird would skin her knickers for a lord where she wouldn't give the next guy the time of day.

William Fluute was in top form all day on the BBC. His limp got worse as the day wore on and the questions came at him one after the other. Fluute was in a wonderful position. This was clearly a Tory fiasco. The security of Gibraltar had been compromised on the Tory watch, he said. The only really honorable action would be for Mrs. Fielding to turn the government over to him.

A leader in *The Telegraph* said Mad Billy and the militant wing of the Labour party—that is, crazies from Liverpool, Manchester, and the unemployed north—were drooling in anticipation of regaining access to the national treasury.

Debbie Fielding had held the line against coal miners, and had even counterattacked. She had fought off hospital workers, garbage collectors, and as the country's industrial north collapsed and deteriorated in a pit of crime and unemployment, she did her best to invigorate the British economy. All this while Catholics and Protestants killed one another with bombs and machine guns.

Sunday evening, Mrs. Fielding, with her customary calm and resolve, had asked her senior military advisers to prepare summaries of alternative plans of attacking Gibraltar, listing both pros and cons of the action. Then they would meet and together choose. They would make up their minds. They would do something. They would take action. Her advisers agreed and committed themselves with all the clichés they could muster. There were tides to be turned. Momentum to be gained. Reverses to be scored. Ground to be made up.

The prime minister, facing a 2 P.M. appearance before Parliament, met with her advisers at 9 A.M. on Monday. They quarreled. Nothing was decided. Mrs. Fielding agreed to pursue a diplomatic solution while the data were fed into computers for a clearer analysis.

At 1 P.M. an attempt to contact Muhammad Aziz was made by Foreign Secretary Sir Ian Tovey-Rundel, using Algerian go-betweens. Aziz refused to talk.

The Norwegians, Costa Ricans, French, Italians, Belgians, Portuguese, Dutch, Israelis, Danes, and Swedes all had consuls on Gibraltar, but Muhammad Aziz refused to talk to any of them. The diplomats were informed, courteously, that if they signed a paper declaring themselves consuls to the People's Republic of Jebel Tarik, Aziz would allow them diplomatic privileges commensurate with their rank. If not, they were to pack their bags.

The consuls informed their governments of this choice. These governments conferred with the British. Moments before she left for Parliament, Fielding instructed Tovey-Rundel to tell those governments that Great Britain preferred that diplomats and their families be evacuated for their own safety. Mrs. Fielding did not wish Jebel Tarik to appear a legitimate government.

Aziz's refusal to work through diplomatic channels meant that everybody from the prime minister on down had to watch the drama on television, one in which posturing and cheap shots were the democratic order of the day. The thunder and roar of the Chevalier d'Arcon's brass cannons in the thirteenth siege of Gibraltar were replaced in the fourteenth by the whip and lash of opinion and analysis, blame-laying and self-justification. But if Mrs. Fielding was roughed up in public, her defense secretary, Roger Jackelforth, was positively savaged.

Poor Jackelforth. Question after unrelenting question fell like a cat-o'-nine-tails until he was forced to retreat

113

into the bunker of his office, defended by unyielding aides and tearful secretaries who repeated, no, no, no, no to requests for interviews. It was as though Jackelforth's upturned public school buttocks were being scourged by a British public furious that Arabs had been able to casually hijack Gibraltar, which everybody had been taught, from grammar school on, was impregnable.

The Fleet Street chaps dug up any number of retired military officers saying on the one hand that the prime minister should be supported and on the other that every day she delayed attacking the Rock, the more costly it would be. The national dailies published stories of a shocking collapse of will in the British military establishment. The Gibraltar fiasco had embarrassed everyone and morale had plunged. If there was any consensus as to how Gibraltar should be retaken, the journalists reported, it was the best-kept secret in the United Kingdom. Furthermore, they said, despite Mrs. Fielding's talk about negotiations and diplomatic channels, there was not a scrap of evidence to show that Muhammad Aziz was willing to negotiate anything.

Prime Minister Deborah Fielding's ordeal before the opposition in Parliament on Monday afternoon made for wonderful listening over BBC radio as listeners were encouraged to imagine campy scenes out of outlandish old movies. Judging from the agitated shouting, stomping, whistling, and jeering, members of Parliament had worked themselves into a perfect frenzy.

FIELDING *(Shouting):* We shall not. . . . We shall not. . . .

PARLIAMENT: *(Jeering and shouting, whistling.)*

FIELDING *(Shouting louder):* We shall. . . . We shall. . . .

PARLIAMENT: *(Jeering and shouting, whistling.)*

FIELDING *(Pushing it through):* We shall stand by the lessons of the Falklands!

PARLIAMENT: *(Jeering and shouting, cheering, whistling, at a lunatic, bonkers level.)*

FIELDING: Will you give me the courtesy?

PARLIAMENT: *(Jeering subsides.)*

114

AN UNIDENTIFIED MP: All that blood. All those lives. No more Falklands!

PARLIAMENT: *(More uproar.)*

FIELDING *(Steady, determined):* We had no warning, I assure you. We had no warning of any suspicious activities, not a hint of conspiracy, much less a plan to seize Gibraltar.

PARLIAMENT: *(Uproar. Jeers and whistling.)*

FIELDING: I believe it must now be admitted that we have put rather too much faith in the myth of Gibraltar's invincibility. Terrorists now occupy Gibraltar. It fairly bristles with missiles. British soldiers are imprisoned inside the Rock. Our fleet is denied access to the Mediterranean. We can neither starve nor bomb Gibraltar without risking the health and lives of Commonwealth citizens. . . .

PARLIAMENT: *(Uproar.)*

FIELDING: If that's the way you prefer.

Whereupon Prime Minister Deborah Fielding excused herself and left Parliament. There followed much speculation in the national dailies as to the reason for her leaving. Was it really out of indignation and protest over being repeatedly shouted down, or was it because she wanted to continue her Hamlet-like dithering over Gibraltar?

A spokesman for Mrs. Fielding said the prime minister decided the atmosphere was not amenable to the discussion of such serious issues, and she felt it was unwise to proceed.

The question addressed in every Tory paper on Fleet Street was, how much abuse and foul manners did a prime minister have to endure before refusing to speak? The situation had clearly gotten out of hand, Tory editors felt; Parliament's harassment of Mrs. Fielding was an indecent, uncivilized display of boorishness.

Labour backers asked just what kind of reaction did Mrs. Fielding expect? She had embarrassed herself and dishonored the country. A brave and honorable people were being made the laughingstock of the planet.

115

3

THE NURSES AND ward attendants at St. Bernard's Hospital adjusted adroitly to the Arab occupation of the Rock. A few minutes after the muezzin completed his morning call to prayer on Monday, the hall lights went on in St. Bernard's. A woman with a cart opened the door and said cheerily, "Good morning, Mr. Schoolcraft. Would you like some nice tea this morning?"

Burlane was impressed by the casual Gibraltarian response to the Arab takeover and his face showed it.

"It's business as usual in a siege, Mr. Schoolcraft. One lump or two?" She sounded as though a siege were like a seasonal disease, the flu or hay fever, say, something to be endured but which would go away in due time.

Burlane was enjoying his tea a few minutes later when nurse Christopher Chipolina, called Chippy by members of the ward, came in to check his blood pressure and pulse.

Burlane didn't like to trust other people. Better, he knew, to do everything himself. But this time it was different. This time he needed help; if Chipolina had even a hint of his ancestors' grit, he was Burlane's man.

Burlane waited until Chipolina had finished counting his pulse, then said, "Any news from out there?"

Chipolina shrugged. "*Nada.* They've got their missiles cluttering up the streets, but that doesn't mean anything."

Burlane was surprised. "It doesn't?"

Chipolina pretended to be offended. "We're Gibraltarians! They've got missiles up top, sure, but we've still got British soldiers down below. The day they dig the British out is the day we'll start worrying. The British have got something up their sleeves, you can bet on that."

Burlane liked Chipolina's spirit. He'd found his man. "Well, let's all hope so."

116

"We'll get them off, one way or another."

"Say, what time does Dr. Maskill make his rounds?"

Chipolina started putting his gear away. "Later in the morning, usually, but sometimes in the afternoon. How does your lung feel, Mr. Schoolcraft?"

"The lung's a lot better today." Burlane tried to breathe deeply but winced from the effort. He settled back on the bed and gestured toward the window with his head. "If I wanted to take a little walk today, I'd have to get Maskill's permission, wouldn't I?"

Chipolina looked surprised. "There won't be any walking for you. You need all the rest and penicillin we can get into you."

"Do you suppose you could talk to Maskill for me? This is quite important, actually . . ." Burlane fell into a coughing fit. "Ouch, that hurts a bit. It'll be pretty hard for Her Majesty's Government to get help in here without exciting Aziz and risking the lives of innocent people. I have some experience that just might help you out. Would you close the door, please, Chippy? Thanks. Have you read very much about MI6? Do you know what it is?"

"Sure. I read thrillers."

"I'm one of their American cousins, as they call us."

Astonished, Chippy Chipolina mouthed, "C-I-A?" Then he said aloud, "I thought you were supposed to be—"

"A birdman, yes, I know." Burlane gave him the clear *seeeee, slipslipslipslipslip* whistle of the pine woods sparrow. He fluttered his lips with his finger to get the *slipslipslip* part just right. "There are some magazines and books in my valise there. Go ahead and take a look."

Chipolina glanced at the photographs of Burlane that appeared on the dust jackets of Larry Schoolcraft's books and accompanied Schoolcraft's magazine articles.

"Genuine," Burlane said. "But run through the press again with my photograph and name instead of the real author's. I do like birds. I really found them interesting once I got into it. I'm not a bad whistler, either." He offered a neat *whip-poor-will* by way of proof.

"That's amazing."

117

"I was hard on their trail when I came down with this." He tapped his right lung with his free hand. "Well, sort of hard. I was sick when I left New York."

"An American spy!"

"Tut. Tut. We never utter those words out loud, never, ever. That's the first rule. I'm a birdman, remember. Flat on my back with the bashers wailing on my ribs twice a day. Are you willing to help, Chippy?"

"Certainly. I'll do everything I can."

"To the best of your ability, that's all I can ask. You must take no notes, Chippy. None. I'll tell you what I want you to do but rarely why. I'll tell you only part of what I'm doing, not the whole gambit. Do you understand why?"

"I think so."

"It's for your protection and for mine. If you get caught, you know a little bit, not the whole thing."

"I understand."

James Burlane lifted the lid on the stainless steel gunk container. He coughed up some grayish sputum and spat it into the purple solution. He closed the lid and winced sharply as he inhaled. "Poops me out. Chippy, my gear is in the closet there. Could you retrieve it for me? You might have to use some of it."

"Me?"

"Sure, you. I bet you have a camera of some kind. Mine's probably more expensive, but it's still easy to use. Go ahead, take a look at it."

Chipolina opened the closet and retrieved two gray suitcases with rounded corners.

"They're made of laminated carbon, incidentally —lighter and stronger than aluminum. Here's a key. You'll need it for the latches."

Chipolina opened a suitcase and whistled.

"That's a parabolic microphone, Chippy. Good for eavesdropping on some turkeys in the middle of a field."

"Or a conversation across the street."

"Or park. A nature photographer has to have good equipment, right? Go ahead, look at it. I've got a four-hundred-millimeter lens in there, and a six-hundred-millimeter, and a night scope that will magnify the

118

available light by seventy thousand." Burlane watched as Chipolina pulled out the telescopic legs of his tripod. "If you push the legs in, you can use it as a mount to shoot documents."

Chipolina pushed the legs in and screwed the camera onto a mount on the underside of the triangle. "Very good."

Burlane unstrapped the digital watch from his wrist. "In the side pocket in there you'll find a mate to this. That's it. Put it on. Go ahead. Push the green button on the side."

Chipolina pushed the button and Burlane's watch began making a small *eeep! eeep!* sound. Burlane punched a stainless steel button on the bottom of his watch. "You shut the alarm off here.

"If the Arabs should ever question you for any reason, you push the green button. You understand why? This works two ways, for your protection as well as mine."

Chipolina nodded yes. He understood.

"Do the Arabs pretty much allow you the run of the Gib? What can you see and what not?"

"All the British military installations are off limits, and of course we have to stay well clear of their missiles and the airfield. And there's the curfew, but they moved it from dusk to eleven P.M. I think the curfew is so the journalists can have the run of the pubs at night."

"Really? That's interesting. Say, you don't know anybody who works at the airport, do you? A city this small, I'd think everybody would know almost everybody else."

Chipolina said, "They almost do, as a matter of fact."

"Well, what do you think, my man? Would you like to help the British take it back?"

"What? Us?"

"Sure, the Brits'll let us know what they'd like us to do. Shoot a few Arabs maybe. Blow a few up."

Chippy Chipolina ran his fingers down his jaw.

James Burlane grinned malevolently. Burlane looked forward to the pleasure of killing a few Palestinian ass-holes. An assassin's equivalent of a ruddy, healthy glow suffused his cheeks. The president's man seemed to be

119

regaining his strength and with it his zest for the administration of justice, a delicate job in the best of circumstances. He was caught in the grip of painful coughs.

James Burlane insisted on going to see Ella Nidech by himself. Chippy Chipolina was both intelligent and eager to help, but he was an amateur. Burlane had to be certain his Larry Schoolcraft cover was still clean before he risked Nidech's hide. In view of the situation, Dr. Michael Maskill agreed to temporarily interrupt the flow of antibiotics into Burlane's arm.

Burlane, weak but feeling better, went downtown by way of the steep steps just below the hospital. The steps went straight down the hill, turned nearly ninety degrees to the left for a longer descent, then took a hard right down to Governor's Street.

He descended the steps slowly, but it was still not easy to breathe. Burlane's lips, which had been dry and cracked from the fever, were once again pliable; his bird calls were interrupted by fits of coughing. It was a balmy day, but he was sweating hard when he reached Governor's Street. He rested and used the rest to check his flanks. He was almost too pooped to pucker, but he mounted a whistle anyway. He bore to his left and went one block down to City Mill Lane to the Israeli consul's office on Main Street. He was in the heart of Gibraltar, just like that.

Arabs in khaki fatigues guarded the entrance to the House of Assembly across the street—now taken over by Muhammad Aziz. More soldiers in khakis smoked cigarettes and watched over the tracked missile carriers that stopped traffic in the narrow streets going downhill from Main Street. Main was a short block from the Moorish wall that flanked the harbor.

Burlane thought the Arabs were a bit optimistic about there being business as usual on Gibraltar when they had blocked traffic on the side streets with their missile carriers.

Downtown Gibraltar had been abuzz with shoppers and activity when Burlane had arrived on Friday. It was now Monday afternoon. The braver residents of the town had ventured onto the streets, peering at all the sleek missiles slanted at the sky like racks of metal snakes.

Burlane whistled *bob-white!* and turned right on Main Street—toward the airport four hundred yards ahead. He checked his watch and his flanks. The guards at the border didn't chop passports, an omission of which Burlane ordinarily approved. This time a chop would have been handy. Luckily, he had caught pneumonia. His Larry Schoolcraft books and his ability to imitate birds explained his paraphernalia. Pneumonia gave him a reason for being on Gibraltar and dated his arrival. Burlane started to laugh at his good fortune in having caught pneumonia, but broke instead into another spasm of coughing.

He hoped he wasn't too late to catch Ella on the back stretch of her pass through town. He wasn't. He saw her up ahead, coming toward him on the sidewalk. She saw him as well and stopped to look at a window display of Gibraltar T-shirts.

Burlane also stopped at the window. "Are you enjoying Gibraltar?" He choked off a cough.

"My mother would be pleased that I grew up to be a belly dancer. How about yourself?"

Burlane coughed. "Pooped, but the penicillin's working."

"And now we wait for the British to tell us what they want done."

Burlane whistled a low warble. "I wouldn't mind killing a few Arabs." He mimicked a gull.

"They say we'll have a gopher in Algeciras tomorrow."

"I have a male nurse named Chippy Chipolina helping me. I think we can trust him to do a job. Also, I hope to be making contact with two writers I saw on my way in to the hospital, a Brit and an American. I know them both."

"I imagine we'll be needing the help."

Burlane looked up the street. "I suppose we'd better be going."

"Thanks for the little date."

"My pleasure entirely," Burlane said.

James Burlane had once almost lost his job because Nidech—in a letter to the chairman of the Senate Intelligence Oversight Committee—had charged Burlane with sexual harassment, all because of one of his pranks. He whistled a mournful, even pathetic *weep, weep, weep, weep* that drooped at the end. This was to let her know he didn't mean to be a jerk.

Ella Nidech said, "Oh, for Chrissake, shut up!"

4

FROM THE MOMENT Muhammad Aziz had assigned him to take care of the Barbary apes, Colonel Terry Holmestead had pictured himself riding at the head of a column of open-topped jeeps. While Aziz and Bobby Nye and the Arabs spent all day Sunday making sure the Rock was secure, Holmestead had stayed out of the way, rehearsing his ape mission in his mind. He suspected he had been given the assignment only to keep him happy and occupied; Aziz needed his computer skills. The ape mission was a chance to prove he was worthy of his new rank.

His dad had always said he was weak and hopeless, worthless, in fact; Holmestead wished his dad could see him now. He also remembered Leonard of the brown eyes in his college algebra class, who had scorned him.

Holmestead vowed to show them what he could do. The sensible thing to do would have been to accompany the British enlisted men for their daily feeding of the apes. Alas, in their enthusiasm to scourge the surface of every British soldier except those with essential technical skills, the Arabs had sent the apes' feeders packing along with everybody else. In spite of that, Holmestead was determined to complete his ape mission with such finesse as to earn the admiration of even Bobby Nye.

There would be no pissing in his pants this time.

Monday came at last, as he knew it surely would. Holmestead brushed his teeth and went downstairs to find the lobby a confusion of Arab officers dressed in proper military uniforms. These were the same cut and olive color as Holmestead's, but with less impressive epaulets, and without stripes down the sides of the trousers. These were lieutenants mostly, and a few captains. Whereas Holmestead had been issued a Western-style officer's hat, the other Jebel Tariki officers wore white kaffiyehs on their heads, tied in place with camel hair akals. Holmestead thought that even with haircuts and shined shoes, the Arabs looked like camel jockeys. He had found Moroccan men exciting in bed, but he didn't want anything to do with Arabs socially.

A private in the Jebel Tariki army was serving strong Arab coffee in small handleless cups. Holmestead, wanting to be part of the group, took one. The coffee was bitter, but he sipped it, smiling as though he liked it. How can they drink this bloody crap? he wondered.

He glanced at his watch. In another forty minutes he was supposed to be at the Naval Sports Grounds where his ape detail was to assemble. He wanted to leave immediately but didn't want to appear eager; the Naval Sports Grounds—at the foot of Gibraltar Harbor—was only two blocks away. The worst thing he could do would be to arrive before the Arabs.

Holmestead fought off the urge to squeeze a pimple that during the night had emerged full-blown and painful at the side of his mouth. Holmestead sat by himself; he was an infidel and was aware of it. He had been proud of the crossed scimitars on his colonel's cap; now he wished he had a kaffiyeh like the others. He wanted to look like T. E. Lawrence. He closed his eyes and pictured himself on a camel loping across the desert, his robes flowing in the wind, crying "Hut! Hut! Hut!" at the animal. He took a second cup of the vile brew.

They had issued him a Czech-made Vz61 Skorpion machine pistol and a shoulder holster. He had never seen anything as exotic-looking, not even in the James Bond movies.

An Arab captain came up to him and said, "Colonel Holmestead, sir. I've been asked to tell you that your ape detail will be postponed until fourteen hundred hours. Colonel Nye would like to keep the streets clear for a while yet this morning. I'm to tell you the light will be better for the camera in the afternoon."

"Certainly," Holmestead said. "Everything proceeds apace, Captain." Holmestead couldn't remember using the word *apace* before. It sounded very Jack Hawkins or Alec Guinness. He wasn't certain he knew what it meant or if there was such a word. Would a colonel use *apace*? He felt anxious. "Will they have jeeps?" he blurted.

"Jeeps, sir?"

"We'll need jeeps for the mission. As soon as they're finished with their other duties, I'd like my men to secure jeeps." Holmestead liked the sound of "secure jeeps."

"Yes, sir," the captain said.

Colonel Holmestead's bladder began to complain of Arab coffee, so he retreated upstairs to his room. Colonels had rooms with toilets. Captains and lieutenants had to use one in the hall. He and the other officers were under orders to remain in their rooms unless they had a specific assignment. Jebel Tarik was not yet secure enough for casual strolls.

Holmestead did have another assignment, actually. He was supposed to train two Arabs on how to operate the perimeter barriers in case Aziz wanted to go in after the British. Now that he had a six-hour wait for the ape mission, he had plenty of time to do it. But Holmestead decided he didn't want to train them just yet. If the Arabs decided to expel the last British soldier, Holmestead wanted to be in on it. He didn't want to train somebody else only to let them have all the fun.

At a quarter to two, Holmestead, unconsciously fingering the loaded Czech Skorpion strapped under his arm, walked across Main Street and down Market Lane to the Naval Sports Grounds. He could see that the RAF complex next to the harbor was alive with Jebel Tariki soldiers who had earlier driven the captured British troops to the Spanish border and turned them loose.

Muhammad Aziz had used GBC radio to announce a temporary closing of nonessential offices and businesses and a public ban on gatherings of more than two Gibraltarians; the populace was reminded that they were as yet hostages, not citizens of Jebel Tarik. Except for Arab soldiers putting the finishing touches on the installation of the howitzers and missiles, the streets were empty. Queensway—which ran along the harbor—was kept free of weapons in case Bobby Nye had to shift his firepower rapidly from Europa Point to the isthmus connecting Gibraltar to Spain or the reverse.

Bobby Nye had allotted Holmestead thirteen enlisted men for his ape detail. These men had been hit-and-run terrorists a few weeks earlier. They were used to hiding bombs that were not detonated until they were safely away; the business of being up-front soldiers wasn't their style. Holmestead thought they looked self-conscious in military uniforms. There were no jeeps, he noted, but his men did carry their Kalashnikov AK-47s in case there was killing to do.

"Fall in, men," he said, his head abuzz with memories of movie officers he had seen: Dirk Bogarde, Sean Connery.

The Arabs, who had received some rudimentary training from Bobby Nye in such matters, fell into a single rank with a sergeant at the end.

"Do you have the video camera, Sergeant?"

"Yes, sir, we did, and we had film too," the sergeant said.

"Had?"

"Yes, sir." The sergeant gestured toward a soldier holding a camera that said GBC on the side of it.

Holmestead wondered if the sergeant had only learned the past tense in English. "Does the private know how to use it?"

"Yes, sir, he did. He knew all about such things. He

was very good. He said the light was very delicious this afternoon. Not as sour as this morning. We had peanuts and blankets to use as scoops if we needed them."

"Scoops? Do you mean nets?"

"Yes, sir. Nets. For fishes. We had boxes to held them."

By "them," Holmestead assumed the sergeant meant the apes, not fish. "And the jeeps?" Holmestead asked.

"Jeeps, sir? Colonel Nye said we were to use taxis." The sergeant glanced at six gray cabs lined up on Queensway.

"Yes, taxis." Holmestead was determined not to show his disappointment. He and the sergeant took the lead taxi, and the rest of the detail settled into cars. Once the column was proceeding down Queensway, Holmestead's enthusiasm returned. Although his face glowed from the untimely renewal of his acne, he ignored it. His mission was to capture the bloody Barbary apes and ship them back to Africa, or kill them if he had to, and that was precisely what he was going to do. He couldn't wait. His men would tape the whole thing, and Holmestead knew very well that the BBC would show the entire humiliating scene to its embarrassed, shamed viewers, poor sods.

Queensway turned left just beyond the Home for the Aged Hebrew, heading uphill; Holmestead was so excited by the missiles at the Home that he almost overlooked the tracked missile carrier backed over the headstones of the heroes of Trafalgar. Missiles in Trafalgar Cemetery! Holmestead did a double take.

The column of taxis turned right—that is, south toward Africa—onto Europa Road which, at two hundred feet elevation, became Engineer Road, hardly more than a ledge carved out of the steep side of the mountain, and rose even more steeply. Less than a quarter of a mile farther, the column of taxis arrived at the entrance to the Med Steps at six hundred feet elevation. The Bay of Gibraltar was blue and luminescent and beautiful far below.

The road switched back and became Queen's Road, heading north, toward Spain, rising higher and higher to

Queen's Lookout at eight hundred feet, then dropping quickly to the den of friendly Barbary apes at six hundred feet.

These were the apes he would capture and videotape for Muhammad Aziz. At first he had wanted to waste the unfriendly pack of apes. He wanted to try out a Kalashnikov AK-47. He also dreamed of writing a letter home telling his old man how he had closed on the enemy with his AK-47 bucking hard against his shoulder. A good little weapon, he'd call it. The Russians knew how to make a decent weapon, you had to give them that.

But after meeting the sergeant who spoke in the past tense, he'd begun having second thoughts about the wisdom of using the assault rifles.

Then he spotted an ape sitting on a low stone wall on the seaward side of the road, and another in the brush on the bank above the road. He was into it, into battle. . . . "Pull over here, driver," he said, his mind full of Bogarde, Guinness, Hawkins, Attenborough, and Connery.

The apes watched as the Arabs got out of the taxis, bearing fishing nets stolen from Gibraltarian fishermen, fruit confiscated from Gibraltarian markets, and their weapons.

Holmestead motioned for the sergeant. "Sergeant, I would like you to tell your men to approach the apes slowly. They are to hold the food in front of them and gain the apes' confidence. When the apes come out of the brush and begin eating, your cameraman is to begin taping them. Is that clear so far, Sergeant?"

"Yes, sir. It was."

"We do not want to frighten them. When I give the word, I want the men to throw their nets at once. To alert the troops, I will give the order in a cadence: get ready; get set; throw. Is that clear, Sergeant?"

"It was, sir."

"Good, then get your men into position."

The sergeant began relaying the instructions in Arabic. As he spoke, Holmestead called softly, "Remember,

127

men, don't spook them. Be very gentle. Be their friends."

The members of the detail slung their weapons over their shoulders and approached the apes with net in one hand, grapes or bananas in the other.

"That's it, men. That's the way." Holmestead's confidence in the Arabs was returning.

The apes looked back at a good-looking, sleek ape who sat in the top of a bush, as though waiting for his instructions.

The sleek ape stirred at the sight of the camera.

Seeing this, Holmestead said, "Sergeant Hassan, tell the cameraman to step back. I think he may be frightening them. We have to gain their confidence first."

"Stood back! Stood back!" The sergeant yelled in English for Holmestead's benefit.

The man with the camera did as he was told.

Suddenly, the sleek ape hopped off the bush and grabbed two female apes, one by each hand, and began scrambling uphill.

Colonel Terry Holmestead yelled, "Fire! Fire! Fire! Fire at will!"

"Fired! Fired! Fired!" Hassan repeated the command in Arabic.

The Arabs opened fire on the confused pack of friendly apes. The slaughter of apes was broken by the screaming of a man.

The soldier who had blown his foot off was packed into a taxi and sent to the hospital. The shaken Colonel Terry Holmestead and his detail then set about the chore of eliminating the wild apes. Holmestead took no chances with the second pack. His men approached with the fruit, and as soon as the pack had been located, they opened fire, killing monkeys for the cameraman.

Holmestead wanted in the worst way to get his hands on the bloody little sod of an ape who had bolted from the first pack. Back at the hotel, he lay back in bed in his underwear to consider his aborted mission. Why did that sodding ape take off?

Shortly after he returned, he received orders to report

to Muhammad Aziz and Bobby Nye. For a debriefing, the note said.

Holmestead had temporarily lost the desire to wear his fancy uniform, but he was going to have to put it on again to see Aziz. Aziz had been one of the few people to treat Holmestead like a human being, but the fact remained that one male and two female apes remained loose on the western slope of Gibraltar. Muhammad Aziz had specifically said that he wanted no loose apes on Jebel Tarik when the international press arrived.

He checked his watch again. It was time.

Colonel Holmestead got up, put on his uniform, and walked diagonally across the street to the House of Assembly that was now the Parliament of the People's Republic of Jebel Tarik. With all the problems of holding almost thirty thousand Gibraltarian hostages and the details of launching an hours-old country, Holmestead had been surprised that Aziz would be so concerned about the apes.

The Jebel Tariki guards were polite, and Holmestead was both surprised and pleased to learn that he didn't have to wait. The prime minister, he was told, was waiting for him.

Muhammad Aziz was flanked by Boris Suslev and Bobby Nye. Aziz rose, his hand extended. He said, "Colonel Holmestead, so good to see you."

Holmestead was relieved to see the prime minister in such a pleasant mood. "You too, Mr. Prime Minister."

"I hear you had some problems with the apes."

"I had three of the little sods take off on me, and one of my men shot himself in the foot," Holmestead said. He glanced at the silent Suslev and Nye, then stared at the floor.

Aziz took him by the shoulder to comfort him. "That's okay, Colonel. A wild animal is always unpredictable; I knew that when I sent you."

Hey! Okay! Holmestead felt a surge of confidence.

"Have you had an opportunity to train your backups so you won't have to be on call twenty-four hours a day? We're going to have to keep everyone rested and fit in the coming days."

Holmestead didn't want to add a second failure to the ape disaster. He could teach them what they needed to know in a couple of hours, no problem. "Yes, sir," he lied. "All taken care of, Mr. Prime Minister." Holmestead felt as if he were in the movies again, the efficient officer reporting to his chief; it was wonderful.

Muhammad Aziz looked at Suslev.

"*Da,*" Suslev said. Suslev was indifferent to killing people.

"Go ahead," Nye added.

Holmestead realized that Nye despised him.

"A worthless queer. No good for anything," Suslev said.

Holmestead heard the metallic click of the safety of Aziz's machine pistol. Muhammad Aziz was pointing the weapon at him. He was going to die. He shouldn't have lied to Aziz about training his replacements. Now they had no reason to keep him.

He remembered Dirk Bogarde holding a soldier cradled in his arms. The confused soldier had wandered away from battle, and Bogarde was under orders to execute him. With his pistol at the soldier's mouth, Bogarde asked why he had volunteered for the army.

"For King and Country, sir," the soldier replied.

Terry Holmestead wondered why his own life had been so accursed. He felt a pimple burning at the corner of his mouth.

The first slug entered his face slightly off center of the bridge of his nose, and the others followed in a torrent, sending his brains *splat!* pinkish-white, against the wall.

5

JAMES BURLANE FIRST heard of Puking Max's escape by way of much excited jabber in the hallway. The nurses recounted the story in Llanito, the Gibraltarian lingo that was Spanish or English depending on the whims and preferences of the speaker; Spanish and English words and phrases mingled in a linguistic stew. Burlane heard the name Max repeated several times. He heard somebody say an Arab television crew had recorded the entire episode on videotape.

Burlane could see Chipolina's back through the open door. "Chippy!" Burlane called.

Chipolina came into the room. "Yes?"

"What's going on out there?"

Chipolina grinned. "You know about the legend of the apes?"

"There'll be British on Gibraltar as long as the apes remain."

"Did you hear the shooting yesterday afternoon? The Arabs sent a group of soldiers up on the hill to get rid of the apes. They took taxis, and the drivers saw the whole thing."

"What happened?"

"They went to the friendly pack first. They had nets and fruit and their machine guns, although the drivers say their commander first ordered them caught. They had an Arab with a camera. One of the apes, one the drivers call Puking Max, bolted with two females, and the Arabs slaughtered the rest. Puking Max is still up there running around with two females. We're all pulling for him. As long as he's out there roaming around with his ladies, we've still got a chance. One Arab shot his foot off; Maskill had to keep him from bleeding to death."

131

"Max sounds like an ape with grit."

"He's up there hiding in the maquis somewhere. They'll never get him. Everybody's watching with binoculars. There're about thirty people watching from down by the dry docks, but the Arabs won't let them out on the mole. Also, the Spanish have positioned tanks on their side of the border. Do you think they're cooperating with the British?"

"Hardly likely. I'd say the northern route is the best way to retake this place, and the Spanish don't want the British to have it. The Spanish want Gibraltar for themselves."

"I was wondering about that," Chipolina said.

"Hard cheese for the British." Burlane coughed again, then said, "Tell me what you found out about the mystery man and his group in the Continental Hotel."

Chipolina used the palms of his hands to square away the sides of imaginary boxes. "They unloaded Sony televisions and videotape recorders from the airplane . . ."

"How do you know?"

"It said so on the outside of the boxes. The boxes were brand-new. They'd never been opened."

"How do you know they'd never been opened?"

Chipolina paused. "Well, I don't for sure."

"They probably were VCRs," Burlane said. "What do you suppose they would be doing with VCRs and television sets on Gibraltar? Looking at skin flicks, do you suppose? Do they have television sets in the rooms at the Continental?"

"Sure. At least I think so."

Burlane, thinking out loud, said, "Sony on the side." This was halfway between a question and a statement. "Brand-new. Tops unopened. What could have been in those boxes, do you suppose? Something else? Computers?"

"Could be computers."

Burlane shifted to his side in bed. "Tell me more about the man. An English speaker, you say?"

"He speaks English with an American accent." Chipolina grinned, having learned that he should report only what he saw, that then they could speculate.

"Did you ask your friends if they thought English was his native tongue?"

"They think so, but they can't be sure. All you Americans sound odd to us."

"Crazed Americans, eh? Tell you what, Chippy. I want to know everything you can find out about this mystery man of ours. When does he go to work? How long does he stay? Does he work at night? I know this is only the third day, but it would surprise you how quickly people establish routines in a new place. He have any? You get what I mean? My cousins will need all the information they can get to free this place."

"Your cousins, sir?"

"The British."

"I'll do my best."

"Find out everything you can without endangering yourself. Also, Chippy, there are two writers who were in town before this all happened, and they may yet be on the Rock."

"And they are?"

"Bob Steele, who may be on assignment from *The Daily Telegraph,* and Jim Quint, who writes adventure novels under a pseudonym. Do you know about the Humper Staab books?"

"Nicholas Orr. *Humper Sticks It In!* Nicholas Orr is on Gibraltar?"

"Nicholas Orr's real name is Jim Quint; I saw him on my way in. Quint and Bob Steele are old pals. If they're still here, I'd like to know where they're staying and what they do at night."

"That shouldn't be too hard. There're only eight hotels in town and they're full of journalists or Arabs."

"But I want you to find out about the mystery man first. Quint and Steele can wait. If they didn't leave Saturday afternoon, they're not going anyplace. We've got 'em on hold, so to speak." Burlane looked amused.

"When do you want all this?"

"How about tonight? Whatever you can find out by tonight."

Chipolina's mouth fell. "Tonight?"

"The longer the British wait, the harder a job it'll be to retake Gibraltar. Time gives the Arabs an opportunity to fix the major weaknesses in their defense."

Chipolina grinned. "How long do you think it will be before the British counterattack?"

Burlane considered that with puffed cheeks. "Oh, I don't know—hours, days. Weeks, possibly. I sure hope no longer than that. The longer the British wait, the tougher it'll be on them. Meanwhile, we ask a few discreet questions and keep our eyes open. For example, it might be critical for the British to know why the Arabs flew all those television sets and VCRs in here. There may be a hint of Russian crude here somewhere, you never know. I'd like to have some dope on the mystery man as soon as possible."

On Wednesday morning, James Burlane propped his pillow up on the adjustable metal rails of the headboard and spread a map of Gibraltar on his lap. He made sure his needle arm was comfortable, then said, "I know you've only had a day, but tell me what you've learned about our mystery man."

"Quite a bit, actually, Mr. Schoolcraft. For one thing, he took over the entire hotel."

Burlane looked up. "Really? Took it over? Tell me what happened."

"The Arabs sacked the entire staff—managers, cooks, waiters, janitors, everybody—then they moved their own people in. The mystery man and three assistants seem to be in charge. But he does all the talking. They defer to him."

"Ahh, the inevitable toadies! Ass kissers are everywhere, Chippy. It's an international conspiracy. But the obviousness of the ass-kissing might be a clue in itself. Russian bureaucrats are at their most comfortable in the posture." Burlane leaned forward and made kissing sounds with his lips: kiss, kiss, kiss. "That makes our work easier, however, because whatever the mystery man thinks

134

and says, the toadies will think and say also. If we can't scope him, we'll scope them. What else did you find?"

"Well, yesterday Muhammad Aziz went to the hotel in the governor's limousine. That was at ten o'clock. After the midday call to prayer, Aziz returned to the governor's residence on Line Wall Road—he's taken it over. The mystery man and his three assistants went for a walk through the center of town."

"Where did they go, south on Main Street?" Burlane moved his finger from right to left toward the tip of the peninsula.

"That's right. Yesterday they went all the way to the Garrison Theatre and returned on Line Wall Road. Then they detoured down Irish Town and had a peek into the shops."

"A peek into the shops?"

"Yes. And they stopped off at a pub to have a pint. They each had a pint, but only two of them talked. The American and a man with a British accent."

Burlane looked impressed. "How did you find all this out?"

"We've been a British colony since 1704. Gibraltar's a small place. Everybody knows everybody." Chipolina grinned. "If you're a Gibraltarian, it isn't too hard to find out what a bartender might have heard in The Angry Friar."

"What exactly did he hear them say?"

"Nothing specific. He kept his distance. But he did hear that the second man spoke English with a British accent."

"And after their walk, what happened?"

"They stayed in their hotel. They stayed up late, I'm told, to midnight or one in the morning. There's one more thing I forgot to tell you."

Burlane raised his eyebrows. "What's that?"

"Yesterday the mystery man, his three assistants, and some others went to the airport to meet a plane that flew in from the east. They unloaded some parcels and drove back to the hotel at high speed."

"They did, eh?"

"They were apparently waiting anxiously for the parcels because they called to ask exactly when the plane was due in."

"Television sets, VCRs, waiting anxiously for some packages. That's interesting, don't you think? Good work, Chippy." Burlane looked out the window at Algeciras across the bay. "If you can, discreetly, I would like you to find out what kind of food is being delivered to the kitchen of the Continental Hotel. Cabbage and beetroots? Black beans and rice? Also, what is it they're drinking? I don't imagine they're teetotalers. Do you think you could find that out for me?"

After Chippy Chipolina had gone, Burlane popped the back off his Mazumo and adjusted the machine to the assigned emergency frequency where a rep, the Company's ears, would be waiting for communications splits. This rep, who was most likely across the bay in Algeciras, would radio the squirts to the American embassy in Madrid, where they would be bounced off a satellite to Ara Schott in Langley. It was Schott's duty to decide what to pass on to Century House, in the Lambeth district of London, headquarters for MI6, the British agency for foreign intelligence, and thence to Mrs. Fielding.

Burlane used the eraser of a pencil to tap a short message on the diminutive keyboard. The words of a single question appeared on the light-emitting diode:

ARE YOU THERE FRIEND? LOOKING FOR AMOS. CHINESE GORDON.

It was up to Burlane how to slug his series of squirts from Gibraltar. Amos was Ara Schott's current cryptonym. The Company rep in Spain might not know who Amos was, but he would know the cryptonym.

Burlane tapped the squirt button.

The delicate man waited. He had not mentioned Ella Nidech. She would be communicating with the Company gopher on her own. Although Burlane was a far more experienced agent than Nidech—he also knew he probably earned far more than she did for essentially the same

136

work—he was not her official superior. He did not want to be superior to anybody. This was, in fact, the first time they had worked together since her appointment as the delicate agent who lacked Y chromosomes.

Was the gopher in place? Burlane hoped so. There was a lot of work to be done. Burlane's wristwatch sounded the alarm. He gave the machine another instruction, and a message appeared on the screen:

CHINESE GORDON. MUSIC IS GOOD. AMOS SAYS SING NOW, PLEASE. KINFOLK'S BLUES TO COME. KOUFAX.

Burlane smiled. His colleague in Spain was introducing his cryptonym and relaying Amos's squirt at the same time. Koufax was obviously Sandy, of the Los Angeles Dodgers. "Kinfolk's blues to come" meant that Burlane would soon be receiving inquiries from MI6 on behalf of Her Majesty's Government. The correspondent was in his thirties, possibly, liked music, and was a fan of the Los Angeles Dodgers.

James Burlane typed "KOUFAX. WHAT AMOS WANTS," and followed with a longer message that rose slowly from the bottom until the eight-line screen was full. The words kept scrolling up as Burlane typed what he had learned so far. Ella Nidech would give her report separately. Ara Schott would put the two together and write a detailed summary for MI6 and Prime Minister Deborah Fielding.

6

THE PILOT OF the Air Libya DC-10 spoke fluent English with a British accent: "Gentlemen, I've been given permission to do a couple of fly-arounds to give you some idea of what Gibraltar looks like, although I'm to remind you that it is now called Jebel Tarik." He banked the plane slightly.

The reporters—scribbling notes, wondering how to spell Jebel Tarik and what it meant—scrambled for windows on the down-wing side of the Air Libya plane.

"You'll see that Jebel Tarik is actually connected to the Spanish mainland by a low isthmus. The British had to push an extension into the bay to accommodate the airport runway. That's the north face of Mons Calpe you see across from the runway." The pilot banked the DC-10 to the right.

One reporter cried "Whoa!" at the sight of the famous monolith. Another said, "Mons what?" Mons Venus, they knew. "Calpe," someone said. Laughing, everybody scribbled. It was nervous laughter as much as anything else; the reporters were still disbelieving that these Arabs had simply grabbed the Rock while the British slept. What had always seemed beyond the pale, unthinkable, had happened, and they were the journalists who had the good fortune to report it to the world.

The pilot said, "The British dug tunnels for their defensive batteries in the solid rock of the limestone there. They were able to fire at nearly point-blank range on the isthmus, which is why the Rock has historically been impregnable from the land. We're over the Mediterranean now. That's the eastern face of Mons Calpe. In the middle there are concrete water catchments. You can understand why Gibraltar has been impregnable from the Mediterra-

138

nean." After a few seconds, he said. "Jebel Tarik, I should have said."

There was laughter in the main cabin. Both still photographers and television cameramen were shooting Gibraltar's famous eastern face.

"We're now approaching Europa Point," the pilot said, continuing his bank to the right. "We're now circling over the Bay of Gibraltar. This is the western face of Jebel Tarik, the backside you might say. At the bottom there is the city of Gib . . . Jebel Tarik, which has a population of twenty-eight thousand. In the eighteenth and nineteenth centuries, invaders from the bay were frustrated by a lack of wind. An easterly wind called the levanter blows for about a hundred and fifty days a year, and it's blocked by the Rock itself."

"Like seeing the backside of the moon," a reporter said, and there was much merriment among the boys on the airplane.

"There is the airport runway sticking out into the bay, and that's it, Jebel Tarik, the whole thing, hardly more than two miles long, barely half a mile wide at its thickest, twelve hundred feet at its highest. The wind's coming off the bay today, so we'll be approaching from the Mediterranean side."

Tony O'Brien finished his notes about the wind and looked up, catching the eye of Harry Gilchrist's correspondent. They smiled in acknowledgment of the coming competition. This was a story of a lifetime, bigger than the grabbing of Israeli athletes at the Munich Olympics or the taking of American hostages in Teheran, and they both knew it. The capture of the impregnable Gibraltar? There were fabulous Nielsens at stake. Even ABC couldn't be counted out; a spirited and imaginative performance could easily send ABC rushing past NBC and CBS.

Tony O'Brien felt like a sprinter toeing the line, or a boxer waiting for the bell. This was show time, shit-kicking time.

A dark-eyed Libyan flight attendant, wearing a Western-style uniform with a trim skirt, gave a brief announcement as the plane descended: "I am to tell you that arrangements have been made for you to stay in the Holiday Inn in downtown Jebel Tarik. Upon arrival at the airport, you will each meet your official host, who will help you with any questions or needs. There will be a press conference with Prime Minister Muhammad Aziz at seven P.M." She thanked them for flying Air Libya and reminded them to stay buckled up until the plane had come to a complete halt at the terminal.

Even the most jaded international correspondents were impressed by the dramatic north face of Mons Calpe just across the airport, and the photographers were clicking and whirring as they left the airplane. The lobby of the airport was filled with Arabs in flowing white cotton thobes and kaffiyehs. As the journalists waited in line for their bags to be checked by Jebel Tariki customs officers, they were descended upon by their assigned hosts.

The hosts bore gifts: a camel saddle and a jeweled scimitar for each of the men; beautiful silk thobes and a handful of solid gold bracelets for those women reporters and photographers who had braved the male world of Islam.

Glancing about him, O'Brien saw that correspondents from *The Washington Post* and *The New York Times* had each drawn a young woman, as had reporters for *The Los Angeles Times, The Chicago Tribune, Le Monde, Der Spiegel,* and *The London Daily Telegraph.*

O'Brien heard his name called and raised his hand. He was pleased to see that he had drawn a brown-eyed beauty whose silk thobe clung wonderfully to her figure. Her veil was made of a nearly transparent white silk that concealed nothing. The veil, in fact, made her face even softer and lovelier than it already was; it was as though O'Brien were looking at a romantic photograph shot through a gauze filter.

She said, "Mr. O'Brien, my name is Zaynab. I am to be your hostess for your stay in Jebel Tarik. If there is anything you want or need, you have only to ask. And these"—Zaynab turned to an assistant who held a camel saddle and scimitar—"are yours, a gift from Prime Minis-

140

ter Muhammad Aziz and the People's Democratic Republic of Jebel Tarik."

"Well, thank you." O'Brien was impressed. The camel saddle would be a prize in his Manhattan apartment.

"We'll have your luggage taken ahead to your hotel room. It's ten o'clock now. You can take pictures if you'd like, or I can arrange some interviews. You might want to have lunch in one of our pubs; the pubs in Jebel Tarik are open as usual. What you want to do before Prime Minister Aziz's press conference is up to you."

"We'll be wanting to work on stories all day."

"Certainly. Whatever I can do to help."

"Uh, interview Gibraltarians?"

Zaynab looked surprised that O'Brien seemed hesitant to ask that question. "Of course interview Gibraltarians. They may not be fond of the turn of events, Mr. O'Brien, but you'll find that none of them are being mistreated in any way."

Tony O'Brien was giddy from the sweetness of Zaynab's perfume.

The room was a snarl of cables connected to the light reflectors on either side of Muhammad Aziz, who was splendid in his black thobe and kaffiyeh—black ordinarily being reserved for sultans and potentates. Both Aziz and the waiting reporters and photographers were patient as the technicians hopped about, making last-second adjustments—7 P.M. in Gibraltar was 3 P.M. in New York, plenty of time to tape and edit what Aziz had to say. "Would you like me to speak so you can check your microphones?" he asked.

One of his assistants nodded, so the prime minister said, "*La illah il-Allah.* Are we ready?"

"The sound's fine, Prime Minister."

Aziz cupped his hand by his ear. There being no objections, he grinned and began as cameras clacked and whirred, and pencils scribbled. "Well, I shall begin by telling you that you're the guests of the People's Democratic Republic of Jebel Tarik, and I am Prime Minister Muhammad Aziz. We have a lot to cover this evening. I

141

know some of you are facing deadlines, so I'll do my best to get directly to the point. First, I suppose you'll be wanting to know who I am and what we're up to. Until two o'clock Sunday morning I was a Palestinian." He paused, and rubbed his nose. "But of course you'll be wondering what Jebel Tarik means. It means 'the mountain of Tarik' or 'Tarik's mountain' as you please. Tarik Ibn Zeyad was the Berber commander who captured this promontory"—Aziz indicated the Rock with a swoop of his hand—"in your calendar year 711. Tarik captured the whole of the Iberian peninsula in battle against Visigoths, who were from Scandinavia originally, not Rome. I would remind you that the Visigoths can in no way be considered the ancestors of the Catholics who now inhabit the Iberian peninsula. They were pagans who worshiped many gods.

"One thing I would like to clear up quickly is the status of the British garrison here on Jebel Tarik. There were about two thousand British soldiers assigned here. We believe about four hundred soldiers were underground at the time of our attack. Sixteen British soldiers were killed in the action; sixty-three were wounded. The dead and wounded were taken to Algeciras; the rest were taken to the Spanish border and released. The soldiers trapped underground are free to surrender and be taken to the border anytime they choose. We are in communication with their commander, a certain Colonel Givings. Our own dead and wounded—twelve dead, nineteen wounded—were flown to Tripoli so as not to crowd facilities here. We are grateful for the generosity of Colonel Omar Qafi and the Libyan people."

Aziz stepped away from the lectern that had been provided for him. "I don't like notes. I prefer honest talk. Am I able to move about?" he asked an assistant.

"Please do, Prime Minister."

Aziz moved in front of the lectern. "If I move into bad light, please tell me. Do you all know the year 1492? Are there Americans here?"

The reporters all laughed.

"That was the year Granada fell and Jebel Tarik, too, and the Moors—our Muslim brethren—were forced back

142

to Africa after a reign of 781 years by my count—almost eight centuries. The Spanish held Jebel Tarik from 1492 until 1704, when it was captured by the British admiral Sir George Rooke, ending a Spanish occupation of 212 years, less than a third of the period of Muslim settlement. The British held Jebel Tarik from 1704 until three days ago —283 years—for a total of 495 years of Christian occupation. This is, correctly, Muslim territory, and we Palestinians have returned it to its proper Muslim owners." Aziz waited for a writer to adjust his tape recorder. "We do this in the name of Tarik Ibn Zeyad, whose followers built the defensive walls you'll find all along the water here in the city. But, of course, all this is explained in your press kits.

"Is that enough for starters? Perhaps you'd like to ask questions? Yes? We have plenty of time. This gentleman over here." He pointed to the reporter for *The Washington Post.*

"Mr. Prime Minister, we have reports that you're fortifying Gibraltar with missiles delivered by Libyan freighters. Sir, could you tell us your precise relationship with Colonel Qafi?"

"He's assisting us in the fortifying of Jebel Tarik, as you can see for yourself." Aziz grinned. "Colonel Qafi is our good friend, as he is a good friend of Palestinians and Muslims everywhere. The Libyan government was kind enough to lend us what we need until we have weapons of our own. We have British, French, and Italian missiles, and Russian howitzers. All of them are available on the world arms market, so this was not difficult. I'm told the French are becoming as famous for their Exocets as for their omelets. Would you like your photograph taken with one of these weapons? You may if you like." Aziz grinned broadly, and this brought laughter from the press corps. "Do you have a question, sir?" This was the man from *De Telegraaph,* of Amsterdam.

"I'm sure we would all like to know your precise relationship to the PLO, to Colonel Qafi, and to the Iranians, Mr. Prime Minister."

"Precise? As the British and American intelligence agencies have no doubt told you already, I'm a Palestinian.

143

Until Sunday, I lived in Tripoli. Colonel Qafi recognized the sovereign state of Jebel Tarik on Monday. The Iranians are our friends as well, and the Syrians—all nations of Islam. I believe we're now the only Islamic country in Europe. Well, there were Muslims in Albania, but I believe religion has been banned there." Aziz pointed to Tony O'Brien.

"Mr. Prime Minister, just what is your relationship to the Soviet Union? Do you have Russian technicians helping with the missiles?"

"We are an Islamic nation, Mr. O'Brien. We follow the laws of Allah as revealed through the Prophet Muhammad and recorded in the Koran. Our missiles, although European, are manned by Jebel Tariki soldiers who were trained by our Libyan friends. Our soldiers trained in the Jebel As Sawda mountains south of Tripoli." Aziz hesitated. "That's spelled *J-e-b-e-l,* as in Jebel Tarik, space, *A-s* —that's with a capital *A*—space, *S-a-w-d-a.* But then, surely your satellites will have photographed the training."

There was laughter at that, with the American journalists laughing the loudest.

"You all have been given a Jebel Tarik media handbook. The first section, printed on the blue paper, contains the proper spelling and translations of Arabic words and phrases. Part two, printed on the light gray paper, contains the Jebel Tarik People's Democratic Constitution. All our laws are based on the Koran. You'll find a pale yellow appendix at the end of the light gray section that matches law with correct chapter and verse in the Koran. Sometimes a hadith is given. A hadith is a quotation from the Prophet Muhammad that has been verified by Muslim scholars. Part three is printed on pale green paper. This pale green section lists the Jebel Tariki aides, assistants, and specialists who will be prepared to answer your questions. Finally, the beige section gives a more detailed history of this promontory than I was able to give you tonight. The beige part has a brief biography of Tarik Ibn Zeyad, and an account of the construction of the Moorish walls and fortifications you'll find around Jebel Tarik. Finally, there is a bibliography, printed on pale orange,

144

together with the names of historians and Arabists we have temporarily assigned to the public library.

"If you would like to talk to any of these people or have someone else in mind for an interview, just ask your press assistant. Are there further questions?" Muhammad Aziz checked his watch, a signal that there would be no further questions.

7

GERARD THOMPSON FINGERED his short gray beard and studied the monitor. In it, an Arab standing by a tracked vehicle was explaining Jebel Tarik's Italian Indigo-MEI missile batteries. As he was talking, in slow, heavily accented English, two sets of three twelve-foot-long square tubes—one set mounted above the other—unfolded until they pointed at a thirty-degree angle above the vehicle's cab.

The camera, following the direction of the sleek missiles, panned the Bay of Gibraltar. The water was being ruffled by a slight breeze blowing from the southwest off the Atlantic and the Strait.

The camera then cut to the soldier who said, "Each of our batteries contains four tracked vehicles, Mr. O'Brien. One vehicle contains search-and-tracking radar. Two launch vehicles, such as you see here, contain six missiles each. And one launch vehicle contains twelve replacement missiles."

The camera cut to a vehicle that contained twelve Indigo-MEI missiles stacked horizontally in banks of three each. The camera zoomed in close up on the missiles. Each had four fins in the middle and the rear.

Cut to an earnest Tony O'Brien, who said, "Can you tell us something of Indigo-MEI's capabilities, Lieutenant?"

Cut to the lieutenant. He was equally earnest: "It is no secret, Mr. O'Brien. All the British have to do is ask their Italian friends. The Indigo-MEI system was designed to protect both airports and armies on the move. We can move them quickly from one place to another on the peninsula, depending on where they are needed. These missiles are eleven feet long and weigh two-hundred-sixty-five pounds; they are very accurate. They can strike up to three miles up"—the lieutenant pointed up—"and six miles across." The camera cut to the hills behind Algeciras.

Back to Tony O'Brien, who looked straight at the viewer. "So we have it. These people of the desert have taken the impregnable Rock and armed it with some of the most advanced weapons on the world arms market. If British Sea Harriers should appear over the horizon tomorrow, Captain Hassan and his men will be ready. If the Rock of Gibraltar turned out not to be as impregnable as the British thought, it sure seems that way now—only it's the Arabs who are dug in. Tony O'Brien, NBC News, Gibraltar."

O'Brien waited a few moments, then said, "Gerard, I think our best bet is to take their missiles in order, beginning with the short-range SAMs and working up to the Exocet, which would be used if Aziz decides to close the Strait of Gibraltar. I thought the Exocet might make a good Sunday piece. Think about it. We can talk about it on the phone."

Thompson punched his remote and Tony O'Brien was frozen on the monitor. The Exocet suggestion made sense to Thompson; then a flush of anxiety washed through his body. What if CBS led with the Exocet and got a jump in the Nielsens? The Argentines had sunk a British ship with an Exocet in the Falklands war. The mere fact that they worked made them sexy in the public imagination—it didn't make any difference if they were the best surface-to-surface missiles or not.

Thompson punched the remote again and O'Brien's second piece was up. Should O'Brien have led with the Exocets and the threat to the Strait? Thompson bit his lip.

146

The camera was now up high, looking down on a flat, narrow, bare isthmus bisected by an airport runway. In a voice-over, Tony O'Brien, with just a hint of Dan Rather, explained the scene: "This is the isthmus connecting Gibraltar with the Spanish mainland, and we're standing in a tunnel carved out of solid limestone in the north face of Mons Calpe, the famous Rock of Gibraltar. These cannon portals were used by British defenders more than three hundred years ago. Now they're fortified by German Cobra surface-to-surface missiles"—the camera panned from the airport terminal by the border, around to the airport runway where it stuck out into the Bay of Gibraltar —"less than a hundred yards from the town itself."

There was a cut to O'Brien in his tunnel. "As you can see, this is point-blank range. Although the technology is different, the rules of warfare remain unchanged: concentrate enough firepower on a small enough piece of real estate and the cost of passage becomes high indeed. Tony O'Brien, NBC News, Gibraltar, or, as it is called now, Jebel Tarik." His closing phrase was definitely Rather. O'Brien waited for a moment, then said, "I thought I'd give you a variety of closings, Gerard. I kind of like this one because of the fortress angle. No change in three hundred years and all that. Again, we can talk about this on the phone."

Gerard Thompson froze the picture again, but for a shorter period this time. He punched the remote for O'Brien's next offering.

The camera moved slowly down a narrow street, past a SAM vehicle next to a church, past more SAMs deployed in a market. In a voice-over, Tony O'Brien said, "This is no longer the Gibraltar touted in the tourist brochures, offering sunshine and palm trees to sufferers of the European winter. These missiles deployed by the Arabs in downtown Gibraltar have radically changed the face of this town of twenty-eight thousand people. Tony O'Brien, NBC News, Gibraltar."

O'Brien paused, then said, "I've got one more bit for you, the best of the day, I think."

147

The monitor was given over to a camel being led off the ramp of an Air Libya airplane. O'Brien's voice-over slid from Rather to a little Charles Kuralt: "The animal you see here is, yes, a camel. And so is the one behind him, and the one behind him, and the one behind him. Camels all. The Arabs are originally a desert people, and they're bringing camels with them. There is no grazing range on Gibraltar, nothing for a humped, ruminant quadruped to do, only a cliff on one side and a steep hill on the other. So why the camels? Well, the Arabs aren't saying. This is just one of the mysteries in this, the fourth day of siege. Tony O'Brien, NBC News, Gibraltar."

Thompson punched off the monitor and checked his watch. O'Brien would be calling any minute now. Thompson dropped to the floor and started in on the damnable push-ups so his stomach wouldn't sag. Instead of doing them all at once, he took them a few here and there when he had the time. This was cheating, he knew, but he didn't care. He wasn't an athlete, but his stomach wasn't bad. Sitting behind the NBC news desk, he looked just fine. The phone rang and Thompson answered.

O'Brien's voice floated dreamlike across the static of the transatlantic hookup. "Gerard?"

"Here, Tony. Good camel bit, I thought."

"I'll follow up on the camels tomorrow. Unless the Brits attack, though, there's not a lot of action, Gerard. This place is incredibly small."

"I think you're right about spreading the missiles out, and the Sunday Exocet piece is a good idea unless Gilchrist starts with them."

"The *Times* guy tells me they're going Exocet on Sunday too, so we're okay."

"Then get your Exocet piece in early and see if you can't find something better. Everybody's got fabulous Nielsens now, but that's not going to last forever. There's gotta be some fallout. Could you tell what CBS got for today?"

"Same stuff as me, Gerard—missiles, the defense of the peninsula, and the camels. The walled headquarters wasn't much, I admit; they always put wire around their headquarters."

"What about the Barbary apes? I'd have thought you'd have something on the apes."

"Ahh, glad you asked, Gerard. That's a possible good one. You know the legend of the apes? Well, Gibraltarians have told me off the record that the Palestinians tried to get rid of the apes. They went up there with AK-47s blazing, but an ape the cabdrivers call Puking Max escaped with two females."

"Puking Max?"

"He's the leader of the friendly pack of apes. Max is from 'maximum ape.' He's supposed to pig out on peanuts from people getting their photographs taken with him. The drivers say he vomits it up so he can eat more. I wanted to get him on tape, but the roads were blocked. That and the fenced movie theater were two of the few places I wasn't allowed to go. I was told Palestinians were scouring the hillside this afternoon looking for Max."

"That could be it, Tony. The fugitive Puking Max. A British ape. A Winston Churchill of an ape. Never say die." Thompson felt the juice. This one had possibilities.

"If Max and his ladies are still up there tomorrow, we'll see what we can come up with."

"We need a grabber before viewers settle in on one network. I want to stick some real numbers up Harry Gilchrist's ass." Thompson paused to think about his problem. "Tony, maybe you'd better give me an ape story for Sunday, just in case."

"What about the Exocets and the Strait?"

"We can go with Exocets on Saturday. If the Arabs shoot Puking Max before Sunday, we'll use the ape piece as an obituary, a eulogy to a legend. If he's alive, we'll have everybody in the country watching us on Monday to see what happened to the valiant Max." Thompson remembered a story he had covered early in his career about West Virginia coal miners trapped a half mile underground. "Tony, will they let you talk to the British soldiers down there?"

149

"I tried that, Gerard. Off limits. They're supposed to let us all listen to Colonel Givings tomorrow, but there's nothing special for us in that."

"Shoot the apes, then, Tony. Do your best." Gerard Thompson was confident. They were in the thick of battle and hadn't fucked up yet. Thompson felt it was difficult to go wrong with an animal story. He wasn't going to beat Harry Gilchrist's Nielsens by being bashful.

Out of a "clearly stated principle" that was in fact never stated at all, and which was understood by nobody, the PLO leader Yasir Arafat had not communicated with the Americans for five years. Arafat preferred to make his wishes known through "exclusive" interviews with friendly journalists. Arafat thus scored points with no rebuttal, while the Americans were forced to deal with reporters from *The New York Times* and *The Washington Post* who were piranhas in neckties.

On Thursday, the fifth day of siege, the American secretary of state, Stuart Kaplan, received a call from Arafat through a telephone connection ordinarily used by King Hussein of Jordan.

"Well, Mr. Arafat. A surprise call." Kaplan suppressed his amusement. He had wondered how Arafat had reacted to his rival's good fortune.

"We will make this brief, Mr. Kaplan. There is no need for long talk."

"I see."

"I want Muhammad Aziz and his missiles off Gibraltar. I want him off *now,* not tomorrow or next week. What are you doing to get him off? I want to know what you're doing to get him off. I want him off, off, off!" Arafat's voice rose.

"I assure you, we're assessing the situation."

"Assessing the situation? Assessing it? If you know what's good for you, you'll work with the British and you'll get him off. You are the United States of America. You get him off."

Kaplan remained calm. "Are you telling me what to

150

do, Mr. Arafat? Do you want to tell me how to get him off as well? Have you any suggestions?"

"I want him off for the love of Allah!" Arafat was furious.

"I see. Well, we're always ready to do a little dealing, Mr. Arafat. What's in it for us?"

The notion of quid pro quo was as foreign to Arafat's imagination as the truth was to Petr Spishkin or sanity to Omar Qafi. Arafat was shocked by Kaplan's chutzpah; Americans and Jews were on the planet to be pissed upon, not dealt with. Arafat demanded or took; others asked or gave. Yasir Arafat took his instructions directly from Allah, who was the only God. "For you?" His voice cracked. "For you? For you? What are you talking about?" he shouted.

Kaplan said nothing.

"If you and your British and Israeli friends don't get him off of there, you're going to have to deal with a Palestinian who can close the Strait of Gibraltar to get what he wants. Have you thought about that?"

"I think somebody raised the possibility the other day."

"The longer Muhammad Aziz stays on Gibraltar, the greater is his claim to the PLO leadership. You have to ask yourself who you'd rather deal with. At least I haven't captured a British colony. Think about that, Mr. Kaplan."

Stuart Kaplan sighed. "Unfortunately, we're doing our very best, Mr. Arafat, and that's the pathetic truth."

8

THE UNITED KINGDOM had lost Gibraltar on Deborah
Fielding's watch. As in the United States, the sport—a
form of dog baiting—lay in the assigning of blame. The
masses couldn't ride to the baying of hounds, being able to
afford neither horses nor hounds. But everybody could
pick up a popular daily or turn on the telly and watch
journalists chase politicians through a thicket of lies and
evasions.

Thanks to the Gibraltar story, circulations were up on
Fleet Street; there were all sorts of sensational charges to
be hawked. This largess was not without problems. For
example, which was the bigger story, the screw-up of losing
Gibraltar in the first place, or the delay and dithering in
getting it back? As each day passed more officers and
officials were pulled into the flames.

The repeated assertion in the dailies that the retaking
of Gibraltar would be a one-battle thing, a tidy little war,
became accepted as fact in the pubs. The logic of the
assertion squirted about like a wet bar of soap, but seemed
finally to rest on the belief that since the Royal Navy had
been posted on Gibraltar since 1704, the British admirals
knew its secret weaknesses and vulnerabilities. The Royal
Navy had the Royal Marines' 3 Commando at its disposal,
and Gurkhas too.

All this meant that anything less than a one-battle,
tidy little war could be claimed by the Labour party as
defeat, shame, and dishonor, one more example of Fielding incompetence. This business of failing to meet goals
had gone so far that politicians refused to predict margins
of victory, because anything less than total triumph was
inevitably regarded as defeat—and the same was true in
America.

This was the wonderful, chaotic game called Democracy, played with as much spirit in Great Britain as in the United States. However, compared to American newspapers, the British dailies entered the fray with far more zest.

By Thursday, the fifth day of the Arab occupation of Gibraltar, writers for the prole dailies pursued the story with bared teeth. The British defense secretary, Roger Jackelforth, had received the first assault because, like an exposed throat, he was an obvious, inviting target. They'd masticated Jackelforth for two days before he became flavorless, after which they flung his ruined career aside and turned to fresh meat.

Given a reason to print anything they wanted because of the enormity of the Gibraltar fiasco, the Fleet Street chaps bared their computer keys to other figures in the military establishment and the Fielding government. Even the solid, responsible British dailies now felt free to report, in good conscience, allegations of homosexuality, philandering, and wife beating on the part of officials whose subordinates—in some cases three and four times removed—were more logically accountable for the lapse in Gibraltar's security.

It wasn't surprising when the senior officers of Her Majesty's Military Establishment—sensing careers at stake—finally let the blood flow in a frenzy of blame laying. Save for the poor flagellants, everybody had fun while pretending to be furious. As allegations and rumors surfaced, inevitably there followed rebuttals. The daily papers, radio, and television were rife with charges, countercharges, rumors, speculations, and allegations of neglect, cupidity, stupidity, criminal incompetence—the adjective *unconscionable* being popular—into which stew of name-calling, cheerfully, were thrown suggestions of drug taking and, in one case, bestiality involving a purebred Yorkshire terrier.

The press divided up the goodies along class lines. *The Daily Mirror, The Daily Mail, The Express, The Sun,* and *The Daily Star* went for the rumors of kinky sex and cocaine snorting among Her Majesty's admirals; alleged girlfriends were shown wearing trousers that were too small and blouses incompletely buttoned. *The Economist, The Observer, The Guardian, The Financial Times, The Sunday Times, The Times,* and *The Telegraph* went for allegations of lying, stupidity, and incompetence. Competing for attention in all the confusion was the monotonous chorus of the loyal, if predictable, opposition claiming that the loss of Gibraltar was obviously so outrageous as to require the resignation of Mrs. Fielding's government.

"This is a matter of honor, as any civilized fool can see," said William Fluute, stalking and glowering for the benefit of the camera. Fluute, who had once called himself a "peacemonger," now called for war.

Although duty-bound to get Gibraltar back, the admirals and generals seemed unable to do anything at all. As the announced favorites in the contest, they were called upon to act swiftly and efficiently. Instead, they argued among themselves, dithered, and wrung their hands.

Thus it was hardly surprising to anybody that Deborah Fielding, determined to keep her attention squarely on the problem before her, named Rear Admiral Sir Cecil Whitehead to head an invasion fleet should negotiations fail and military action become necessary. Sir Cecil was no national hero; those were becoming rarer now that the Second World War receded into the past. He had served ably in the Falklands, however, and had a solid record. What was most important was that Sir Cecil had once been in command of the British garrison on Gibraltar and so knew the Rock intimately.

Alas, it turned out—after Mrs. Fielding's announcement—that Sir Cecil, on his tour of duty at the Rock, had spent most of his time screwing two different mistresses in Algeciras while his incompetent second-in-command —later eased out of the navy—ran the garrison, or rather presided over the deterioration of its competence and morale.

Sir Cecil refused to resign his position without a proper hearing, and since there was no time for a proper hearing, Fielding was stuck with him.

Undeterred from what had to be done, Fielding asked
154

the government in Lisbon for permission to assemble an invasion fleet in Portuguese waters just south of Faro. The Portuguese leaders were traditional friends of the British. Also the Portuguese valued the trade that would pass through the Faro airport to supply the fleet as it assembled for action. On top of that, there was the delicious opportunity to make the Spanish squirm, something few Portuguese politicians could resist.

9

FRIDAY MORNING, TONY O'BRIEN—accompanied by a tall, bearded cameraman named Jack Brooks, and his broad-shouldered pal, Eddie Figueroa—rented a cab and started up Europa Road on the way to the ape den, but found their passage blocked at the bottom of Engineer Road.

O'Brien got out of the car to talk to the sergeant in charge. "My name is Tony O'Brien with NBC News. Would it be possible for you to check with your superiors? We would like to videotape the site of the extermination of the apes, if that is possible."

"NBC News?"

O'Brien showed him his NBC card with his photograph on it.

Saying nothing, the sergeant returned to his post at the roadblock and made a call on a field telephone. After a short conversation, he hung up and ordered the roadblock opened for O'Brien's car. The driver began the steep ascent. At the observation platform overlooking Europa Point and the Strait of Gibraltar—this was about three quarters of the way to the tip of the peninsula—the narrow lane, renamed Queen's Road, doubled back to the north and leveled off.

The road began to descend slightly, and four hundred

yards later—approximately midway in the peninsula, above and to the left of the casino—they saw a helicopter gunship hovering above the side of the hill.

"Would you pull over, please?" O'Brien said.

Brooks, who was the senior of the two photographers, yelled, "Get the camera! Get the camera! Get the camera!" This was directed at O'Brien. Because of union rules, reporters were reporters and cameramen were cameramen, never the twain shall meet. There were times, however . . .

This was one of them. O'Brien dove for the extra camera they always carried.

The three men were out of the car before it stopped, and sprinted downhill, keeping their cameras aimed at the copter. The copter hovered in the air; just then, terrible machine guns, modern Gatlings, exploded the side of the hill with an awful hail of slugs: *VROOOOM!*

"Jesus Christ!" O'Brien said. A death hum; he had never heard or seen anything like it.

The Gatlings erupted in a second satanic roar. Then a third. *VROOOOM! VROOOOM!*

"Did you get that, Eddie? Jack?"

His cameramen, still taping, nodded their heads yes.

O'Brien was elated. "My God, what luck! We got here just in time. Just in time."

The helicopter started moving their way. The AK-47s opened up. Dirt exploded from the hillside not ten feet to O'Brien's left. O'Brien hit the ground, defending his camera with his elbows, as did Brooks and Figueroa.

"Watch, watch, watch, watch for apes!" O'Brien yelled.

Then, in one of the luckiest breaks of Tony O'Brien's career, Puking Max and his women vaulted over the low stone wall on the outside of the narrow road.

"Got 'em! Everybody on the apes!" Brooks yelled.

The apes scurried up the hill straight at the three whirring cameras. They saw the cameras and bolted to their left, uphill, grabbing for low branches which they used to vault onto the high side of the road. They disappeared into the maquis.

156

"Did you get 'em? Did you get 'em, Jack?"

"Did I get 'em? Shit, man." Hey, Jack Brooks was a pro.

Brooks pivoted on his hips, not taking his eye off the camera, following the direction of the fleeing apes. He finally put it down and said, "Fucking A. John, we got 'em. Eh, Eddie?"

"Got the little skedaddlers," Figueroa said.

"Keep 'em rolling, keep 'em rolling. You take the copter, Eddie." Brooks, slapping a new lens onto his camera, followed the skedaddlers.

Figueroa took the copter.

A babble of expletives in Arabic could be heard beneath the chopping of helicopter blades above the road.

Troops were coming. "I got the ragheads." Brooks turned and zoomed in tightly on the soldiers who appeared below him on the road. The lead soldier, exhausted from the uphill run, dropped to his knees and laid random swaths in the brush above the road. He was angry and determined. His shoulder bounced from the kick of his weapon. His colleagues dropped to their knees also and fired in the direction the apes had fled. Judging from the whine of ricochets, they hit plenty of limestone boulders.

Brooks was nervy and good. He established the scene: the narrow road, the town low and to the left, scrub brush and limestone rocks above the road. He zoomed in on the group, framed the Arabs head to knees on the road as they knelt, firing in the direction of the fleeing apes. Through the lens, he could see their chests heaving. Then quickly, moving rhythmically from soldier to soldier, he framed them head to knees on the road. He closed in on their faces as they swore in Arabic.

He adjusted the lens with a knob he rolled with his right forefinger. Up tight and close; down, back and wide. The control was tricky; it responded to the slightest nudge. He worked the camera like a jazzman; his finger was one with the knob.

The soldiers, still babbling in Arabic, got to their feet and started running up the road.

Brooks backed out of their way, his finger still working the lens. He taped them clumping past in their boots, taped them struggling up the hill. Up above, the helicopter suddenly moved north, its Gatlings roaring: *VROOOOM! VROOOOM!*

The Arabs reversed themselves and ran back down the hill. They were now exhausted. Mouths open, gasping for air, they dropped to their knees again and fired at the slope below the helicopter. The helicopter hovered, then went uphill, then downhill, then south toward Europa Point, then north toward Mons Calpe.

The apes had escaped.

Brooks turned and raced back to the car, yelling, "Got it! Got it! Got it!"

The Americans and the Gibraltarian piled into the Peugeot.

O'Brien said, "Back to town, go back, go back. Turn around. Turn around. No, no. Put it in reverse. Put it in reverse. A thousand American dollars. Gerard Thompson's paying. Whatever. Anything. Anything." He dove for his wallet.

The Gibraltarian cabdriver loved a good tip but didn't need a bribe. He turned his neck and laid smoke in reverse. He said, "They could evaporate us with that thing up there if they wanted."

O'Brien and his colleagues were aware of that. They bit their lips. They peered back at the helicopter. The helicopter hovered, as if it were uncertain what to do next.

Would the cab be stopped at the roadblock? O'Brien and the photographers turned their attention to the bottom of Engineer Road; the Arabs at the base of the hill had abandoned their barricades to get a better look at the action above the Rock Hotel.

Bob Steele looked up and down the bar to make sure they could talk in privacy. He ran the palm of his hand over his thinning hair. He shook his head until his jowls shook. "I don't know, Jim. I just don't know what we should do. It seems like there must be something we can do other than get sloshed in the pubs every night."

"You saw him shoot two Russians, and you helped him push the corpses off the Trans-Siberian Express. The CIA paid me to take a hike, so if he said he was me, he's CIA. If he's CIA, he has to be here on business. Has to be."

"Lower your bloody voice, Jim."

"What if he needs help?"

Steele belched and took another swig out of his pint. "I think that pasty gave me gas. It's impossible to get good pasties in the colonies. We don't know if he's still there, do we? And even if we did, we don't know his name. He surely isn't using yours still."

"No, no, that's over. They gave me my money, and I took off. I never heard from them again, not a thank you. Nothing."

"We could go to the hospital and ask if they had admitted a tall blond American recently. We could say we met him on the train coming down from Madrid or something . . ."

". . . and say we forgot his name. Sure, Bob."

Steele raised his voice. "Another, please, miss. Look at that, Jim, a woman who knows how to pour a pint." Steele ran his tongue along the outside of his front teeth and said softly, "The bloody Rock's probably crawling with your CIA chaps and our MI6 blokes. What would he be doing anyway, besides skinning the knickers off some bird's bum? You're right; we should at least offer to help them out."

"If we were smart, we'd start researching a book on all this. You know, Bob, I wouldn't mind skinning the knickers off the bartender. Is that what you call them, knickers?"

"She has a nice bum, yes." Steele raised his hand. "Another pint, please, miss." The portly Steele stood with his feet slightly apart, an athlete ready for action. "The Fleet Street Flash and Bison Jim. We could do it, you know, blast them with Uzis." A young man was coming their way; Steele shut up.

The young man said, "Are you Bob Steele and Jim Quint?"

"Yes, we are," Quint said.

159

"My name is Chippy Chipolina. I'm a nurse at St. Bernard's Hospital."

Quint and Steele looked at one another.

"An American acquaintance there says he saw you standing in the street on his way into the hospital."

"Old friends?" Steele said.

"His name is Larry Schoolcraft." Chipolina looked momentarily disconcerted. He glanced about him.

"It's okay, we're alone. You can talk," Quint said.

Chipolina looked relieved. "Mr. Schoolcraft wonders if you might not like to pay him a visit."

"When would be the best time?" Quint asked.

"Mr. Schoolcraft says in the morning would be good. Do you think you could make it?"

Bob Steele said, "Oh, I think we can make it okay. What do you say, Jim?"

Jim Quint motioned to the bartender. "Another round, please, miss, and a pint for our friend here. For Queen and Country."

10

THE SATURDAY MORNING attention of the media was directed at the arrival of even more camels at the airport. These weren't dilapidated zoo models; they were sleek, one-humped beauties. What in heaven did the Arabs have in mind? There was hardly any level ground on the peninsula that was not covered by buildings, streets, parking lots, tennis courts, cemeteries for fallen heroes, something.

There was sandy open space on both sides of the airport runway—if the government wanted to add wandering camels to the hazards of takeoff and landing.

There were beaches, but they weren't much more than

160

an occasional fringe of sand at the base of the rock. Did Muhammad Aziz have in mind turning camels loose on the beach in front of the Caleta Palace Hotel? Yes, he did. The camels were evenly dispersed among Gibraltar's several small beaches. Small trucks of grain and hay arrived from Spain.

None of the Arabs who handled the camels knew what the animals were for. It wasn't that the handlers were uncooperative; they hadn't been told.

The routine in most press conferences was that Numero Uno, or the Famous Person, would begin with his or her boring, self-serving, unintelligible, stupid, petulant, or lying little say. This was endured by reporters in the name of civility; in fact, they waited as dogs tensed for meat. Muhammad Aziz now reversed this format. The reporters were obliged to ask questions first; this was followed by Aziz's pronouncement of the day—if he had anything to say—which signified the end of the conference.

On Saturday, Prime Minister Aziz's press secretary, a man named Ali, announced a 1 P.M. news conference rather than the usual 7 P.M. gathering. Considering the light and time zones, this was good.

The first question came from the grinning correspondent from *Le Monde*. He stood. "Monsieur Prime Minister, you have us all wondering about the camels that have been arriving at the airport. *Mon Dieu!* What are you going to do with all those camels?"

When the laughter had died, Aziz, who was himself clearly amused, said, "I thought you might ask that question. When you recover a country that has been occupied for four hundred years, you have to reestablish the traditions of its people. The only traditions we have are those we brought with us, like socks in a valise, and so we decided to start some of our own. You'll be seeing a lot of those camels. They'll be in training for a sporting event, to be held two weeks from today, undertaken by our Muslim friends. As you know, we're at the western end of an Islamic population that extends from the Sulu Archipelago in the east, to Morocco and Jebel Tarik in the west."

161

Sporting event? The which archipelago? Scribbling hands hopped like hungry pigeons.

Ali, the press assistant, spelled it aloud: *"S-u-l-u."*

"Since we are in the west, with Morocco, Mauritania, Algeria, and Mali, we have devised a contest derived from the skills of the Tuareg, Reguibat, and Tibbut nomads. Before the Europeans came, the *razzia*—a raid—to steal camels or treasure—was a way of life in the western Sahara." Aziz paused. "Or for women sometimes, that was also true," he added with a disarming smile.

A contest? What the hell was this?

Aziz consulted a paper on his lectern. "We are told that the attacking party always dismounted before firing their rifles, so we have fashioned our own Razzia rather after your Olympic biathlon, which combines cross-country skiing and shooting. Razzia will substitute camels for skis. Only we won't be competing for slaves or women."

Biathlon? Substitute camels for skis? The reporters taking notes glanced up. Compete for what? Muhammad Aziz was on a roll, giving the details of the competition.

"A biathlon course is twenty kilometers, almost eleven of your American miles. There are four one-hundred-and-fifty-meter shooting ranges. These are stationed between the fifth and eighteenth kilometers. Twice around Jebel Tarik, as it turns out, is twenty kilometers." Aziz looked up from the paper. "I'll give it to you briefly here; Ali has a press kit for you that will give the details." He studied the paper again. "The participants will leave five minutes apart, from the sundial. They will head for Main Street and downtown Gibraltar. They will fire in the prone position at Catalan Bay, which is seven kilometers from the start. That's about four miles out. Isn't that correct?" Aziz looked at Ali.

"That's about right, Prime Minister. The kilometers-to-miles conversions are all contained in the Razzia press kits I'll be distributing."

Aziz said, "At ten kilometers, they will fire from the standing position. The range will be located behind the

162

sundial and parallel to the airport runway. On the second lap around Jebel Tarik, they'll fire prone at Sandy Bay at the sixteenth kilometer, and standing at Eastern Beach, eighteen kilometers from the start. What size are those targets, Ali? I don't see it here."

Ali consulted a copy of the Razzia press handout. "The prone target has a twelve-and-a-half-centimeter center ring and a twenty-five-centimeter outer ring. The standing target has a thirty-five-centimeter center ring and a forty-five-centimeter outer ring. If a shot hits the second ring, a competitor is penalized one minute," Ali said. "If a shot hits outside the second ring, the competitor is penalized two minutes. The weapon must not be larger than eight millimeters and must not be loaded until the competitor arrives at the target station. No optical sights are allowed."

"Isn't this fun?" Aziz asked the reporters.

The members of the press corps found it impossible to restrain their amusement at Muhammad Aziz's chutzpah.

"Are the competitors allowed to fire any type of weapon they choose, Mr. Prime Minister?"

Aziz held his finger up. "Oh, yes. That.. Ali?"

"As long as the rifle is not over the allowed caliber and doesn't have optical sights, it can be any brand, size, or shape the shooter chooses. Biathlon shooters use specially crafted twenty-twos with heavy barrels, I'm told. Contestants in Razzia can use a twenty-two if they want, or an eight-millimeter Mauser. We don't care. A shooter has to take one shot at each of five targets at each stop. The scorers check the holes and total the minutes to be deducted from the rider's elapsed time at the end of the race."

Aziz put on his reading glasses and exchanged his Razzia fact sheet for another paper. He looked up. "Those nations who have been contacted and have agreed to participate in Razzia include . . ." Aziz looked down again. "I'll read them from *A* to, let's see, to *Y* so as not to discriminate on anything other than the alphabet. They are"—Aziz read the list—"Albania, Algeria, Afghanistan,

163

Bahrain, Bangladesh, Chad, Djibouti, Egypt, Ethiopia, Indonesia, Iran, Iraq, Jebel Tarik, Jordan, Kuwait, Libya, Malaysia, Mauritania, Morocco, Niger, Oman, Pakistan, Qatar, Saudi Arabia, Somalia, South Yemen, Sudan, Syria, Tunisia, Turkey, the United Arab Emirates, and Yemen." He looked up. "Would you like me to read that list again?" He did his best to appear innocent, but broke into a grin.

In a few seconds everybody in the room was laughing. Racing camels? Shooting? Qatar?

Aziz read the list again, but more slowly.

Tony O'Brien glanced at the CBS correspondent and their eyes locked momentarily, combatants out of Hemingway.

Aziz said, "That's thirty-two entries, counting our own rider. Some of our fellow Islamic countries, like Malaysia and Indonesia, don't ordinarily have camels. Some are selecting marksmen and training them to ride. Others are selecting riders and training them to shoot. Remember, a Tuareg on a camel raid had to do both. Sir?" he asked the man from *Le Monde*.

"Did we hear you correctly, sir, that Albania has agreed to participate?" The Frenchman seemed incredulous. The Albanians participated in nothing, had in fact isolated themselves from the world. Although it was officially without religion, Albania in fact had a large population of Muslims.

"We are pleased to say that, yes, the Albanians have agreed to participate. All we Muslims are determined to act as one in this, to show the world that we are capable of unified action. He hasn't arrived as yet, but we're told there will be an Albanian marksman with experience on horses on his way to Jebel Tarik for training on a camel."

"May we ask what is the prize of this competition, monsieur?"

"A good question. In the last few years you Europeans and Americans have developed the practice of holding concerts to benefit charity. Your rock-and-roll musicians have made millions for relief in Ethiopia. In America, your country-and-western singers held benefit concerts for your

164

farmers. The Koran discourages music, so we Arabs do the best we can with what we have at hand. The Prophet Muhammad tells us we must give alms to the poor. In fact, the third pillar of Islam is zakat, an obligatory tax for the needy. The Koran tells us, 'And what you give in usury, that it may increase upon the people's wealth, increase not with God; but what you give in alms, desiring God's Face, those—they receive recompense manifold.' Since we are unable, for this first contest, to invite people in and sell tickets, we have decided to sell television rights. The sums paid for the rights will be used for relief in areas of the Muslim world hit by famine or drought."

"What sort of sums are those, Mr. Prime Minister?"

"This depends on the size of the market and whether the network is private or public. In the case of the United States, the largest television market, we expect twenty million U.S. dollars. We want all the networks to share: five million for each of the majors, two and a half each for public television and Mr. Ted Turner. That's entirely reasonable, I'm assured. This is a charity event, ladies and gentlemen. We mean to be fair, not greedy. In fact, for small or very poor countries, the fees will be nominal or waived entirely. The wealthier countries will be generous in this matter, I'm sure."

Aziz motioned to an assistant on his right who rolled in a blackboard mounted on casters; upon the blackboard was hung a map of the course, showing the target sights, rules, and other details of Razzia.

11

IF TONY O'BRIEN felt there was any kind of crack in the real world, where the surreal poured forth at Gibraltar, he did not allow it to show. Men were riding camels behind him at the side of the airport. O'Brien was there, on the spot, during the siege. He was determined to be ultracool, calm. American viewers regarded emotion as unheroic, possibly sissy, which accounted for the successes of actors Sylvester Stallone and Chuck Norris.

A serious, unemotional face was needed so that his viewers would know that this was dramatic and serious. This was siege, dammit! O'Brien had always envied Barbara Walters her ability to talk without moving her lips —as though she were the ventriloquist rather than the dummy.

A camel rider shouted "Hut! Hut! Hut!" in the distance.

O'Brien felt slightly heroic, and thought of Edward R. Murrow in London during the blitz. With Spitfires and Messerschmidts rat-a-tat-tatting in the skies behind him, Murrow had delivered. There could very well be a book in the siege story, he knew. A publishing house with a little class. Simon and Schuster or someplace like that. Sure. Add a little touch of respectability there. "Tony O'Brien on the Rock," he could call it.

At his side was a gentleman in his sixties wearing a beret and sporting a beige, polka-dotted ascot at the throat of his jacket. His mustache was properly trimmed. He was a gentleman.

"Are you ready, Colonel?" O'Brien asked.

"*Oui*. I am ready," said the man.

"Okay?" O'Brien nodded at his cameraman, Jack Brooks.

"Whenever you're ready," Brooks said.

"We are standing at the edge of the airport runway here on the isthmus between Gibraltar and Spain. Behind me is Mons Calpe, the famous Rock. Behind me also are camels, as you can see."

Brooks said, "Good, good. Now the colonel."

"This is Colonel Henri Le Cocq, who was an officer in the French camel corps in Algeria in the 1950s. Colonel Le Cocq, who is now retired, is here on Gibraltar as . . ." He turned to the colonel.

"I am what you call the consultant to the camels," Le Cocq said. "I was hired by Monsieur Ali."

"What should people know about camels so they can appreciate the complexities of the upcoming race, Colonel Le Cocq?" O'Brien winced inwardly. Should that have been *complexity* instead of *complexities*?

"We are talking about many kinds of camels. There are twenty kinds of dromedary camels in Africa."

"You're talking about one-humped camels."

"*Oui*. Thirteen of these varieties are used for pack animals. They are too heavy or slow to ride. Six types are suitable for riding, and you'll find them all represented in this race. They are the Anafi, a light, leggy and small-humped camel from northeastern Sudan, and the Bishari, also of northeastern Sudan. The Bishari is stronger than the Anafi. You'll see the long-haired Tibesti, the smallest riding camel in Africa. Tibesti is in northwestern Chad. You see the Aïr, from Niger—tall, slender, small-humped —a fast camel. You'll also see the Adrar, from southern Algeria, and the Sehel, from Mauritania. The Adrar is gray and has a moderate hump; the Sehel is fawn-colored and smaller."

O'Brien faced the camera: "Colonel Le Cocq has promised to show us the various types in a few minutes."

"That is why I am here, monsieur. I have a rider, Abdul, who will give us a riding demonstration."

"Good. Good. Tell me, Colonel, what kind of camels did your troops use in the Sahara?"

"We used the Adrar, a strong camel—perhaps not as swift as the Aïr, but with better range. The camel's hump

167

does not contain water as children sometimes believe, but rather fat that shrinks as the animal begins to dehydrate. During the six or seven cool months on the Sahara, camels get most of the water they need in the plants they eat. A camel can go ten days to two weeks without water at eighty-five to ninety-five of your American degrees Fahrenheit. When it gets above one hundred degrees—about a six-week period on the Sahara—a camel has to drink at short and regular intervals. In the summer, free-grazing camels can usually go for a week without water. A camel can lose up to forty percent of its body weight from lack of water, so a dehydrated camel can hold a lot of water. A thirsty camel can drink twenty-five to thirty-five of your American gallons in one turn at the water. A large, thirsty male can drink up to fifty gallons."

"What can you tell us about their running, Colonel? How far can a camel go and how fast?"

"I'll do the best I can. The answer of course has to do with the temperature, the surface, the load, the type of camel, and so on. First of all, let me tell you that camels are unique in one sense. They are the only species that generally paces—by that I mean that their front leg and rear leg on one side move forward and backward simultaneously and opposite the legs on the other side. In animals that trot, the front leg on one side moves simultaneously with the diagonal rear leg. Horses and dogs can pace, but they usually trot. A camel's feet are broad pads with two toenails; because of the weight of their long neck, their front feet are larger. Are you ready for Abdul, monsieur?"

"What do you think?" O'Brien asked his cameramen.

Brooks said, "I think we should do the camels now before we start losing our light." He held up a light meter and checked it. "We can always come back to the colonel."

"We can have the colonel in a voice-over as Abdul rides. Yes, it would be nice if Abdul could ride now, Colonel."

Colonel Le Cocq turned and yelled something in Arabic to Abdul, a swarthy Arab waiting by a kneeling camel. Abdul put his foot on the camel's neck and hopped aboard the saddle placed slightly forward of the hump. He

168

began digging his sandaled feet into the beast's shoulders. The camel began to rise, the rider holding on . . .

O'Brien said, "It might be good if you talked along as Abdul rides, Colonel. Gives it a little more interest that way."

"The truth is, I don't watch a lot of television, monsieur." He looked slightly embarrassed. He cleared his throat. "But I'll do my best if it will be of help." He yelled again in Arabic and the camel began to move. "This is the camel's slow pace, from four to about five and a half of your American miles per hour. A camel can travel at this speed without tiring for ten to twenty hours."

He yelled in Arabic. The camel moved faster. "This is a medium pace, from six to about seven and a half miles an hour. And here Abdul's camel is changing into a fast pace, from ten to about twelve and a half miles an hour. A very strong male can sustain a speed of about fifteen miles for an hour or perhaps two at a maximum."

He motioned to Abdul with his hand. Abdul turned the camel and brought it back at a gallop. "A camel cannot sustain a gallop for long, and it is difficult for the rider to stay in the saddle, as you can see. The camel's hind legs are hitting the ground in front of his front legs, and he may be supported during a stride by any one of his legs or by none at all." The camel changed back into a fast pace, then slowed even more.

"How about the running surface, Colonel?"

"A camel does not have hooves, so stones or hard surfaces are ordinarily not good for them. If they have to walk long distances on stones and rock, their feet will crack and bleed. But, due to the development of special pads in recent years, racing on Gibraltar's paved roads will be no problem at all. A fast pace will be quite comfortable for them."

O'Brien said, "What about this race, Colonel Le Cocq? What would be the proper stride here?"

"A fast pace certainly, using a gallop only at the finish."

"And who do you think will win the race, Colonel?"

"You want my prediction?" Le Cocq smiled broadly.

"I think Algeria will win, of course. My old Algerian riders—meharistes, they were called back then—would be disappointed if I said anybody else. They have pride, monsieur. They think they are the best camel riders in the world. They just might be."

"Who will be the competition, in your opinion?"

Colonel Henri Le Cocq thought about his answer. "They ride camels in the western Sahara more than in the other parts of the Arab world. I should think that Mauritania, Mali, and Niger might field a strong camel and rider. Morocco perhaps has an outside chance. You have to consider that the Arabs in the eastern Sahara and the Middle East don't ride camels as much. The nomads of Somalia regard camel riding as outrageous. When they do ride farther east, they use a saddle that puts them directly on top of the hump. They are so high they have to use a stick to guide the animal. In central Sahara they use a terik saddle that sits forward on the hump and allows the rider to steer with his feet. That's what Abdul was using."

"Whether they steer with a stick or with their feet, Muslim riders from all over the Islamic world are arriving on the Rock for what promises to be one of the most colorful and unusual sporting contests ever held. One thing is certain about Razzia. Handicapping a race of these long-legged beasts with the awkward gait is a chancy business indeed, even for an old hand with camels. This is Tony O'Brien, NBC News, Gibraltar."

12

OWING TO ITS location at Gibraltar, St. Bernard's Hospital was a natural dropping-off point for ailing sailors from all over the world. Add to that its nearness to the Spanish Costa del Sol and the Portuguese Algarve—both favorites of British tourists—and it was obvious why the private ward was an international hodgepodge of races and nationalities. Chippy Chipolina had befriended stricken travelers many times before, and if the nurses and sisters of the private ward saw anything unusual in his visits to the American, Larry Schoolcraft, they said nothing.

Chippy Chipolina said, "I brought you a copy of *The Gibraltar Chronicle* like you asked. A special edition. I thought you might want to study it before we go on our birding outing." He handed Burlane the paper. "Twelve pages. It tells all about camels and how they're ridden."

"And how many pages to a regular edition?"

"Four."

Burlane looked at the Sunday front page, which was given over to an account of the upcoming camel race. "Very slick. The Rock's first daily, first published in 1801; there's a history for you." In addition to the race story, the front page carried an ad for J & B scotch whiskey, and for Piccadilly cigarettes. The article didn't carry a byline. In fact none of the articles did. "No bylines in the *Chronicle,* eh, Chippy?" He gave the paper back to Chipolina.

Chipolina looked at it and said, "I don't think so. It's not much of a paper when you come right down to it."

"Well, not a whole lot happens on the Gib, I wouldn't imagine. Can you find out if a *Chronicle* reporter wrote all this Razzia copy or did someone else? Aziz only made the announcement yesterday. Doesn't that seem like a lot of work for a paper like the *Chronicle*?"

"Yes, it does, come to think of it."

"I'm not putting it down, mind you, but this is a town built mostly around four parallel streets at the base of a mountain, and Fleet Street isn't one of them."

"I bet I can find out."

"I'm asking a lot, I know, but we have to take advantage of whatever opportunity they give us. That takes a little watching and listening and paying attention."

"Maybe I can get work with MI6 when this is over."

Burlane grinned. "I know people in MI6. I can put in a word." He reached for the paper. "Razzia's quite an undertaking, wouldn't you say? Can you imagine the politics of getting all those countries to agree on something

171

that complicated? Aziz surely had to be thinking of the race before he jumped the Brits. That was just a week ago."

Chipolina studied the front page. "It says here they'll ride counterclockwise from the sundial on around the peninsula."

Burlane consulted his map. "Chippy, if you find that someone other than a *Chronicle* reporter wrote the race story, I want you to back right off. Pursue it no further."

Chipolina looked concerned. "Why is that?"

"I've got a feeling, a hunch." Burlane twisted his face in thought.

"Which is?"

"You want clues?"

"Sure."

"Well, let's see. The Irish sweepstakes. Thoroughbreds at Pimlico. The Triple Crown. Le Mans. The America's Cup. The American presidential elections."

"The American presidential elections?"

"In Great Britain a politician stands for office, Chippy. In the United States he runs."

"What?"

"I have this little hunch. We'll see." Burlane grinned mischievously.

Later, James Burlane was lying in bed staring at the awful painting in his room, when *"La illah il-Allah"* echoed up from the loudspeakers on the mosque. It seemed to Burlane as though the volume of these calls had increased with each prayer. It seemed as though the muezzin was jacking the sound higher and higher, prayer by prayer, intent that his homage to Allah should float across the Iberian peninsula and penetrate Europe if possible.

The muezzin got real dramatic when he hit the *lah* of *illah,* a gargle with timbre, reminding Burlane of the similarities in sound among Jahweh, Jehovah, Allah, Dumbalah of West Africa, and Jah of the Rastafari in Jamaica. Hey, even Godzilla, deity of five-year-olds watching television on Saturday morning.

From the moment the polls said he was certain to be elected, President Charles Barbur's aides had told him he needed a woman in his cabinet. This was so he could invite Gloria Steinem to the White House for the swearing-in ceremonies and picture taking—thus demonstrating to women everywhere that he was in the forefront of the women's rights movement.

All presidents felt obliged to complete this drill; ordinarily they chose a woman for the Department of Education, or Human Services, where, it was believed, the duties were congenial to their sex.

When his advisers suggested Hannah Callaghan for attorney general—saying she was a helluva fine lawyer and a good administrator to boot—Barbur had balked. The women had gotten Sandra Day O'Connor, hadn't they? Justice was no place for a woman, the president said, although not loudly or in the presence of anybody but his wife. In the end, he agreed to at least talk to Callaghan. Even if he had no intention of appointing them to his administration, interviewing women candidates was part of the president's drill as well.

Before the interview was finished, Barbur—adopting the goony grin of a man smitten—asked Hannah Callaghan if she would please consider being his attorney general. What brought about the goony grin was a mystery to Barbur's aides and assistants. Callaghan was no beauty in the usual sense; she was slender, it was true—to the point of being skinny—with short black hair and intelligent brown eyes. She was a lively, spirited woman, given to splendid laughter, and seemed to find something funny everywhere. She was the only member of Barbur's team besides Secretary of State Stuart Kaplan who had the nerve to be herself in his presence. When she laughed she laughed with gusto, showing a mouthful of braces.

President Barbur awaited her appearances at cabinet meetings with his goony grin in place. He was grinning goonily when she appeared before the extraordinary Sunday morning meeting of the National Security Council. She was there to brief the president and his advisers on the possibilities of preventing the television networks from

173

entering into commercial agreements to telecast the camel race on Gibraltar. When Barbur began licking his lips rapidly—a sign his brain was off his coffee and onto the business at hand—the NSC members quieted. "Mr. Kaplan. Ms. Callaghan. I . . . We . . ."

"Yes, Mr. President?" Kaplan said.

"Boy, isn't this good coffee. It has almond in it. Ms. Callaghan, is it possible for us to prevent those, those . . ." He seemed uncertain if he should say what was on his mind.

Callaghan looked up from the papers in front of her, and addressed Barbur over the top of her glasses. "Bastards?" Callaghan led the laughter around the table.

"Can we stop them from participating?"

"We can try, Mr. President."

"Try?" Barbur looked disappointed. He had obviously been thinking of a stronger response than that.

"We could use the same statute Jimmy Carter used to freeze Iranian bank accounts in the United States and to prevent American citizens from doing business with Iran. That would be the authority of 50 USC Section 1701."

The president sipped his coffee. "You know, one of the great American traditions is the endless cup of mud. What does that law say, Hannah?"

"It gives you the authority to declare an unusual and extraordinary threat to the national security, foreign policy, or economy. This threat has to be from a source outside the United States. For extraordinary threats here, you have the possibility of the Sixth Fleet being trapped in the Mediterranean."

"Now we're getting somewhere," Barbur said. Then he looked worried. "This isn't a declaration of war or anything like that?"

"It's not a declaration of war, Mr. President."

"Because if we declared war on them, we'd have to . . . we'd have to . . ."

"We'd in essence have to admit that Jebel Tarik is a government, a sovereign entity. That's correct, Mr. President. However, 50 USC 1701 gives you the right to

174

prohibit commercial transactions if you want, or prohibit the exchange of currency. You can ban loans, credit, the sale of goods and services, or the shipping of specific products."

"Ahh. Now, suppose I declare this emergency and prohibit the networks from . . . from doing business with the Arabs. What if they decide to do it anyway? You know, go ahead with their plans. Could they get away with that?"

Callaghan held her hand up for the president to slow down. "Not so fast, Mr. President. There are a couple of steps along the way. First I have to file an injunction in federal district court seeking a declaratory judgment giving 'equitable relief,' that is, prohibiting the networks from doing business with Aziz until the emergency is over."

"And if we get that and the networks go ahead, we can do what?"

"Well, if the district court actually did give us a judgment and the networks broke it, they would be in contempt and I could throw their buns in jail." Callaghan rubbed her hands together with much enthusiasm and giggled at the thought. "But it's highly unlikely that it would work that way, Mr. President."

Barbur's face drooped. "Unlikely?"

"The networks would very likely object."

"Well, on what grounds? On what grounds could they possibly object?" Barbur looked confused.

"The First Amendment, Mr. President. The First Amendment. The question is, does the government ever have the authority to suppress news before it is published or broadcast? This is called prior censorship. Can we legally stop them? The answer is maybe yes, but probably no. The networks will say never, under any circumstances. But they'll also add that this is a charity event and doesn't enrich the Arabs."

"Under any circumstances?"

"It will be our burden to demonstrate a direct, immediate, and irreparable damage to national security. The network lawyers will reply that Razzia is a camel race with target shooting; how could a camel race have anything at
175

all to do with national security? In any event, the district court will very likely give us a temporary injunction only so the other side can organize its reply."

"What then?"

"The usual course would be that we would then have to take it to the court of appeals for yet another temporary injunction, and then to the supremes. Since they'll be wanting to sew up the television rights tomorrow, we can petition for a direct review by the supremes, and probably get it by Tuesday. They met over a weekend to rule on the Pentagon Papers case." Callaghan laughed her splendid laugh, her braces catching the light. "Nobody knows what will happen once it gets to the supremes, Mr. President. That's why God made lawyers."

"Aarrrr," said Barbur.

"As it stands now, we have to trust on the honor, common sense, and good taste of television executives. Perhaps you could invite them in for a lunch or something, Mr. President. You could talk to them."

Barbur was surprised. "Honor? Common sense? Taste? Television executives? We'll base our injunction on the Sixth Fleet thing. Muhammad Aziz is threatening our freedom of movement on the high seas."

Callaghan made a note on a small pink pad. "External threat." She glanced at Stuart Kaplan, who, like herself, respected the First Amendment and was opposed to the legal bullying of the media.

"We'll say if the networks have to pay to televise this thing, then it's clearly entertainment, not news, and we can prevent the transaction. Ms. Callaghan?"

"The network lawyers will argue news-schmoos, what difference does it make? They've got the right to televise what they wish and where they wish, as long as it's not libelous, thank you. Whether they pay or don't pay, it doesn't make any difference."

Barbur didn't think the media should have that right if it wasn't to his advantage. He narrowed his eyes.

"It's a tradition, Mr. President."

The president said, "We'll throw in that there's no

guarantee that this money will ever be spent on any kind of charity. Just what guarantee is there that any of it will ever benefit anything other than Muhammad Aziz's bank account? None."

"Mr. President . . ." Hannah Callaghan did her best to hide her dismay. She didn't want her name associated with this lawsuit; she didn't want the public to think it was her idea.

President Barbur's stomach growled audibly, as though he were having an internal thunderstorm of some kind. Everybody in the room heard it, a great cracking boom of a stomach growl. "Mmmm." The president glanced at his watch. He looked concerned. "I think it's time for lunch," he said.

13

IN ORDER TO scope the mystery man on his Sunday afternoon walk, James Burlane settled in by the flower sellers on Main Street. He started whistling loud enough for the vendors to hear, but not loud enough to be obnoxious. He chose some mellow calls, some cheery *tweet*s, and some mixed *tweet-twit, tweet-twit*s—a medley of optimism and good cheer.

He opened his equipment case. Still whistling, he set up a tripod, mounted a 200mm lens on his camera, and began shooting pictures of house sparrows in the slender trees at the curb in front of the flower stalls. *Click, clack. Tweet-twit. Click, clack.*

Then he got his parabolic mike out and snapped it to the center of the concave collection mirror. A thin wire from the mike ran to a tape recorder on his belt and to a headphone. He checked his watch.

He opened the lid of his equipment case. He leaned

the back of the collection mirror against the inside of the lid. He studied the sidewalks on either side of the narrow street, then faced the lid—and the parabolic—north up Main Street.

He checked his watch again. *Tweet, tweet, tweet.* He looked up the street.

The mystery man and his three toadies were coming his way, out for their daily walk.

Tweet, tweet. Burlane turned his back to his target and stepped to one side of the open case. He slipped a small joy stick out of his pocket. *Tweet-twit. Tweet-twit.*

He stopped whistling. He used the joy stick to sweep the sidewalk with the parabolic—listening to the babble of street noise searching for the mystery man and his three-toady entourage.

He heard ". . . ielsens and Arbitrons."

". . . ould have seen Gerard Thompson and Harry Gilchrist smile."

He whistled *tweet, tweet,* and coolly backed up on the joy stick. He lost the conversation. Hah! Caught it.

"Did she like to fuck? Irina? Does a bear shit in the woods?" This was a Russian voice speaking English with a British accent.

"Ivan was a drinker, I'm told." This voice had an American accent.

"Oh, yes, old Ivan could put away the vodka if he wanted," said the Russian with a British accent.

"Let's try this one today," the American accent said.

"*Da,* Leonid," said his friend.

The sound was gone. No more. Burlane scoped left, right, with the joy stick. Nothing. He turned. They were gone, disappeared into a pub. Burlane sighed and put away his gear. Nielsens and Arbitrons, Gerard Thompson, Irina's libido and Ivan's drinking.

James Burlane packed his gear and began the hike up the hill to the hospital. This was less of a chore than it would have been even yesterday. The delicate man was feeling stronger.

When he got back to his room, he sent a squirt to Ara Schott via the Company man across the bay:

178

President Charles Barbur knew that members of the Supreme Court watched television also, and so knew how to judge a poll. Barbur considered Stuart Kaplan savvy about numbers also, and when the president had to take a hard look at the trends, he liked to have Kaplan on hand. Thus poor Kaplan had to return to the White House Sunday evening.

Barbur's assistants had purchased a machine that arranged the data visually for him with brightly colored graphs. If the trend of the data was heavily bullish, the graph was colored red, a hot color. The stronger the trend, the brighter the red. The bearish data plunged in shades and hues of blue. The correct colors were specified by a computer that controlled dye mixtures according to the numbers.

The secretary of state always gave Barbur time to consider the full impact of the trends. Stuart Kaplan wondered whether this was how it had been when Winston Churchill was handed new figures on the dead and dying, how many Messerschmidts had appeared over the skies, how many tons of bombs had landed on Coventry—death and suffering rendered in neat figures at the bottom of columns.

"Take your time, Mr. President."

"A person doesn't realize sometimes. Just doesn't realize." Barbur cleared his throat and began leafing through a summary book.

Kaplan felt sorry for Barbur. In the good old days, all national leaders had to do was count heads and ships and divide by distance, or some such formula. The country with the biggest army and navy did what it wanted.

The bomb altered the formula. Use the bomb, and you risked losing everything.

The other thing that made life different for foreign ministers everywhere was the emergence, in the twentieth century, of two particularly cancerous ideologies, one secular, the other religious. The first was the Russian belief—nursed in that frigid empire from the medieval age—that it was their destiny to rule the world. Stuart Kaplan did not believe the Bolsheviks were revolutionaries at all. On the contrary, he thought they were profoundly conservative. They conserved the czar's bureaucracies, secret police, and labor camps. The lash of their whips was just as painful as that of the czars'. The czarist conceit of Russian destiny became a Leninist conceit. Kaplan wondered just what it was that the Bolsheviks were alleged to have overthrown. Nothing. They had overthrown nothing.

"These numbers don't look good," Barbur said.

"They could be better in places."

Studying the summary, Barbur fell into a trancelike silence.

The second calamitous ideology, that of the the Shiite Moslems, had been unleashed by the Ayatollah Khomeini in Iran. *La illa il-Allah*—there is no God but Allah —meant literally that to a Shiite. This belief was made worse by the Shiite doctrine of *Kerbela,* wherein a life sacrificed to the cause—a practice ennobled by the martyr Hussein—was guaranteed heaven.

It was the perverse logic that so horrified Kaplan. No act was too crazed or bizarre if it resulted in heaven. Suicide was the ideal. Believers in *Kerbela* walked into mine fields to detonate Iraqi mines. Believers drove car bombs into embassies and hotels.

Kaplan knew Barbur didn't pay any attention to Arab logic. The president felt that if someone acted like an asshole, he was an asshole. Barbur adhered to the belief that countries ought to behave honorably and advance upon one another with proper armies, flags flying; Kaplan saw it as one of his jobs to remind the president that, in the 1980s, this would mean ICBMs launched, sirens wailing.

Barbur made a low rumbling sound in his throat.

Was the president about to speak, or was he just clearing his throat? Kaplan waited.

President Barbur rumbled again. Barbur knew his polls. He regarded polls with fascination. He approached each new result with a wary, slightly squinting eye —visually pawing the numbers for possible new voters and checking for hints of decisions gone wrong. The computers were so fast that bad numbers were onto you faster than an adder, truth's venomous teeth clamping hard.

When Barbur liked the results of a poll, he used it to close the mouths of complainers. When he disagreed, he kept his mouth shut and changed his position. When Barbur succeeded in agreeing with the largest number of voters, he denounced anything to do with his original position, denying that it had ever been his. This ability to rewrite the past was a perk that had evolved over years of presidential history.

"What on earth can people be thinking of?" Barbur murmured at last. This was directed at himself as much as to Kaplan.

"They like races, Mr. President."

"They say paying the Arabs money to televise the camel race is wrong. They say it helps the Arabs. They . . . They . . ." Barbur made no effort to hide his dismay. "You read it, Stuart."

Kaplan had, several times. He looked at the figures in front of the president. "Fifty-three percent think the race is entirely entertainment. Thirty-one percent say it's entertainment first, news second. Thirteen percent say it's news first, entertainment second. Three percent think it's all news."

"We've come upon hard times, Stuart." Barbur put a hand on Kaplan's shoulder.

"Sixty-nine percent say the networks should be allowed to participate."

"They still want to see the damned race!" Barbur shook his head.

Under the circumstances, Kaplan thought the trend line looked rather like a stiff prick. He said, "But look at your personal approval rating, Mr. President. Seventy-two percent, and a solid, if not to say glowing, red." Barbur's personal approval in spite of his policy setbacks continued to be amazing.

"What do you think I should do, Stuart? If we . . . If we . . . This is . . . How can we fight these people? What

181

...What are we supposed ... Paying them all that money. This is like the damned movies! And what about the damnable Supreme Court?" He doubled up his fist.

"*Theater* is the word you're looking for, Mr. President. The Court has agreed to a direct review on Tuesday."

"I don't know how long we can take this kind of punishment. Just look at those numbers."

"These are extremely short trends, Mr. President." Kaplan didn't mention color; in truth, the line of the people who wanted to see the camel race was Chi-Com red. Whereas the president's line of personal approval was a wonderful scarlet, the approval line for his response to the Gibraltar crisis—going to the Supreme Court—was a purplish color, still engorged but draining fast.

Barbur didn't like to lose, so he was careful how he picked his fights. "You know, Stuart, this happens sometimes. The polls get deranged, if you know what I mean; it's like some kind of fever or something. How can we have correct policies if we don't know what people want? They're not sending us clear instructions: what is it that we have to do?"

"It's complicated, Mr. President."

"We could say that Gibraltar is a British colony. It is a British problem. We could say we stand by our British allies and that sort of thing. When the camel race is over and the numbers come down, the P.M. can make her move. The people over there are just as worked up as they are over here. What do you think the Court will do, Stuart?"

"Support the networks," Kaplan said. He adjusted his eyeglasses.

"I . . . I appointed most of those b-bastards. How, how can they . . . They just can't." The president's face turned as purple as the approval line for his court action.

14

THE GRAND HIGH Muckamucks at NBC were ecstatic when they heard about the Puking Max story. Thompson's new image was perfect, made to order for this tale of high heroism. The writers and editors had drunk coffee or tooted coke to stay awake all Saturday night. They had tape from three cameras to play with and orders to go for all the flash and dazzle they could muster.

Two cameras had shot a four-second monkey run. A third had taped a helicopter gunship going *VROOM!* Out of this, an hour special. It was a clear-cut masterpiece of writing and editing—done with unacknowledged indebtedness to Canadian masters of film documentaries. They drank French champagne at a catered NBC viewing party.

Corks popped and a cheer went up as a dog food commercial gave way to their main man, the grizzled, handsome Gerard Thompson. Thompson gave not a hint that he was under any strain from Harry Gilchrist's Nielsen assault. He exuded confidence and masculinity. He was Ernest Hemingway's clone, an intellectual, father, lover, and reporter. The solemn Thompson, affecting a slight growl that was the essence of a no-bullshit kind of guy, said:

"The United Kingdom hasn't seen anything like it since Winston Churchill and the British people stood fast during the German blitz of World War Two. You saw the first pictures last night. Palestinian terrorists using machine guns and helicopters tried in vain to rid Gibraltar of one of its most enduring legends of resistance: the Barbary apes. Stay tuned for a dramatic NBC exclusive on Max and his ladies. This is Sunday, February sixteenth, day eight of the siege of Gibraltar."

183

" 'Max and the Siege of Gibraltar,' an NBC Special . . ."

". . . with Gerard Thompson."

On the screen behind Thompson a helicopter with Gatlings tore crater-sized divots in the side of a brushy slope. "Good evening. This is Gerard Thompson. The Arabs in these helicopter gunships are not firing at a British soldier. No, they are trying to kill an ape named Puking Max—who in just one week has become the symbol of Gibraltarian resolve to stand fast under siege."

There had been much discussion over whether or not to retain the Puking. Thompson had been for it on the grounds that it added color. NBC executives initially overruled him because millions of viewers like to eat snacks when they watch TV. Sunday afternoon was a prime time to advertise beer. Thompson replied that Hollywood had discovered that teen-agers loved gore and the outrageous, hence the success of the *Halloween* movies, and such movies as *The Texas Chain Saw Massacre*. Teen-agers would insist on watching the Puker, he said. The executives saw the truth in this and didn't want to lose advertising dollars.

"For an NBC exclusive on the action, we go to Tony O'Brien on the Rock."

"Behind me you see the famous profile of Mons Calpe, the famous Rock of legend. And here"—the camera panned to the right—"is the back side of Gibraltar. You see the town there by the water. Above the town —somewhere on that steep, brushy hillside—a male Barbary ape and two female apes are on the run today from these . . ."

A helicopter gunship fired Gatlings. The camera cut to a dark green bush that exploded under a hail of slugs.

On the monitor, Gibraltarians with binoculars looked up at something in the distance. In a voice-over, O'Brien said, "Giving these people, and these people, and these people, courage . . . and hope." The camera cut from the people with binoculars to shoppers walking past missiles to people watching the telly in a Gibraltar pub. "And who

184

is giving them courage and hope? Max and his ladies. We call them apes, as is the practice on Gibraltar. They don't look like apes; they look like monkeys, which they are, in fact—the rest of their tribe lives in Morocco, fourteen miles across the Strait of Gibraltar."

Puking Max's head appeared over the top of a low stone wall. The tape froze, the camera moved in. Max's face was shown close up, a mixture of terror and determination.

"He doesn't command fleets or smoke cigars, but he has become a candidate for that distinguished pantheon of British heroes that runs from Admiral Nelson to Winston Churchill. His motto: Fight on!"

The camera drew back from Max's face, and his body appeared in graceful slow motion as he vaulted over the stone wall and onto the narrow road.

"These Arabs want to rid the Rock of its apes once and for all." Arabs were shown firing machine guns at a fleeing target.

Tony O'Brien was on the screen in a cutaway. "Yes, a Barbary ape named Puking Max. The two females in the drama, Virginia and Jane, so named by a British army lieutenant in honor of Virginia Woolf and Jane Austen. They are, we are told, the comeliest of Max's pack that was slaughtered by the Arab occupiers on the second day of siege. This is Virginia . . ."

Virginia's head appeared above the stone wall. Her face was frozen as Max's had been.

". . . and this is Jane."

Jane's frightened, straining face was shown.

Virginia, then Jane, completed the vault in slow motion.

"The legend is that the British will be on Gibraltar as long as the apes remain. Well, the remnants of the British regiment are trapped inside the Rock."

The camera showed Europa Point under which four hundred British soldiers were imprisoned.

"Gibraltarians will tell you that as long as Max, Virginia, and Jane are on the loose, then the British soldiers inside the Rock are not prisoners of anybody. Listen to Pedro Smyth-Wickwire, the owner of a bookshop in downtown Gibraltar."

The camera cut to a middle-aged Gibraltarian with an empire mustache and wearing an ascot with his blazer. "*Sí, es verdad.* As long as Max and his ladies are running free, we are under siege. We have not succumbed and we bloody well shan't."

O'Brien, in a cutaway, said, "The Arabs, however, are determined to see that they don't."

A helicopter hovered, its Gatlings going *VROOOM! VROOOM!* Close up, explosions of powdered limestone and dust echoed the vrooms.

"NBC news blundered onto the action you are seeing. We don't know how many Arabs were involved because they were around the curve of the hill and out of sight. However, thanks to the accident of chance, we're able to share these exclusive shots. You see the action as we saw it."

With machine guns rattling in the background, Max ran in slow motion. The Arabs fired their AK-47s. Max ran in a close-up. All three apes ran in slow motion.

"Gibraltarians say Max, who is also called Puking Max, named for his habit of regurgitating after overindulging, is the leader of the pack on the Rock."

On the screen: three apes running.

"Today these heroic primates are the sole surviving members of the Barbary apes on Gibraltar. The question is, how long can they survive the pursuit of Arabs flying West German helicopters and firing high-speed American Gatlings?"

Helicopters vroomed. A hillside exploded. Craters and ditches were ripped from the side of the hill. Max ran. Virginia ran. Jane ran. Puking Max grabbed a branch in slow motion. The Arabs fired their machine guns in slow motion. In slow motion, Max swung onto the bank on the uphill side of a narrow road. Still in slow motion, he landed. Arabs fired. Helicopters went *VROOM! VROOM!*

Tony O'Brien stood at the edge of the runway at the

Gibraltar airport, a handsome profile of Mons Calpe behind him. "The plucky Max has become a symbol of Everyman here on Gibraltar. It's not easy being under siege, and the pride of a Gibraltarian is inevitably stirred when his name is mentioned. Gibraltarians will tell you the Arabs won't get the apes tomorrow, either. Gibraltarians say they've been leaving food out for Max and the ladies every night. Each morning the food is gone. For NBC news, this is Tony O'Brien at the Rock."

Gerard Thompson said, "Coming up, reactions to the story of Max from President Barbur and Prime Minister Fielding, plus Londoners say what Max means to them. That and more stories of the heroic apes. You're watching the siege of Gibraltar, day eight." The red light went off and the monitor was given over to a handsome, smiling man standing by a shiny black Nissan sedan.

Thompson relaxed. He didn't like to claim Nielsens before they were tallied, but he felt NBC had done it —inserted a little action into a story that had threatened to go flat on them. He felt jubilant. There had been the usual assholes, sure—NBC executives who argued that viewers didn't know symbols from diddly-squat; one even objected to comparing Max to Winston Churchill! He said only old farts knew who Winston Churchill was, and they weren't a decent market. He suggested comparing Puking Max to John Lennon, a more familiar figure to the baby-boomer population bulge.

But Gerard Thompson, Tony O'Brien, and all the editors had believed. They had stuck by Winston Churchill. And they had made it work. It was a sensational start on the ape story.

Now, if the Supreme Court came through, Gerard Thompson would take his new masculine image to Gibraltar and kick ass, finish Harry Gilchrist and CBS once and for all.

Alas, because of the latest employee of the National Security Agency to sell secrets to the Russians, President Charles Barbur could not talk to Prime Minister Deborah

Fielding over their "safe" phone. There was no time for the safest way, which was to have couriers shuttle notes across the Atlantic by Concorde.

Barbur didn't like having to communicate through codes. That wasn't his style. He liked to negotiate with a hot dog in his mouth or with a bowl full of ice cream in his lap.

There were those presidential aides who claimed that Barbur, far from being a bit drifty in the head, or somehow befuddled, was in fact shrewd, calculating in the extreme. They said his fascination with food was a tactic, if not a strategy. They always cited a chat that Barbur had had with the West German chancellor. The two had been talking about free trade and American attempts to limit the importation of West German steel, a subject that really mattered. Barbur had recalled having eaten barbecued chicken at the volunteer fire department of Linkwood-Salem, Maryland, in the summer of 1973 or was it 1974; he couldn't remember for sure. But it was delicious. Vinegary, he remembered. The Germans liked a lot of vinegar in their food, didn't they? One of the aides memorized part of the exchange that followed in the official transcript:

CHANCELLOR: I think we should talk very frankly about the issue of steel, Mr. President.

BARBUR: It could have had lemon in it too, but I'm sure it was mostly vinegar. I know it had lots of black pepper in it, and I like black pepper.

Stuart Kaplan, Peter Neely, and Ara Schott went to the White House on Monday afternoon prepared to eat while they read what Mrs. Fielding had to say. It was their job—Kaplan's mostly—to assist the president. Mrs. Fielding would be surrounded by her foreign secretary, the head of MI6, and her minister of defense.

The American secretary of defense, Henry McArthur,

was excluded from the American side. This was ostensibly because he was needed at the Pentagon, where everybody was poring over contingency plans. These plans, for one reason or another, were never worth a damn. Yet they were always demanded and always produced—at great cost to the taxpayer. Unlike farmers who planted seeds and watched their plants grow to fruition, McArthur's people had nothing to show for their work and so felt guilty. Although they almost never worked in practice, contingency plans were something tangible his officers could point to as having accomplished.

The truth was that the admirals and generals were doing all the poring over contingency plans, not Henry McArthur. McArthur was excluded from the White House on nonceremonial occasions because he was a couple of bales short of a full ton and everybody knew it. He was dogged and forceful, which was what was needed in appearances before Congress. He came across on television as very, very sincere, the kind of man needed in charge of the nation's defense. That he wasn't very smart wasn't commented upon in the public papers; he merely took stupid or mendacious positions; lack of intelligence was genetic bad luck, but a condition easily concealed in a democracy.

Because he was secretary of state, Stuart Kaplan ate well; there was no question of that. Kaplan even had his own cook at his town house in Georgetown. But there was something special about the treats the president provided his guests in times of emergency. Perhaps he had concluded, after all the years of his administration, that the prospect of ICBMs in launch position, or Debbie Fielding ready to do battle, was best savored over a soothing mousse or fresh peach ice cream made by White House chefs.

The order of arrival was in reverse to the order of rank: it was Ara Schott first, in a proper dark blue suit, then Peter Neely, in a splendid three-piecer of British cut and cloth.

Stuart Kaplan joined them in the communications room and they said their hellos, waiting for the man with the food cart. After the food arrived, the president would come and they could learn more of poor Debbie Fielding's anguish and rage.

"Hah, strawberry shortcake!" Neely said.

As though on cue, Barbur, beaming, strode through the door. "Oh, strawberry shortcake! The chef makes these shortcakes according to a recipe handed down in my wife's family. You're probably looking at a little lard mixed in there with the flour, but that's what makes it good. I say the hell with Ralph Nader." Barbur looked jolly indeed.

Barbur's chefs came up with some of the most amazing concoctions. They looked like magazine illustrations —so fresh and good-looking it was unreal. As now: succulent strawberries, sliced in elegant little slices, in a polished silver bowl. And little pitchers of cream Kaplan knew would be so sweet and good it would make him grin. "It does look good, Mr. President," he said.

Kaplan waited while the steward set about making *café au lait* with a special machine that his assistant had wheeled into the room.

Barbur said, "I had a hankering for *caffelatte*. You know I like that business of adding hot milk to strong coffee, all that hissing and wheezing when they heat the milk." The president pursed his lips and made a hissing sound to imitate the sound of a *caffelatte* machine. He nodded toward the decoding machine. "Do you want to turn that on and give us the gist of what she has to say?"

Kaplan understood the president's request; it was not without precedent. He was being asked to read the decoded message, drink his *caffelatte*, eat his pioneer-recipe strawberry shortcake, and at the same time give Barbur a summary of Mrs. Fielding's remarks. Kaplan assumed that the sugar somehow soothed Barbur's nerves and relieved his anxiety over the possibility of taking some action that would end with rockets going up. If that was the case, Kaplan figured, eating strawberry shortcake was a small enough price to pay.

The steward dished up their shortcake, beginning with Schott, then Neely, then Kaplan, then the president. When Barbur began eating, they all began eating, and Kaplan punched on the monitor of the decoding machine; the monitor was taken over by print, and Kaplan began reading while he ate. Behind him, Barbur and Peter Neely talked about riding horseback at Jackson Hole. Ara Schott, who was along in case Neely was required to think with any degree of sophistication, ate his strawberries in silence.

"Aren't these good?" Barbur said. "They're so good they're disgusting."

Kaplan said, "Well, she says she's going to invade and recapture Gibraltar and will let us know so that we may notify our Sixth Fleet of activity in the area. She says this is a British problem and the British will take care of it. She does ask that we assemble our Sixth Fleet in a show of force off Gibraltar's Mediterranean side on the date chosen by the Royal Navy for S-Day."

"This was the way it was when I was a kid, you know, sweet cream like this, sugar."

Kaplan paused. "She says when this is over and the British have Gibraltar back, they will never, repeat never, never cede it to the Spanish under any conditions whatsoever. She wants to know if I might pass that on to the Spanish."

"You have to add sugar to the strawberries; otherwise they're too tart." Barbur smacked his lips.

"Mr. President, she wants to know if the Royal Navy should by any chance run into unforeseen difficulties, can the British call upon the Sixth Fleet for help? She says the Royal Navy is preparing contingencies, and her officers say that possibility—it is remote, she says—has to be factored in." Kaplan looked up, frowning. He adjusted his spectacles.

"I think . . . I think . . . What do you think, Stuart?"

"I think we should say yes, we'll help them out any way we can."

The president, who was ordinarily a tough talker, an admirer of Teddy Roosevelt's famous big stick, studied his loaded spoon. The polls continued to be confusing. The president was a poll junkie. He needed a quick fix of unambiguous numbers. A poll fix gave the president a high
191

in which he was confident of action, knowing in advance that it would be approved of by the voters. "I think . . . I think we should tell them we support our traditional Anglo-American commitments. Our common heritage." President Barbur started to say something more, but didn't. He took another bite of strawberry shortcake.

"Perhaps I should give her an answer that doesn't make any sense," Kaplan said dryly.

President Barbur, sucking on a strawberry, brightened. "An answer that doesn't make any sense. She could hardly be sore at that. That's not a bad idea! Beautiful, Stuart. Beautiful! Yes, do just that. Do it. You're the best secretary of state a president ever had."

Stuart Kaplan's mouth fell. It was a joke. A joke! God, what had he done?

15

GERARD THOMPSON WAS a longtime, savvy watcher of polls. Like President Barbur, he watched the subtle numbers in the background. The relationships. By Monday evening, he thought it possible that an incipient conscience was developing. In the past, he knew, public conscience was unpredictable, and could spring overnight into full-scale backlash.

Whether Gerard Thompson was going to go *mano-a-mano* with Harry Gilchrist in Razzia coverage had been delivered into the hands of the Supreme Court. Thompson, confident and comfortable, was ready to flash his stuff. But the justices, he knew, watched television, and the poll results appeared to be reported with the same regularity as the weather and basketball scores. If the justices detected the slightest hint of backlash, they could scuttle Razzia with the stroke of a pen.

On the television screen a large-beaked man swung his leg over the bridge of the saddle and leaped off a camel's hump. He started running with long strides, his eye on the next camel. His white thobe looked wonderful trailing in the wind. Thompson felt Felicia's presence behind him. Without taking his eye off the television set, he held up his hand for hers.

"They'll back you, hon. They have to, it's the First Amendment, and this is clearly a First Amendment case. Everybody says so."

He pulled her onto his lap and sighed. "It should be okay if the justices aren't watching those poll results too carefully. It's hard not to worry."

"I think I'll do a line, okay, hon?"

"Sure," Thompson said. He gave her an affectionate tap on the rump as she slipped off his lap to get her gear; Thompson poured himself another neat shot of scotch.

"You have to admit, the race sounds like it'll be fun to watch," she said. "I'll just bet you the justices are watching the action too. Do you think they'll want to pour water on everybody's fun? If they cancel Razzia coverage, everybody'll hate them for it, and they want to be loved just like everybody else." She took a tiny plastic envelope of white powder and dumped it onto a small mirror. The cocaine was ready to toot, but Felicia liked the ritual of mincing it with a single-edge razor blade and shaping it and reshaping it into neat little lines.

"My career in the hands of nine old farts." Thompson shook his head.

"Uh-uh. Eight old farts and Sandra Day O'Connor." Felicia drew two lines. She squinted at them and redrew them more nearly even. "Those justices'll have their grandchildren leaning on them, sweets. Oh, no, Grampa, not the camel race! You can't stop the camel race! How do you think old Sandra Day will react when her little grandchild slips onto her lap and asks her if she's going to stop the camel races? You've got it grooved, hon, mark my word."

"I suppose if all they're watching are camels . . ." Thompson didn't sound confident. ABC's cameras zoomed in on a group of six Arabs unpiling from two Mercedes-Benzes. He thumbed the sound up with his remote:

"And this is the team from Chad, which has been training its rider at Abeche. Which one is the rider, Faoud?"

"That would be Abdul Saud; he's the one on the left there, Bill. He's a Tuareg nomad, twenty-six years old, unmarried, a rider, not a shooter. He just wants to get acquainted with his camel, then it'll be back to the range. But he's a natural shooter, they say. Both his father and grandfather were camel drivers, Bill. The Chadians say Abdul was born on caravan and has spent his entire life on a camel."

Bill Richards laughed. "No lack of experience there." The team from Chad was replaced by a map of the Sahara. Everything was pale yellow except for Chad, which glowed with a pulsing beige. "This is Chad, just below Libya. If Abdul Saud beats anybody, he wants to beat the Libyans. Omar Qafi has had his eye on Chad for years and has twice tried to invade his neighbor."

"The Chadian army was rescued by the French both times."

"It'll be a real grudge match between the Libyans and the Chadians," Richards said in his famous Bill Richards voice.

Thompson sighed and thumbed off the sound.

Felicia pushed her left nostril closed with her forefinger and sucked a line into the other side with a small, silver straw. She tilted her head back to let the coke spread into her sinuses. Her head still back, her blond hair fell nearly to her rump.

Thompson thought Felicia looked sexy with her head back like that. It did wonders for her chest. Of course she knew this, knew that he liked to watch, which is why she did it. Thompson knew he wouldn't have a beautiful blond wife twenty-seven years younger than himself were it not for his fame and his $1.5 million NBC salary. Wealth and fame made men handsome.

Would Felicia stay with him through bad Nielsens?

194

What would she do if he were sent down to run a Sunday-afternoon bullshit session with a bunch of ugly and repugnant print journalists?

Looking back, Thompson saw very few really good NBC efforts. NBC had produced *The A-Team,* that was true, but look at some of the gems the competition had come up with: *The Love Boat, Lifestyles of the Rich and Famous, Divorce Court.*

Dammit, he wanted to take on Harry Gilchrist in covering the camel race on Gibraltar. He took a slug of scotch and held Felicia close with his arm.

"Good toot," she said. Then she added, "Maybe the Puker will give you an edge."

"I wish it were so, hon." Thompson ran his fingers through his wife's hair. The story of Puking Max had started out well enough, but it was rough for Tony O'Brien to follow up on it because the damnable apes spent most of their time in hiding. Day after day, lugging their cameras and sound gear, O'Brien and his cameramen had followed Arabs up and down the steep hillside overlooking the bay. Always, it seemed, Max and his ladies appeared somewhere else. On the surface, this looked promising. The reality was that the viewers never got to see apes. They did get to see camels and so clamored for the camel race.

Felicia Thompson slipped her hand onto her husband's crotch and began massaging it. A few minutes later she looked up, and without unobstructing her mouth said, "Wai' an' 'ee. Su're'e 'our' yus'ices wa'ch 'ee'ee 'oo."

16

ON TUESDAY MORNING, Secretary of State Stuart Kaplan waited in the television room for the call from Attorney General Hannah Callaghan, who was at the Supreme Court where the decision in the Razzia case was to be announced shortly.

Kaplan had felt a little foolish about the television room, but in the end he relented because he knew that the trappings of power had meaning in Washington. Only those cabinet members with reason to be following the Gibraltar crisis had any reason to have a room full of television sets upon which to watch the story develop.

To emphasize his importance, Henry McArthur had such a room over at Defense. Questions would be asked. People would be wondering. Who has the president's ear in this one, Defense or State? Kaplan's aides argued: should not Kaplan have a television room if McArthur has one?

Trapped, Kaplan, at some expense to the taxpayer, had a room stripped and refurbished with television sets, chairs, and a table with computer terminals. This was so hardworking State Department officials—getting the latest word off television—could ask questions of various State Department experts.

Having approved of what he thought was an absurd expenditure of money and displaced a number of State employees for no good reason, Kaplan felt a need to actually use the television room.

Kaplan knew that if Debbie Fielding said she was going to invade Gibraltar, then by God she was going to invade Gibraltar. But unless the intransigent Spanish prime minister changed his mind and cooperated, the British were in a lot of trouble.

Kaplan considered the circle of five television sets: NBC, ABC, CBS, cable news, public television.

On NBC, Arabs fired AK-47s at the fleeing Puking Max, who grabbed a branch and swung himself onto the high side of the narrow road. A freeze-frame photograph of Max grabbing a branch had been on the front page of *The Washington Post*.

On ABC, a man was riding a camel at the foot of Mons Calpe.

CBS switched from a shot of the brushy hillside where Puking Max was presumably in hiding to a group of shooters on the airport target range.

Cable news did this in reverse, moving from shooters to apes.

On the fifth set, public television, three intense, serious men were being interviewed by Robert MacNeil.

Kaplan changed channels again, back to ABC. Colonel Henri Le Cocq was being interviewed.

Kaplan couldn't stop himself. He turned the sound up.

". . . They pull themselves when they run, you see. So do giraffes. It's because of those awful necks of theirs. Those muscles there. A bull will push himself up a hill with those rear haunches of his. A camel will pull itself up. In answer to your second question, their pace is not pretty, I agree, but it is quite efficient to a point. Camels are at their best in a steady, patient walk, to be honest. My point is that the winning rider will keep his camel at whatever pace is fast enough to be one of the leaders. There'll be no galloping early or a camel just might collapse. A camel just seems to fly apart at a gallop. One has to whip them."

"Colonel Le Cocq, what about these complaints we're getting from the Iranian delegation, among others, that the terik saddle favored by the Tuaregs of the western Sahara gives the Algerians and Moroccans an unfair advantage? Is there any justification in their argument that all riders should be required to sit directly on top of the hump?"

Le Cocq's hand went to his bow tie. "I should think the main difference is that it's a little wilder ride up top than down front, although in a gallop I don't imagine it makes any difference where you ride. This is all foolishness anyway. If a rider can't shoot, he can lose ten minutes at each range—forty minutes for the contest. There's no camel or camel saddle that will make up for a deficit of forty minutes in a twenty-kilometer race. That's why the camel riding trainers are having to work these long hours. These contestants are almost all shooters learning how to ride. As far as I'm concerned, any camel in the race is capable of winning it if his rider is a good enough shot."

"You think it's a well-designed contest, then."

"Let me say this, Bill. When I was a young lieutenant—"

Kaplan silenced ABC and turned up the sound on NBC, where an ape was being pursued by helicopters and automatic rifles. A man narrated the story in voice-over. "In this exclusive and now famous sequence by NBC photographer Jack Brooks, we see Max on the run from Arabs just down the road." The camera cut to the soldiers firing their weapons, then panned the steep hillside. "Up there somewhere, the keeper of Gibraltar's legend of British invincibility hides. The question is where? Arabs are combing the Rock from dawn to dusk."

The camera showed a tight line of soldiers moving through thick brush, a helicopter hovering overhead. "One of the stories associated with the Barbary apes is that nobody has ever discovered the bones of a dead ape. People say there exists on Gibraltar a burial ground that has withstood centuries of efforts to find it. Could the secret burial ground be in one of Gibraltar's famous caves? Is that where the three apes are hiding from their Palestinian pursuers?" The camera showed the entrance of a limestone cave, then moved closer.

Kaplan turned off the sound. He wondered how long they could work the ape story with no apes to be seen. He tried ABC, where a man in flowing Arab costume was riding a camel.

Sportscaster Bill Richards described the action, assisted by a man named Faoud Abu:

"This is the Somali contestant, Abdul Kareem, who has agreed to take time out from the shooting range to let us watch him ride. Tell us what you think of his style, Faoud."

"Kareem is one with his camel, Bill. Note how he reassures the animal with his left hand as he beats it with his right. If he can learn to shoot straight, Kareem could be a factor. But if I were a betting man, I'd stick with the shooters."

"I'm told we have another rider starting the course." The camera cut to a camel rising from the ground. The camel began moving fast, then started into a loping gallop. "We're told this is Jabbar Abdul, a shooter who is riding for Jordan. What do you think, Faoud?"

"He may be a shooter, but don't let them kid you; he's spent some time on a camel before, Bill. You'll note how quickly he gets his camel moving at full speed. He's deceptive."

CBS and cable news had both apes and camels. Shaking his head in disgust, Kaplan turned to public television.

Robert MacNeil was asking a question of an older, taciturn man. Kaplan turned the sound on as lettering under the man identified him as Dr. Woodward Reed, a curator from the Smithsonian Zoo:

". . . ollowing the instincts of their ancestors. There have been studies in Algeria on monkeys very close to—"

Kaplan turned the sound off. Kaplan's friend Sir Ian Tovey-Rundel, the British foreign secretary, said the Puking Max story was by far larger than Razzia in England. In England, the action was in the newspapers. Part of the fun of Puking Max in England, Tovey-Rundel had told Kaplan, was the repeated claim that a Barbary ape was more heroic, and more representative of traditional standards of British behavior, than were the monkeys working in the wretched mess that was Mrs. Fielding's government under crisis. If this claim was not accepted as the literal truth in the pubs, it came close, Tovey-Rundel said.

Alas, Kaplan had to admit to his British colleague that in America, the only game was television. Kaplan's was a nation of starers. Television lacked the sport of watching a skilled writer negotiate the truth in pursuit of drama, and the facts in the pursuit of truth. Kaplan liked to visit London. In his opinion some of the writers for the British tabs showed unusual chutzpah and crass inventiveness in the way they inflamed the proletarian imagination. It had to be a joke to the writers and editors, sneering cynics, their newspapers in fact drunken practical jokes. In this literary sense, the performance of the British press had a certain ragged, amusing class.

Americans, alas, preferred the pleasures of the cathode ray tube, and so had channels running around the clock. Razzia now dominated American television, because the camels provided constant action for minds that needed joggling to stay awake. Americans now seemed bored with the indomitable Puking Max; perhaps they were tired of watching Arabs paw through maquis.

The phone rang. Stuart Kaplan answered, "Yes?"

It was Hannah Callaghan. "Well, we got the decision."

"And?"

"Five-to-four supporting the networks. Mr. Chief Justice wrote the majority opinion. Unfortunately, for anybody interested in First Amendment rights, his brief was so badly written, stupidly argued, and obscure that it doesn't make any sense."

"No sense?"

"None. It's not even clear if the majority thought the First Amendment was involved. Reading it is like trying to crack some kind of code. It's a joke, worthless as a precedent. By the way, do I give the president the news, or do you?"

"That's your job, Hannah. You're the attorney general. I'm the secretary of state. Actually, I think the Supreme Court has gotten Barbur off the hook. He made a good-faith effort at being the fearless leader. His wife likes watching the camel racing stories on television, and I think he's getting into it also."

"Ahh. Everybody wins then, sort of."

"Sort of," Kaplan said.

When Muhammad Aziz stalked angrily into his Tuesday conference, scowling, glaring at his assistants, the members of the international press corps, who had been babbling happily about the previous night's bed partners and hangovers, shut their mouths immediately. They had never seen Aziz so exercised. Ordinarily, he was fair-minded and polite if a bit evasive at times. They had never seen him lose his temper.

Had something happened? Were the Brits about to attack? The reporters and photographers checked their tape recorders and cameras.

Was it to begin like this, then? Was this history, upon them suddenly in this storied fortress? The journalists surrendered a heady moment to the cocking of ballpoint pens: *click, click, click, clickety-click,* on down the line.

Muhammad Aziz stepped up to the microphone. The lights went on. Aziz squinted, waiting for his eyes to adjust. He looked at his feet. He looked up.

The tape recorders were turned on: *click, click, click, clickety-click,* on down the line. The red lights were on.

"Something has happened that affects my honor directly, and I want to get the matter cleared up before I take other questions. When I first announced our camel race, I said we had riders from thirty-two countries with large Islamic populations, including Albania; I had an agreement with the government in Tiranē. Albanian officials had said they would provide a marksman if we would provide a Tuareg trainer to teach him how to ride. We agreed.

"Then they said, would we guarantee that they have the best camel in the race? Their rider is a beginner, they said. We said we couldn't do that, out of fairness to the others in the race; there were others with no experience with camels. We would get everybody the best camel possible. Anyway, who's to say which camel is best? We can't handicap them like horses. If that's the way it's going to be, then absolutely no. The Albanians said they were finished with the matter. Then we promised to get them the best camel we could get our hands on. We guaranteed to do our best to see that they were competitive. The Albanians said maybe—maybe yes, maybe no. Finally, they called today and said no: they will not be participating in the

201

race. There is a conspiracy against them, they say." Aziz shook his head in disgust and looked skyward in a mock appeal to Allah.

The reporters and photographers all laughed—not so much at the mule-headed Albanians as at themselves for being so stupid as to think history was going to start at a press conference. They all knew this was caca, manure, but there wasn't anything they could do about it.

Aziz grinned, amused at himself for getting so sore at paranoid Albanians. It was a charming moment, wonderful for photographers who were alert, and they all were; the adrenaline fairly squirted among the reporters and photographers.

Aziz held up his finger. "But let it be recorded before councils of just men that Jebel Tarik upheld its end of the bargain. We retained the services of an army lieutenant from Niger to tutor the Albanian. This is an experienced rider. Plus we leased the services of a camel that, by the way, placed second in the annual camel races staged by the army of Niger, and we went to all the expense and effort to fly them here from Niger. Now then . . ."

Muhammad Aziz's face was colored. He waggled his finger at the journalists. ". . . I am a man of my word. I promised you Albania will be in the race. Albania will race. If the people of Albania had been asked—as they were not, as we all know—they would surely have sent a rider." Aziz paused. "Therefore, as a gesture of solidarity with our Muslim brethren in Albania, the People's Republic of Jebel Tarik will select a rider for Albania. We want to be fair about this, so we've decided to hold a shooting contest to determine the rider. The details will be published in *The Gibraltar Chronicle* tomorrow, and we'll hold the contest on Saturday. Everybody is invited to compete. The winning shooter will ride for Albania. We will furnish the camel and teach the shooter how to ride."

The reporters bobbed up and down like pistons in some bizarre machine. They either stood immediately and waved their hands, then sat, not wanting to appear too pushy, or sat and waved their hands, then stood, still waving. The camel story was getting good.

"You ladies and gentlemen are welcome to cover the shooting to assure the Albanians that we're doing the best we can to make sure they have the best rider in Razzia." Muhammad Aziz turned the floor over to his press assistant.

There followed a tumble of questions.

17

THE TELLY WAS on, but with the sound turned off, in the Debbie and Harold Fielding household on Wednesday afternoon. Mrs. Fielding, assisted by her stolid, pipe-smoking husband, spread maps of Gibraltar across their dining room table and considered the problem of retaking Gibraltar.

The colorful blimps were a momentary diversion for television. The BBC was doing a story on the blimps that had been contracted by the American television networks to provide aerial coverage of Razzia. They were all hiring European blimps, now that they'd been able to buy television rights. Blimps! Mrs. Fielding preferred stories about Puking Max. It was almost as though she had equated Max's survival with her own as prime minister. She was convinced that Max was still alive, and whenever the cameras began panning the maquis where he was allegedly hiding, she turned up the sound with her remote.

The Arabs kept telling the reporters that Max was dead, but the Gibraltarians, who were still leaving food out at night, still reported it gone the next morning. Puking Max was very much alive, the Gibraltarians said.

Harold Fielding put the pencil down and tilted his head to adjust to the middle level of his trifocals. He had a natty, studious look about him. His hair spilled down over his ears like ivy at an old college. He dug at the bowl of his pipe with a neat little penknife. "I think I'll have a cup of tea. Would you like one?" Harold adjusted his comfortable old robe and padded off in his slippers to the kitchen. He nipped into the loo on the way.

"A little port might be nice. What it takes is a clear analysis of the problem and an imaginative solution. It's a very small place, really, hardly anything to it." She glanced at the telly: an Arab was riding a camel.

"What did you say, my dear? You know I can't hear you when—"

"Why don't you close the door when you have to relieve yourself, Harold?" Mrs. Fielding yelled. Her voice had an edge to it.

The door closed.

"I said Gibraltar's a very small place indeed!" she said loudly. "Hardly anything to it!"

The door opened, and a minute later Harold returned with his tea and a bottle of port for his wife. "I forget," Harold said. He poured her a glass of port, and checked the zipper on his trousers. "That comes from being raised in the country, I suppose."

"You sound as though you're using a fire hose. My word! Sometimes I wonder."

When Deborah Fielding was a little girl she'd gone through a period of fascination with the heroics of the British navy in its glory years—this followed her chess phase, in which she was the scourge of old men at the park. She used her collection of agates to represent various vessels in famous sea battles. Once, she had told her father she wanted to become a naval historian. Her father told her that was a noble ambition, but unfortunately impossible. There were no women naval historians, he said. Older men groomed younger chaps for what few appointments there were as naval historians. How on earth did she think she was going to crack that kind of monopoly? He told her to buck up, however. She was very clever and there was always a future for clever people.

Now that she was prime minister, Debbie Fielding, infuriated, if not downright disgusted by the indecision and bickering among her military advisers, decided to have a go at the Gibraltar problem herself. After all,

Winston Churchill had a love of maps and maneuvers, why not Deborah Fielding?

Harold refilled his pipe out of a leather pouch so old it was worn shiny. He refilled and lit up. The room was filled with the aroma.

"Oh, that one smells good, Harold. Nice and sweet."

"Chap at the club recommended it. Regis. I've mentioned Regis. His gout's at it again." Harold puffed contentedly on his pipe; the sound was not unlike that of a hound smacking its chops in front of a comforting fire. Using the stem of his pipe for a pointer, Harold took another look at the classified plans for wresting Gibraltar back from the Arabs without furthering any Spanish claim to the colony. He had been made Almost Royalty, so he could look at classified documents. "Well, I don't know, luv. We've got the parachutists, but we talked about that. We've got the landing on Eastern Beach, but that would involve moving everything over France or around Africa. We've got American and Israeli fifth columnists."

"Charles Barbur says his people are literally the best he has. The Americans are literally waiting for us to tell them what to do. But Jackelforth is cautious."

Harold Fielding was a good *mmmm*er. He communicated by inflection. An *mmmm* that was a question rose like the curve of a bull market. A noncommittal *mmmm* was as straight as no-brain activity. When in Harold's opinion his wife was in danger of getting herself in trouble politically, these *mmmm*s dropped ominously in tone. There were intricate subtleties and variations on his *mmmm*s that only his wife understood. "Mmmm?" he asked.

"Jackelforth says that the Americans are unknowns, despite Barbur. Barbur would never admit to having bumblers on the Rock, would he?"

"Mmmmm."

"He says you can't trust them for an operation that has this much at stake. There are only two of them; if something happens to one of them, there goes fifty percent of their capability."

"Mmmmm." This *mmmm* dropped slightly. "Tea gets

to me." Harold shuffled off to the loo, this time shutting the door behind him.

When he got back, she said, "With maybe one exception, they aren't showing any imagination. If they had been this constipated in the Falklands, I hesitate to think what would have happened." She had ignored Harold's dropping *mmmm*. This meant either that she had already taken it into account or thought it was a stupid or jackass *mmmm*.

Harold never took offense at being ignored. His wife was the prime minister, after all. "What's the exception?"

"A plan submitted by Brigadier Tomlinson and the chaps over at Three Commando. The idea is for lads with light motorcycles to land here at Camp Bay and here at Little Bay. The Camp Bay detail goes north, taking the high streets. They do this very quickly on their bikes. All this talk about how their missiles and troops can be switched quickly from the border to the point or from the point to the border. The Three Commando chap says a bloke clever with explosives could hold things up for a while. I quite agree."

"Deep enough hole, I suppose."

"It's easier to shoot down on people, he says. The commando chaps get above them very quickly."

"Mmmmm. I should think."

"There really aren't many streets at all, and if you look carefully, they come together at key points. As Tomlinson sees it, the Camp Bay chaps keep the Arabs pinned from above, and the Little Bay lads free the Gibraltar regiment from under Europa Point. Instead of trying to mount a large and costly amphibious landing, we free the soldiers trapped under Europa Point and let them have a go at the Arabs."

Harold looked shaken. His teacup rattled. "You're looking right at Bobby Nye's Exocets!"

"We use Wellington-class Hovercraft. A Wellington will do fifty-eight knots, Harold; they're both quick and maneuverable."

Harold was not convinced. "You mustn't forget the missiles, Deborah. You mustn't."

"Harold, you have the same problem as Jackelforth, who doesn't like this either, by the way, and for the same reasons. Hear me out, please. Nye will have to move his missiles on the Mediterranean side because of the American Sixth Fleet. What Tomlinson says we need is for the Spanish to fake an attack from the north."

Harold looked surprised. "I thought you didn't want to deal with the Spanish."

"Harold, the Spanish don't want us to win, do they? They want us to lose. We move the fleet into the Strait of Gibraltar. What do they do when they see us moving to attack?"

"You're the P.M., luv. I hide out in the British Museum all day." Harold Fielding was a gentleman archivist at the British Museum; that is, he was given the title of archivist but never actually worked. In fact, he spent most of his time at the track or getting pissed with his pals at the club.

Deborah took a sip of port. "I say they'll gather their troops at the border to watch the fight. If it looks like we're going to win, they'll attack at the last moment and lay equal claim to Gibraltar. Remember, this is how Russia got Sakhalin Island: after Harry Truman dropped the bomb, Stalin bravely invaded Japanese Manchuria. If it looks like we're going to lose, they'll make a halfhearted attempt to cross the airport and retreat with a minimum of casualties."

"To strengthen their future claim no matter what."

"Exactly. Spanish blood has flowed on behalf of Gibraltar, they'll say. So when Bobby Nye sees Spanish tanks lining up on the border, what will he think, Harold?"

Harold gestured with the stem of his pipe. "He'll think we made a deal to give Gibraltar to the Spanish for their help in evicting Arabs."

"That's Brigadier Tomlinson's belief, and I agree with him. And Bobby Nye's response will be . . . ?"

"I'd say to reinforce the northern wall at the Moorish Castle there and load up the galleries on Mons Calpe."

Deborah Fielding grinned. "Well. You see how it goes." The prime minister leaned forward, studying the map, considering possibilities. She said, "Which leaves us, alas, at the mercy of Bobby Nye's Exocets."

"Mmmm. Yes, well . . ."

"They would be like the clichéd ducks in a pond."

"Mmmm."

"The Royal Navy chaps say Tomlinson may know his battle tactics on land, but his idea is out of the question. They said we would be lucky if any of the Hovercraft made it."

"Mmmm." Harold puffed rapidly on his pipe as a gesture of concern. "How on earth do they defend against those things? Did your navy chaps tell you that?"

"They can present a smaller target by turning their bow or stern toward the missile, and they can use chaff, they say. Chaff is the best, the more the better. They fire rockets that burst into metallic chaff to decoy the Exocet's radar guiding system. The hydrofoils are too small to carry troops and much in the way of chaff. They tell me if we tried to carry the chaff rockets in helicopters, the Arabs would use their Sea Wolfs to swat the helicopters like flies."

The colorful blimps were back on the television.

"For the want of chaff the war was lost. You'll think of something, luv." Harold Fielding had confidence in his wife. She was a clever woman and would come up with something.

The BBC chap was obviously telling his viewers about the colorful blimps. They had been looking at Dutch blimps. These were French.

Prime Minister Fielding, her mind on chaff rockets, was curious about the blimps. She used her remote to turn the sound up on the telly.

18

FROM THE MOMENT Razzia was announced, Prime Minister Deborah Fielding's advisers told her that the most propitious time for an invasion of Gibraltar would be at the scheduled start of the camel race. Even if the Arabs suspected an attack on that day—and they most likely did—they had committed their energy to the needs of the press, and so both their resources and attention would be stretched to the weakest since they had seized the Rock. The day following the race, security would inevitably tighten once again.

On Thursday morning, with ten days remaining before the Arab charity race, Mrs. Fielding requested a private meeting with 3 Commando's nervy Brigadier Harry Tomlinson and told him of her variation of his plan to attack the west slope in Hovercraft.

When she finished, Tomlinson blinked, astonished. "It's either disaster or it's brilliant, Prime Minister."

"What I want to know from you is, will it work technically, with the chaff rockets and all?"

"I can't imagine it wouldn't work, Prime Minister. We'd have to get some chaps at work designing mounts for the rockets."

"Consider the logic carefully, Brigadier."

"If you can convince the War Cabinet, I'll get the necessary volunteers."

"How long will it take you to train your lads on those things?"

"A week to do a proper job, although it could be done more quickly."

"The longer we wait, the more difficult it is to extricate ourselves from the Gibraltar fiasco. We've all agreed on this. British honor is at stake. If I rang you this afternoon and said, yes, I have the approval of the War Cabinet on this, how long would it take your chaps to get started? You said a week to train. I know how these things work. The next question is, how soon you can begin training?"

"This afternoon, ma'am."

"I don't want you to begin until I call, however. If you start before the meeting and somebody finds out, I'll be accused of pushing people around." Mrs. Fielding grinned. Of course she was going to push people around. The U.K. had to act.

"I'll wait in my office and keep my lines clear, Prime Minister."

"If we don't have the proper motorcycles, I want you to go out and buy them from dealers if necessary. Don't go through the bureaucracy. There'll be some fool at every level who will have some reason why it can't be done. I'll see to it that you get the cash to buy what you need. I want good new ones that work—Japanese if necessary."

"Yes, ma'am."

"I shall call by four."

Tomlinson smiled. "We'll have the lads doing wheelies on Suzukis by lunch tomorrow, Mrs. Fielding."

The War Cabinet met at three in Foreign Secretary Sir Ian Tovey-Rundel's house at No. 11 Downing—across the street from the prime minister's residence. The room was fusty and pungent with age and tradition. On the walls were first-edition histories, biographies, and autobiographies of British statesmen who had built the empire, and who had lost it, good reading for a foreign secretary on a rainy winter's night.

The seven-member War Cabinet included Mrs. Fielding; Sir Ian Tovey-Rundel; Sir Edwin Price, Tovey-Rundel's predecessor as foreign secretary, whose job it was to prepare papers for the War Cabinet (officially it was the Western Mediterranean Defense Group, but the acronym WMDG, pronounced Woomdig, was so awful it was never used); the home secretary, Michael Fearn; the defense secretary, Roger Jackelforth; Chief of Defense Staff Sir

Nicholas Facer; and the Cabinet Office head of foreign and defense liaison, Robin Crumbley.

They sat around a table sipping small glasses of sherry, although Crumbley, an ostentatious abstainer, drank tea. Each had a summary of proposed actions, together with estimates of strengths and liabilities—both from a military and a political standpoint. There were four main proposals: an attack by parachute; infiltration by frogmen and commandos; an amphibious landing from the Mediterranean; a helicopter landing at Europa Point.

In addition there was a fifth proposal, a new version of Brigadier Tomlinson's quick strike that the War Cabinet had discarded earlier after giving up on the thorny problem of how to keep the Hovercraft from being blown out of the water by Exocets fired at virtually point-blank range. There was also a reluctance to go to the Spanish hat-in-hand, asking please would they fake an attack from the north.

"And whose is this?" Mrs. Fielding asked. She reread the new proposal and arched one eyebrow, a sign that she was very curious indeed. All proposals forwarded to the War Cabinet for consideration were required to identify the sponsor in case there were questions that needed to be answered quickly. The sponsor of the new variation of the Tomlinson proposal was not identified. "Sir Edwin? Surely, you must know."

Sir Edwin Price blinked and cleared his throat.

Her advisers and officers looked at one another. Nobody had any idea.

"A joke, I think," said Roger Jackelforth, the defense secretary.

The prime minister reread the mysterious new proposal. "What do you think of it, Roger?"

One hand at his necktie, Jackelforth looked at the proposal again. "Well, it . . . I think. I think it's a joke. Who did write this?" He looked at the others.

"The question again, who is the author? Perhaps it was the gentleman who served the sherry," Mrs. Fielding said.

211

Nobody said anything.

"Of course the whole thing's absurd on the face of it. Outrageous," said Jackelforth.

"Really?"

"Of course," said Jackelforth.

"Although I'm annoyed that the sponsor won't speak up, I think it has merit," Mrs. Fielding said.

Jackelforth said, "Prime Minister, I don't think it makes any difference who modified the plan. The additions to Tomlinson's proposal are based on a reading of Spanish and Arab minds. A misreading in either case would be disastrous. We have a fleet involved, so there will be no element of surprise. Under the circumstances, we have little else to do but mass as much firepower as possible at their weakest spot and land troops and suffer the consequences."

Debbie Fielding had a stubborn set to her face. "There were two problems with Tomlinson's original plan, Roger: having to deal with the Spanish, and Bobby Nye's Exocets. As I recall, the critical issue was the lack of chaff. That appears to be solved here."

"If it doesn't work, my God, you'd have those lads out there naked. I'd hate to take the responsibility."

"There is a catch, remember, a way out with minimum losses. We'll have ambulance boats standing by to pluck the lads out of the water. Roger, would you be willing to try this up to the bail-out point? If it doesn't work, then we can turn to one of the other plans as we see fit."

"Please . . ." Jackelforth looked around the table for support. His colleagues were staring at their cuticles.

"There are times one uses one's imagination. What better time to try it than this? What better time, I ask you, Roger? Show you anything different, anything with a hint of imagination, and what do you do?" Fielding's voice rose. She waggled her finger at the embarrassed Jackelforth. "You defended Gibraltar primarily from a sea invasion and allowed Arabs to walk in and take it over. Now we're back to it again, aren't we? If we revert to the same old ways this time, it will cost us very heavily indeed. We're talking about the lives of British marines and the

212

Gibraltarians we were supposed to protect and didn't. They've got every right to be angry with us, and I will not put their lives at risk if I can help it. I refuse. I will not. Everything that's in there applies to this problem. The use of Hovercraft, everything."

"Mrs. Fielding, I—"

Deborah Fielding wasn't finished. She cut him off. "No, you listen, Roger. All of you listen." She looked around the table. "You're afraid of being laughed at. Isn't that right? Isn't that the truth? Speak up, now, if that isn't the truth." She looked around the table again, but more slowly, looking each member of the War Cabinet straight in the eye.

Nobody said anything.

"As I understand it, we at least had the foresight to see to it that the pilots and crews were working for us in case we needed them. Isn't that so?"

"Well, yes, Mrs. Fielding, the crews are Royal Navy."

"Then why wouldn't this work?"

Jackelforth colored and laughed nervously. "Mrs. Fielding . . ."

"Then it might be done, mightn't it?"

Jackelforth cleared his throat.

"The truth is, this really is our best hope, isn't it? The losses involved in any of the other alternatives would bring down the Conservative government."

Nobody said anything.

"If we give the American agents a little notice, perhaps they'll show a little imagination in helping us out. President Barbur says they're very clever and skilled. Also, I think we should allow the BBC to televise this along with everybody else. There is something unseemly about all the hotels in France being booked solid by Englishmen wanting to watch Razzia on television. A camel race is one thing, but I don't want it said that we kept military action from the British telly when everybody else in the world was watching."

"They're paying for the battle. They might as well watch it on the telly," said Jackelforth.

Deborah Fielding clenched her jaw and narrowed her

213

eyes. Roger Jackelforth was being deliberately surly. Everybody in the War Cabinet knew this meant he was positioning himself to take over Mrs. Fielding's job. Jackelforth, in short, was gambling on debacle. "You're thinking this is a scheme worthy of the Chevalier d'Arcon, don't you, Roger? Doomed to failure."

"When a prime minister bypasses command and has a chat with a brigadier, word gets out, no matter how careful the brigadier." Jackelforth pressed his lips together.

"You know the consequences if I'm right and you're wrong, don't you? It's not too late to work together on this. I want to try this plan up to the fail-safe point. If we have to back off, we have to back off."

The War Cabinet voted to approve Brigadier Tomlinson's plan, with precautions understood. If the Tomlinson plan failed, the Royal Navy would mount an air strike on the Europa Point missile sites to support a helicopter landing on Europa Point. Once the Strait of Gibraltar was safe for passage by the Royal Navy, an amphibious landing would follow at Catalan Bay and Sandy Bay on the Mediterranean side.

The Company rep in Algeciras timed Ara Schott's Thursday split to coincide with the muezzin's midday call to prayer. Although the messages were scrambled, the Mazumo was a field device, not a maximum security transmitter or receiver, so Ara Schott had written a very special message he knew Ella Nidech and Burlane would easily translate.

WILL BOOGIE AT THE CARNIVAL. (The British would attack during Razzia, Nidech understood.) FROGGIES GO WALTZING ON AIR WHEN GARY TOOK HIS WALK. (Frogs? The *French*? No, it must mean amphibious. British Hovercraft! Gary Cooper faced down the bad guys at high noon.) BELIEVE BAD GUYS WILL BOOGIE NORTH TO GREET BOB'S BOYS. ALL HOO HOO. (The Spanish prime minister's first name was Roberto. The Arabs would go north to meet a fake attack by the Spanish.) FROGGY ONES ON MCQUEENS GO HIGH: SOUTH PAVILION ROAD; GREEN LANE; QUEEN'S LANE. (Nidech looked at her map. Steve McQueen rode motorcycles. The first detail would land at Camp Bay and go north on motorcycles to the high ground above the Arab howitzers and missiles at the Moorish wall.) FROGGY TWOS BOOGIE ONE STEP SOUTH, GO DIGGING FOR HELP. (A second detail would land at Little Bay and free the British regiment under Europa Point.) GRAND LADY SAYS EXTREMELY URGENT THAT BAD GUYS NOT BE ALLOWED TO BOOGIE SOUTH. NEED LANES CUT. (If the Arabs were able to respond to the south, the Royal Marines might be pushed back into the bay.) ALL BEST FROM GRAND LADY, EVERYBODY HERE.

The "grand lady" was Deborah Fielding, of course. Nidech unfolded her map of the Rock completely. The key to the plan was an attack or a fake attack from the north by the Spanish. Had the Spaniards changed their position and agreed to help the British? Nidech was surprised.

Theoretically the plan made sense. But how did Mrs. Fielding and her admirals figure on dodging Bobby Nye's Exocets while Her Majesty's Navy positioned its vessels for the attack?

Nidech wondered what the British officers thought of an operation that might be televised live in both Europe and America. That could happen with all the television people assembled to cover Razzia. In the past, civilized admirals and generals in all armies had always come to a consensus on a scapegoat so as to soften the harsher judgments of history. This was considered a gentlemanly, courteous thing to do—a fraternal tradition.

Ella Nidech knew James Burlane would have received the same message. The delicate couple had work to do. Nidech set the Mazumo's transmitter to Burlane's frequency and sent a squirt:

METHINKS WE NEED TO MEET, CLAUSEWITZ.

19

WITH A NOTE from Dr. Maskill in his pocket directing him to take an afternoon walk to "expand his lungs"—and with a copy of *The Gibraltar Chronicle* under one arm —James Burlane set out to meet Ella Nidech in Alameda Gardens. Burlane insisted on composing the note himself, although Maskill wrote it so that the handwriting would be correct. Burlane had him add the French phrase, *aux grands maux les grands remèdes*—desperate diseases need desperate remedies.

Burlane left St. Bernard's in his Larry Schoolcraft outfit: chinos, old penny loafers, a veteran cotton shirt, tie askew, old sweater, tweed jacket, binoculars around the neck, sleek black walking stick. This could be quite effective in the British Commonwealth, hinting as it did of public school casual. In the United States it would be considered Yalie Gone to Seed.

He was getting stronger and no longer coughed; in fact. He practiced bird calls as he walked. He took Prince Edward's Road to Trafalgar Cemetery, then strolled south on Red Sands Road; this was uphill from a housing estate, and level with the Alameda Parade. Although there were low bleachers on the far side, Her Majesty's Regiment didn't spend all its time marching, and so the parade was usually a large parking lot.

Burlane walked on the bay side of the street, and just as he drew near the bottom terminal to the tram that went to the peak of the Rock, Ella Nidech stepped up from the stairs descending to the housing estate.

"I've been watching. You're clear, as close as I can tell," she said.

"Shall we take a little walk, then?"

216

They crossed the street, passed the fire station, and turned left up the short, narrow road to the monumental phallus, a bust of General George Augustus Elliot—who masterminded Gibraltar's defense in the Great Siege —sitting upon a marble column. They stood and looked up at Elliot. They walked uphill into the shadow of large trees in the park.

"If their plan works and the Arabs take the Spanish feint . . ." He was lost in thought.

"Bobby Nye would deploy his people north and south."

"Leaving the town open for us."

Nidech said, "There's no reason for them to leave anybody in town. But if they hear somebody driving around in here, you can bet they're going to check it out."

"We have to cut the streets in three places, as I see it."

"That's how I see it."

"But we have to cut all three. If we leave just one street open, it could be disaster for the British. By the way, do you by any chance know how to ride a camel?"

Nidech looked surprised that Burlane would ask such a stupid question. "Of course I can ride a camel. Can't everyone? A man in Baghdad taught me how. I was there to dance."

"You know a camel doesn't make a whole lot of noise. No internal combustion engine or any of that. And they can climb stairs." Burlane unfolded the *Chronicle*. "Have you been reading about the contest for someone to ride a camel for Albania? They're going to hold a shooting match Saturday morning. I've done a little shooting."

Nidech laughed. "Talk about a ringer! I just bet you'd get the hang of camel riding too, wouldn't you?"

"I'm a fast learner, ma'am."

"Are you well enough?"

"I've been hiking back and forth in the hallway at the hospital, and taking laps up and down the stairs. I can do it."

Nidech said, "I can steal the explosives and timers. They don't think I can do anything except roll my belly."

217

"Chippy Chipolina can get me the drill and bit extensions I'll need. We want to get those charges as deep as we can. Say, did you ever get inside the Continental Hotel?"

"I thought you'd never ask. Once, with Boris."

"You did?"

"Only for a few minutes. It was in and out again. Some men in the lounge were watching an American news program on television."

Burlane looked shocked. "They were being tortured? Right out there in the open? That's barbarous!"

"One of them was taking notes," Nidech said, as though Burlane had said nothing unusual.

"I think our mystery man is named Leonid Borodin, but I haven't received any confirmation from Ara. The Russians are getting to be worse than mosquitoes. Everywhere you turn, there they are, the bastards." James Burlane whistled *trit, trit, trit! Weet, weet, weet! Trit-weet, trit-weet, trit-weet!*

Three years earlier, a man had shown up on Jim Quint's doorstep in the District of Columbia asking if Jim would like to have breakfast with the Big P occupant in the White House.

Breakfast with President Charles Barbur? Quint was not wealthy. He had no connections. If the president wanted an author, he would get himself Paul Theroux or Mary Gordon or somebody who counted. One morning when Quint was high on hashish and rolling on an outrageous Humper Staab, he had fallen in love for a couple of hours with Mary Gordon. This burst of emotion was based on a review of one of her novels and her photograph on the front page of *The New York Times Book Review*. Such a good-looking woman, and a talented novelist to boot! Groan. Alas, Quint's entertainments were for the beach.

Quint knew he was going to be called upon to do something odious. Still, he said yes, thinking: maybe it'll be a surprise breakfast for authors and Mary Gordon will be there, a closet Humper Staab fan.

The president and Jim Quint had their breakfast and chat in a wonderful little room back in the White House that was off limits to tourists. This was the private White House, where Lyndon Johnson had once let sweet farts and drunk his morning coffee, and where Richard Nixon, eating cottage cheese with ketchup on it, had contemplated the siege of his administration.

Quint tried to memorize every detail so he could have Humper Staab eat breakfast with the president also.

Over eggs Benedict, and lovely little melon balls in a syrup, the jolly president had gotten directly to his point. The president said the government would like to use Jim Quint's identification as an author and journalist as cover for a "Company field representative" on a mission of "grave importance" to his countrymen.

Most of what Barbur had to say, he said without saying anything. His face and the tone of his voice said: Look, I know this is chickenshit, but you have to trust me; if this wasn't for the larger good of the country, I'd have called you on the telephone.

Jim Quint, unable to say no to the affable Barbur, sighed and said yes.

While the real Quint was hanging out in Jamaica, his journalist friend Bob Steele had been riding the Trans-Siberian Express to an arms signing in Vladivostok. On the train, he had met a tall, disheveled man who was calling himself Jim Quint and telling stories about growing up in Bison, Montana. On the last night before Vladivostok, Steele had blundered onto the American spy shooting two Russians.

Now, at the spy's request, they were here, summoned by the American's apparent man Friday, a male nurse named Chipolina. He took them to Room 5 but stopped short of the door, saying, "I'll be in the hallway so you'll have your privacy."

A bird whistled inside the room.

"His name is . . . ?" Quint asked.

"Larry Schoolcraft."

A second bird began whistling.

"He writes books about bird calls," Chipolina said.

Quint and Steele went inside, where the man calling himself Larry Schoolcraft was doing push-ups. He stood and began mopping his sweaty forehead with a towel. His hair was tousled, as Steele had said it would be. To Quint he looked like a middle-aged Huck Finn. Still breathing fast from his exercise, he held out a long arm and said, "Larry Schoolcraft's my handle. Bison Jim Quint, my main man!" His eyes acknowledged the past. To Steele he said, "So, I pop up again. We spooks are everywhere, you know. We're fighting a war out here."

Schoolcraft said, "Sit, you two. Sit. Sit. I'm sorry I don't have a whole lot of furniture; the bed'll do for me." Schoolcraft hopped onto the center of the bed and sat squat-legged, while his guests sat in the two chairs in his room. "I bet you two've got it figured, haven't you: here it is, kismet, fate, that old flying fickle finger. I suppose there's no reason why we can't get straight to it. Bob, you jolly Brit?"

"No reason."

"Bison?"

It was obvious to Quint that Schoolcraft had no intention of going into the details of his ride on the Trans-Siberian. "Fine," Quint said.

Schoolcraft whistled *seebit seebit seebit titititi*. "Did Chippy tell you? I'm an expert on bird calls." *Seebit seebit seebit titititi*. "My books are in the valise there."

Quint opened the valise. He glanced at Schoolcraft's picture on the dust jackets and passed the books to Steele.

"Those are Schoolcraft's books with my picture on the dust jacket. You know, I saw you two by the side of the road when I was on my way here."

Quint said, "We thought about visiting you, but we didn't know what name to ask for." After this little display of the Company man's whistling skills, Jim Quint began to wonder about Larry Schoolcraft. Was he, by any chance? No, he couldn't be.

"They call me Schoolcraft the birdman." Schoolcraft whistled a pretty trill. "You two might be interested in my gear there in those two large numbers. Go ahead, open them up." Schoolcraft did imitations of excited sparrows while Quint and Steele opened the heavy latches to see the

220

receiving mirror for the parabolic, the fancy tripod, the lenses, cameras, and tape recorders.

"Ooof! Look at this, Bob," Quint said.

"My heavens!"

Quint said, "Do you people always carry all this gear with you?" His eyes were wide in disbelief. He was. Quint was sure of it now. Had to be.

"Almost never. This gear is called peeps, by the way."

"For the voyeur," said Steele.

"That's it," Schoolcraft said. "Jim, did you do any shooting when you were growing up out there in Montana? Most kids do, out there in the sticks. My folks gave me a twenty-two when I was eight years old." Schoolcraft hopped down from the bed, retrieved a black walking stick from the closet, and resumed his squat on the bed. He used the screwdriver of a Swiss army knife to unclip the metal caps on either end of the slender black stick. It turned out to be hollow, a tube. He gave the tube a whack against the metal rail of the bed and tossed it to Quint.

Quint aimed the tube toward the light on the ceiling and looked down the middle. "Oooh! A gun barrel! Lightweight."

"A barrel for a very special twenty-two. I put a weight on it and use a laser scope when I'm doing fine work, looping a slug into someone's eardrum, say. Makes 'em sit right up."

Quint looked at Schoolcraft with mock admiration. "Well, I'd think so. This is made of what?"

"A wonderful little alloy developed by a lady at Cal Tech. It's expensive, but I'm worth it. Hey, the taxpayers're springing, who cares how much it costs? Make 'em pay, I say." He laughed mischievously. "My employers commissioned a gunsmith to turn it into a special weapon for me. An artist deserves good equipment."

Quint turned the barrel toward the light again. The mirrorlike interior was neatly rifled.

"Let me show you something." Schoolcraft knelt at his opened gear cases and began removing various parts. It became clear that the skids on the underside of one case were in fact a wire stock for a rifle. He removed a black trigger guard from the inside of one handle, and so on, saying, "Isn't this a honey of an idea? Isn't this neat? Isn't this the damnedest thing you've ever seen in your life?" Then he assembled all the parts into a lethal-looking little rifle, saying, "Isn't this sweet how this works? See here how this goes? It works just like that, see? Full automatic if I want: *vvvvvvvtttt!* Screw on a silencer, and who's to know? Now let me show you something special."

Larry Schoolcraft suddenly restrained his enthusiasm. He looked up at Jim Quint and Bob Steele. He looked very serious indeed. "We've known from the start that the British weren't about to let the Arabs keep Gibraltar forever. Well, I have a colleague here in Gibraltar, and we've been asked to serve hors d'oeuvres at a little party to take it back." Schoolcraft's shoulders slumped. "The problem is that we need a little help, a few good men to maybe ambush some Arabs. This will be dangerous work." He looked from Bob Steele to Jim Quint. "This invitation comes from Prime Minister Deborah Fielding herself." Then he grinned. Of course they would help. He gave the harsh cackle of the American bald eagle: *kleek-kik-ik-ik-ik-ik.*

Quint said, "There's a question I have to ask you that, I . . . I think maybe Bob better not hear." Quint looked embarrassed. "Sorry, Bob."

"Oh, no. No problem. I'll step outside and have a chat with Chippy." Bob Steele joined Chipolina in the hallway.

Quint cleared his throat. "About the time I started writing these cockeyed Humper Staab thrillers, I fell in with a guy who had retired from the Company. We used to shoot the breeze once a week, and have a few. He had been a translator of Czech and Hungarian at Langley. Anyway, he started telling me these nutty stories about a legendary Company spook. He said the joke at Langley was that if this guy wasn't humping somebody, he was stabbing them. That's why I named my man Humper Staab. He said this agent was said to have been taken under by dysentery in Mozambique, but everybody at Langley thought that was an official rumor."

Schoolcraft smiled. "Your friend was naïve. Everybody at Langley has heard those stories. They also know the guy doesn't exist. He's a joke."

"I have to ask this because he's the model for Humper Staab. I want to know. You understand. Is your real name James Burlane?"

Larry Schoolcraft burst out laughing. "Me?" He looked incredulous at the stupidity of the question. "Oh, come on. Get serious." He waved Jim Quint away with his hand and yelled, "You can come on back now, Bob."

20

THE SHOOTING TRYOUTS for the Albanian camel rider were held on Eastern Beach, and it was there that James Burlane joined the hopefuls. He wore brown contact lenses, black hair, and a mouthpiece that made him look as if his teeth were a tangle of cypress roots. The mouthpiece, which changed the shape of his face, made him sound as though he were Flem Snopes doing imitations of Marlon Brando's godfather.

The man called Leonid—the mysterious Borodin, Burlane was sure—was slouched in a canvas director's chair watching the prospective riders for Albania line up, his feet tucked up on the rungs. He wore Nike running shoes, fashionable blue jeans, and a light gray sweat shirt. An English-speaking Arab had been assigned to oversee the competition among the volunteers, but Leonid was obviously in charge.

Leonid's trio of toadies stood back respectfully. He was a master, they apprentices. He was casual and confident. They were a bit stiff, perhaps a trifle insecure.

The line was a beaut, but Burlane, who ordinarily hated lines and crowds, did his best; his aversion to crowds came from his having grown up in eastern Oregon where a man had the privacy by God to take a leak or scratch his nuts anytime he felt like it. He waited in line behind a young Gibraltarian, who was eager to try his hand at the firing range.

Burlane listened as the Arab asked the Gibraltarian his name, his age (twenty-two), his occupation (mechanic), his experience as a camel rider (none), his experience as a shooter (none), why he wanted to represent Albania in the camel race (unstated—fame), and his address and telephone number on Jebel Tarik.

The Arab was not quick with a pencil, which Burlane thought irritated Leonid. When the Arab finished, he looked up at the Russian.

Leonid nodded.

The Arab handed the man a heavy target rifle. "Five prone. Five standing."

"Which?"

"Fire from your belly first, then you stand up," the mystery man said.

The Gibraltarian started to get on his stomach, not knowing for certain what to do.

Burlane, laconic in his hillbilly/godfather mode, said, "I believe Ah'd sprhed mah legs if it twas me. Sprhed yoah legs. Elbows on the ground. Cheek agin' the stock. Then y'all put the sling unduh your arhm and over yoah hand. Let the sling hold it, not yoah hand."

The Gibraltarian, who had struggled to understand Burlane's muffled southern lingo, said, "Thank you." Burlane had such a mouthful of awful teeth that nobody wanted him to say anything.

Leonid watched Burlane as the shooter did his best prone first, then standing. The scores, called back in, were not good.

It was Burlane's turn.

The Arab said, "Name?"

"Obadiah Jones. Ah'm foaty-foah yeahs old, it's so but Ah'd be surhprised if any of yoah volunteahs can outshoot me or outrhide me." Burlane snaked his tongue out over his cypress-roots Obadiah Jones teeth and licked his lips. He laughed, "Heaugh, heaugh, heaugh!"

224

Leonid grinned at the colorful southerner.

The Arab had a form to complete. "Occupation?"

"Ah think unemployed is the word at prhesent, but Ah reckon Ah'c'n hit a coon's ass at two hundred yahds without stirh'n' the fuh. That's if youah lookin' for shootahs. Heaugh, heaugh." James Burlane sounded as if he were trying to talk with a mouth full of dog turds. Burlane was running what he called a spook's riff, a jazz improv of the secret world. Obadiah Jones was Burlane's rube riff, the amiable southern redneck dumb shit. If Burlane's adversary regarded Obadiah Jones as one brick short of a full load, well then, advantage Burlane.

The Arab clearly didn't like the idea of some out-of-work American participating in the contest, especially this insane-appearing individual.

Burlane continued amiably: "Ah had me this place outside of Charhleston, but Ah sold it. Got me a little fritterin' money. Always had a hankerin' to take a trip to Europe to see the ruins and castles. Wanted to ride me a gondola and stuff. Heaugh, heaugh." He pronounced it You-rope, two syllables.

The Arab didn't know what a "place" was in this context. He glanced at Leonid. The Arab didn't want the Russian to let Obadiah Jones participate.

"Ah was in the hospitahl when this all happened. Ah'm okay now, but Ah have to hang around for tests and to take these shots in the rhump. Ah got a puhmission slip from Doc Maskill." Burlane whacked himself on the rear with the palm of his hand. "Heavens, y'all want a good shootah to ride for them Albanians, Ah'm yoah man. My great-granddeddy fought with old Jeb Stuarht."

Leonid nodded his head yes, let Obadiah Jones take his turn.

Reluctantly, the Arab handed Burlane the target rifle.

"Slack out'n the triggah?" Burlane asked.

Leonid said, "They say it's been adjusted, the trigger and the sights."

James Burlane—thinking about Leonid's straight, clear American English—settled into the prone position, took a good breath, paused, slowed his pulse, snapped a

225

shot during the lull between heartbeats, then four more, in a dirge of a rhythm, following the lulls. Then he stood, keeping his left elbow down, right elbow high. Again he took a breath, paused, concentrated on biofeedback, and snapped out a lead shot, followed by four more in an unhurried roll.

When he finished he waited for the scores. All bulls. All dead center.

Eyes wide, the Arab looked at Leonid.

Leonid said, "Where did you learn to shoot like that, Mr. Jones?"

"Shootin' 'coons," Burlane said. "Ah' c'n ride a hoahse, too. Had me a couple out on the place. Had me a big old stud named Bodan. What a hoahse! Reckon Ah' c'n learn how to hold on to a camel. Ah do promise to do mah best to make them Albanians proud, y'all c'n bet on that."

Leonid turned to the Arab.

"Sir?"

"This is our man. Obadiah Jones. He will ride and shoot for Albania."

The Arab looked surprised. "An American, sir?"

"He shot a perfect score, didn't he?" The mystery man said to Burlane, "You won't mind participating in Prime Minister Aziz's press conference this evening, will you, Mr. Jones?"

"Oh, hell no. Obadiah Jones'll give 'em a show if y'all want. Heaugh, heaugh."

"Ahh, good. Then the prime minister will present you with your rider's pin on behalf of the People's Republic of Jebel Tarik."

"Ridah's pin?"

"For your lapel, Mr. Jones. Every rider gets a pin in the shape of the first letter of his country. In your case that will be a bright red *A,* for Albania."

"A scahlet lettah? Foah me? All right!"

The mystery man and James Burlane, grinning broadly, swung their right hands high and shook, thumbs up. "And yoah name is . . . ?" Burlane asked.

"You'll begin your lessons in the morning—from a Nigerian army lieutenant. That's Niger, not Nigeria."

"Ah'll do my damnedest."

"You'll be getting some real exercise in the next few days. You should do a little running before you go to bed tonight. You got yourself some shoes?"

"Fact is ah shoot bettah in mah barh feet. Didn't have no shoes when Ah was a young'n. Heaugh, heaugh, heaugh." James Burlane flashed his impossible mouthful of Obadiah Jones teeth.

Stuart Kaplan and the foreign ministers of Albania had never been amiable old partners, it might be said. Despite the late Enver Hoxha's most passionate slogans and fervent pledges of socialist progress, to Kaplan's knowledge horses never did sing in Albania, nor did pigs fly. Those were Kaplan's minimal standards for sainthood as he understood the term. All he knew was that the Albanians remained one of the most isolated, pissed-upon people on the planet.

Now then, the foreign minister of Yugoslavia, Albania's neighbor, called to say that his Albanian counterpart, yet another Hoxha, but with an unpronounceable given name, would please like a word with the American secretary of state. The Albanian was apparently there, at the Yugoslavian's side, demanding the telephone.

Kaplan—suspecting as he opened his mouth that he was about to do something stupid—said yes.

The Albanian foreign minister shrieked oaths in Serbo-Croatian and other languages, sputtering as he did.

A smooth, suave voice cut in: "Mr. Hoxha says good evening, Mr. Kaplan. He says Palestinians, umm, he says Muhammad Aziz sucks the penises of hogs."

The Albanian made sucking sounds into the telephone. He began yelling again. Kaplan furrowed his brow and held the receiver back to spare his ear the ranting.

The well-mannered translator returned, determined to pursue the course of civility. "Mr. Hoxha said that while Albanians and Americans have not talked much in the past, which is, umm, your fault, as is internationally acknowledged. Lizard snot"—the translator coughed softly—"et cetera, I believe would cover it. Mr. Hoxha

227

said Albania has plenty of marksmen specially trained to, umm, hit capitalists right between the eyes, but he doesn't have any to, umm, fuck around, I believe the American phrase would be, on Gibraltar. And he adds, umm, right between the eyes of Yugoslavians, too, and the Russians, and Chinese, and the Italians and Greeks. Right between all their, umm, fucking eyes, sir."

Kaplan realized that the Albanian foreign minister was drunk. The Albanian had been drinking with the Yugoslavian foreign minister, and had demanded to talk to the Americans. Kaplan grinned. He thought the translator was a kick. "Well, I see . . ."

The smooth translator said something to Hoxha.

Hoxha entered into an even longer tirade.

Kaplan, amused, listened patiently.

The translator said, "Mr. Hoxha made several references to what he believes is an Arab affection for, umm, sex with various animals, sir. Hippos and ducks, I believe he mentioned. To answer your question, what he says is that Muhammad Aziz never once contacted Albania about any camel race. He says Aziz's whole story is a damnable lie. He mentioned, umm, sucking pig penises again, lizard, ahh, phlegm, and said good luck."

"Good luck?"

"Yes, sir. Mr. Hoxha said, 'Tell my American comrade, good luck!' Those were his very words, sir."

"Well, tell him thank you! Tell him to call again whenever he feels the urge. No problem." Was this to be the unlikely beginning of some kind of breakthrough in the Balkans? The thawing of Albania? Kaplan grinned at the thought.

The Yugoslav came on the line again. "Thank you, Stuart. I'm sorry to surprise you like this, but he insisted. He hates the Russians but loves their vodka. He's furious at Muhammad Aziz."

"Can we talk now?"

"He's been, umm, taken under, Stuart."

Kaplan mimicked the wonderful translator, "He passed out then?"

228

"Yes, he has, I'm afraid to say." The Yugoslav sounded melancholy.

Kaplan burst out laughing. "Well, that's one for my memoirs. The call from the drunken Albanian. A thaw in Albanian-American relations."

"We do the best we can with the Albanians, Stuart. Our border surrounds them on three sides. They're paranoid. I'm able to talk to this one until he drinks too much vodka, then it's impossible. Talk to people, I tell him; you'll be surprised. Get a little trade going. People like a little comfort; you'd be surprised how they respond. I say, listen: old Karl, well, his heart was in the right place; we're not saying he's a fraud or anything. The same with Lenin. But they were off a little on their predictions, I tell him. We're marketing a cheap little car in the United States. We figured if the South Koreans can do it, why not us? Give the workers a little incentive there. Make bread toasters or something. You know what he said? Toasted bread is capitalist decadence; we'll never make bread toasters. Stuart, I've been telling you for years they're crazy. Can you imagine having to deal with people like that? Can you?"

Stuart Kaplan, who had to deal with President Charles Barbur every day, said nothing.

The squirt from Ara Schott came during the Saturday afternoon call to prayer. James Burlane's watch gave the alarm three seconds after the first *"La illa il-Allah"* echoed past the hospital. Burlane used his thumbnail to pop the back of the Mazumo and watched as Schott's report scrolled up:

CHINESE, SCHEHERAZADE: LEONID ILYICH BORO-DIN, THIRTY FIVE CITIZEN OF THE USSR: BA, AMERICAN HISTORY, GEORGETOWN UNIVERSITY; MA, TELECOM-MUNICATIONS, UCLA; PH.D, AMERICAN STUDIES, YALE UNIVERSITY. BORODIN'S FATHER, ILYA, AN AIDE AND CLOSE FRIEND OF ANATOLY DOBRYNIN, WAS EM-PLOYED AT THE SOVIET EMBASSY IN WASHINGTON FOR THE THIRTY YEARS OF DOBRYNIN'S TENURE AS AMBAS-

SADOR TO THE US. WITH DOBRYNIN'S APPOINTMENT
TO THE POLITBURO, ILYA BORODIN RETURNED TO
MOSCOW; HIS SON FOLLOWED. LEONID BORODIN, A RUS-
SIAN YUPPIE, DOES PUBLIC RELATIONS FOR PREMIER
PETRSPISHKIN AND THE CENTRAL COMMITTEE OF THE
POLITBURO. FYI: COMPANY COMPUTERS, PRO-
GRAMMED BY IGNORAMUSES, REJECTED BORODIN AS A
SUSPECT BECAUSE HE IS A PUBLIC RELATIONS MAN.

21

JAMES BURLANE'S SHOULDERS and ribs complained when he
reached to shut off the alarm on his digital travel clock. He
lay back, wide awake. His muscles had settled into knots
during the night. First pneumonia, now camel rider's
thighs. He lay there thinking about camel saddles. The
sides of Burlane's terik saddle were so deep it was like
riding atop a four-by-four. His guru, Mahut Madaaua, said
the reason was that a rider's weight had to be distributed
lower down on a camel, on its ribs or shoulders. Direct
weight deformed the hump.

Burlane felt deformed for sure. He tried to move his
legs. The insides of his thighs were slabs of pain. He
wondered what would happen if he asked for a different
saddle on the grounds that Lawrence hardly had any hump
at all. It struck Burlane as possibly stretching things to call
Lawrence a camel at all. But he had seen the equally leggy
and humpless Saudi Arabian and Iranian entries, and knew
better. Madaaua said Lawrence was classy camel flesh.

Burlane counted three, gritted his teeth, and sat up,
his body protesting. He should have known. He creaked
down the hall to the shower, wincing with every step. He
was scheduled for the range in the morning and camel
riding with Mahut Madaaua in the afternoon. Burlane
would have to get loosened up for the shooting, especially

standing, and he didn't want to disappoint Mahut Madaaua by not giving his all.

When he was finished with his shower, he checked the coloring of his new black hair. He then exaggerated the slight turn of his nose with theatrical putty—gave himself a real beak. This was his Obadiah Jones nose, an original, Burlane felt, not just a Karl Malden copy. He applied a hint of makeup—just enough to alter his complexion slightly and to ensure that his nose and beard could take a close-up. He popped in his brown-tinted contact lenses and slipped his artificial teeth into place. Obadiah Jones was ready, although his mouth was a little sore from having to wear the teeth. He took his time walking from the hospital to the shooting range.

Burlane smiled to himself when he saw the crowd of reporters assembled at the shooting range. The photographers, glancing at light meters, adjusted portable reflectors. A bank of clouds was moving in and the photographers were anticipating diffused light. Burlane giggled when he saw the reporters begin moving in his direction, led by none other than Gerard Thompson, the network anchor at NBC, and his counterpart at CBS, Harry Gilchrist. Thompson and Gilchrist were accompanied by photographers who orbited the famous men like human moons.

Thompson got to Burlane first. "Mr. Jones! Are you ready for the range this morning?"

"Reckon Ah'll do my damnedest, although Ah didn't have any ghrits for breakfast. How about y'all? Heaugh, heaugh, heaugh." Thompson's two photographers taped his reply, one kneeling, one standing.

Harry Gilchrist was now upon them, saying, "Are you a bit sore today, Obadiah?"

The CBS cameramen joined in the drill of taping Obadiah Jones stretching his long arms. Burlane was then surrounded by photographers and reporters asking him questions. Burlane, grinning his aw-jeez-boys grin—his mouth tender from the apparatus that warped his face —allowed himself to be led to the firing line, where his Iranian range instructor waited.

An Iranian teaching an American how to shoot! The

press corps loved it. With cameras whirling, bathed in reflected light, Burlane took the custom-built Spoel-3 Belgian target rifle that was to be his for the contest, accepting the piece with as much stereotypical southern hick admiration as he could summon.

He was introduced to the Iranian, whose name was unpronounceable as far as Burlane was concerned.

"In contest, shoot you wery good," the Iranian said.

"Reckon Ah never did learn the rhight way to shoot. Ah just like to shoot's all. Heaugh, heaugh."

"Prone first position begin will we. So that. Adjust strap you how know, Mr. Jones?"

Burlane knew how to adjust the strap, but he said no so the Iranian would have something to do, and so the cameramen would have something to film. Then he allowed himself to be shown how to use it. When he got into the prone position, he put his elbow out to one side so the Iranian could tell him to put it under the rifle so that the bone of his arm supported the weight.

"Reckon good form makes things a whole lot easier," Burlane said. "You know, this feels nice, real nice." Burlane listened and followed directions in sighting in his Spoel-3 and adjusting the trigger pull to his liking.

Then came the practice shooting, with Burlane's instructor giving him directions in English that was so convoluted that Burlane mostly didn't understand. Burlane went into his sniper's trance—his heartbeat slowing, slowing. He put a couple in the outer ring on purpose, hit some bull's-eyes, then deliberately laid a couple right on the line. The Spoel-3 was dead-on accurate, a fine piece. "Left mah shootin' eye in bed this mawhnin'," he said.

"Fine, you'll do, Jones," the instructor said. "Breath no, you can't shoot when."

Burlane decided to give them a treat. He slowed his pulse again and *snap, snap, snap, snap, snap* —rhythmically, in the lulls between heartbeats—laid five in the bull, five so tight it was like Jimmy Stewart putting a shot through that coin in *Winchester '73*. "Heaugh, heaugh. Hey, theah, pahdnah, thank ya!" Burlane called to his firing instructor.

The Iranian beamed proudly for the cameras. See there, see how good my lessons are, his smile said: I tell the American man how to shoot; he shoots; he hits the bull's-eye. Iranians know how to shoot!

Burlane thought: Raghead, the Prophet Muhammad taught you how and what to eat and drink, and how to sleep, and when to wake up, and how to clean your ass, and how and when to pick your nose, how to wash your face, what to wear, how to walk and talk, and how and when and with whom to screw, yet your principal delight is the rifle. Burlane was dismayed by all the alleged prophets who had risen from the Middle East. He grinned and said, "Say, this Eye-rhan-ian fella shuah does know his shootin'."

The cameras turned to the proud instructor who said something that was apparently one-third English, two-thirds Farsi.

Burlane said, "Ahm just a old South Carolinah boy."

Gerard Thompson said, "Tell us how you learned to shoot, Obadiah."

"Muh deddy got me a BB gun when Ah was six and Ah practiced on sparras' eyes. Pretended they belonged to Yankees, you know. Heaugh, heaugh. On a bright day you could see the copper BB a loopin' through the blue. Poetic, sort of. Heaugh, heaugh." Burlane gave Thompson a goofy grin to show that he was properly contrite and had learned a lesson young people were not to repeat. "When Ah got a coupla years olduh he gave me a twennee-two and Ah went out aftah jays and squirrhels. Courhse that was a terrible thing, too, and Ah was wrong to do it."

"Times were different back then." Gerard Thompson was solemn.

"Ain't that the trhuth," Burlane said. "Ah hadn't picked up a gun in yeahs until Ah lucked out in the contest these nice folks was ahavin'. Ah guess it must be like ridin' a bicycle; once a fella learns, he nevah foahgets."

After target practice and lunch, Burlane reported to his riding mentor, Mahut Madaaua. It was obvious that Madaaua knew a lot about camels and was fond of them. Even if it was Burlane and not he who rode in the big race, Madaaua would share in the glory of victory.

233

"We rhide as one, a team," Burlane said. "Togethah. We win togethah. We lose togethah. We southerhn boys may have gone down in th' end, but Ah reckon ain't nobody ever said we went down easy."

When Madaaua heard the translation, he beamed and they shook. *"Oui!"* he said. That was a word he knew Burlane understood. Madaaua jabbered enthusiastically in Arabic.

The translator said, "Lieutenant Madaaua says the Albanian Flyer has stiff, uh, wings this morning. He says we will work twice as hard today. The more you practice, the faster you'll ride, Mr. Jones. You and the camel need to get to know one another."

"Oui!" James Burlane held his thumb up and tried to look eager. He mopped the sweat from his forehead. What a bum roll of the dice this was for a man just recovered from pneumonia. Mahut Madaaua was out of the Vince Lombardi school of preparation.

Ara Schott just could not believe it. No. It couldn't be. Just could not be. Was it possible? Behind those insane teeth?

He started changing channels looking for yet another interview with the colorful South Carolinian, Obadiah Jones. He found one. He popped a tape into his video tape recorder and punched the record button.

He looked at the black-haired man being interviewed and felt momentarily relieved. The poor man's teeth made it so he could hardly talk. It wasn't Burlane. Or was it? Burlane with his mouth twisted out of shape. Schott leaned close to the screen and put on his reading glasses. It was Burlane, right here on the Monday evening news. The teeth had made him almost unrecognizable. Schott turned the sound up as Burlane was replying to a question from Harry Gilchrist:

"Oh, shuah! Huntin' them coons is greaht spohut. A man gets hisself a old dawg and lights out into the swamp with a grin on his face and a pinta bouahbon in his pawket. Reckon that's one a life's sweetest pleasuahs."

Schott turned the sound off. Yes, it was Burlane

. . . Burlane, running hillbilly riffs behind those teeth. Ara Schott sighed, thinking that warping his face that way must be hard on Burlane's mouth. Some years earlier Burlane had been sent to a studio in New York where he had learned method acting. Burlane really got into his roles. If he was playing Obadiah Jones, James Burlane thought and felt Obadiah Jones; he was Obadiah Jones.

Schott turned off the television set and started looking for his shoes. Peter Neely would have to tell the president that his delicate man was appearing on television all over the planet. James Burlane wouldn't have entered the competition without a reason. Schott wondered just how James Burlane and Ella Nidech figured to use a camel to help the Royal Navy.

In his Gibraltar hotel room late that night, Jim Quint strode back and forth very dramatically, even grandly in his Arab getup. "Very Peter O'Toole, don't you think? Grim, tight lips. Squinting as if constipated. Much enigma there. A mysterious loner is me. An adventurer. What is this man all about? What drives him? The ladies out there eating popcorn want me to undo their skirts, Bob, want to grab my throbbing member." Quint narrowed his eyes and turned, twirling the skirts of his thobe. "Schoolcraft got us scuffy beards, too, so we'll really look like Arabs. To the attack, men! They say women like short beards like this. You use it for a whisk broom on their thighs."

"Dust off the lint there."

"Sure, dust off the lint."

"You're not writing your Humper Staabs now, Jim. This chap Schoolcraft's going to get us bloody killed, he is. You Americans're bloody nutters. I don't know why I have anything to do with you, I really don't. Bloody nutters is what you are! It's all because of California!"

"Tut, tut, Bob, I'm from Montana. Where's the stiff upper?" Quint tapped Steele on his lip. "Keep it up there, now, sharp as a plowshare."

"He's a sodding loony is what he is, dressing us up like Arabs. Arabs! Fine-looking Arab I am." Steele slapped his stout tummy with the palm of his hand. "When was the

235

last time you saw an Arab with one of these? Arabs eat boiled wheat, don't they? Couscous and so on. And that awful bread. Such a diet." Steele shook his head vigorously. "Eat with their hands. No wonder they haven't made any bloody progress in the world."

"You're a stout Arab, Bob, not fat. Remember that. There're stout Arabs; I've seen them. I see you as a merchant or a slave trader. It's not to worry anyway. No problem. Schoolcraft says they'll be under attack and too excited to notice. He said this was the way we beat George III, and he's right. It's your basic chickenshit-sit-back-in-the-weeds-and-ambush-people style. Made to order for us, Bob."

"If we pull it off, perhaps Charles and Di will have us pop over for tea. Maybe we could even meet Fergie."

"Do they give titles to heroic journalists? Will you be Sir Bob?"

"Let me understand this, Jim. Arabs on foot will have to take one of three flights of stairs to get to this route . . ."

"That will take the commandos directly to the high ground above the city and the Arab defenses at the Moorish wall. That's right, one for you, one for me, and one for Chippy Chipolina."

"We hide in the maquis and shoot the buggers as they come struggling up the steps."

"Until the guys on the motorcycles get by. But the guys on the motorcycles should be past before we have to shoot anybody, Schoolcraft says."

"What if we get in the way of those commando chaps zooming along? They're killers, you know? How do they know we're on the good side? Sure! We're a couple of writers running around with AK-47s."

"We won't wear these getups, for God's sake, and we'll have the flag. And once we're relieved we go hide in the brush . . ."

"Maquis."

". . . hide out in the maquis until all the shooting stops."

Bob Steele looked at himself in the mirror. "Well, I guess I can see where I might make an Arab. No merchant or slave trader, though. I see a wealthy sheik or some kind of an oil minister."

Steele had been a little boy in London during the blitz and so knew firsthand of the British courage that had seen his country through that awful time. There was no way he wasn't going to stand in there and shoot a few Arabs from ambush. Help Debbie Fielding out.

22

THE FIRST LADY rose to help President Barbur, but then saw that he had everything under control. "I'm glad you could make it," she said. "They haven't started yet. That man, that Frenchman . . . Henri. Colonel Henri Le Cocq. They had him on last night. Look, here he is again, Chuck."

"What'd he say?"

The sound came on again. ". . . amel in the race."

Mrs. Barbur lowered the sound with the remote. "You've certainly developed an interest in Razzia. They were just talking about Obadiah Jones's camel." She accepted a pineapple-and-black walnut sundae from her husband. "Mmmm. Thank you. That poor man. Those teeth. Isn't it terrible he didn't get them fixed when he was young?" The First Lady turned up the sound on Colonel Le Cocq.

". . . ride, as you can see," Le Cocq said. The camera turned to a man riding a camel.

"That's Obadiah Jones there," she said.

"He'll win it," the president said.

"Really? You think so, Chuck? Wouldn't that be fun?"

The camera cut to two Arabs watching the action. After conferring with the apparent teacher, the second Arab, using a hand-held microphone, relayed instructions to the rider. The second Arab was a translator.

Le Cocq described the action: "This man Mahut appears to be an organized instructor. He's very patient with Jones, who, incidentally, is a good student. Here the lieutenant's showing him how to roll with the movement of a pacing camel. The faster the pace, remember, the more the hump sways. A horse is far more stable and faster but less efficient over long distances."

"It doesn't look like it has much of a hump," said ABC's sports reporter, Bill Richards.

"That's why it's a good camel, Bill."

"They'll be going a lot faster than this, I imagine."

"This is a slow pace. They'll race at a hard pace. Mahut's starting Jones out at a slow pace. He did this yesterday too. He's teaching him the basics. When Jones is comfortable with the motion, the lieutenant will move him into faster speeds. Jones has to pay attention here. A camel has to know the rider is in control."

On the screen was a close-up of Obadiah Jones riding a light fawn camel. A long-legged, slender beast. It had a big nick taken out of one ear. The camera moved in on the nicked ear with Le Cocq still talking. "This nick was probably caused by a fight with another male. A camel can open its jaws very wide and literally put its mouth around an opponent's head." Le Cocq used his hands to demonstrate a wide-open camel's mouth.

The camera pulled back as Obadiah Jones slowed the camel for a return to his instructor. Richards said, "Both the instructor and the camel were originally contracted for an Albanian rider. For those of you who have just joined us, we're watching the Albanian rider, former South Carolina farmer Obadiah Jones, an old bulldog, and his instructor, Mahut Madaaua, who is a lieutenant in the camel corps of the country of Niger in the central Sahara. This is the camel Madaaua rode to a second-place finish last November in the annual army races at Agadem. The camel that placed first is being ridden on behalf of Niger by his fellow army lieutenant, Abdul Tessaoua."

"I told you it was a good camel," Henri Le Cocq said. The First Lady turned the sound down slightly with her remote. "Isn't this fun? They showed him on the firing range a little while ago. He didn't do too well at first, then he really started hitting them."

"Bull's-eyes?"

"They were saying he's a natural."

The president said, "I think I could go for another sundae."

Janet Barbur turned the sound up again, leaving her husband licking his lips. "Another one? Oh, Chuck!"

Richards said, "Tell us more about the evolution of this gait, Henri."

"Well, Bill, the camel doesn't have any natural enemies on the desert, so if it is left to him, he just walks a slow, steady walk, as Monsieur Jones is letting him do now. A desert is flat and one can see a long way. Evolution has provided the camel a walk that sacrifices maneuverability and stability for a long, efficient stride. In the walk, the feet on one side of a camel move forward almost simultaneously. A camel does not trot, as horses do. A horse, by the way, can usually pace slightly faster than he trots. Good, Monsieur Jones has his animal up to a slow pace again so we can see.

"The pace evolved from the walk. One has to whip a camel to make it pace. In the pace, the camel's feet land in a rhythm of back foot–front foot on one side, back foot–front foot on the other. In a slow pace the camel always has its weight on one set of lateral legs or the other. In both the long-legged camels and giraffes, the hind feet land well in front of the front feet in a fast pace; its footprints land in pairs rather than scrambled fours."

"Obadiah Jones seems to be getting the hang of it," Richards said.

"Indeed he does, Bill. The camel's weight shifts from side to side, although you'll notice that it compensates for this by keeping its neck low. There is less swaying in Monsieur Jones's terik saddle because he's sitting forward on the hump, but he has to help, too. He's a tall man. He has to squat low and allow himself to go with the rhythm of the camel."

"I think he looks good, don't you, dear?"

"He'd better pay attention to the Arab," the president said.

"This one's an army camel, Bill. He's been taught to steer with a stick. This is a very responsive camel, a bit of good fortune for a beginning rider."

The camera cut to Bill Richards. "In a few moments we'll be interviewing both Obadiah Jones, who has been selected to ride on behalf of Albania, and his instructor, Lieutenant Mahut Madaaua of Niger. Right now, a word from our sponsors."

The president said, "Hey, I forgot. I had them marinate kiwi fruit in light rum. We had some about a month ago, remember? Boy, they're good."

"I'll pass." The First Lady watched a troup of bikinied young women wiggling their sleek bodies to show how sexy and fashionable drinking diet beer made them. Then the handsome Mexican actor, Pedro Lunes, told the viewers how sexy and fashionable it was to make monthly payments on a new Ford.

Then it was back to Gibraltar for ABC's "continuing, live coverage of the racing event of the century."

The camera cut to Richards, who was standing in front of a black-haired, toothy man wearing a beaten old fedora. Richards said, "The man standing behind me is forty-four-year-old Obadiah Jones, an unlikely participant in this otherwise all-Arab race."

"Mahut says Ah'm gonna win it, and he's my padnah."

"What will be your strategy, Obadiah?"

"Reckon Ah c'n hit bull's-eyes if Ah put mah mind to it. As to mah camel and mah ridin', y'all'd be better off to ask coach. Heaugh, heaugh." Jones repeated a question to the translator, who communicated with Mahut Madaaua. The camera cut to Madaaua, who nodded gravely to the question that was being put to him, and replied in a mixture of French and Arabic.

In a voice-over, the translator said, "Lieutenant Madaaua said his camel would have won the race if it had

240

not been for a problem with cheating by Abdul Tessaoua, who, he says, took a shortcut. But this is an issue he prefers not to get into. He says this race will prove once and for all which camel is the fastest. To answer your tactics question directly, Lieutenant Madaaua prefers not to answer."

"He seems confident of his camel. Ask him what kind of student Obadiah Jones is?"

The camera cut to Mahut Madaaua, who glanced at Jones. Madaaua was very serious. He went into a long monologue in Arabic, which the translator solemnly rendered:

"He says Monsieur Jones is an excellent student. Although he is an American, he listens. I beg . . . He begs your excuse . . . pardon. When Monsieur Jones rides, he pretends he is one of Monsieur Madaaua's men riding into battle. He says he is a Muslim and cannot gamble, for this is forbidden by the Koran, but if he could, he would bet on Obadiah Jones."

"Y'all'c'n bet yoah sweet cheeks on it. Heaugh, heaugh, heaugh."

Bill Richards was back, grinning at Jones. "Well, we have a little subplot developing here. An unexpected rivalry has surfaced between two camels from Niger. Obadiah Jones's soldier-trainer, Mahut Madaaua, charges that his rival won Niger's annual army camel race by cheating. Madaaua says his camel is the best in the race. He's confident Jones will redeem his camel's honor."

The First Lady said, "Wouldn't it be something if Jones really did win it? He can shoot, you know."

Bill Richards said, "Say, Obadiah, does your camel have a name?"

"Mah man Mahut says yes, it has a name, and he told me what it was, but it was in Arabic, and Ah didn't unduhstand it and cain't prahnounce it. Mahut says that's fine, because it nevah rahsponds to its name anyhow. Y'all have to whack a camel to get its attention, he says. He says to rename it if Ah want, so Ah'm calling it, him, Lawhrence, out of the movies."

241

Richards said, "Okay, Lawrence it is!"

"Mah man's been calling me the Albanian Flyah, isn't that right, Mahut? Heaugh, heaugh, heaugh."

The translator asked the question of Madaaua, who stuck his elbows out and flapped them like wings, grinning and nodding his head yes. The translator, suppressing his amusement, said, "It comes out something like that, yes."

"The Albanian Flyer!" Richards said. "Tell us, Obadiah, did growing up on a farm prepare you for this?"

"Us southerhn boys'll rahd anythin'. Heaugh, heaugh, heaugh."

Janet Barbur said, "Doesn't he have a wonderful laugh?"

Jones said, "Just get me in the saddle. Doesn't take much to get me started. Heaugh, heaugh."

President Barbur and the First Lady, enjoying their ice cream, laughed along with Obadiah Jones.

The camera cut quickly to Richards, who said, "Most of the countries are participating here in the spirit of celebration and as a way of showing their support for the Arabs who occupy Gibraltar. But a few countries are taking it very seriously indeed. We take you now to ABC camel racing expert Faoud Abu, who is with the Iranian team."

"Bill, the Iranians are taking the race very seriously indeed. We are allowed to tape the Iranian rider and camel—Jebel Tarik officials have insisted on that—but the Iranians themselves are talking to nobody. They have acquired a very tall, sinewy camel with a beautiful, long stride."

A man in a black thobe was shown riding a powerful camel at a fast pace.

As the camera followed the camel, Abu said, "Insiders are saying this camel is from the Bishari region of northeastern Sudan. It's obviously well trained and it has a perfectly lovely stride. Look at the rhythm and power of those lateral legs as they swing forward together. Look at the efficiency. This animal's fast pace is a thing of beauty, believe me, Bill . . ."

242

The camera remained on Abu, as Bill Richards said, "The race favorite, do you think, Faoud?"

Abu laughed. "Not by any means, Bill. If you think the Iranians are going to a lot of expense and trouble, you haven't seen anything yet. The Iraqis are racing a camel imported from Mauritania, and is he ever a beauty. Here's a glimpse of him."

The Iraqi was shown running his animal at a full gallop.

"The thing that is remarkable about the Iraqi camel is that it seems downright eager to run. Most camels are not that way. If the truth were known, most camels would rather walk. And look at the animal in the Saudi camp."

The Saudi rider was shown atop a strong, sleek camel running at a fast pace.

"Experienced camel men are picking this one, Bill, the camel flown in to represent Saudi Arabia. Nobody knows where the Saudis got this animal, and they aren't saying, but one thing is certain: the Saudi camel is a running machine. It was born to run. Finally, there is this camel . . ."

A rider in a white thobe whipped at the neck of a pale, leggy camel with the longest stride of any of the camels yet shown.

"This is the camel Omar Qafi has judged the fastest camel in the Arab world. It was loaned to Qafi by a Bedouin chief in southern Libya who has been breeding camels for speed for years. Back to you, Bill."

Bill Richards said, "Coming up, Faoud Abu will take a closer look at the riders and handlers of the camels of Iraq, Saudi Arabia, and Libya. Those camels, as well as the Iranian entrant, are fast emerging as the favorites in this race. But the wild card, remember, is the shooting. A rider may have the fastest camel in the race, but if he can't consistently score bull's-eyes, he won't be winning Razzia."

"Do you think Obadiah Jones has a chance?" the First Lady asked her husband. "You know, they were saying before you got here that more money has been bet on this

243

race than on any other sporting event in history. Bookies are astonished both in London and New York. The Koran prohibits gambling, but it seems that the sheiks and sultans are letting pride get in the way of good sense."

"The most money in history? Really?" Charles Barbur glanced at the door, then put one finger to his lips for his wife to be silent. With the other finger he beckoned her close.

Janet Barbur leaned toward her husband.

Barbur whispered to her.

Mrs. Barbur's eyes widened. "No!"

PART THREE

Borodin

1

ONE OF THE first things the Russian students had wanted to do on their trip to Gibraltar was to try out some of the local food. On the plane down there had been talk of beefsteak and kidney pie, and of Spanish paella. But no. For security reasons they had been virtually imprisoned in the Continental Hotel immediately upon their arrival. Their chef, if he was to be called that, ordered beets when he could have had Valencia oranges.

Less than an hour after the students arrived, Leonid Borodin slapped videocassettes into their hands and dispatched them to their rooms to watch the Kennedy–Nixon debates and films of students rioting on the steps of Sproul Hall at the University of California at Berkeley.

The first night they watched Borodin teach Muhammad Aziz how not to move his hands when he talked on camera. He told Aziz to "pretend you're playing hide the salami with a beautiful woman. Look that red light right straight on. Mmmm, my love!" A Leningrader whose English wasn't the best asked Borodin what a salami was. It was just one of many stories that would one day make these sessions legendary and everyone knew it.

They crowded around the makeup man when he did Muhammad Aziz's face for his television appearances. The dresser told them about fabrics and television lighting and the need to dress the prime minister in Western suits in cool colors—muted blues and grays.

At night they retired to their rooms to read Jerry Rubin and watch what were seemingly endless videotapes. They watched tapes of Premier Petr Spishkin and his glamorous wife, Anna—who had even had a sexy feature on her printed in the American magazine *Cosmopolitan*
247

—but also tapes of Franklin Roosevelt, Winston Churchill, Harry Truman, John Kennedy, Ronald Reagan, Stokely Carmichael, and the American hostages in Iran. It was Borodin alone who was credited with elevating Anna Spishkin to the international stage of hoo hoo and nonsense, the *Cosmo* article being the capper, changing the image of the socialist woman from that of a bag of potatoes to a stylish bag of potatoes.

Borodin treated his students to a running commentary the first time he played the Ronald Reagan tapes. "Look at that hearty Dutch face," he had said. "Look at those jolly eyes. That's personality, of course; he was very likely born that way. But look at his jet-black hair, comrades. See how young and vibrant that makes him look. See what a good makeup man can do. People think this was because he was an actor, which is wrong, of course. He's being himself and the American television watcher senses that."

The Soviet students watched more than tapes of national leaders. Actually, they were all of Russian birth, the Politburo being chary of teaching The Power to a Georgian, Armenian, Ukrainian, or Latvian. Borodin had them watching tapes of American news programs and documentaries, as well as such offerings as *Bonanza, Monday Night Football,* and Road Runner cartoons.

Few of them would ever forget—in fact most of them had on tape—Leonid Borodin's introduction of Razzia. "What is it that the Indianapolis 500, the Boston Marathon, Pimlico, and Hialeah all have in common?" he asked. He looked from one furrowed brow to the next. "You don't know?" Borodin shook his head with disgust. "They're races, comrades. Action, action, action all the way. The tapes you were assigned to watch included cross-country skiing, quarterhorse races, stock car races, and the explanation of why political races are literally that, races where each contestant's position relative to the other is precisely known, measured by the Gallup Poll and Lou Harris."

Each day Leonid Borodin reminded his students that almost everyone watches television in America, the president, and—as was perfectly clear from their decision

248

supporting the American television networks—members of the United States Supreme Court.

Comrade Leonid Borodin made his final appearance on the Wednesday before Razzia, addressing his students after their midday borscht. They took careful notes; there would be an examination when they got back to Moscow. A career in PR was a career with a future in Moscow; they all knew that.

"Need I remind you, comrades, of the difficulties of a low score on the upcoming examination?" Borodin bowed his head, pointed to the northeast where Siberia lay, and covered his face with his hands. He opened two fingers and peered between them. Then he removed his hands. "If I were you, I would pay close attention to my review. You'll need to go over your notes again and pay close attention to the examples I've given you.

"The American television networks are not in the business of reporting the news, comrades. Whatever they say, the truth is they're in the business of delivering viewers to advertisers. That's how they make a profit." Borodin waited for pencils to stop.

He said, "They may air or not air as they see fit. In fact, they air what will bring them the most viewers, hence the most profit. Since news that moves gains the most viewers, news that does not move is by definition no news at all. This is a function of the market, comrades, and the reason for the success of our experiments with the apes and Razzia. From their standpoint our capture of Gibraltar is profitable—and for them, free—entertainment. If we are to overcome the capitalists, we must understand this and take advantage of it."

Borodin waggled his finger at his students. "The value of Razzia is incalculable. Remember, after Georgia's former governor won the New Hampshire Democratic primary, he was the subject of such intense media coverage that his opponents never caught up. What did the American public get?" Borodin held up the palms of his hands and shook his head sadly. "Yes, Jimmy Carter. On Saturday: Razzia!" Borodin grinned broadly, pleased with the success of his imaginative "overt," which he described as "up-front P. T. Barnum," as opposed to a "covert," which he defined as "secretive manure."

Borodin remained modestly silent on what everybody in the class knew was far and away the most sophisticated aspect of the overt, namely the idea of reserving a spot in Razzia for an American or European contestant. Borodin had told them about professional basketball teams in the United States whose support waned when all their players were black. White sports fans liked at least one white guy on the floor, he had said. It didn't make any difference if the guy was a half-step slow. They liked to have someone with whom they could identify or it was difficult for them to work up enthusiasm.

It is said some men are born lucky, others make their luck. Borodin's luck had held when the toothy South Carolinian, Obadiah Jones, had stepped forward to ride Albania's camel. Both the Americans and the European television viewers took to him immediately. The introduction of Jones shot the ratings sharply upward—overnight, in fact. He was a Rebel sharpshooter. He was just about perfect.

After Jones had surfaced, Borodin swore to the students that he was not a deliberate plant, a KGB agent passing himself off as an American. Borodin had absolutely no way of knowing that Obadiah Jones was on Gibraltar when it was captured or that he would volunteer.

"The importance of understanding television is critical, comrades. You will remember my example yesterday of the so-called 'Symbionese Liberation Army' in the United States in the late 1960s. It turned out that this 'army' had just six members. Yet the American journalists referred to it as an army and even called one of its leaders a 'field marshal.' Similarly, it doesn't matter if Muhammad Aziz's government is not recognized by the United Nations; if American television reporters call this peninsula Jebel Tarik, then it is Jebel Tarik." Borodin had attended first-rate schools in the United States; he had learned from the best. He swiveled left, and tilted back. He was on the cutting edge of Soviet policy, forging it, in fact—all the

250

clichés of Soviet pamphleteers. There would be stories later of him swiveling dramatically on his chair, directing the Jebel Tarik experiment.

"Comrades, Premier Spishkin returned Anatoly Dobrynin to the Soviet Union and the Politburo after thirty years in the United States. He did that because Dobrynin knows his Americans." Borodin took a sip of coffee while his students struggled to keep up in their notebooks.

"Comrades, picture a circus, if you will. You start with clowns and go to pretty girls and then the aerialists and tigers. The band plays exciting music. The spotlight sweeps from here to there, from one colorful, dizzying act to the next. The performers keep the show moving: laughter, sex, danger, or some combination. You've watched your tapes, you know: *The Gong Show,* Benny Hill. In America, some of the smaller circuses, those called carnivals, those that travel to small towns and out-of-the-way places, display fat people and freaks—a man with flippers for arms and legs, or a woman with four breasts—and men called geeks, who bite the heads off live chickens. Keep in mind your videotapes now: *The Dating Game, Lifestyles of the Rich and Famous, Miami Vice,* the Solid Gold dancers, the presidential elections, *Ripley's Believe It or Not.*" Borodin paused, grinning. "A geek, comrades, is the operative definition of an American politician, such is their determination to be reelected and remain in the limelight."

Borodin, who had natural timing, waited for the laughter to subside. "Alternatively, in America, television may be regarded as a form of public theater with a self-generating script, a series of small dramas that enter the public stage and stay there until there is a resolution or the excitement and newness fades. You will find, if you look at it with clear eyes, that one or two stories dominate any given day, while the lesser stories are interwoven much as the strands of a rope. The principal lesson I offer is that the Soviet Union—if it is clever enough—may intervene and write the script to benefit its ends. Comrade Gubunov, what is the most important thing to remember when you're planning a media event?"

251

A serious-looking blond man with a square jaw looked up from his notebook. "The importance of movement, comrade. Constant motion is necessary for the networks to keep people watching television. Action. Without action, viewers get bored. The average length of a shot on *Charlie's Angels* was two point five seconds."

Borodin was pleased. "The attention span of American viewers is steadily diminishing. Today, even *Charlie's Angels* is dated. A two-point-five-second shot on American television now would seem like Ingmar Bergman. Movement, movement, movement, comrades. Never forget it. In the soap operas the actors and actresses go in and out of doors and back and forth from the coffeepot. In the game shows they spin big colorful wheels or have banks of blinking lights. After that come the guns and car chases. This is needed to keep their attention and stop them from going to the bathroom during commercial breaks. Conversely, Gubunov, what is it you avoid?"

"Talking heads, comrade."

"That's right. Viewers get bored with talk. They're not interested in subtlety or the complicated gray areas of public issues. You want to give them movement. You did so well, Gubunov, how about another one? What are the two kinds of staged events?"

"The covert and the overt," Gubunov said.

"Good for you, comrade. Puking Max was a beautifully handled covert. First, I assigned an incompetent to get rid of the apes. If no apes escaped, we'd simply have grabbed some from Morocco." Borodin grinned. "The Arabs caught the NBC reporter's attention with a helicopter gunship. After the cameramen had an opportunity to get out of the cab and get their gear ready, the hook was set. It was smoothly executed. All our Arab friends had to do was release the three captured monkeys from below the road. The Arabs were never seen. The NBC cameramen thought they had stumbled onto the chase. An accident, Thompson told his viewers. An NBC exclusive. And the result of that, Comrade Zargov?"

The attentive Zargov adjusted his spectacles on his nose and repeated the conclusion given earlier in the week

252

y Borodin. "Airtime spent covering Puking Max is air-ime not spent on debating the political and military issues f the Arab occupation of Jebel Tarik."

"Yes, very good, comrade. We've seen how easy it is. he Arabs had fun firing their weapons at the hillside. JBC got the myth of Puking Max. Meanwhile, Muhammad Aziz has done his best to secure our hold on Jebel arik. Everybody's happy. Right, Gubunov?"

Gubunov grinned. "*Da,* comrade."

"May I have another cup of coffee? Comrades, I can't tress how important it is for us to know our Americans. hese lessons are no good at all if you don't learn what americans are all about. That is why Razzia is working." orodin stopped to savor Razzia, a classic overt—the american television networks knew they were being used ut didn't care. The Razzia overt just might have earned orodin the honor of becoming the youngest member of he Central Committee of the Communist party. "So, Comrade Zargov, what is the functional purpose of polls in Western democracy?"

Zargov blinked from behind his glasses. He said, "The unctional purpose of polls is that the viewers are spared aving to think. There is no ambiguity or confusion. americans have found that reporting politics as sport is he most profitable way of retaining the interest of a nation hat never reads."

"Correct. The polls tell the American public how nany people support which politician on what issues. omeone is ahead. Someone is behind. There will be a vinner and a loser. Americans like winners and avoid osers, no matter how intelligent or honorable."

The efficient Zargov, basking in the warmth of praise rom Borodin, took another note.

Borodin said, "You and Gubunov must be spending ll your time studying, comrade. Good for you. The american television networks know perfectly well that Razzia is a public relations setup, but they don't care. I beg ou to remember H. L. Mencken's observation that no-ody has ever gone broke by underestimating the intelli-ence of the American public. One could substitute taste for intelligence and Mr. Mencken's observation would still stand."

The students made a note. Mencken was one of Borodin's favorites. The students were attentive in the first place; they were the best and the brightest from Moscow University. They were honored to be part of Borodin's extraordinary laboratory. One thing was certain: this was a bold experiment in Soviet policy. They were also highly motivated. A blessing by Borodin almost guaranteed a career in the Soviet foreign service, and that meant a life abroad, away from the horrors of actual life in the paradise of socialism.

Leonid Borodin said, "Comrades, our goal here on Jebel Tarik is to show that Muhammad Aziz will make a pleasant and constructive neighbor. Arabs have a terrible image in the United States. It is far easier to fight the Americans with polls than with bullets. If we plan our images carefully and execute our stunts properly, the A. C. Nielsen Company, the Gallup Poll, and the Lou Harris Poll will do our job for us." Borodin laughed. "Remember, comrades, Arabs can be fun."

Borodin suddenly shouted: "There are two kinds of bayonet fighters, comrades. The quick and the dead. What kind are you?"

"The quick!" the class roared back. This was an exercise practiced by drill instructors in armies all over the world. The students grinned and laughed along with the animated Borodin.

He shouted even louder: "There are two ways of fighting the capitalists, comrades! The smart and the doomed! What kind are you?"

"The smart!" the class roared back, louder than before, then laughed along with Borodin.

PART FOUR

. . . action!

1

THE CELEBRATION OF the Razzia fund-raiser actually began on Friday with the sunrise appearance of television blimps over the southern coast of France. These blimps would guarantee that the viewers got to see the camel riders from every possible angle and advantage. No detail would escape the hovering bags of gas.

The blimps had wonderful swirls of color twisting around their jolly big bellies. There were two each blue and gold; black and yellow; red and silver; green and orange. What merry blimps! Gay blimps! A formation of clowns, they were, delighting the inhabitants of small French towns as they made their way to the Mediterranean Sea. Frenchmen waved at the happy balloons passing overhead.

The eight blimps met in stately rendezvous at Marseille, and crossed the Golfe du Lion, heading southwest. Later, ever splendid, they appeared over the Spanish seacoast twenty miles northeast of Barcelona. There they formed a single file—alternating combinations of colors—for the parade down the Costa Brava and the Costa del Sol. It was a grand procession.

Madre de Dios! Where were all the blimps going and why?

The procession of blimps was covered by Spanish radio and television, which is where the Gibraltarians first heard of it. Do these blimps have anything to do with us? they wondered.

When the blimps could be seen over the Mediterranean headed for the Rock, the Arab on the Gib radio explained what they were all about. In the United States, he said, it was standard practice for television networks to use blimps to provide their viewers aerial coverage of grid football matches, car races, and other sporting events. In fact, a blimp advertising a tire manufacturer had become famous in the United States for floating above a football stadium every Monday night each autumn of the year.

The colorful procession, about a hundred yards offshore, followed the Rock's Mediterranean coastline to Europa Point, circled the point, and moved over the Bay of Gibraltar, which they also circled, giving both Spaniards and Gibraltarians a little show. The blimps began weaving up and down, in and out, in a broad, coarse maneuver that the pilots had practiced on their way across the Golfe de Lion. The pilots were parodying the tight-flying formations of high-performance jets, having fun as they guided their blimps into imaginative patterns of color.

The Americans had agreed to share expenses with the European and Asian television systems, whose pockets weren't nearly as deep. Some of the European networks were government run, and so spent all their budget on the feeding and care of self-absorbed bureaucrats. The cost of such appeasement meant their photographers often had to make do with dated and insufficient equipment. The private networks didn't have such vast markets as the Americans and therefore had more modest budgets.

NBC, sharing its feed with the BBC, the Spanish, and the Italians, had rented blue-and-gold blimps from a firm in Milan. CBS, taping with a French crew—working with the Swiss and the Austrians—had secured black-and-yellow blimps from Paris. ABC, working with the Chinese, Scandinavians, and Germans, turned to Munich for red-and-silver blimps. Ted Turner, the Canadians, the Japanese, and the Dutch pooled their resources to acquire handsome green-and-orange blimps from Amsterdam.

When the blimps had finished their grand parade they headed for Gibraltar, where they were tethered around the peninsula in alternating colors—quite a show. As viewed from across the Bay of Gibraltar, the Rock had taken on a carnivallike atmosphere that bordered on the surreal, in the territory of Salvador Dali, say, or Luis Buñuel.

2

WITH THE MUEZZIN'S broadcast of *"La illah il-Allah!"* ringing in his ears, Gerard Thompson set out on his morning jog on the day of Razzia. The Arabs had put him up at the Caleta Palace Hotel on the Mediterranean side, so he set about jogging along the tidy little beach at Catalan Bay. It was a fabulous place to run, what with the eastern face of Mons Calpe high above him on his right, the limestone reflecting the colors of the sun as it edged above the water.

The British had an invasion fleet assembled south of Cadiz, and NBC had its allotted number of reporters and photographers on board the vessels. Whether the British attacked that day or the next, it didn't make any difference to Thompson. Razzia was a nothing story compared to a military invasion. It would be fun to handle both, but if he had to choose, he wanted to cover the British attack.

Thompson was at long last in the right place at the right time. A television newsman could spend a career trying to be there at the whacking of history's funnybone —at the sinking of the *Andrea Doria,* say, or the assassination of John Kennedy—and never make it.

This would be a lovely test, a perfect measure. For the first time ever, to Thompson's knowledge, an entire military action was to be televised live, sort of a mini-war. All the gear was in place on Gibraltar complete with blimps for aerial coverage. This would be something of a set piece and so easy for viewers to understand. Cameras with telescopic lenses on the peaks of Mons Calpe and O'Hara's Peak could provide panoramic views of the geography of battle: the Rock; Europa Point; the Bay of Gibraltar; Africa to the left; Spain to the right.

Thompson felt ready. His suffering in Nicaragua, his

eye job, his gray beard and hairy wrists had apparently done some good, because his masculinity scores had edged to new highs. He was ready to take Harry Gilchrist on Nielsen for Nielsen, Arbitron for Arbitron, and bury the son of a bitch.

It had been a long time since television had had a really good war. Jaded viewers now regarded people exploding in Beirut with the same indifference as people freezing to death in a Wyoming blizzard. It was getting so it took real imagination to keep people riveted to the television set. There were people, alas, who insisted on talking to one another and who regarded the bedroom as a place to screw rather than watch television, but those people remained in the minority.

The Vietnam War had offered some good shots, that was true—footage of people being burned alive and executed on the street—but it was hard for the viewers to put the action in context. The enemy was everywhere, so it wasn't possible to have maps—in the manner of television weathermen—depicting various skirmishes, battles, units, and their disposition. Then there was that awful William Calley business. Also, the damned thing lasted too long. Viewers got so inured to violence that the Nielsens hardly rose during Tet.

There was one problem with covering the British attack and Arab defense. The crews had been chosen to cover Razzia, and so the networks had hired expert commentators on camel riders and target shooting. What they needed now were some articulate field-grade officers or navy commanders. Thompson knew he'd have to make do with the tactics he could remember from ROTC.

The road around Gibraltar seemed to change its name every kilometer. At the base of Mons Calpe it was called Catalan Bay Road. Thompson jogged up onto the road, where he was joined by a second jogger.

He was Stan Meyer, chief foreign correspondent for *Time* magazine, a small man with curly red hair and eyeglasses kept on his face by a band around the back of his head. Meyer said, "You mind if I join you, Gerard?"

"Sure." Thompson looked quickly away, ostensibly to cough, but really to make sure Meyer didn't see him swallow. Very few newspapers or magazines impressed him. Two that did were *The New York Times* and *Time* magazine. He had run this same path every morning since he had arrived on the Rock. This was the first time he had seen Meyer. Had Meyer seen him or heard about his morning runs? Was that why he was here, an "accidental" meeting?

"The network anchor jogging out the kinks on the morning of the big story, eh?"

There were reporters, and then again there were reporters. Some had no clout, so their stories were more likely to be cut. These people were to be avoided. The bespectacled Meyer was a very good man to know. Thompson laughed a laugh that sounded natural, if not downright amiable. "The camera adds fifteen pounds, they say."

"Did you hear the British have been assembling an attack fleet in the Atlantic? Yes, just south of Cadiz. Can you believe?" Meyer fell in beside Thompson.

The "just south of Cadiz" meant something, Thompson knew. "Really, just south of Cadiz?" Thompson's tone suggested that he knew everything there was to know about Cadiz.

"In almost the exact same place where Nelson assembled his fleet."

Thompson's mind went blank. Nelson? Was that Waterloo? No, Napoleon was at Waterloo. Napoleon and who else? Nelson? If Stan Meyer wrote in *Time* magazine that on the eve of the big battle Gerard Thompson didn't know what Nelson did south of Cadiz . . . There'd go his rating of trustworthiness, pissed down the drain. A quiver of fear shot through his stomach. "Maybe Mrs. Fielding has a sense of history."

"Every British schoolkid learns about Trafalgar."

Trafalgar! That was it. Thompson remembered reading somewhere that Stan Meyer had a photographic memory. He could recall conversations word for word, a talent that allowed him to remember candid, revealing details.

Thompson tried to remember what Trafalgar was all about. He vaguely remembered a painting with a pale, dying admiral on deck being ministered to by the ship's physician. Or was that Horatio Hornblower? Thompson couldn't remember. He wished Meyer wasn't such a smart little fucker.

Meyer said, "This is a beautiful place to run, isn't it?"

Was Meyer just being friendly? Was he just out for a run at sunrise, or was there something more to this? Was he getting color for a feature about Thompson? Jogging details were the stuff of cover stories. "I love running," he said. "The solitude gives me a sense of who I am." There, that was a good quote, Thompson thought. A quotable for Meyer. He had a flash fantasy. What if *Time* featured that as a blurb to draw readers into the story? Yes! Then he had second thoughts: maybe it just sounded stupid. *The solitude gives me a sense of who I am.* What the hell did that mean anyway?

"I bought these running shoes in the shop there, Spanish-made. Pacos." Meyer laughed, shaking his head. "They feel real nice on my feet." Meyer watched his feet for a few strides. "They look good too."

Thompson wanted to turn the conversation around to himself if he could. "Just about every city of any size in the United States has a television station featuring 'eyewitness' news. We just might have a little more eyewitness here than we bargained for." There, that was better, Thompson said. More modest. Never, never, never make promises or predictions. Never. Be modest, then deliver in spades.

"What do you say, shall we run down to the sundial and back? I bet it's still dark on the other side of this mountain."

Thompson felt thwarted. Was Meyer just being a friendly jogger? Was that all? If all he wanted to do was jog, why didn't he do it with somebody else? Thompson was a network anchorman, for God's sake! Asshole scribblers just didn't butt in and jog with a network anchorman. Thompson thought Meyer looked like some kind of odd cross between Woody Allen and Danny DeVito. He bet Meyer didn't have a woman as good-looking and voluptuous as Felicia to chase around the bedroom.

"This business of covering Razzia must be a complicated business for you network people. All that coordination and pressure. Live feeds."

Okay! Thompson perked up. He'd misjudged Meyer. "It damn near takes a field marshal to make it all work. Good special-event coverage takes an experienced producer and a lot of talented people, let's face it." He had praised others without mentioning himself. That kind of modesty came across good in print, he knew. Yes!

"You do an amazing job for the pressure you're under, I have to admit."

Stan Meyer was a helluva guy. Thompson liked him. "We do the best we can; it's a complicated, expensive operation."

"I was thinking of having one of our people do a sidebar on the problems of television coverage."

The problems of television coverage? A sidebar? Thompson had in mind a detailed feature on himself. Thompson thought Stan Meyer was a prick with thick eyeglasses, a fucking print snob.

"Hey, look, coming up," Meyer said.

Coming at them around the curve of the bend was Obadiah Jones out riding the camel the whole world was now calling Lawrence of Gibraltar. When Jones saw them, he slowed his camel to a stop. "Such a pleahsant suhprise. What a wondahful mawning," he said as he slipped off the camel. He advanced toward Thompson and Meyer with his hand outstretched, grinning his huge, toothy grin. Both of them had interviewed him several times. They were all old pals by now.

It was a treat for the two newsmen to bump into the Albanian Flyer, complete with Arab garb and scarlet *A*. Here, perhaps, was a colorful anecdote that would be theirs alone, a juicy tidbit denied their competitors.

"Say, reckon if'n I was y'all and was a bettin' man, Ah just might lay a few bucks on muh numbah. Ah know

263

damn well Ah'c'n outshoot them A-rab fellahs, and now that me'n old Lawrhence here are gettin' to know one anothah, well . . . hey!" Obadiah Jones treated Meyer and Thompson to one of his hillbilly laughs: "Heaugh, heaugh, heaugh."

As James Burlane rode Lawrence on his slow-pace warm-up around the Rock, it was 2 A.M. in Washington. The lights were on at 1600 Pennsylvania Avenue, as they inevitably were in times of international crisis.

True, there were people manning the communications room so that anxious commanders of the Sixth Fleet —bobbing like impotent corks in the Mediterranean —might be told what to do if the Royal Navy got itself into a serious jam.

However, most of the activity was in the White House kitchen, where Charles Barbur's chef was spending the night preparing treats for the president to enjoy while he watched the British recapture Gibraltar on television. The chef had had smoked eel flown in from Amsterdam for one little snack. He had roasted squabs in pear brandy for another. His list of goodies was elaborate and complicated. The president, for example, liked his ice cream made minutes before it was served and only with tree-ripened fruit.

The chef, knowing the president regarded this as a bigger viewing event than the Superbowl or World Series, was determined to please Barbur. The White House chef was one of the few chefs in the world with groupies, and Barbur's man wasn't about to risk that status with a second-rate performance for the Battle of Gibraltar. For example, he insisted that the Norwegian salmon was line-caught, not scooped up in some barbaric net. The squabs were delivered live in a large cardboard box. While the delivery man watched, the White House chef selected the squabs he wanted—succulent, plump little numbers —and wrung their necks himself so that it was done properly.

Barbur had just the day before had a new state-of-the-art television set installed for the viewing. This set, a Sony, took up an entire wall and had a picture as sharp and clear as a thirteen-inch screen. Flowing blood would look like flowing blood, not like strawberry soda or thin ketchup.

3

DEBORAH FIELDING DECLINED the offer of an escort back to her stateroom. She knew the way back, she said. She wanted the privacy of a little walk by herself. The sea was calm, the ship was stable. "I might be the prime minister, Admiral Whitehead, but I am still an adult. Please send word as we approach Cadiz. I want to be up top for the show."

The route back to Mrs. Fielding's stateroom took her past a small room where her Royal Navy escorts waited. She heard the man on the BBC talking about the pending attack before she saw the open door. Upstairs with Admiral Whitehead, she'd gotten the impression something was being kept from her.

She proceeded on tiptoe so she could hear what the BBC announcer was saying:

". . . although Mr. Jackelforth's personal aides denied it. For reasons of security no details of the plan were given. Members of the War Cabinet are not discussing the action, but the question of the architect or architects of today's action remains unclear. Is it, as is alleged, the inspiration of Brigadier Harry Tomlinson, commander of Three Commando, and Prime Minister Deborah Fielding herself? Labour party leader William Fluute said that if the rumor is true, quote, 'Let's all hope Mrs. Fielding has better luck in the Bay of Gibraltar than did the Chevalier D'Arcon.'"

The results of the Chevalier d'Arcon's fanciful scheme in the Great Siege was by now common knowledge of the television watching world; the details of his colorful failure were frequently repeated by television journalists to show they were well read and hip to history and stuff. To compare the prime minister to the Chevalier d'Arcon was to provoke hearty grins and jokes in every pub in the United Kingdom.

"Meanwhile, we are told, the British flotilla is approaching the Spanish coast where, as every schoolboy knows . . ."

The prime minister set down her heels as the announcer began the obligatory rehash of the Battle of Trafalgar. She could hear the escorts scrambling to attention. She said, "Relax, gentlemen," and passed on by the open door. The radio was nowhere to be seen on the small table, but a single playing card remained, evidence of gin or poker. Ordinarily her assigned escorts would have been wearing dress uniforms with shoes polished to mirrors. But not these escorts. They were dressed in combat gear, as was everybody else on board, except for Mrs. Fielding, who now faced the question of what to wear for the invasion.

She continued on to her stateroom to consider that bleeding Roger Jackelforth, the backstabbing sod, and the question of what to wear. She poured herself a hard shot of Tanqueray and sat back in the best chair. No sooner had she relaxed than someone knocked on her door, *tap, tap, tap.* The tapping, barely audible, was accompanied by a polite clearing of a throat.

"What is it?"

"We're told Cadiz is coming up on the port, Mrs. Fielding."

"Admiral Whitehead knows my instructions."

"He does indeed, Mrs. Fielding. We've had our orders, ma'am."

"I'll be up in a few minutes, then, thank you."

Jackelforth would have to wait. Fielding stepped back and looked at herself again in the mirror. What to wear? The question had been a burden for Deborah Fielding ever since she took over the leadership of the Conservative party. She was a woman and proud of it. If she was to lead her party and her country, she would be both strong and graceful. She refused to go the route of Golda Meir, who looked like Lyndon Johnson in drag. God!

Mrs. Fielding wasn't young or coltish, but she wasn't sexless by any means; there was a huskiness to her voice that was held to be attractive. Harold liked her caboose. He talked about it as if it were part flower, part melon, part return to the womb. He couldn't keep his hands off it.

Fielding was determined to make a good show for the invasion of Gibraltar. Ordinarily she chose a tailored woman's suit with a scarf at her throat to show she was a woman. This, apparently, was so that no one would be fooled into thinking otherwise; a skirt and the bulges caused by female appurtenances were insufficient notice of gender in modern circles. This was a solemn occasion —men's lives were at stake, not to mention her government—and the question of what to wear was of no small consequence. What would look well in a bronze statue in the park? she wondered.

Thinking of Winston Churchill, she tried on a dark blue suit with elegant pinstripes. She tried it on first with, then without, the vest. Mmmmmm, she thought.

Tap, tap, tap. A throat cleared again. A hesitant voice said, "I am to remind you, ma'am, that Cadiz is coming up on our port." Her escort had obviously been ordered to tell her again and he was embarrassed.

"Rest assured, I'll be right up," Fielding said. Men were the same everywhere. Just like Harold, her escort was out there pacing, waiting for her to get dressed. It was at Trafalgar, off Cadiz, where Admiral Nelson had closed upon the combined French and Spanish fleet and entered the ranks of the immortals. It was comforting to Mrs. Fielding to think that the ghost of Nelson was at her side as she led the British flotilla into battle. The blue suit. Would Nelson approve? She thought he would. The skirt had a weighted hem so there would be no inadvertent sideshows.

Should she put a touch of rouge on her cheeks? She thought not; the sea breezes would bring a natural blush to her cheeks.

She tried on a red, white, and blue scarf that matched the Union Jack. She pinned a tiny Union Jack on the lapel of her suit. She stepped back to see how that looked. She would be on television, she knew. Was it too much Union Jack? Would the red, white, and blue jump right out at the camera? She was leading them into battle, so a little patriotism was in order, was it not? Or was she opening herself up to ridicule by Mad Billy Fluute and the Fleet Street cartoonists?

She replaced the Union Jack with a tiny gold lion. That was better. Besides, she liked the image. Next, her panty hose. She had found the question of panty hose to be critical when she was around military aircraft and ships. Submarines were the worst, having to squeeze through ridiculously small passages with pipes and corners everywhere and all those stairs. She felt the fact that men actually volunteered for submarine duty to be evidence of an intellect inferior to women's, although she kept this to herself.

Mrs. Fielding put on a pair of her special underpants. They were her lucky underpants, actually; she wore them when there was a major vote in Parliament or she gave a major policy speech. They were provocative knickers—jet-black, translucent, with little ruffles around the legs.

She had several pair of these underpants, and although her husband, Harold, knew she wore them on tense occasions, he was gracious enough not to say anything. She loved her husband; he was a good friend and companion, although he had his little ways. The reason Mrs. Fielding wore the underpants was because of her passionate first love, Rory, a young veterinarian whom she had helped nurse one spring after he had suffered a horrible kick from Madame Queen, a maddened Holstein. After he died, she had written him a poem, "To a Veterinarian Dying Young."

Tap, tap, tap! "Mrs. Fielding!"

Prime Minister Deborah Fielding.

She started to open the door, then closed it quickly. "Just one moment." She hurried back to her closet. Nelson and Trafalgar and tradition be damned. She wasn't a pretend man. She was a woman and proud of it. She was going into battle with skirts flying. She put on a print dress, pink roses on navy blue. There was no wind; the sea was flat. There was no reason for weighted hems and all that nonsense.

She stepped out into the corridor, and joined Admiral Whitehead on deck.

"Cadiz up ahead, Mrs. Fielding," he said, and nodded toward the Spanish shoreline.

"Close by, as I said. Give them a show, Admiral."

"A good cricket batter will be able to hit shore, ma'am."

Cadiz was situated on a peninsula on the seaward side of a natural bay. It was an attractive city in the Spanish manner, white buildings with red tiled roofs. The masts of fishing boats could be seen inside the bay.

It was said that Nelson had had the ship's band play "Rule, Britannia!" as he sailed into battle.

Admiral Whitehead said, "Mrs. Fielding?"

"Any time, I should think."

Whitehead checked his watch. "We'll proceed as planned, then." He nodded at a subordinate. The party waited. A few seconds later, "Rule Britannia!" began over the loudspeaker, not only on the flagship, but simultaneously on all the vessels in Her Majesty's Fleet. The stirring, patriotic music floated across the calm waters where amazed and excited Spaniards gathered on the shore to watch.

"Well, we'll see."

"Would you like some tea, Mrs. Fielding?"

Mrs. Fielding suppressed a nervous sigh. "I think we probably all could use a spot of tea." In the next few minutes, she knew, they would all know if the Spanish gambit was going to work.

The prime minister and her officers waited while their tea was poured. They shifted nervously from foot to foot. If the Spanish gambit didn't work, they were in for a long, long day, and Deborah Fielding's turn on the public stage would very likely come to an ignominious end.

A few minutes later word came in from an MI6 chap

in Algeciras. Admiral Keyes read the message: "Spanish responding in earnest. Putting all La Linea forces on the border, more coming."

The Spanish had responded. The command party on the bridge of the H.M.S. *Bountiful* was joyful.

Admiral Whitehead escorted the prime minister to the fo'c's'le where they stood, watching the Spanish shoreline.

Deborah Fielding felt a surge of adrenaline and confidence. Her dress felt good pressed against her thighs. Her breasts pushed through the air like the bows of dreadnaughts plowing the cold waters of history.

The next question:

How would Bobby Nye respond to the Spanish gambit?

Bobby Nye found it hard to believe that the sodding Arabs were insane enough to think the British would let them keep Gibraltar without a fight. But that's what they apparently believed. They professed bewilderment at the turn of events, in fact seemed offended that Deborah Fielding wanted her colony back, the bitch.

Alas, this was the morning Nye had known would one day come. Major Habib would be calling shortly, and then Nye would have to earn his money, command a ragtag army of ragheads under attack by the bloody Royal Navy. He had led units of undisciplined wogs out of some pretty hairy scrapes in Zimbabwe and Angola, but the Battle of Gibraltar promised to be something else again.

Nye always charged the maximum rate for his services and then some. He wasn't some gung-ho kid who masturbated over articles in *Soldier of Fortune* magazine. He was a graduate of the Royal Military Academy at Sandhurst. He was a professional. The wogs and ragheads all knew they could work with him, and he always got the job done.

The seizing of Gibraltar was a fabulous professional coup, the stuff of legend in the world of mercenaries, and he was proud of it. Nye kept a stiff upper as he received the reports of the advancing British fleet. He was rather like a football manager who had put every man on the pitch in front of the goal, hoping to weather the inevitable barrage.

It was good defense that won football matches. Let them take their shots. Let them.

The Arabs first got a call from a British-hating Spaniard in Cadiz. The Spaniard said the British looked determined. They were playing "Rule, Britannia!" on the ship's loudspeakers. Deborah Fielding herself was leading the flotilla, the Spaniard said. They could see her with binoculars, standing on the deck of the H.M.S. *Bountiful,* wearing a print dress. Yes, a dress, with skirts blowing.

Then Aziz's Arabs called Nye: Spanish tanks had begun warming their diesel engines on the border, and half-tracks with field artillery pieces were being put into position behind the tanks.

This was followed by word from lookouts with binoculars in Tangier: advance vessels of the British fleet could be seen just off the Spanish coast.

He looked at his maps of the Spanish coast. Ordinarily, the British fleet would have passed well south of Cadiz—certainly not within view of the shore. They had turned from the straight shot at the Strait of Gibraltar. Then there was all that "Rule, Britannia!" business. Nye wondered why they had done that.

They were possibly doing it because they were British and had read too much history and were sentimental; they wanted to go into battle with peckers and knockers up—a British way of showing solidarity with their brand-new Spanish allies. Had they really made a deal with the Spanish? That would almost certainly result in the cession of Gibraltar to Spain. Would Mrs. Fielding do that?

Or were the British luring the Spanish armored division to the frontier as a feint?

The Arabs, he knew, were eagerly waiting for him to tell them how to thwart the Royal Navy. They had paid him a fortune, after all.

The telephone rang.

It was Major Habib, sounding anxious.

4

THE CAMERA TRACKED a lean, thin shadow back to Gerard Thompson standing tall, à la Clint Eastwood, in the middle of an airport runway. Thompson wore a many-pocketed cotton vest of the kind presumably worn by adventurers and hard travelers. Thompson clenched his jaws, the muscles bunching with the tension of the pending drama:

"So"—he paused a beat—"we come down to it."

In New York, the NBC crew gathered around the monitors, knowing this was television history. Jesus Fucking Christ, Gerard Thompson was standing in the middle of the airport like a referee awaiting kickoff! Unprecedented hair!

With the camera tracking to his description, Thompson said, "To the south, over there, behind those Moorish walls, await the Arabs with German Cobra antitank missiles. The Arabs have surface-to-surface missiles up there too, and there, and there." The camera tracked the artillery positions high on the northern face of Mons Calpe —"To the north, there behind the customs building and the air terminal, are Spanish tanks, lined up tread to tread from the Bay of Gibraltar to the Mediterranean Sea" —and panned the row of tanks.

The camera turned to Thompson's grave, bearded face. "I am standing in the middle of the Gibraltar airport, the no-man's-land here, in these final moments before the battle that was inevitable from the moment Arabs seized Gibraltar. It was clear from the first that the Americans and Europeans could not allow Arab domination of both entrances to the Mediterranean Sea. So . . . war. We'll be seeing the battle from the moment the treads of those tanks dig in and they begin the charge of the Spanish brigade."

In New York, the NBC people had champagne and hors d'oeuvres to celebrate Thompson's promised rout of Harry Gilchrist. Boy, oh, boy, Thompson wasn't letting them down, either. This was Edward R. Murrow stuff. Thompson's striding coolly to and fro on the tarmac suggested to the viewer: Christ, what if the Spaniards blew the starting whistle before that asshole got off the runway? He was a matador awaiting the charge of *el toro* Spanish *tanques*. The thrill of watching him standing there like that, between missiles and tanks, was akin to the kick viewers got out of watching the Indianapolis 500, secretly wishing a racer would flip over and explode.

"And farther out, past the Bay of Gibraltar there, the British fleet will arrive to challenge the Exocet missiles of former British officer Bobby Nye. The British trained Nye. Can they anticipate his moves? We'll find out shortly. We'll be covering the Exocet action via NBC blimp, and we'll have aerial coverage of the action here on the isthmus. You'll be seeing surface-to-surface missiles from launch to target."

The camera panned slowly from tank to tank on the Spanish border.

"When those tanks move, and the planes begin to fly, we'll be following all the action at once, including video replays of combat highlights. For complete details by the most accomplished cameramen in the world stay tuned to NBC. Gerard Thompson, on the line in Gibraltar. Right now, a word from our sponsors."

Corks popped like farting buffalo as Lee Iacocca appeared on the monitors hustling Chryslers. The NBC staffers were joyous. What a start! Yes! Lay it to 'em, Gerard! When the ads were finished and Thompson was on the monitor again, the level of babble got even louder.

Gerard Thompson was strolling casually in front of the tanks—a matter of two or three yards in front of the tanks. The huge barrel of the tank loomed above his shoulder. "These are M-60 tanks purchased from the United States. The critical tanks are these, lined up on Churchill Avenue, which crosses the airport runway. Their job will be to race down Churchill and into the city while the tanks on the flanks and Spanish howitzers just behind these tanks lay down a barrage of fire at Arab missiles at the Moorish walls there, and Arab missiles high up on Mons Calpe there . . ."

The camera cut to the Moorish wall and moved in tightly in a slow pan, then cut to the precipitous north face of Mons Calpe for a series of close-ups. Thompson said:

"Those are called the galleries, the first of which were dug by Royal Engineers during the Great Siege of July 1779 to February 1783. This one is called Windsor Gallery. Here you see the King's Line. There is, of course, a Queen's Line; here it is. Those objects you see are surface-to-surface missiles, aimed at the tanks behind me. There are missiles here, called the Notch, and here, St. George's Hall. During World War Two, the Royal Engineers added thirty miles of tunnels in the Rock."

Behind Thompson, a Spanish officer began yelling in Spanish and waving for him to get off the no-man's-land. Thompson said, *"Sí, sí, señor,"* and began walking down Churchill Avenue, a dramatic figure, the camera pulling back, coming with him, then moving to one side and finally settling over his shoulder as he walked across the airstrip straight at the missiles behind the Moorish walls. Thompson was casual, even grinned when the Spaniard yelled at him—fabulous for his masculine image.

As Thompson walked, he told the viewers: "So here they are, Spanish and Arab, eyeball to eyeball, staring at one another across an airport tarmac. They wait as armies have always waited—at Runnymede, at Chickamauga, at Pork Chop Hill. You can, well . . . feel the tension." Thompson shuddered and gave himself a little hug to demonstrate the chilling effects of the tension, a wonderful little visual. "Later, the British fleet will arrive . . ."

Viewers were given a low shot, over the bay. The lens of the camera enabled viewers to see Africa in the distance.

". . . there. We're here to see all the action from opening shot to closing taps, an entire war, for the first time live on TV. For the best shots by the best cameramen in the business, stay tuned to NBC. Coming up: What the

Arab Exocet technicians will do when the British fleet is detected on radar."

In the minutes before he moved his command center to Europa Point, Colonel Bobby Nye seemed to be everywhere along the Moorish wall and in the galleries on the north face of Mons Calpe. If the Spaniards dared so much as budge, they would be crippled by a coordinated Arab response.

This was not to be fire at will, or fire in confusion or without plan. No, no, no. Nye assigned the responsibility for specific sectors to his Arab subordinates. There were backups to backups, each with an assigned sector and firing order so that rockets and howitzer rounds wouldn't be wasted on the same target in the confusion of battle. The first charge would be carnage. Bobby Nye would return from Europa Point for any subsequent attack, during which he would direct rocket and howitzer fire from a vantage point on Mons Calpe.

The Arab rockets and howitzers were in limestone tunnels or behind the Moorish wall. The Spanish tanks and armored personnel carriers and field artillery pieces were completely exposed, naked. Even an Arab could hardly be expected to miss at that range. If the Spaniards called in air cover, they risked Arab SAMs and the deaths of Gibraltarians whose favor they wished most ardently to cultivate. If the Arab rockets and howitzers worked at all as advertised, it would be one of the most ruinous attacks on record.

In fact, if the Spanish tanks tried to breach the Moorish wall, it would be testament to the spirit of that wonderful old warrior, Don Quixote. With rockets to the left of them, and with rockets to the right, and with rockets high above, it would be a charge deserving even of Tennyson.

Onward would clatter *los tanques bravos*.

With missile carrier half-tracks *click-clack*ing north on Main Street, Muhammad Aziz and Boris Suslev remained at their headquarters in the House of Assembly. This was the location of the Russian communication equipment necessary for them to receive their instructions. Since Borodin's hasty departure when the British fleet reached Cadiz, the source of authority had followed him—to Libya. As the Spanish gunned the engines of their tanks on the north and the British flotilla entered the Strait of Gibraltar, Aziz and Suslev waited for Leonid Borodin to tell them what to do.

Bobby Nye went to Europa Point, because at Europa Point the expected battle could very well be a classic. Whatever happened, Nye wanted to be the one who called the shots when the shots had to be called. This was a matter of pride with Nye. As he knew, a good spoiler could claim a spot in history. Who was the guy who beat Napoleon at Waterloo? Who was the guy who beat the Royal Navy at Gibraltar?

Not bad company.

This wasn't the first time Bobby Nye had had his bum on the line, not by any means. He'd led shiny-faced wogs into battle in Zaire, Angola, Namibia, and Zimbabwe, and so knew what the business of keeping tight sphincters was all about. A successful defense of the Rock was in the cards if the ragheads firing the missiles did their job.

The stunner came at 1 P.M., just as radar blips showed that the British flotilla had progressed well into the Strait of Gibraltar.

Bobby Nye was informed that the television chaps would be using their blimps to provide overhead coverage of the confrontation between Arab Exocets and the Royal Navy that was expected at the Bay.

Nye could hardly believe it. He rang Muhammad Aziz at headquarters.

"Is there some kind of problem, Colonel Nye?"

"You bloody bet there's a problem! We've got a battle to fight in a few minutes. We don't need blimps in the middle of everything. All that will do is add more radar blips to the confusion. We do not, I say again, *do not* need blips taking pictures. Blips, blimps. Which is which?

276

Which one will the missile choose to hit? It's impossible, Mr. Prime Minister, I implore you!"

Aziz sounded surprised. "Impossible? I'm afraid I don't understand. They want to televise the battle. I can't imagine that you would have any objection to that. They're neutral."

"Just keep the bloody things on the ground! This is war, not theater."

"I'm not so sure the issue is all that clear, Colonel Nye. However, I do understand your anxiety. Will you please stand by? I think I should confer with, uh, Boris Suslev on this." He hung up.

Nye waited, knowing full well that Aziz and Suslev were ringing Leonid Borodin and Omar Qafi in Tripoli.

Two minutes later Aziz rang back. "Colonel Nye, if we are assured, guaranteed, that the blimps will remain well above the action, so that there would be no possible confusion for your missiles, would you be satisfied? It really is difficult to see the harm in their taping the action on the bay if they understand the problems involved. They don't want to get shot down any more than you want to shoot them down."

"I want them on the ground."

Aziz sighed. "Colonel Nye, do you feel we have a chance against the British navy? With all our missiles and planning. Do you feel we have a chance? You've been telling us we have a chance. We've paid you a lot of money to see that we have the best chance possible."

"If our rockets score, yes, we have a chance. We're in control, in fact. We've got Mrs. Fielding by the short hair, and the Royal Navy knows it."

"Colonel, I ask you to consider this. If our rockets do score their hits, wouldn't it be wonderful to have all of America and Europe watching it on television? You would be the architect of victory, would you not? Certainly not me."

"All those bleeding—"

"We've talked to the television producers, Colonel Nye. They understand our problem fully, they say. The
277

pilots have agreed to stay at least two hundred meters above the battle. They don't want to get in the way of Exocets either. They'll make up the distance with their special lenses. How does that sound, Colonel? Colonel?"

It had been due in no small measure to Gerard Thompson's influence at NBC that Tony O'Brien had gone as far as he had, but now that it was time to divvy up the coverage for the war, Thompson had to be careful. To cultivate a friendship among correspondents was one thing —it enabled Thompson to learn in advance of any discontent among the troops—but he knew it would be a mistake to give O'Brien too much of the action.

The bearded Thompson wore splendid war correspondent/battle gear for the big show. His olive fatigue pants had pockets on the hips, deep, bellows pockets at the thighs, and pockets on the outside of the calves. His long-sleeved, sand-colored shirt had bellows pockets at the breast, and pockets on the forearm. Over the shirt, he wore a beige photographer's vest with pockets stitched upon pockets, including a big one on the back to accommodate maps. The pockets were snapped, buttoned, and zippered; the material was one hundred percent cotton—polyester was prole—the colors complementary. Over his beautiful salt and pepper hair, Thompson wore a floppy but utilitarian British desert hat.

Tony O'Brien was clean-shaven, had no hat or vest, and his shirt and fatigue pants had fewer pockets.

NBC now had four correspondents on Gibraltar, including Thompson and O'Brien, plus eight photographers—two for each correspondent. A guy named Higham had been brought in from Miami. In order to appease the Friedan-Steinem flank, the fourth correspondent, Laura Lynne-Dell, was a woman. Now that the nature of the pending battle was becoming clear, the journalists met at the sundial. The eight colorful blimps were now moored around the sports stadium between the sundial and the Prince of Wales Cinema, ready to cover the sea battle.

Thompson said, "The Arabs are saying the Spanish

ay just be bluffing. It would be insane for them to try to reach the wall without shelling the town."

"They'd kill half the population of Gibraltar."

"I think you should cover the northern front from up n Mons Calpe. You take it from the Arab side, Higham rom the Spanish side."

O'Brien had wanted the sea battle but tried not to look isappointed. Maybe Lady Luck would smile his way and ie Spanish would try to breach the Moorish wall. "I've got ommo with the people up top so I can direct their shots, o problem." O'Brien was cool under pressure, a pro.

"I'll take one blimp out and Laura Lynne-Dell the econd." It annoyed Thompson that Lynne-Dell had a fty-fifty chance of drawing better action than himself, but iere was nothing he could do about that. "If the Spanish inks move, one of us will move over to help out the Mons alpe and ground cameras." Thompson wanted to reserve iat decision until he knew where the action was.

O'Brien glanced nervously at the Spanish tanks and ie Moorish wall.

Thompson said, "I'd better get going. The Arabs want s to get the blimps out of their firing line."

They shook hands, and Gerard Thompson began otting to the blue-and-gold blimp that waited like a huge olorful toy. Live coverage of the Battle of Gibraltar! He as a professional, a veteran. He wore a salt-and-pepper eard and a vest with seventeen pockets.

Across the way, Gerard Thompson saw Harry ilchrist jogging to a yellow-and-green blimp. Thompson ondered if this was how British pilots had felt jogging to ieir waiting Spitfires during the Battle of Britain.

279

5

THE CABIN OF NBC's blimp was loaded with large plywood boxes held together by metal strapping tape. Gerard Thompson wondered what the boxes were for. They didn' need that much gear to photograph Razzia.

Thompson was usually the immediate center of atten tion everywhere he went; this recognition was of the contours of his face, not the sublety of his mind, although he had come to believe they were the same. It seemed tha everybody in the United States knew what he looked like People watched him secretly at parties, he knew. He wa deferred to. Heads nodded vigorously whenever he made a point. Thompson flattered by listening. He thrilled merely by saying something, no matter how stupid or banal. In passing on the remark, the listener got to bask in the reflected glory of having been spoken to by Gerard Thomp son.

Here, nobody paid any attention to him at all. It wa as though he were a sack of potatoes thrown aboard the blimp for provisions.

There was a crew of six inside the blimp, including the pilot and copilot. Thompson found this odd; he had been in blimps before, and a pilot and copilot were all that wer needed. The four extras were busy popping the strapping tape with bolt cutters.

Cameramen Jack Brooks and Eddie Figueroa, who were used to being ignored, set about stashing their gear Finally the captain said, "Good morning, Mr. Thompson my name is Captain Ted Mahar, of the Royal Navy. Would you sit, please? I'd like a word with you in a moment. You also, please." He beckoned the two photographers with hi hand.

The Royal Navy? Thompson sat, watching the men with bolt cutters. He watched the captain and his copilot go to the cockpit in the front of the cabin.

Captain Mahar left the copilot in the cockpit and came back to Thompson and the two photographers. He squatted by Thompson's seat and said, "Welcome aboard, Mr. Thompson. And you would be Mr. Brooks and Mr. Figueroa." Mahar stopped to listen to the copilot's radio conversation with the ground. "Are we ready, Ian?"

"Shall I take her up, sir?"

"Take her up. I won't be but a second." Mahar turned to Thompson and the photographers. "You will be participating on a mission of the Royal Navy, gentlemen. I'm to tell you that your President Charles Barbur asks you to please help us on this matter, and our Prime Minister Fielding most urgently requests it as well." The men unpacking the boxes worked with a frenzy. The blimp was released and began rising.

Among the boxes a slender white rocket was exposed, and one of the men began making an adjustment with a screwdriver.

Mahar eyed it mildly and said, "That's a chaff rocket. I'll explain presently. We would like for you to cover this story as you planned, Mr. Thompson. Give your viewers your usual nonsense. Omar Qafi is watching this on television in Tripoli, and he's telling Muhammad Aziz what to do. It is essential, I say again, essential that there be not a clue or hint over television about what we're really doing. They musn't suspect. They must not. If they believe you, and this plan works, perhaps thousands of lives and millions of pounds will have been saved.

"Now then. We're to fly above and just in front of a Hovercraft loaded with Royal Marines and motorcycles." Mahar gestured to the huge box being opened. When the square launching tube became visible, he said, "A chaff rocket explodes into bursts of foil to confuse the Exocet's radar guiding system. We fire, fire, fire to port, the Hovercraft pulls hard to starboard, or we fire, fire, fire to starboard, the Hovercraft turns hard to port. Neat, eh? The

Arabs don't have experienced crews. If they dawdle too long before they fire their first rocket, the Hovercraft will be home before they can get a second off. You follow me?"

Gerard Thompson was getting to cover the Battle of Gibraltar from a blimp riding shotgun on Hovercraft. What a fabulous break! If Tom Brokaw knew what his successor had lucked into, he'd be twisting with envy in his grave. Harry Gilchrist was certainly no Dan Rather. Rather would have been good on this one, but Thompson thought he was better himself.

"If the Arabs use a SAM to shoot us down, we'll go *plop* in the water and the Hovercraft will have to turn back. The Royal Navy will have boats standing by to fish us from the water. If you could please keep our chaff launcher out of your pictures until it's been used once, it would help. But we must, *must* have your cooperation in our ruse."

"We'll do our best," Thompson said.

"Thank you all." Mahar shook their hands and returned to the cockpit. The four men had the launching tube fully exposed now and were frantically making adjustments. The cabin had a bay door for loading cargo, and the tube had been fitted with a mechanism that would swing the tube down from the belly of the blimp's cabin. Another large box contained radar equipment needed to track incoming Exocets.

Jack Brooks began shooting the airport and the Moorish wall receding below them. Turning his back to the chaff launcher, Eddie Figueroa taped Gerard Thompson in his many-pocketed adventurer/journalist's outfit. He was getting a chance to earn his pockets.

Thompson, his face serious, solemn, said, "This is Gerard Thompson in the NBC blimp that will be providing aerial coverage of the dramatic Battle of Gibraltar this afternoon. Colonel Bobby Nye waits on Europa Point with deadly French Exocet missiles. And the British, well, the Royal Navy will be coming into range quickly now. You folks back home can settle back in your easy chairs and watch the action unfold. For the best photography in the business, stay tuned to NBC News."

Bobby Nye could hardly believe it. How in the hell did he Arabs expect him to save their hides when all they wanted to do was watch themselves on television? Arabs at he Moorish wall had commandeered television sets from Gibraltarian households, and were staring at the telly.

The Spaniards across the airport were no different. One of them, finding himself on camera, waved happily and grinned, calling, *"Hola, Mama!"*

When one of the Arabs at the Moorish wall did the same thing, called, "Hello, Mom," in Arabic, Nye almost lost his cookies. This was impossible, just impossible. A man couldn't fight a war this way. This was insane. But then, Nye realized, he must be an old-fashioned man, out of date.

Even his Exocet technicians, with the Royal Navy gathering for the attack, were trying to watch radar screens and television at the same time, with the telly getting just a tad more attention.

Every time a television cameraman came by to photograph them waiting with their Exocets, the Exocet technicians adjusted their kaffiyehs and tried to look all heroic and professional. When there were no cameramen around, they were just as apt to turn around and casually piss on the wall.

6 _____

THE BATTLE OF Gibraltar was to be a neat and tidy engagement—thoroughly modern and old-fashioned at the same time. The players wore identifying costumes, stayed in their assigned areas, and could be described with a few agreed-upon cultural stereotypes and clichés. The British, for example, had upper lips that were said to stiffen under adversity, a physiological response found in no other nation. They bore no empire mustaches now, however. Their lips were naked, bared to the world. The Arabs were formidable enemies because they were suicidal fanatics, as everybody knew.

This was a dream of second-unit directors, real Yakima Canutt stuff. The action was centered on and above a bay surrounded by hills on two sides and the western slope of the Rock on the third, so that it resembled nothing so much as an enormous theater in the round. The Royal Navy would enter from the Strait of Gibraltar, that is, from stage south.

The best Spanish seats were on the west side—on the hills above Algeciras. The hills behind La Linea were farther back and unfortunately in line of sight for errant Arab artillery rounds and missiles fired from the Moorish wall. Spanish confidence in Arab accuracy was not great, so it was behind Algeciras that most of the Spanish audience gathered with blankets and binoculars and picnic lunches to watch the action. This was much as their ancestors had assembled to watch the Chevalier d'Arcon engage the British defenders in the Great Siege, a fact radio and television announcers were quick to point out at any hint of a lull in the action.

Moderns on the sides of the hills got to listen to the action described live over Walkmans and diminutive radios, some no larger than credit cards. The Spaniards who watched the action from the upper floors of buildings in Algeciras got to follow the battle on television also. Owing to video replays, slow motion, and aerial coverage, there were Spaniards who said later it was more exciting over television, because they knew what they were seeing. On television, there was no confusion as to the strategies, and the viewers got to hear interesting technical data such as the range and speed of the missiles involved, and the bed capacity of St. Bernard's Hospital. Also, television was able to run videotape replays to keep the action rolling.

Before each commercial break, announcers reminded their viewers that the cameras aboard the blimps were capable of tracking an Exocet in flight and to stay tuned.

The choice seats were on the steep western slope of

Gibraltar. In the town itself, the streets were lined up terracelike on the hillside so that not only were spectators close to the action, but they looked down upon it as well; a theater architect couldn't have designed better viewing.

The television crews had the problem of being where the action was, plus reporting it swiftly and clearly so that the viewer could understand the developing battle in the simplest of terms. NBC, for example, chose to place two cameras at the site of Nye's Europa Point Exocets in the event of a strike by British Sea Harriers—one to follow Nye's SAMs skyward, the other to record the British hits on the Exocets. There were two cameras aboard each NBC blimp, and three cameras high on Mons Calpe to provide overhead coverage of any attack by the Spanish.

Cameramen who delivered the action sequences did so at the risk of their lives, although they were able to use their lenses to keep some distance. Such was their seeming calm in the face of death that some of these cameramen had acquired reputations as legendary fools. However, they were generally not good-looking, often downright scruffy, and so were kept on the wrong side of the camera, unknown to the public.

One thing NBC was able to do—this was at Gerard Thompson's suggestion—was to string a system of microphones along the Moorish wall so that viewers might hear the screams of maimed and dying Arabs in voice-over.

The Spanish television announcer could be heard through the open windows of Gibraltarian households:

"The flotilla is proceeding single file now, following the curve of the Spanish coastline. We're into the Strait of Gibraltar. In this shot you see Africa across the way. In this nice shot you can see Prime Minister Deborah Fielding here at the helm of the *Bountiful* conferring with Admiral Whitehead and his assistants."

The second announcer said, "We're seeing history in the making, Paco."

"We're told, although this has yet to be officially confirmed, that the prime minister has assumed personal command of the flotilla. The water is quite deep here and

285

they're no more than two hundred meters offshore. You see the bustle of activity on deck there as the sailors of the Royal Navy are getting their ship ready for action."

"One can imagine Nelson's men scrambling about the deck in similar preparations."

The first announcer said, "Up ahead there, in a few minutes, we'll be seeing the coast turn abruptly to the southeast. This will be Punta Marroqui, the southernmost point in Europe, Raul. The protection afforded by Punta Marroqui is believed to be the reason for the single file."

"The Prime Minister is a determined lady, isn't she Paco? Look at her face there, calm and resolute. The pressure must be just incredible."

"The Battle of Gibraltar is shaping up to be a short affair, depending on the accuracy of the much-touted French missiles, so don't go away. We'll be right back after a word from Coca-Cola . . ."

The more nervy of the Gibraltarians, including Nigel Helgado and his family, took to the rooftops for the best of all view of the expected panoramic action. Nigel was a camera nut, having gained himself some notoriety if not celebrity by his pictures of oiled tourists.

Nigel worked in a camera shop on Irish Town, and had begun shooting oiled tourists as a teen-ager. He was interested in the way light reflected off oiled skin, tourists at Catalan Bay and Eastern Beach being handy subjects. When he got his first car, he made oiled-tourist forays up the Costa del Sol, where sun-starved Germans, oiled up, strolled to the beach with a rolling gait to accommodate plastic beach slippers. When Nigel was twenty-five, a London publishing house issued a book of these grotesques, oiled Swedes, oiled Dutchmen, oiled Brits and Germans in insane swimming trunks, some with great white, oiled bellies.

Come time for the Battle of Gibraltar, Nigel Helgado had all the photographic gear he needed for what was to be his moment of destiny. It was not the angle of his moon or the plane of the stars with Uranus or Pluto that made his luck, but rather the location of the apex of his tripod with respect to one of history's merry tics. The Helgados lived t the southern end of Red Sands Road. Shooting west, Nigel had a perfect shot of the entrance to the bay. Nigel ooked nearly straight down on Rosia Road as it flanked he Admiralty Dockyard. His view of the Moorish wall to he north was not as good. To the north lay Alameda Gardens.

Helgado, opting for naval action, had set his outfit up n the roof as soon as the Arabs had shooed the residents ndoors.

With Arabs gone north and south, the center of the own was strangely silent. Arabs in a Gibraltarian police ar made one last pass through town using a loudspeaker to rder lingering civilians off the streets.

"You can see perfectly well from the roofs or the indows of your houses," said the Arab with the loud-peaker. "You can watch the battle on television. If you are the streets or the hillside, you will be shot, please. We sk you to be sensible and watch the action on television. hank you very much."

A few minutes after the final warning to be sensible nd stay put, Nigel Helgado saw them, saw the two camel ders on Rosia Road below him.

The tall man in the Arab costume rode with a saddle hat was slightly forward of the hump. Nigel Helgado ted that because he had been watching Colonel Le Cocq n television. The woman rider, whose camel matched the an's stride for stride, wore Muslim garb and was veiled. he rode her camel on top, a technique which Le Cocq had lso described, and which meant she had learned to ride rther east.

There was nothing happening yet on the bay, so elgado followed the anomalous pair through the tele-hoto lens of his camera. Just south of the Red Sands ntrance onto Rosia Road, the riders pulled their camels to stop in the middle of Rosia.

"Mama! Papa! Susan!" Helgado yelled, Susan being s sister. "Down there—look!"

The Helgados watched while Nigel shot pictures with e enormous lens he had bought to zoom in on nude

287

beaches in Portugal. His Nikon was tripod-mounted and he triggered the camera by remote as he framed his shots. His parents and his sister shared his father's Japanese binoculars.

The woman got off her camel, slipped an assault rifle onto her back, and pulled a Union Jack out of her saddlebag and held it high for everybody to see. The man removed a drill and a roll of cord from his saddle and ran the cord into a house on the hill side of the road. He returned shortly and set about boring a deep hole in the middle of the street. Glancing both ways on Rosia, holding the flag high, the armed woman walked slowly around the man who knelt, concentrating on his work. He bored three such holes across the street, slipping a metal tube into each, and cleaning up his mess quickly.

When the man was finished with the last hole, he turned, lifted the lady's veil, bent her over backward, and gave her a slow kiss.

Through his telephoto lens, Helgado could see the woman's arms close passionately around the man's back.

Then the lovers were finished. They got on their camels and started north up Red Sands Road. British agents riding camels! Nigel Helgado could hardly believe his luck. He hustled his tripod to the back side of the roof and shot pictures of the pair atop their handsome camels striding confidently past his house.

The Arab battle plans—ABC's prepared in advance by Bobby Nye to answer all possible questions about what had to be done and why—called for the impressment of all mechanics on Gibraltar to help repair the expected battle damage. Mechanics and other essential Gibraltarians had been identified in the first days of Muhammad Aziz' takeover, and told that in the event of an emergency, they would be ordered to post via the Gib radio. Aziz was democratic about the matter. They could decline to report if they chose—it was up to them—but in that case they would be relieved of their heads.

From the beginning, the Arabs, themselves experts in
288

the manufacture of Molotov cocktails, had wanted to frustrate unhappy Gibraltarians planning to get their hands on gasoline. Accordingly, they had placed two armed guards at each station. There were four petrol stations in the northern end of town, two in the southern, including the British Petroleum pumps and garage on Europa Road by the Rock Hotel, and below and just southwest of the casino high above town.

The four mechanics at the Europa Road station had been told to bring food and bedding in case they had to spend one or more nights at their post. They were old friends and talked this over in advance so as not to duplicate their fare. With hurriedly packed bags of fruit, bread, cheese, sausages, and cans of olives, they walked to the station, carrying rolls of blankets and Thermos bottles of hot coffee. In their pockets—in case they were called upon to weld a broken rocket launcher in the middle of the battle—the reluctant mechanics carried cameras of varying degrees of complexity. Gibraltar was a duty-free port and almost everybody owned some kind of camera. Also, so as not to miss out on the fun, one of the mechanics brought with him his daughter's portable telly.

The mechanics were in the garage with the doors open—they had a view of the bay from the windows in back—drinking coffee and listening to a hyperbolic Spanish television announcer describe not-to-be-missed action that hadn't taken place yet but just might, just could, maybe, perhaps happen, when an Arab woman rode into the station on a camel.

She stopped her camel near the two Arab guards and slipped easily off. She said something to the guards in Arabic. The guards both laughed. The woman took out a silenced machine pistol and lashed the laughers in the face on full automatic. She whipped out a knife and slashed their throats lest either one be inclined to scream in his death throes. Almost before their bodies hit the ground, she whipped out a Union Jack and displayed it for all to see.

Just then a second camel pulled into the station, this

one ridden by the toothy American hillbilly, Obadiah Jones, as the mechanics all knew from television. Jones, with the scarlet *A* glittering on the breast of his costume, was laughing "Heaugh! Heaugh! Heaugh!" He closed his fist and gave the mechanics a triumphant thumbs-up. Yes! He walked over and kicked a dead Arab, laughing his demented laugh. In his hillbilly–Don Corleone voice, he said, "Ain't she a kick? Fun kind of woman. Pahticipates, if'n y'all know what Ah mean."

He got back on his camel and, followed by the woman on her camel, rode to a spot on Europa Road just south of the entrance to the Rock Hotel. This was a matter of thirty feet from the petrol station.

Jones removed the drill and cord from his saddle. He turned and addressed the mechanics who had followed the camels out onto the street. "Reckon Ah'm gonna have to drill a few holes heah in th' street. Obliged if'n y'all could help me with the corhd. You ah to be asshuahed the lady and mahself are in th' serhvice of Huh Majesty's Govahment. Ms. Fieldin's people."

The mechanics scrambled to help Jones with the cord and in minutes he was hard at work on his first hole. As he started the second hole, he looked up at the mechanics who hung back uncertainly, cameras in hand. Seeing this, Obadiah Jones said, "Y'all want to take pictchuhs, go ahead. No reahson why not. A-rabs'll love 'em latah on. Heaugh! Heaugh!"

When he finished drilling and loading the third hole, Jones cleaned up his mess, a proper craftsman. When his drill and cord were strapped onto his saddle, he adjusted the assault rifle on his back and suddenly grabbed the woman, embracing her as he sang:

> Frawgie went acoawtin' an' he did rhide, uh
>   huh, uh huh,
> Frawgie went acoawtin' an' he did rhide, uh
>   huh, uh huh;
> Frawgie went acoawtin' an' he did rhide,
> Swoahd and pistol by his side, uh huh, uh huh,
>   uh huh.

Then, with his amazed gallery still taking pictures, Obadiah Jones kissed the woman most passionately.

"Obadiah!" the lady responded in a voice that was both shocked and pleased. She returned the kiss with emotion of her own.

Even the camels regarded the clinch with interest.

When the lovers broke their kiss, Jones said, "She is a hanhdsome womahn, is she not? Did you see huh in action? The totahl womahn."

The pair then mounted their camels and were off to the north.

Later, it was learned, the couple had planted similar explosives high up on Willis Road.

7

OF ALL THE bleeding! Colonel Bobby Nye could not believe, just could not! The television sets were now showing Spanish and Arab soldiers staring at television sets hoping to catch a glimpse of themselves.

They showed another Spanish soldier waving at his mother. *"Hola, Mama!"* he called.

Bobby Nye wondered when it was that men would fight like bloody men and not like a bunch of pussies! Watching for themselves on the telly! What had become of honor? Sweet Jesus! Nye wanted to drive up to the Moorish wall and find those Arabs and shoot their bloody bleeding balls off. *Hola, Mama!* Nye could hardly believe, and yet did.

On the screen, Hovercraft circled wide for their run into the bay. An NBC camera zeroed in on the deck of a Hovercraft.

Commandos and motorcycles.

What the bleeding?

The blimps weren't staying two hundred meters up as

their pilots had promised, not at all. They were right on top of the buggers. Right on top.

The windows suddenly rattled from explosions to the north, in the town.

Bobby Nye said, "Will you please find out what that's all about, Captain Hassan? Also, splash the blimps, all of them. Do it now. Fire at will."

The Exocet technicians looked at him, then at Captain Hassan.

Captain Hassan regarded him mildly. "The blimps are providing aerial television coverage—"

"Television coverage?" Nye shouted. "Television coverage? What are you talking about? We've got a battle here! Would you rather win unseen or watch yourself lose on television? Now then, let's be very clear and rational about all this and take the proper course of action, which is to splash those fucking blimps right now!"

"It has been forbidden."

"Shoot them! Fire! Fire! Now! Now!" Nye was furious. He didn't have time to explain to a bunch of bleeding ragheads what the British were up to. The British had chaff rockets mounted in the bellies of the blimps. Chaff. Had to be.

"I said, forbidden, forbidden by Comrade Borodin." Captain Hassan took a pistol from his hip and shot Colonel Bobby Nye four times square in the chest, and turned to watch the approach of the Hovercraft on television. He said, "Ignore the blimps. When the Hovercraft get halfway into the bay, fire your missiles and sink every one."

Hassan stepped over Nye's corpse for a better view of the television set. He adjusted the color, which was too blue for his taste. The Spanish announcer had been promising slow-motion action of an exploding British Hovercraft; Captain Hassan wanted to make sure the ball of flame wasn't some stupid, unreal color.

Gerard Thompson glanced at Laura Lynne-Dell's blimp on his left. If she drew the first Exocet, he'd be pissed. He wanted first blood. First action.

292

The radar man said, "Fire up on our port."

An Exocet! Thompson scanned the bay with his binoculars. There it was, sleek and white. An Exocet on its way. Amazing! He could see the orange of its rockets as it slipped over the water like a serpent. ". . . That's chaff you see," he heard Lynne-Dell say over his audio linkup. "A miss. Yes! Thank God!" Laura Lynne-Dell was openly pro-British and made no apologies for it.

In Thompson's cabin, Captain Mahar, who had been listening also, was jubilant. "Your colleague did a wonderful job, Mr. Thompson. Wonderful job. Not a hint of where the chaff is coming from. Not a hint." For all the Arabs knew, the Hovercraft crews could have found some way to carry their own chaff.

"Fire up dead ahead, sir," said the radar man. An Exocet coming their way!

The chaff gunner chewed at his lips, staring at a spot on a screen.

Gerard Thompson told his viewers, "Exocet up and coming toward the Hovercraft beneath our blimp. We're waiting for the Hovercraft to fire its chaff . . ."

"Bleeding!" the gunner yelled.

A jam.

No chaff.

"Bleeding!" the gunner screamed.

A hit below. The Hovercraft exploded directly beneath the blimp.

Jack Brooks was hard on it, his camera whirring a high-tech *mmmmmmmmm.*

Gerard Thompson, staring at the corpse of a British soldier looping up toward the blimp, its head and one leg parting from its torso like errant moons, screamed, "Slo-mo! Slo-mo! Slo-mo!"

"Gotitgotitgotit!!!" Brooks yelled as he stared intently into the viewfinder of his camera.

NBC had delivered with a direct hit of an Exocet. A direct hit! Slow motion by the best man in the business. Lynne-Dell had drawn chaff. He'd drawn an Exocet hit. Thompson was almost beside himself at his good fortune. He doubled up his fist in triumph, yes! He turned . . .

. . . and,
.
.
he realized,
.
stupidly,
.
in his
.
.
excitement,
.
had stepped
.
.
through
.
.
the open bay
.
.
of the cabin.
.
.
He fell,
.
.
remembering
.
.
Felicia in the
.
.
presenting position
.
.

on her
.
.
Day
.
.
of Fabulous
.
.
Hormones.
.
.
Then,
.
.
knowing
.
.
he was about
.
.
to die,
.
.
he wondered
.
.
if Jack Brooks
.
.
was taping
.
.
his
.
.
descent
. .

in slo-mo.

.

.

Jack Brooks did indeed get Gerard Thompson in
slo-mo. In fact, a freeze-frame from his tape provided one
of the most startling images in the history of photojournal-
ism.

It was a frame of the many-pocketed intellectual/
adventurer/journalist Thompson, upside down, his head
about to plow through the wreckage of the sinking Hovercraft. In this instant before Nielsens no longer mattered,
Gerard Thompson looked serious, solemn, concerned, just
as he did every night on the six o'clock news.

8

EVEN THOUGH BOB Steele had been warned, he jerked and
made an inadvertent yelp when the explosive charges went
off. Larry Schoolcraft had told them they would hear the
explosions first, followed by the buzzing of motorcycles.

He heard the motorcycles coming up the hill. They
sounded like large mosquitoes at first, then the sound got
louder and louder.

Steele's mouth was dry. Below, he heard the engines of
Arab vehicles starting up, on their way to discover what
would block their way.

It would be after this, Schoolcraft had said, that the
Arab commanders would realize their only chance was to
block the cyclists with small-arms fire.

That was when the Arabs would turn to the stairs.

By the time the Arabs turned to the stairs, the first
commandos should be past, Schoolcraft had said. The
commandos' first objective would be to seize the Tower of
Homage and Willis's Road above the Arab defense.

When the main strike force passed, Bob Steele, Jim Quint, and Chippy Chipolina would be relieved.

Bob Steele waited at the top and to one side of the route leading from the Devil's Gap Steps to Green Lane. Jim Quint waited on the other. There was a smaller, unmarked route guarded by Chippy Chipolina. These stairs were where the Arabs would turn first.

Steele had the Union Jack spread out by his side, as Schoolcraft had instructed. The commandos had been told that three men would be guarding the tops of the two stairs, but they needed clear identification.

"They're coming! Listen to them roar! Good chaps!" Bob Steele licked his lips and looked down the steep steps through the sights of his assault rifle, a Kalashnikov AK-47 with a folding stock. It had been stolen for his use by the whistling spy. The Arabs would be very nearly defenseless trying to climb those steps. Schoolcraft had decided that the next steps over—a matter of thirty yards—could be defended by one man if the heat were turned up. Chippy Chipolina, armed with Molotov cocktails in addition to his AK-47, waited there to uphold Gibraltarian honor. God alone knew how Schoolcraft had gotten hold of the gas for the cocktails.

The first riders up, grim under their helmets, acknowledged Chipolina, Steele, and Quint with a nod of their heads as they passed, heading for high ground as quickly as they could.

To the south, at the Europa Point entrance to the British underground command, there was the sudden chatter of automatic gunfire.

Looking down the barrel of his AK-47, with motorcycles *zoom, zoom, zoom, zoom*ing behind him, Jim Quint wondered if a human being jumped and kicked around in its—his, her—death throes like a jackrabbit or mule deer back in Montana. He'd lost his taste for hunting when he'd gotten older, had in fact gotten so bad that he went out of his way to avoid stepping on spiders. He couldn't see the point in killing something for no reason.

But Quint remembered. He remembered watching a

buck mule deer on its side, dying, remembered it twitch, and jerk, stiffen and shudder in awful spasms, farting, shitting, jaws wide, remembered his brother circling the animal, standing clear of the thrashing hooves, remembered his brother being careful where to put one more slug, careful so as not to mess up the antlers, which were a trophy rack. Quint wondered: Had Mother Nature conspired to make the human nervous system somehow different, so that a corpse dropped as neatly in battle as in the movies?

To the north, suddenly, every automatic rifle in the United Kingdom seemed to be firing down on the Arab missile and artillery batteries at the Moorish wall.

Waiting for the Arabs to figure out which stairs they had to climb in order to stop the hemorrhage of motorcycle-riding Britons, Jim Quint tried to remember a war movie, even one ballyhooed as antiwar, that had shown a dying human being flopping like a rag doll. What would happen—in the filming of an otherwise good, clean action movie, a few hundred corpses, give or take a score—if a director told a beautiful actress to lie on the floor and twitch and jerk and shudder for the camera, eyes rolling, tongue stuck out, jeans wet from urine and feces, while recorded farts played on the soundtrack?

A motorcycle zoomed behind him.

Quint shook himself awake. There was an Arab clambering up the steps, followed by a second and a third.

Another motorcycle.

Bob Steele seemed taken by surprise also.

A group of motorcycles went *zoom, zoom, zoom* up the hill.

The Arabs were coming closer.

Both Quint and Steele opened fire at the same time, and the figures—they were the lead four of a larger party—were blown backward down the steps. Three were clean kills.

The fourth was a flopper.

Quint thought, Aw shit! He swung his weapon at the flopper, but more heads appeared above the horizon of the steps, and these were firing uphill. The flopper jerked and flopped. Quint fired at the heads. The flopper began twitching. The heads went down. Heads up. Twitch. Jerk. Quint fired. Heads down.

Quint screamed: "YYYYEEAAUUUUGHHHH!" A hand had clamped his shoulder.

"Sorry, mate. Didn't mean to scare you like that. You're free to go." The commando settled into position. He snapped off a single round, and the twitching Arab rested.

Down the road, there was an explosion over on Chippy Chipolina's stairs. Smoke rolled skyward.

"You'll roast their little weenies with the first throw," Schoolcraft had told Chipolina, gesturing at the Molotov cocktails. "Then keep the fire roaring. If it starts to wane, add another bomb. That's a narrow passage; they can't attack you through a wall of flames. Keep throwing gasoline on it until you're relieved."

Chipolina was a nurse, a healer. This was not good training for throwing Molotov cocktails, but Chipolina was determined to do his best.

Chipolina, too, had been startled to see Arabs suddenly coming up the steps. Curiously, without panic or even anxiety, he had lit the wick of the first jar of gasoline and lobbed it high, watched it loop into the blue, heard motorcycles passing behind him, watched the jar score a goal in the passage, bursting orange, touching off a symphony of screams.

He hurled another jar of gasoline to the pyre.

Chippy Chipolina was wiping vomit off his mouth when a commando pulled over to relieve him.

Thanks to the network television blimps, the Helgado family on Red Sands Road—which had moved its telly up to the roof—didn't miss any of the action. In fact, Nigel Helgado had brought his camera up; he wanted to shoot some of the television coverage for his scrapbook.

The blimps, having finished with the Hovercraft action, now floated over the inferno that was the Moorish

299

wall. Nigel Helgado, and his parents, and grandparents, and sister, and brother-in-law all watched the telly: Brigadier Tomlinson's commandos were laying down a perfectly insane hail of small-arms fire from the rear and above the Arab defenses facing the north.

And from the south, in what in some ways was an even more awesome display, Colonel Givings's troops triple-timed it up Rosia Road—passing in front of the Helgado house—to attack the Arabs from the south. Squad after squad tromped north on Rosia, which became Main Street, high-stepping it in camouflaged combat gear and shined boots. The blimps followed the progress of the British troops, so the Helgados got to see two views at once.

Givings's soldiers had been trapped underground for two weeks, and had worked themselves into a frenzy. Never mind that they were radar and communications specialists and missile technicians. They were soldiers, and apparently now had themselves believing they were the toughest of tough Royal Marines. Viewers back home got to listen to British sergeants lead a four-beat cadence that alternated with the tromping of boots. The cry echoed up the narrow streets and alleys of Gibraltar, to cheering in every household:

"Kill! Kill! Kill! Kill!"

Tromp. Tromp. Tromp. Tromp.

"Kill! Kill! Kill! Kill!"

Tromp. Tromp. Tromp. Tromp.

In the middle of all the excitement, with the *rat-a-tat* of assault rifles still echoing from the north, with the television announcer shouting, with his family cheering, and with British soldiers below yelling "Kill! Kill! Kill! Kill!" Nigel Helgado happened to look east, at Alameda Gardens next door.

Nigel Helgado saw something on the grass that he did not believe at first. He looked at it through the lens of his camera. Yes. *Click. Click. Click.*

Hardly taking his eyes off Alameda Gardens, he reloaded his camera.

The majority of the British troops had now passed up

Rosia, so the rest of the Helgado family turned to the television set, which was showing the battle close up. A British soldier with clenched teeth was raining slugs onto Arabs trapped below him. Cut to a close-up of the Arabs: bodies everywhere. Nobody seemed to be in charge. Men lay twisting in pain. The announcer said:

"As you can see, the Arabs are being ripped apart by this terrible onslaught from above. They've somehow got to get organized if they're to defend themselves from the British troops you saw triple-timing it up from Europa Point. As the British regiment gains momentum, it's a time of decision for the Arab command."

Nigel Helgado moved his camera to the best angle for shooting Alameda Gardens. He swiveled his big lens and focused on the man and woman.

They were both naked, on their sides, screwing lazily, as their grazing camels waited behind them. They humped with slow, delicious, unselfconscious abandon.

Nigel Helgado had seen the camel riders before the action and had wondered who they were. The couple had now thrown their Arab outfits to one side. A Union Jack was lying on the grass. On it, clearly through the 400mm lens, Helgado could see what appeared to be a mouthpiece containing outrageous teeth. The grass around the lovers was littered with assault rifles and bandoliers.

Helgado photographed the action in the park, sorry he couldn't see their faces.

A spontaneous cheer went up behind Helgado; he looked around. The television showed the flag of Jebel Tarik being lowered. The Union Jack was once again hoisted over the House of Assembly. This was followed by the frenzied honking of horns all over town. The excited announcer said:

"It's over! It's all over! The Arabs heard the British coming up Main Street shouting that chant of theirs, and suddenly there were white flags everywhere. The Battle of Gibraltar is history, finished with a stunning, clear victory by the Royal Navy under the command of Prime Minister Deborah Fielding."

The lovers in Alameda Gardens were also finished;

301

they lay on the grass holding hands, cooling off. Helgado was patient, not wanting to run out of film, but he snapped more shots as the two got up and embraced. The lady had such a wonderful figure—such a rump! Helgado groaned aloud as she turned to get dressed. He was so attracted by the rump that he stayed there, *click, click, click,* following underpants and blue jeans as they were slipped into place over those wonderful hillocks. She happened to turn —Helgado's good luck—when she put on her bra and blouse.

While Helgado was shooting the woman's derriere, the man had also put on blue jeans and a shirt. Thus casually attired, the lovers got on their camels and rode off toward Europa Point, the gentleman steering with his feet, the lady with a stick.

Nigel Helgado realized, too late, that he had missed an opportunity to photograph the faces of the lovers. He'd had his opportunity when they had stood. Now the moment was gone. He cursed his stupidity.

9

THE DAY BEFORE the battle, public relations man Leonid Borodin was a hero, a source of much glee, to the Central Committee and the Politburo. Alas, after the battle, MI6 and the CIA—humiliated by the fact that a PR man, an odious flack, had orchestrated the entire Gibraltar episode —cooperated in keeping the fact secret from the public. The group of Russians in the Continental Hotel were said to have been "Soviet technicians." There was too much excitement for anybody to ask technicians of what.

The Battle of Gibraltar had been goose-bump time for the viewers back home. This was war. Live. The real stuff. Viewers had gotten to kick back with a cold beer and watch Royal Marines reclaim British honor.

The following days were wonderful for video-replay on television. What stories there were!

Prime Minister Deborah Fielding returned to London in triumph, her Gallup and Harris approval numbers pushing past the unheard-of ninety mark. Once the media learned that mounting the chaff launchers on the blimps had been Mrs. Fielding's idea, all responsibility for the loss of the Rock in the first place fell on Roger Jackelforth. The prime minister was held blameless for the loss and was virtually guaranteed another five-year term in office.

Mrs. Fielding obliged the photographers by standing on the bridge of the H.M.S. *Bountiful* as it slipped up the Thames to its London berth. As bands played "Rule, Britannia!" and Union Jacks waved, viewers were told this was how Mrs. Fielding had stood when she led the flotilla into battle.

Royal Navy officers who had been there on the deck of the *Bountiful* affirmed that yes, it was true, she had stood resolutely on the bridge in that same navy blue print dress, her chin up, her eye to the task before her.

"God, it was something. Seeing her standing there like that, leading the flotilla. It was extraordinary. Gave me chills, I can tell you," a young officer was quoted. The headline writer assumed that these chills were of inspiration and admiration rather than of fear or terror.

The BBC announcer said Deborah Fielding had joined the company of the immortal Nelson among British heroes, and inevitable comparisons of the Battle of Trafalgar and the Battle of Gibraltar followed, including the playing of "Rule, Britannia!" on the way to the enemy. In reply, a Labour partisan wrote a letter to the editor of *The Guardian*:

> As I understand from reading and watching the many accounts of the Battle of Gibraltar, Deborah Fielding's claim to the pantheon of heroes and saints rests on her idea of firing chaff rockets from the bellies of television blimps. Given a choice between possible victory and seeing themselves on television, the Arabs opted for

television. For this, apparently, we are to add "military genius" to Mrs. Fielding's political dossier? For observing that the circus prevails over logic? Please!

The Guardian published a second letter, representative of many in the editor's mailbag:

> Surprise! Now we have it unmasked. War, the ultimate man's game; who is it who saw the obvious, knew intuitively the enemy's weakness? Who was resourceful? Who took responsibility? I thought we had long known from *Gray's Anatomy* that one's genitals have nothing to do with intelligence or the ability to lead.

Poor William Fluute. He thought he'd had Debbie Fielding on the ropes. The indefatigable peacemonger had been elated, had felt wonderfully youthful and vigorous as he had pushed for full-scale invasion to throw the barbarous Arabs off the Rock. Then, reversal: a certain five more years of Tory rule. If his detractors had once called him Mad Billy, they knocked off that practice now, because Fluute was admitted to a sanitarium in Bath suffering from depression. Electroshock treatments were needed to bring him around. Stories surfaced in the popular press that Fluute was listless and uninterested in public quarrels.

Gerard Thompson was another hero. All Gerard Thompson had really done was fuck up. Instead of knocking over a glass of wine or tripping on a doorstep, or whacking his head on a door like Gerald Ford, he had stepped into an open hole. Those things happen. But he had done something. His Gerard Thompson persona, impeccable under pressure, had helped the Royal Navy pull off its ruse. Thus Thompson was a hero in America on a scale appreciated best by aficionados of the surreal.

The Americans, whose Sixth Fleet had bobbed up and down impotently on the Mediterranean side of the Rock, not helping a damned bit, just went crazy for the Thompson heroism story. A psychiatrist at Georgetown University

304

ty claimed this Thompson enthusiasm was akin to the efforts of the French, while singing the praises of the Resistance in World War II, to ignore French anti-Semitism and cooperation with the Nazis.

Nevertheless, there were proposals before Congress to erect a "national media statue" on the Mall in Washington honoring Gerard Thompson and other heroes of journalism who had given their lives in pursuit of the truth. The Vietnam veterans had gotten their statue, the logic went; why not the journalists as well? In the excitement of the moment, this logic was not examined closely. Judging from the stories in most American newspapers, a reader freshly landed from Mars would have concluded that Gerard Thompson alone was responsible for fooling the Arabs. Once again the Americans had rescued the bumbling Brits.

Thompson's funeral was spectacle at its most wonderful, highlighted at the end by eulogies both by President Charles Barbur and Thompson's colleague Harry Gilchrist. Gilchrist, speaking last—suggesting that he and Thompson had been old drinking buddies on faraway, exotic assignments—broke into tears, a moment that touched the nation of viewers, especially women. Gilchrist's Nielsens shot up to unheard-of levels the next day.

As the American television networks geared up for various "specials" on the Battle of Gibraltar, so they could make more money off their videotape, they were horrified to learn what the viewers really wanted to see. They had apparently OD'd on Arabs being shot and burned alive by Royal Marines. What everybody really wanted to know was, who were the phantom lovers who had made it all possible? Still photographs by Nigel Helgado and the other Gibraltarian photographers were turning up everywhere in newspapers and magazines.

Because the story of the romantic fifth columnists didn't move on the screen, the television networks couldn't use it effectively. Their Nielsens waned, even though earnest announcers with heavy, dramatic voices did their best to convince viewers that more replays of the battle were not to be missed.

Desperate, the networks began promoting these as "collector's programs," historic action that must be recorded on VCRs and saved for the education of children in the family. This was followed by a modest run on VCRs by families using history to justify buying something they couldn't afford. In fact, the action shifted to newspapers and magazines, where Nigel Helgado's photographs were to be found.

The British popular press had an especially good time with the story. *The Daily Mirror,* for example, ran a Helgado shot of the nude lovers on the front page under the headline: "Joint Action!" *The Sun*'s headline said simply: "Allies!" Both *Playboy* and *Penthouse* announced special spreads on the couple locked in sexual congress. Descriptions of the lady in question began with "striking," and progressed to "beautiful," "sensational," and all manner of hyperbole.

No one could come up with any clue to her identity, but everyone could see that the man was Obadiah Jones. There was a mad run of journalists to South Carolina, many of them ending up in North Carolina by mistake, to track down the elusive cracker. Not a trace of him could be found. And as for the woman . . .

The more it became clear that nobody had any idea who the couple was—or would ever say—the more insistent was the public that their identities be found out. *The New York Times Book Review* got in on the fun by running a sonnet for the occasion written by John Updike.

The annoyed president of ABC Television was so irked that he wrote a letter to *The New York Times*:

> Was there any real point to our "phantom lovers" being quite so dramatic in carrying out their mission in the Battle of Gibraltar? What was Obadiah Jones's "Froggie went acourtin'" nonsense really all about? Did our heroic couple really think they could copulate in a public park in the middle of a battle without anybody seeing them? Well, I think we all know that Obadiah

Jones and his friend are pranksters, if professionals, who decided to rub it in the face of television, then ride off into the sunset on camels.

Nobody seriously believes a British agent could have faked the southern accent we all heard repeated daily on television. That's as difficult as an American trying to mimic a cockney. This leads us straight to the CIA. I think we have a right to expect better behavior for our tax dollar. If Obadiah Jones and his companion are employees of the CIA, their antitelevision bias is unconscionable and outrageous for public servants. They should be fired.

President Barbur failed in his attempt to silence us through the courts. I think a few questions might be asked of Mr. Barbur. Did he have prior knowledge of this television baiting? If he did, there ought to be an accounting.

A writer in *The Guardian* speculated that the mystery man and his lady were sent by the gods to intervene on behalf of the Torys. There was no other answer. A psychic told the *Mirror* that she'd had a vision; in fact, she said, the couple were jinns escaped from a bottle left by Tarik Ibn Zeyad in A.D. 711. Despite Obadiah Jones's accent, reports persisted in London that the couple were MI6 agents, suggesting that the British secret service had done something right for a change. MI6 officials, hoping the rumor would become accepted as fact, declined to comment.

Steele and Chipolina, both being British subjects, were cited for heroism by the Queen. The American author Jim Quint—er, Nicholas Orr—the subject of a media blitz, insisted on being called by his nom de plume, Nicholas Orr, and manfully mentioned his Humper Staab novels every second or third sentence. Steele, Quint/Orr, and Chipolina all announced plans to write accounts of their fifth-column activities, Chipolina having his choice of ghostwriters. These books, it was said, were all sold for giddy sums of money. Nigel Helgado pulled down handsome publishing contracts all over the world for a book of his photos of the phantom lovers.

The final story in the glut that followed resolution had to do with Puking Max and his ladies. The Barbary apes emerged shortly after the tourists returned. Max looked poorly. He had not done well on the healthy fruits and vegetables left by his Gibraltarian supporters.

All that changed immediately.

It seemed as though every camera on the planet converged on Gibraltar. They were eager to photograph Puking Max, who had been rendered mythical, for the moment surpassing Winston Churchill as a symbol of British pluck. In fact, the British command on Gibraltar assigned armed guards to protect Max from possible kidnappers—at least until they could import new apes from Morocco.

The celebrity puker had never experienced anything like it. He was surrounded by black snouts. Max did his best to handle the bounty. When his stomach filled, he emptied it and returned for more. Max loved Bah. He held out his hands for more, more, more, and Bah saw to it he was fed chocolate-covered peanuts. Max ate, and ate, and ate, and it was good.

With the world watching on television, Prime Minister Fielding made a trip to Gibraltar to dedicate the site where a statue would be erected in Max's honor. On this occasion there were black snouts beyond imagination.

However, in the excitement, nobody told Mrs. Fielding about Max's preferences, and she tried to approach the ape straight on.

Max went, "Bah! Bah! Bah!"

Mrs. Fielding retreated. The photographers all laughed. Nobody knew quite what to do next. A Gibraltarian cabdriver with thick eyeglasses was consulted. An aide then murmured in the prime minister's ear. Mrs. Fielding, listening, nodded her head gravely. She turned her back to the ape. She stepped slowly backward.

The indomitable Max was pleased and to the delight of everyone hopped up on Mrs. Fielding's shoulder. The two heroes of Gibraltar stood gaily, resolutely together, pals.

It was a grand moment. The cameras clicked and whirred. Max, surrounded by images of himself, loving what he saw, reached out to the black snouts, reached out for the blessings of Bah.

THE BEST IN SUSPENSE

BESTSELLING BOOKS FROM TOR

ELIZABETH PETERS